Tom Watson is the former deputy leader of the Labour Party and the MP for West Bromwich East between 2001 and 2019. He first folded Labour Party leaflets in the family kitchen in Kidderminster at the age of seven and has been involved in every single General Election since then. Tom served as a Minister for Tony Blair and worked at the very heart of Downing Street with Gordon Brown. In September 2015, he was elected as Labour's Deputy Leader. Tom is well known as a campaigning politician. He took on the tabloid newspaper industry during the phone hacking scandal and more recently has campaigned against exploitative and addictive practices in the gambling industry. After changing his diet and getting fit, Tom now has the sugar industry in his sights and is committed to raising awareness about the dangers of excess and hidden sugars, and improving public understanding about conditions like type 2 diabetes.

Imogen Robertson is a writer of historical fiction. Now based in London, she was born and brought up in Darlington and read Russian and German at Cambridge. Before becoming a writer, she directed for TV, film and radio. She is the author of several novels, including the Crowther and Westerman series. Imogen has been shortlisted for the CWA Historical Dagger three times (2011, 2013 and 2014), as well as for the prestigious Dagger in the Library. She has also written *King of Kings*, a collaboration with the legendary international bestseller Wilbur Smith, and *Liberation*, a wartime thriller, with Darby Kealey.

TOM
WATSON
& IMOGEN ROBERTSON

The
HOUSE

sphere

SPHERE

First published in Great Britain in 2020 by Sphere
This paperback edition published by Sphere in 2021

1 3 5 7 9 10 8 6 4 2

*This is a work of fiction. Certain institutions, public offices, events
and public figures are identified, but are used fictitiously. Other characters
involved are wholly imaginary and any similarity with actual persons
living or dead is unintentional and coincidental.*

The quote Owen is trying to remember on pg 182 is:
I recalled what Imo said about size and attraction and felt it
like a gun quite close to my head, by which I mean cold and true.

From *Farewell to Bread* by Roddy Lumsden, published in *Not All Honey* (Bloodaxe Books
2014), used with with kind permission of the publisher.

A CIP catalogue record for this book is
available from the British Library.

ISBN 978-0-7515-7880-5

Typeset in Simoncini Garamond by M Rules
Printed and bound in the UK by Clays Ltd, Elcograf S.p.A.

Papers used by Sphere are from well-managed forests
and other responsible sources.

MIX
Paper from
responsible sources
FSC® C104740

Sphere
An imprint of
Little, Brown Book Group
Carmelite House
50 Victoria Embankment
London EC4Y 0DZ

An Hachette UK Company
www.hachette.co.uk

www.littlebrown.co.uk

To Ned and Sarah

'May they never lead the nation wrongly through love of power, desire to please, or unworthy ideals but, laying aside all private interests and prejudices, keep in mind their responsibility to seek to improve the condition of all mankind.'

from the Daily Prayer of the House of Commons

Chapter 1

Monday 7 March 2022

Philip Bickford gets to his feet and takes the magic half-step forward. He opens his folder and places it on the despatch box then rests his left hand on it, index finger brushing the figures he needs.

The honourable members scattered behind him are quiet. It's an ordinary morning and no one is expecting much drama during Oral Questions to the Minister for Patient Safety. Philip is not a dramatic performer. No one perks up waiting for him to be funny or cruel, or both. They are expecting bland words and his usual flurry of percentages delivered in – well, it's not quite a monotone, but sometimes it gets close.

This is 'local press release fodder' questions. This is 'get your MP a line for his Facebook page' time. It's celebrating the NHS, welcoming this, reviewing that, consulting widely and acknowledging tough choices will be made without getting into the weeds of what those tough choices will actually be.

Philip's senior, the Secretary of State for Health, will make any important announcements and probably in front of a bank of cameras rather than in the Chamber of the House of Commons, so these regular sessions of parliamentary questions are usually mere skirmishes on the edge of the battlefield. Still, an opposition backbencher might try to make a name for themselves by inflicting a flesh wound with a flourish of their rhetorical blade, or open a campaign which could make the whole government bleed with an innocent-sounding enquiry into something local, specific. The sort of thing you might miss. The ground is treacherous.

In the warren of corridors and committee rooms the enquiries into the government's handling of the outbreak are continuing. The Royal Commission on Virus Control daily demands further disclosures of emails and minutes of meetings and the civil servants parry and prevaricate; across the river the Commission takes day after day of evidence from nurses who didn't get the Personal Protective Equipment they needed even as their colleagues started dying around them, and care-home workers weep into the microphones as they talk about their residents left to die alone in their rooms; then there are all the public consultations as regulations made in haste are unpicked with tortuous slowness. Unexploded ordnance is still scattered over the field, in other words, so Phil, swallowing to clear his throat to speak, has to be careful where he treads.

Phil knows he got this job after the 2019 election because nobody in government was paying much attention. The Brexit hardcore had got the top jobs and they still had dozens of junior Cabinet positions to fill. A working-class boy whose mother had been a nurse, and who hadn't made too many enemies in the party? He'll do somewhere in Health. The Prime Minister's political secretary shrugged, scrawled Phil's name on a Post-it note, stuck it up on the whiteboard in the 'Health' column and then got back to the really important business of Brexit. Those were the days.

Phil was never going to be a great parliamentary performer, but he turned out to be competent and reassuring when that's what people needed. He kept his job. Won the grudging respect of his colleagues and the opposition, and got on with it.

So, OK, this isn't one of the grand pitched battles of parliament, it is a dawn patrol, a routine survey of the battleground. A warning exchange of fire as the pickets and snipers remind each other they are still there.

But. If you've never been there you can't know what it feels like, that half-step into the glare surrounding the despatch box, the feel of the New Zealand hardwood under your fingertips, the blank, hostile faces of the opposition and the sudden jolt of adrenaline, of fear which makes the hairs on the back of Phil's neck stand up. He gives it a beat, then speaks.

'I thank my honourable friend for her question and am delighted to join her in congratulating the staff of NHS Kent on the opening of the new wing of Kent Central – another demonstration of this government's ongoing commitment . . .'

He trots out the phrases, hardly needs to glance down for the numbers. The jackals on the opposition benches have nothing to cling onto, no room for a heckle, no hook for a joke. They grumble and sulk their way through his answer, scratching at their cuffs, hunching their shoulders.

Philip sits down to polite 'hear, hears' from the men and women on his own benches. They sound like sheep when they see the hay truck winding up the hill. So far so good. He controls his expression. Don't look smug. Don't look scared. Don't look nervous. Don't look bored. Look calm. Look engaged. Don't smirk. The battlefield is quiet, but the cameras are still on and the snipers are still watching through their scopes even while they smother a yawn. Spot who among the bobbing MPs the Deputy Speaker is turning to next and listen.

'Donald Black!'

The Deputy Speaker raises her voice for the first time this session. More members are coming in to find their places before the next item on the order paper. The Prime Minister is coming in to make a statement about the tortuous progress of the trade talks and offer some bullish bromides about great days ahead. Jam tomorrow. Just ten minutes of topical questions left and Phil can get out of here and back to work. An afternoon of meetings in his parliamentary office, then a strategy session at the department which is scheduled to run till seven, but will probably bleed on until nine.

Yes. The Honourable Member for Southampton West, face like a misshapen orange with tiny dark eyes – cloves stuck in the pith of his pockmarked skin. Collar too tight, knot in his tie too small. Voice nasal.

'Would the Honourable Member agree with me that as we approach the second anniversary of the peak of COVID-19 in the United Kingdom ...' What's left of it. The thought, heavy with the bafflement and fear of those first weeks, hits heavy behind Phil's eyes. He thinks of the camp beds in rows in sports stadia, that photograph of a nurse coming off shift in Lewisham, his face gaunt and grey with exhaustion. The slow unravelling after the first crisis passed. The spiralling unemployment figures, shuttered restaurants and bills. The endless brain-aching bills. ' . . . that now is the time to commemorate that moment in some significant way, and particularly offer some public memorial to the frontline NHS workers who lost their lives in their heroic struggle against the virus.'

An easy one. Surprisingly easy from the opposition. Phil stands up. Half-step forward again, the words ready behind his lips. More people are coming into the Chamber and a movement in the visitors' gallery catches his eye.

A man in his late sixties, wearing the open collar, thin sweater and jacket of a retired white-collar worker, is finding his seat behind the glass panel. He nods politely to his neighbour as she lifts her scarf and bag out of his way.

Something deep in Philip's brain twitches into anxious, vigorous life. The man sits and faces into the Chamber. Dark eyes, pale brown skin. A stutter of memory. A summer's evening. Distant pounding music. Owen's voice shouting something, Georgina crying. The yelp and squawk of a siren. Philip's brain goes white. He's frozen for what feels like minutes. Two point three seconds, he'll learn later. Long enough.

The tricksters and hecklers on the opposition benches snap to attention. Blood in the water. Say something, Philip tells himself. Stop looking at that ghost in the gallery and say something.

He clears his throat.

'The government believes that a lasting public memorial would indeed be appropriate to celebrate the deaths of frontline workers whose selfless actions . . . ' Laughter, cries of 'Shame' bouncing off the walls. What has he said? How has everything

5

changed? Three minutes ago he was listening to the birdsong and now the air is full of explosions. Order papers rolled into clubs are being pointed, fingers stabbing the air like knives. Keep going. '. . . saved thousands of lives. But the Mayor of London must cease distorting this simple sign of national recognition into a political football.'

It redoubles. The Deputy Speaker is looking at him with barely disguised contempt. Why? Then he hears his own words repeated in his head and he feels the blood rush to his face, the prickle of sweat behind his collar. *Sauve qui peut.*

'Madam Deputy Speaker . . . I . . . with many apologies. We wish to *commemorate* those workers. I . . . misspoke.'

Too late. Too slow. The moment has flown. The opposition benches are fake roaring themselves purple, but among them he sees faces twisted with genuine rage. They have the full sentence. *Government ministers didn't just allow the deaths of our nurses, they celebrate it!* He can see the newspaper and social media headlines next to a picture of his own sweating face.

Phil sits down, knowing he looks like a child. He doesn't know what to do with his hands. Humiliation runs through his arteries, pumps through his organs and poisons them. He folds his arms and looks at the benches opposite him with loathing, then upwards. He needs a moment, just a moment to stare at the vaulted roof.

It's fine. It's fine. These things happen. A slip of the tongue. How many times have people warned about the perils of breakfast rather than Brexit? Appeals to aid the shitting industry rather than shipping? God, his own mother is a nurse! They can't forget that, can they? Of course they can. The opposition were bored and are now going wild for it.

The pith-faced member for Southampton West can't believe his luck, and has just enough nous to act on it.

'Point of order, Madam Deputy Speaker!' The idiot can't help licking his lips.

She allows it.

'The minister has just revealed the government's true thoughts on the hundreds of thousands of public sector workers who were ground down by a decade of austerity then forced to risk their lives daily to save others. What remedy does this House have to force the Minister to apologise to the families of every lost public servant?' He reaches a near hysterical pitch. 'Isn't it the case, Madam Deputy Speaker, that no one will ever trust the party opposite to run our public services again?'

He sits. His eyes have almost entirely disappeared, he is smiling so broadly. The MPs behind him reach over the bench to pat him on the shoulder. He's the most popular kid on the playground. It was a mistake! A simple mistake!

Phil gets to his feet and says words. Reminds them that the government knows better than anyone what is owed to the NHS, the exemplary care given to the Prime Minister, and thousands of others. Reminds them about his mother, about the record investment in the NHS, the pay rise for the frontline, the writing off of its crippling debt, yanking hospitals out of the financial black holes the opposition had driven them into with its private financing initiatives when in government.

It should be a strong recovery but nobody hears him – they don't even pretend to listen. In Hansard this sensible, well-constructed answer will be printed in full and look no more or less important than his last answer. But right now he's the kid who's spilled juice down his crotch in the playground, the girl

7

with her skirt caught up in her knickers walking through the office, the cuckold, the viral pratfall, the gazelle at the back of the pack with the injured leg.

Final question. The Deputy Speaker has called someone else. Christ, they are actually going to make him stand up again. It's another of the government backbenchers who looks, as he's thanking Phil for his department's swift action on something or other, as if he's going to throw up. Phil knows how he feels. Phil lurches back onto his feet. Muscle memory. He says more words. He speaks for the microphones, hardly audible in the Chamber. He is on automatic pilot now and feels like his own ghost as he gives a lacklustre answer to the follow-up under the cacophony of heckles and sneers, pausing only when the Deputy Speaker, her voice starting to crack, calls for order again.

Philip looks up again at the man in the balcony. Remembers being young. Remembers the sirens and the smell of damp grass, the feeling of drying mud on his hands. The interview room. The man stares back at him then leans towards a woman sitting next to him and says something. She nods, then flicks her long braids back over her shoulder.

What in God's name is Sabal Dewan doing here?

His hair has gone completely white, and even sitting you can notice the slight stoop in his shoulders.

The Deputy Speaker moves on to the next item of parliamentary business. Phil can escape. He passes the Prime Minister as he leaves the raucous Chamber behind him. The Prime Minister blanks him. No – worse than blanks him: lets his eyes flicker over Phil then his expression resolves into one of mild disgust. That chancer, that scatterbrained blustering . . . It was a mistake! One mistake! After years of dutiful shit-eating during

Brexit and then twenty-hour days and sleeping in his office for half of 2020 trying to save lives! Then Sabal Dewan turns up and brings back the memory of the worst night of his life, his losses, and in that sudden moment of reliving it he made *one* mistake and now the mop-haired martyr of Westminster looks at him like he's the excrement on his shoe.

Damn it. Damn these people, damn them to hell. Let the sodding building collapse in on itself, cordon off the Palace with yellow tape and leave it to rot, let sewage flood the basements, let the frayed wires flame and consume, leave the statues for looters and let the busts of parliamentarians serve as garden ornaments, let the terrace tumble into the Thames and take all these failed comedians, nonentities, intellectual lightweights, tribal warriors and braying asses with it.

Phil needs a minute. Just a minute to clear his head and recover from the solar plexus punch of it, to get his game face back on. Out of the Chamber he risks touching his forehead. Good. Not clammy. Maybe it wasn't as bad as he . . .

Owen McKenna, Labour Member of Parliament for Warwick South, is standing in the Central Lobby with his researcher. Damn. Phil hears the throbbing music again. It just had to be Owen, didn't it? Owen will take one look at him and know exactly how nightmarish the last fifteen minutes have been. And it will make his day. His week. His month.

Owen sees him and grins wolfishly then turns slowly back to his researcher. Philip has a sudden memory of Owen in the house in Lambeth, a can of Stella in his hand and seeing that same grin. They are both in suits now. They both have staff and homes and status and, compared to most people in this staggering, staggered country, power. Phil has stayed slim, Owen still looks like a brickie but he's kept his hair, while Phil is afraid he is beginning to thin at the temples. Whatever. It's the same grin, the look Owen got when he'd really managed to get one over on someone, his hungry delight in the fall of an enemy – and now it's directed at Phil.

Owen's researcher nods, writes something down on the legal pad held across her chest, asks a question. Phil wants to walk across the lobby, grab the pad and strike Owen across the face with it, send his owlish glasses flying onto the patterned tiles. How many punches could he get in before security reacted, the cameras and phones came on? How would the squeals of Owen's researcher echo up the gothic stonework? How would it feel for once to wipe that self-satisfied vicious smirk off Owen's face?

'Mr Bickford? Minister?'

'What?' Phil turns round and finds himself looking into the face of a dark-haired woman he doesn't know. He manages a tight smile. She has a visitor's pass. She fingers it with neatly manicured nails.

'Can I help you?'

The woman is with a group. Students, Phil guesses. He tries to breathe through the humiliation, the flush the fantasy of smashing Owen's glasses off has given him. Two of the girls, probably the ambitious ones, wear boxy jackets. Mother Hen must have been taking them on a tour. Phil nods, keeping the smile going while he scans the perimeter to see who their guide is and recognises the researcher for the Member for Maidenhead, the constituency next to his own.

'Good afternoon,' Phil says. If they've been on the tour, they probably didn't see his meltdown in the Chamber. That is some sort of blessing. A temporary one.

'These are some of my best students doing the A-level politics course at Jude Levy College. Can we ask you just a quick question?'

Phil nods again. 'Of course. I have to get back to my office, though ...' What was his next appointment? Where was Ian? 'So we'll have to be quick.'

The teacher thanks him and points to one of the girls in a boxy jacket. Long dark hair, Indian parents probably. Eager look to her. She reminds Phil of his last researcher, now working in Conservative Central Office in Matthew Parker Street and looking for her own seat to run for. He waits. It will probably be something technical, designed to ingratiate and impress, but as the girl draws breath a taller boy, his hair long and curled on top, his T-shirt patterned with cartoon characters, gets in first.

'What's the point of all this?' The boy waves his hand around, taking in all Westminster, the arches and mosaics, the statues and the security guards, the researchers fast-walking up the shallow steps, the TV screens showing the committees in progress, the BBC Parliament feed from the Chamber. 'This Punch and Judy nonsense carrying on as usual while the world goes to hell?'

'Jason!' the teacher says sharply. Jason shrugs. Thirty seconds ago Phil was feeling the same way, but now his anger switches back and runs the opposite way. Phil's been answering this question ever since he ran for his seat in 2012, offering the usual words, sincere but apologetic, acknowledging past failures and promising to do better, but now suddenly, today, who knew? He's had enough.

'Yes, sometimes I think it's a complete waste of time,' Phil says. Angry Boy's eyes open wider and Keen Girl bites her lip. The teacher's apology for her student's rudeness stops in her throat.

'I mean, democracy – we gave it a good go, but it is basically reality TV, isn't it? Celebrity politicians who make used-car salesmen look trustworthy, advisors knifing each other in the back, journalists who don't know or care about policy but just want to make politicians sweat under the studio lights and voters who are led up the garden path. You say parliament is Punch and Judy? Spend half an hour on Twitter and tell me you still support universal suffrage. What do you think?' The boy gapes at him. Phil shrugs. 'Maybe we should put every policy to the popular vote. Free beer to everyone and we put the PM in the stocks if the market drops two per cent?'

He waits. The boy says nothing. 'No? Or maybe we could ask a bit more from the people. From the voters. Maybe *you* could actually think about who you were electing and why, rather than acting like it's a game show where you vote for your favourite four-word slogan, or don't vote at all and tell yourself politicians are all the same because you are too lazy to find out what the differences, the profound differences, are? Maybe if you want us to be better you should better yourself.'

The shock on Jason's face acts on Phil like a drug. So this is what it is like to say what you mean! He remembers it now, like a reformed smoker taking a long, filthy drag.

'I—' Jason begins, but Phil cuts him off. This feels too good. His blood is up. He will, for once, say what he thinks.

'Because this place matters. It is the mother of parliaments. You saw what happened in some countries – cities and states fighting each other over masks, authoritarians grabbing power. The roots of democracy run deeper here. Centuries deep. And they start here. Our system has emerged out of wars, rebellions, plagues and struggle. It adapts. And that culture of fierce debate and challenge, that stuff that looks like nonsense and Punch and Judy to you – that's what makes us strong. We bend but we do not break because a system grown up over centuries might look eccentric but it is adaptable and it is resilient. You want efficiency and nice packaging? Go to the Apple Store. Where were your Silicon Valley disrupters when the virus came? Letting the usual lies spread along with COVID and tinkering with their apps. We were here. Risking our lives to do everything we could for the frontline workers, the terrified and the sick. And fighting to come up with the best solutions to impossible problems where there were no good answers. So don't you sneer at this place, young man. Don't you dare. And while we are at it, learn some manners. Young lady, I think you had a question?'

Phil turns from the boy, who is staring at him slack-jawed, to the girl in the jacket. She blinks.

'Yes ... I ... I just wanted to ask, why did you want to be an MP in the first place?'

Phil smiles again and he means it this time.

'I wanted to do something that mattered. And it does matter. If the last couple of years have proven anything, they proved that. We haven't managed to save everyone, we haven't managed to save every job or business but the people who work here come in to fight for their constituents every single day, give us the room to build, to put lives together again. Whatever side of the floor they are on. You want to make life better for ten people? Fine. Be a good person. You want to make life better for a million people? Get into politics.'

The teacher and her students offer slightly dazed 'thank-yous' and Phil heads towards the stairs up to his parliamentary office. His senior researcher, Ian Livingstone, is waiting for him.

'What was that about?'

'Students.'

They keep moving, taking the shallow stairs two at a time.

'You seemed quite worked up. And one of them was filming you.'

Phil doesn't answer. What had he said? Some stuff about democracy. A brief respite from the shitshow of his day. He sees the jeering faces on the opposite benches again, like cherubs floating in the air in front of him.

'Did you see it?'

'Yes. What the fuck happened?' Phil doesn't reply so Ian ploughs on. 'And I wanted to warn you Toby Dale is waiting in your office. That vein in his forehead is popping.'

Perfect. Of course Toby Dale is waiting for him. The current favourite special advisor shovelling crap in and out of Number 10. Must have sprinted to Phil's office before he even got out of the Chamber, his lips puckered and head down, his hand-made shoes thrumming along the carpet like a wind-up toy in leather brogues.

He nods. 'OK. Thank you for the heads-up.' He pauses in the committee corridor and stares out of the window at the crumbling stonework of Cloister Court. He has to know. 'Ian, can you find out why a man called Sabal Dewan was in the visitors' gallery in the Chamber today? Do it quietly if you can.'

'Of course, boss.'

Chapter 2

Owen McKenna watches as the students swarm round Philip. When Owen arrived here, first walked the corridors in the glory days at the turn of the century running messages between parliament and party headquarters in Millbank, the older Labour MPs had taken it in turn to share a worn-out shibboleth with him: 'Remember, son, the opposition is in front of you – your enemy is behind you in your own party.' Maybe. As a rule. But Philip Bickford is an exception. He *is* Owen's enemy and that meltdown in the Chamber was bloody delicious.

Phil is listening to one of the students now, a lanky kid with a *sod-you* look about him, like the goths and playground anarchists Owen grew up with. Philip hadn't needed to grow up. He'd been born on a rough Essex estate with the mind of a forty-year-old Tory junior minister. He'd fooled Owen for a while, but then finally the scales had fallen from Owen's eyes and he'd recognised Phil as the arrogant, narrow-minded self-hating, traitorous . . .

Pam, his researcher, is waiting for an answer.

'Sorry, Pam. That all sounds good.' She has been briefing him about the social media grid for the week. She is good at it. A digital native, and a smart strategic thinker. Witty, too. He won't be able to hang on to her for long.

'Are you going back to Portcullis House now?' she asks. 'There are a few constituency emails which need your attention.'

There are always 'a few' constituency emails. Owen looks at his watch. Better to launch into the inbox when he's had a chance to shake himself out of this bitter mood. God knows, you always had to make sure you were feeling emotionally robust before diving into the constituency work, but now? With half his people up to their necks in debt and scared with it? Walk fast. Breathe the air. Get back to the desk with the fizz and pop of oxygen in the blood.

'Quick walk first,' he says. 'Did you remember to have lunch?' He sounds like a dad.

He heads down St Stephen's Hall and his phone rings. Christine.

'Hey, Chris.'

'Where are you?' Christine has a good telephone voice. Low pitched, but clear. Those elocution lessons her mama made her take. Sounded good in the Chamber too. Not for the first time, Owen silently curses the voters of Newcastle South West for kicking his ex-fiancée out of office. She should be on the front bench by now. So should he.

'St Stephen's Hall, being looked down on by those weird statues.'

She laughs. 'I like them. I found it very inspiring to tell every one of them to sod off on my way into the Chamber.

Look, Owen, any word on the written question to the health department yet?'

Damn. He'd meant to ask Pam to chase that up, but enjoying watching Philip get shredded in the Chamber had distracted him.

'No. I'll get Pam on it.'

'What about getting the Select Committee to report on data security?'

Another reason the emails kept piling up. Owen was glad to be part of the Select Committee which shadowed the work of the Department for Digital, Media, Culture and Sport, but its remit was mind-shatteringly wide.

'I've raised it, Christine. But we've got other fish to fry and the chair would rather punt the data issues over to the health department.'

'Of course he would.' Christine sighs, and Owen stops, moves to the side to let another tour group pass. He finds himself staring up at one of the mosaics. Not his sort of thing. The artwork in his flat is mostly classic band posters and street art. Framed now, rather than stuck up with Blu Tack, because you have to start acting like a grown-up sometime. These weird Edwardian murals have always left him cold. He knows about them, though. He gave the tour a hundred times when he was working in Labour headquarters in his pre-MP days. This one shows Richard the Lionheart heading off on a crusade. A culture war. What sort of message is that? A man heading off on a fatal fool's errand and leaving his country to shift for itself. Not Owen's sort of hero. Maybe when they get round to rebuilding this gothic palace they should replace the murals with protest signs. BLACK LIVES MATTER, TAKE BACK CONTROL, bring a bit of the chaos and battle of Parliament Square into the bubble.

'Owen, don't you think it's strange?'

For a moment he thinks she means the mural. He turns away from it, rubs the side of his nose, pushing up his glasses as he thinks. Six weeks since the Select Committee had poured cold water on the idea of an inquiry. Four weeks since he'd filled in the form and pressed submit. Most answers to parliamentary written questions come back in a fortnight. Sometimes you get a message saying the answer will be delayed because they need to collate complex data. But this time ... silence. Owen keeps thinking. The minister gets the question and his civil servants draw up an answer, then if the minister approves of the answer he or she puts their name to it and back it comes. But if the minister doesn't like the answer the civil servants have suggested, if it reveals something sensitive or politically damaging, back it goes for redrafting. The more dangerous the question, the longer the pause.

'Could be.'

Her voice snaps. *'Could be?* Oh, give me a break! It's been weeks. I'm telling you, Owen, there is something going on. They promised a formal consultation on the loosening of the data protection laws months ago. And now they aren't even answering a simple question about when it might be?'

Data laws. Even the opposition members on the committee had shuddered at the idea. Important, of course, but people need to be fed and housed, the economy propped up before it collapses entirely. Not for the first time he finds himself about to ask if it is really important? Why does it matter?

'I'll chase it up, Chris.'

'Fine. Don't over-exert yourself.'

'I'm doing it now.' He taps out a WhatsApp message to Pam and it swooshes away. 'Done.'

'Thank you. Let's see if anything happens before I see you tomorrow.'

That catches him out. 'Tomorrow?'

'We're having lunch. It's in your diary. How about the Strangers' Dining Room?'

'So a public affair, is it? What are you doing, Chris?'

'What the idiot who replaced me in parliament should be doing – and you!'

Owen glances at his watch. His window to stretch his legs is closing.

'Fine. Tomorrow. How are Rob and the kids?'

'Fine. Phil is trending on Twitter, by the way.'

'Yeah, he fucked up good and proper in the Chamber,' Owen says with a certain relish.

'No, not that. Something he said to a bunch of students in the lobby.' She goes quiet and Owen can hear her listening to Phil's voice. Weird. He was standing two yards away when it happened. Now Phil has ghosted his way into Christine's home office in the Newcastle suburbs and Owen can hear the trace of him over her phone. 'Hmm.'

It's the noise she makes when someone has managed to impress her. Owen feels a wave of jealousy, then a backwash of guilt. She married someone else. She has a family. You had your chance, McKenna.

'What's the arsehole saying, then?'

She sighs. Owen hears a tap at the other end, imagines her with her afternoon tea in her hand, setting the mug onto the table top. Would he recognise the mug? Do you ditch all your old mugs when you break up? What's the shelf life of a mug? Is twelve years unreasonable?

'A spirited defence of British democracy. Twitter is lapping it up. See you tomorrow.'

She cuts the connection. Owen puts the phone away, feeling weirdly rejected, and he's back in St Stephen's Hall staring up at the bearded knights in chain mail off to right imagined wrongs in the Holy Land. Walk. He nods to another backbencher in the doorway to Westminster Hall and one of the Leader's Office political advisors cruises by him without a flicker of recognition. Owen is pretty sure he helped get that arse hired. Now he's got a decent tie and a serious expression and he thinks he's saving the country. We're all trying, fella.

He walks down the shallow stone steps to the landing overlooking Westminster Hall. A change of mood. Hits him every time. The Victorian gothic fantasy is replaced with the austere grandeur of the oldest part of the parliamentary estate. A vast space the length of a football field, its hammerbeam roof a masterpiece of fourteenth-century engineering. Guy Fawkes and Charles I were both sentenced to death here. It's been a shopping arcade, a courtroom, a church, a concert hall, a feasting chamber. It is full of ghosts.

Owen sees one.

He stops in his tracks, rocks back slightly to let another group pass by him. He's older, a little frail perhaps, but it is him. Sabal Dewan. Owen feels the years disappear, leaving him cold and afraid, suffering those first punches of guilt and horror.

Sabal looks up and sees him. Owen tries to smile, but Sabal just looks away. Should Owen go and speak to him? It's been what, thirteen years? He can't cower here behind a bunch of schoolkids. He wonders who the woman with the braids is, standing at Sabal's side. She is wearing a claret sheath dress, high heels, dark raincoat. Go and ask if you're interested, he says to himself. He takes a deep breath, rehearsing the questions in his head, then Sabal turns away; his narrow face is transformed by a wide smile, a warm smile. It triggers another memory, another punch in the stomach. A day in the shared house when Sabal came to have lunch with them in the garden. To meet Jay's friends. Summer of 2008 when even the banking crisis was just a shadow on the horizon and all they could talk about was Obama's nomination. Happy days. Sabal holds out his hands, palms up ready to embrace . . . who? No. No way.

Sabal is greeting Georgina Hyde like she's a long-lost daughter. They've kept in contact? Georgina opens her arms and then bows, all smiles, and leads them both away, staying close to Sabal.

'Owen? Got a sec? As you're just standing there.'

The voice is coming from behind him. He takes a second to put some sort of professional smile on his face.

'Charlotte! How are you? I was just contemplating the future of democracy.'

Charlotte Cook. Lobby journalist for one of the many papers who loathe Owen, his party and his leader, but Owen suspects Charlotte is not as loyal to the party in power as her bosses believe. She keeps her reports factual, calls for comment before she runs something. Also a *very* careful gossip. She is wearing TV make-up, which makes her look a decade younger than she is under TV lights, but disconcertingly 'done' in the greyish natural light of the hall.

'Yeah, like you care. And don't try that democracy nonsense, either. One – we both know it's empty cant, and two – Philip Bickford is our knight in pound-shop armour today.' They are in danger of causing an obstruction. Charlotte sighs noisily at a middle-aged couple who brush her shoulder. 'Off for one of your walks? I'll keep you company to the edge of the estate.'

'Fine.' They walk down the steps together and the ceiling rises above them. Owen notices she's wearing trainers. A lot of women in parliament do this, switching into heels for any time the cameras are nearby, keeping their Converse and Nikes handy for the rest of the time when they are wandering the endless corridors, chasing division bells, bills, stories. 'And why would a lowly backbencher like me deserve such an honour?'

'I must have started drinking earlier than usual today,' she replies. Owen's never seen her drink anything stronger than mineral water. 'I'm giving you a heads-up. And you'll owe me one. The Labour Party leadership are launching an anti-bullying investigation.'

'OK.'

She shoots him a side-eye. 'The word is a slightly skeezy freelancer called Edward Barns has whipped the editors of the *Chronicle* into a frenzy with the prospect of a damning exposé. Your leadership wants to get out in front of the story.'

Owen feels a tight knot of anger in his stomach. A government with unprecedented powers, a country reeling and wounded by the social and economic shock of the century and all his party can do is disappear mournfully up its own arse. Whatever it is, publish and be damned. Trust the people to work out what matters.

They go out through the doors and into the spring air, damp

and chill. Three steps out onto the tarmac, she puts a hand on his arm.

'2009, Owen,' Charlotte says, looking up at him with her heavily mascaraed eyes. 'It's Jay Dewan's case they are investigating.'

That hits him like a punch in the gut. He should have known. So that's why Jay's father is in the building.

'Why? After all this time?'

Damn. He normally has a good poker face but Charlotte is watching him, sees the shock. He wonders what she remembers about those times.

'It's a good story, Owen. The former housemates. Jay makes a great tragic hero, and now you and Georgina are on one side of the house, eager to govern, and Phil is on the other, rising through the ranks. Human interest and a whiff of dark deeds. Of course the *Chronicle* is eager.'

'There were no dark deeds,' Owen says, as firmly as he can.

She watches him, professional cynic, but then so is he. 'You might need a better line than that, Owen.'

Now they are on the tarmac forecourt, the echoing space of the ancient hall is replaced by traffic noise, the smell of the caramel-nut vendors, the chants of the protestors. The sky is overcast.

'Thanks, Charlotte.'

'Pick up when I call you, Owen.'

Is that a threat, or a promise she'll tell him more when she can? Probably a bit of both, knowing journalists, and Charlotte. She releases his arm and turns back into the hall. Owen leaves through the turnstile and heads straight across Westminster Bridge. For the first time in a year he doesn't take note of the number of tourists, tally them with the month before and pray for continued growth. He walks towards County Hall and the Southbank, head down.

2009. The Jay Dewan case.

The past is coming for him.

Chapter 3

Phil doesn't look at his secretary as he passes through the outer office; she half gets up before she catches Ian's 'not now' signal, and sinks back miserably into her seat as Phil shoulders his way into his own office. Toby bloody Dale is sitting in his chair. Behind his desk.

'Get out of my chair, Toby.'

He does.

'What in God's name happened? Did you have a stroke? Did your brain literally start bleeding in there? That was the most humiliating thirty seconds of TV I've seen in my entire life.'

Phil walks past him, throws his folder on the coffee table then drops into his chair. The office, with its high narrow windows and tatty panelling, feels like a prison today. There is a letter on his letterhead lying on the blotter in front of his keyboard.

'What's this?'

Toby is typing something on his phone, he finishes then

shoves the handset into his pocket. 'It's your apology, of course. And you should be bloody grateful it's not your resignation. Did you hear your dear old friend Georgina Hyde on the *Today* programme this morning? Slagging us off again on behalf of all the key workers – you'd think they'd be happy to be in work without another pay rise – and then, just when the press are getting bored rehashing her thought-for-the-fucking-day-touchy-feely-bollocks you hand them a gift-wrapped cherry for a second bite.'

Phil reads the letter. It's snivelling. Abject. He's exhausted. 'I'm not signing this.'

'You are. Or the PM will sack you himself.'

Phil looks up. Toby is the sort of person who wears a Union Jack waistcoat at fundraising dinners, can't stop banging on about the Great British spirit but despises from the depths of his soul the fifty per cent of the British people who think he's full of shit and his plans for the future wishful bollocks. They lack pluck, apparently.

'No, he won't,' Phil says. 'Not now, anyway. It'll make him look panicked. Just like this letter does. It was a mistake. It was corrected. You're the one turning a five-minute story into a whole news cycle, Toby.'

Toby goes purple. Patches of it in his cheeks. A miracle he's survived the virus so far with blood pressure like this.

'Listen to me, Philip. You've managed not to screw things up till now, but I know at heart you're not just a remoaner, you're a socialist and I can't believe we were stupid enough to let you into government. If I scratch you, you'll bleed red.'

'We all bleed red, Toby.'

That doesn't help. The vein in his forehead is throbbing.

'You are hanging on by a thread, *a thread*. We need a united party, and the PM doesn't trust you. Neither does the Secretary of State and neither do I! If I go back and tell the PM you won't sign this, you won't be sacked tomorrow or next week. First we'll have a good trawl through the archives for every fuck-up, every sin being laid at the health department's door and then work out how every one of them was your fault, *then* we'll throw you out. Sign this letter or I will personally see to it you are the sin-eater for the whole fucking department.'

Philip has to take a moment now. This was always the danger. What had made him valuable to the Cameron government and useful to this one – his past as an activist on the other side, his working-class roots – also made him vulnerable when someone was looking for a scapegoat and God knows, they need a farm full of them now. He looks back down at the letter. Maybe it's not so bad. Toby is breathing hard, sensing a win.

A knock and the door opens.

'What?' Toby shouts over his shoulder.

Ian comes into the room and stands between them, cradling his phone in two hands.

'You have to see this,' he says to Phil, then to Toby. 'The Minister is trending all over Twitter.'

'No sodding surprise there,' Toby spits.

'No. Not the fuck-up. The thing you said in the lobby. It's all over. *The Times* is on the phone, and Ian Dunt's just retweeted the clip. He says "Fuck yeah."'

Again Philip tries to remember what he actually said.

Ian's voice rises with enthusiasm. '*Telegraph* says Minister's off-the-cuff defence of parliament strikes chord with patriotic voters. The original tweet's already got two thousand retweets. You're a meme, Phil.'

Phil picks the letter of apology off the table and hands it to Toby, unsigned. Toby folds it and tucks it into his inside pocket, his jaw working like he's sucking an arsenic-coated lemon.

'Minister, the chief executive of MenCap is here, and what shall I say to *The Times*?'

Philip nods. 'Show him in, Ian. And tell *The Times*, like all my government colleagues, I'm proud of our parliamentary traditions and will always speak in their defence.' He looks back at the crimson special advisor. 'Goodbye, Toby.'

Toby can't get any words out through his spasming lips. Who is having a stroke now? It's over. He leaves and Philip has a whole ten seconds to enjoy the moment before his next meeting begins.

Owen is lucky to have an office in Portcullis House. Not many backbenchers do, but he's been helpful on a couple of key votes, does his committee work diligently and this was his reward from a grateful whip – a room of his own where he can get to the Chamber for votes in an easy four minutes. His executive secretary Debra and researcher Pam share the room next door with staff of the chair of another committee. No outward-facing window onto the Thames, but it's a step up from his first office where the cleaning staff were still shifting out their mops and buckets when he turned up.

Twenty-five minutes after he left for his walk, Owen is back at his desk working through the emails and trying to ignore the flood of notifications on WhatsApp. Everyone has an emoji reaction to Phil's speech in the lobby they feel the need to share. Eye-rolls, fingers down the throat. The leader has tweeted a 'Though I don't often agree with the Right Honourable Member, on this occasion . . .' Bit pompous.

Pam and Debra have triaged the emails, sent standard replies to the form letters ('press here to email your MP!') and individually tailored replies to the ones who bother putting their opinion in their own words. And a lot of the constituency casework he won't even see – Angie in the constituency office will deal with it and send him a summary at the end of the week.

He still has a mound of desperate appeals to deal with, though. He rolls his shoulders and cracks on.

The shredded social safety net continues to let people drop through the holes. The hurried legislation to deal with the virus, and the knock-on effects from shuttered offices, courts and schools, has left bureaucratic chaos in its wake. The stunted system is more capricious, labyrinthine, cruel than ever. An MP on his own has little power, but it's amazing what a letter to the council or the bank can do if it comes on official House of Commons stationery. And a reputation for being a good constituency MP? A two per cent extra personal vote at the general election.

Pam comes in and offers to do a coffee run, then returns and talks him through local press campaigns, an update from the food banks in his constituency and he checks through and signs off on her draft responses and tweets.

'And I got your message about the data review question for the Secretary of State for Health. I've sent the follow-up.'

'Thanks.' Owen is already reading the next email. 'Any other business?'

'Yes,' Pam says slowly. 'The Leader's Office called. They want you to meet a lawyer called Chloe Lefiami at six. I was ordered to put it in your diary. Anything I should know?'

Owen looks at her. She looks so bloody young sometimes. Did he look like that? Back then? He remembers thinking he knew it all, and his anger when his elders wouldn't listen and came over all world-weary at him. Now he's doing it. He resists the temptation to ask Pam to define 'should' in this context.

'Have you heard the name Jay Dewan?'

Head on one side. A frown. 'Vaguely.'

'Google it. If anyone asks, I look back with great fondness on our friendship and will do anything I can to assist Ms Lefiami in her enquiries. That's it.'

She gets up to go.

'Pam?'

'Yes, boss?'

'Be careful on the phone and in the bars. The whisper is there's a story coming about Jay, and me. That the investigation has been launched as a response.'

She nods and he wonders if she realises just how bad this could be. Every MP has some crap printed about them, but this could be a lot worse than that. A lot worse.

'Anything in particular I should be on the lookout for?'

He breathes out slowly. He's been going over it in his head as he strode along the river with his head down. 'Yeah. Anything about me being a bully,' he pauses. 'Or violent. The working-class thug dog whistles.'

Her eyes widen and her breath catches, but she doesn't say anything, just nods and retreats from the room.

Six o'clock comes round fast. The coffee is cold but

untouched, a sad skin on its surface, when Pam knocks and ushers Chloe Lefiami into the room.

Owen gets out from behind his desk, smooths his tie and shows Chloe towards the tight coffee table and armchair set up that look like they were nicked from the nearest Travelodge reception area. Lefiami is older than he first thought, seeing her across Westminster Hall.

Chloe takes a seat and pulls out a yellow legal pad from her briefcase.

'Mr McKenna. Thank you for seeing me so quickly.' As if he had any choice in the matter. She's calm, efficient. 'Have the Leader's Office team explained to you what this is about?'

Owen crosses his legs, worries that it will make him look defensive, but uncrossing them will make him look shifty and nervous. He goes with it and folds his arms too.

'No. One of the lobby journalists told me an investigation had been launched into the Jay Dewan case to get in front of a hit piece in the *Chronicle*.'

A flicker of amusement or mild contempt crosses her face. He can't tell which it is.

'I'm not sure about the hit piece, but your leader has asked me to run a formal investigation into what happened to Jay Dewan and any other historic accusations of bullying and intimidation that come to light as a result.'

She reaches into the briefcase again and produces a card. Passes it over to Owen. He has to lean forward to take it and finds himself, elbows on his knees, sitting forward and staring at it.

'You're a QC?'

'Are you surprised that *I'm* Queen's Counsel, or that the

Leader of the Opposition's office is concerned enough to *appoint* a Queen's Counsel?'

He puts the card on the table and leans back again. Looks straight at her. Lets himself be assessed for flickers of racism.

'Bit of both. You look too young to be a QC and I imagined LOTO would have asked one of their own many, many lawyers to run the investigation.'

Chloe writes something down and Owen fights the impulse to ask what it is. She uses an ordinary pen. A plastic Fineliner. He thought all QCs got a Montblanc fountain pen with the wig.

'So, Mr McKenna, could you tell me how you came to share a house with Jay Dewan?'

He sees it. The traffic-clogged street on the borders of Lambeth between Elephant and Castle and the Imperial War Museum. A stumble from the Kennington Tandoori and the Dog House pub. He can smell the diesel in the air, the fat and spiced temptations of the chicken shops. Then the house itself. A Victorian three-storey with tall windows, a broken mosaic path and a high hedge. The long shabby back garden which backed onto someone else's back garden, full of foxes and lost children's toys.

Chloe is waiting.

'Georgina Hyde – Maxwell, she was then – found the house through friends of her mum and dad.' Though Georgina would call them Mother and Father. 'The owners were academics who had gone to teach at Yale for a year. She and Jay were at university together. They knew Philip Bickford from Oxford. I knew Phil from when we were both on sabbatical running Labour Students a few years before.'

'You weren't at Oxford?'

Owen feels himself bristle. 'I was at Manchester. You?'

Now she looks up at him and flashes a quick smile. 'Sussex.'

He relaxes a little.

'And your job at this point, Mr McKenna? When you were sharing the house?'

Hours under strip lighting in Charlotte Street open-plan offices, staring at focus group reports and polling data, making weekly PowerPoint presentations of local by-election results, pulling quotes from the emails of Constituency Labour Party chairs and their volunteers. Following up donor leads, harassing CLPs for donor leads. Trying to build a war chest without selling his soul. Any more of his soul.

'I was Head of Field Operations at Labour Party HQ.'

'And Jay was a junior advisor to the Treasury team?'

'Yes.'

'Important job in the middle of the financial crisis.'

Owen resists the temptation to repeat 'junior'. It was a big job for someone Jay's age, even if most of his work was admin. Oh, and obsessing about getting Alistair's message out, trying to manage the story of the relationship – fissured and fracturing – between Number 10 and Number 11. Jay had been right in the middle of things, though. In Downing Street. He couldn't help reminding his housemates of that, and however much they had taken the piss out of him as a tea boy, they couldn't help resenting it. A big job. Too big. Too close to the sun. The gravity and pressure of the space he occupied was crushing.

'And Philip Bickford?'

He can't talk about Phil. 'I'm sorry, I should have offered you something to drink. Do you want a tea, or a coffee?'

'I'm fine, thank you, Mr McKenna.' She waits, looking at him with her head slightly on one side. Calm. Neutral. Some of her braids have sliver thread running through them.

Fine.

'He was Research Director at the Centre Ground Institute.'

'Which is now defunct . . . '

'He destroyed it when he left to become a Cameron crony.' The words come too fast, too hot. She doesn't react, just writes on her pad.

'And Ms Hyde was Political Officer of the Public Sector and General Workers Union at this point?'

He nods. Easier to be off the subject of Philip, push aside the swirl of uneasy and bitter memories his name provoked, the raw feeling of his knuckles. God, they sounded like high flyers – head of this, officer of that, advisor. Still just a bunch of over-eager political junkies in their twenties, trying on responsibility and job titles like teenagers experimenting with their looks.

'Georgina was impressive even then. The unions were still a difficult place for a young woman, but she'd found a way of working with the team.'

Chloe looks up. 'In what way "difficult"?'

The question surprises Owen. Surely a black female QC doesn't need to ask him that? It takes him a beat before he realises that Chloe is checking that *he* knows.

'Institutional sexism, of course. It was a pretty macho culture. I don't remember anything specific. I was just aware it was hard.'

Owen spots a micro-shrug.

'How did she get on with her boss?'

Is that a trick question? 'Well, she married him just before the 2010 election. So pretty well, I guess.'

'It's my understanding,' she goes on, flipping a page in her notebook, 'that things started going wrong for Jay in the autumn of 2008. Is that your recollection?'

Owen's memory feels hazy. He tries to remember the first time he saw Jay ruffled. Tries to find some anchor in his memory.

'It's difficult to ... It's like going bankrupt, isn't it? What happened to Jay, I mean? It happens slowly, then suddenly and all at once.'

If she recognises the quote she gives no sign, and Owen feels a need to explain he's never gone bankrupt himself, it's just ... He squashes it. He can do calm.

'What about the week Lehman Brothers collapsed?' Chloe goes on. 'That was 15 September 2008. You had a party. Do you remember that?'

Of course he does.

Chapter 4

Monday 15 September 2008

'It's crazy. Have you seen this, Owen?'

Phil's taken the armchair opposite the TV and has pulled the curtains against the early evening sun so he can see the screen. He's leaning forward, like he might see something new in it if he concentrates hard enough. His backpack is dumped on the floor next to him, his latest pamphlets slithering out round his feet.

Owen puts his bag on the sofa and shrugs off his coat.

'Of course I've seen it. It's on a loop.'

He can't help watching it again, though. The woman comes through the spinning glass doors of Lehman Brothers in Canary Wharf, her expression dazed, and squints against the light. She has a cardboard box in her arms, a pot plant drooping over its edge.

You can imagine her, picking one of her variations on the city slicker uniform ready for a day at the desk doing whatever it was she did just as dawn broke, and now at 10.30 a.m. she's out on the street.

She's baffled, caught by the waiting cameras looking left and right. Owen guesses she's probably deciding between the Tube or the bus as her taxi account would have been cancelled, but they keep showing it. Her confusion. Her cardboard box. He can feel it being etched into his brain a bit deeper every time it comes on.

'It's crazy,' Phil says again. 'What on earth is going to happen? Have you spoken to Jay today? I've been trying to commission a pamphlet from one of the LSE professors and when I called him he was almost in tears. He thinks the whole financial system could buckle any moment. It'll be anarchy.' Then he looks. 'You OK? You look like crap.'

'Thanks for that. Yeah. Everyone's running round like headless chickens and picking through the copy on the website to make sure we don't still have language about "financial innovators" in the city for the hacks to find.'

Owen picks up his bag and goes to hang it and his coat in the hall. This is the nicest house he's ever lived in, and his mum would expect him to treat it with respect. He can't tell if the world is collapsing or not. The buses and cabs still cruise by outside, the bars are filling up. The sun rose this morning and the cash machines are working. But somehow the foundations are gone. Everyone is living on really thin ice, on surface tension, and they just don't know it yet.

What's better, warn them? Cause panic, make them look down? The illusion shatters and we all fall through into who knows what? Or do what they are doing? Send in teams to prop it up, emergency joists under the structure made of solid gold and hope the people never know how close the abyss got to sucking them all in. Present them with the bill later? Human beings cannot bear much reality.

'You going to the kitchen?' Phil calls out. 'There are beers in the fridge. Grab one for me, will you? And help yourself.'

Owen walks through the house to the kitchen, walking carefully like he might fall through a crack.

The kitchen is large – a huge wooden table at the house end – not like the polished table in the dining room. This one is rustic. What Owen has learned to call 'rustic'. Ten years ago he'd have just called it a bit knackered. A door on the right leads to the long, narrow back garden and beyond the table is a generous U-shape of units, sink, stove, cupboards. It's an extension built by the current owners, practical but a bit boxy and low in comparison with the high ceilings in the rest of the house. He's learning the language of the middle classes and to pass in London, in Westminster, you need to get the words right. In every house big enough there is the room for special occasions only. It was the 'lounge' where he grew up, the 'front sitting room' here. 'Serviettes' there, 'napkins' here. 'Toilet' at home, 'lavatory' in Westminster. Then there were the little shifts in the things themselves. Figurines v. *objets d'art*. Family photos and reproductions v. limited-edition prints bought from the artist. Antimacassars v. spindly dining chairs with fluted backs.

Phil has bought Stellas. A lot of them. Not Red Stripe, but good enough. Owen takes two and glances at the post on the table. Doesn't spot his name on anything. Mostly junk mail, a couple of bills. Georgina will deal with them. She'll tell them what they owe and make sure everyone coughs up. Phil grumbles sometimes; he's got a weirdly picky attitude about money, how to split the bill in the restaurant, or if he should pay as much electric as Georgina because of her hairdryer. It's uncool of him, weird and he can't help it. Owen is a spend-it-while-you've-got-it man himself and he trusts Georgina to be fair. He pays less rent because he's in the back bedroom, and it was Georgina who worked out some formula about floorspace and proportion of utility bills.

He goes back into the lounge, sorry, sitting room – gives Phil his can and sets his own on the coffee table before he goes upstairs to change. Indoor and outdoor clothes. You wear the good stuff on the street only, then change to save the wear when you get in.

His room might be the smallest, but it looks out over the back garden and he prefers that to the main road. There's a crappy wardrobe, a chest of drawers too big for the room and a bed with a decent mattress. He changes into chinos and polo shirt on automatic pilot and then it hits him. He sits down suddenly on the edge of the bed and stares out of the narrow window.

It's *not* going to be OK. All those mighty ships of finance crashing into the rocks. All those wise men and wizards of the City were drunk at the wheel and charged at the rocks with a bottle of Perrier-Jouët in one hand and a cigar in the other.

And who is going to pay? He hopes it will be them, the financiers, but he's been in London long enough to think that's unlikely.

The front door opens and closes, knocking him out of his funk. He wants that beer now. He heads back downstairs. Jay is home. A despatch from the frontline.

Jay Dewan is perched on the far arm of the sofa when Owen

comes in, a bottle of Peroni gripped in his hands, staring intently at the screen and picking at the label. As Jay hears Owen he turns and smiles. He's excited. They exchange greetings. Jay looks like he's ready to spring to his feet and into action at a whistle. Like a hunting dog.

'Can this get any worse?' Phil says.

'Yes,' Owen and Jay say in unison.

'How did you get home so early, Jay?' Owen adds.

'I've been there since six and all weekend. Clive sent me home. We're sort of working in shifts, looking after Alistair, fielding calls from bankers having nervous breakdowns. Half the time I think I should be giving them the number for the Samaritans.' Owen laughs darkly. 'How is it at headquarters?'

'Lots of people asking each other what's going to happen next and no one having a clue.' He takes a long swig from his can. 'But you holding up, Jay?'

He runs his hand through his hair. 'Yeah, cheers. I wish I could work out where these stories about me are coming from, though.'

'What – are there more?'

They've been on his mind for a few weeks now, these stories. Owen found him working in the dining room last week, upset because someone had told someone that Jay had said something off about a mutual friend. He'd explained he'd never say anything like that and been believed, but it had rattled him.

'Tess asked me how I was coping, given my "party schedule". Told her I haven't been to a decent club since July in Ibiza, but I don't think she believed me.'

'Probably just someone jealous of you,' Owen says.

He smiles. 'True. Well, who wouldn't be? But, I don't know,

there are still plenty of people who think if you are gay and under fifty you must be out having sex with strangers in clubs five times a week. Chance would be a fine thing.'

'Your team can't think that. Just ignore it.'

'Yeah, I know. I'll try. Just grates a bit, you know.'

Phil gestures at the screen. 'What *is* going to happen to this country? We can't just save the banks and ask them nicely not to do it again. There have to be consequences.'

Jay picks at the label of his beer bottle. 'There will be consequences,' he says firmly. 'But if we don't support the banks they will collapse and that means no cash in the cash machines, no way to get your wages paid or buy your shopping. If the banks go, the whole bloody thing goes.'

'So we bankrupt the country to save the City?' Owen asks.

'I know, I know!' Jay replies. 'But if the City goes, everything goes.'

Phil reaches for the remote and mutes the news. No one protests. 'That's it, isn't it? If the government does its job properly, life will carry on as normal for most people. It's what we have to do, but we won't get any credit for it.'

'Gordon had a meeting about the party conference today,' Jay says. They all refer to the Prime Minister as 'Gordon'. They'd be lucky if he could identify any of them with more than a vague nod. Owen hates it. Knows he does it himself, nose up like a terrier when one of the Cabinet breezes through the office, yipping with the other office juniors for the chance to make an impression.

'And?' Phil says.

'It was supposed to be five minutes.' Jay's voice is dry. 'Then his executive secretary went out to grab lunch and the junior didn't dare bust in and say the Bank of England and Treasury teams were waiting. Scared shitless of Gordon tearing him a new one. We waited forty-five minutes before Gordon looked at his watch and buzzed through to see why we hadn't turned up.'

His voice is hollow now, wondering. Owen gets interested. 'And?'

Jay pushes his hand through his hair again and it falls immediately back into place.

'They needed Gordon's OK to the new banking guarantees. In those forty-five minutes nearly 450 million pounds' worth of deposits in UK banks were transferred abroad.' He drinks the rest of his beer. 'That secretary's sandwich cost the UK economy almost half a billion quid.'

They are all silent for a minute.

'Fuck,' Phil says. And he means it.

Someone laughs on the pavement outside, footsteps on the path, then the front door opens. Georgina swings into the room. She's got one of her work friends with her and her phone at her ear. She finishes the call.

'Thanks – yes, that's great. Glad to help. Bye!' Phone down. She holds up a catering sack of soft white rolls. 'We're having a party. Owen, help us get the barbecue going, will you? Jay, Phil, be heroes and go raid Sainsbury's for sausages? I got the burgers and buns.'

Phil points at the silent TV.

'World is on fire, Georgina.'

She rolls her eyes. 'Hence the barbecue. It's a theme.' She leans against the edge of the sofa. Owen can smell the lemon of her shampoo and the stale office air on her clothes. Her phone starts ringing again. She glances at the screen. 'Look it's all our people. Everyone's been run ragged and there's more to come. Let's give them the chance to blow off some steam, eh?'

The man behind her in the doorway shifts the bag of charcoal in his arms and curses under his breath at the black smear on his shirt. 'Georgina, where do you want this?'

'Out back. Just go on through.' She turns back to her housemates. 'Come on, Owen, you can help us get the fire going. Jay, Philip, go hunt and gather.'

Jay sets down his beer and stands up. 'Actually, it's not a bad idea. Let's call some people. Everyone needs a night off. Come on, Phil. Georgie, did you get any snacks? I'll pick up the hummus and crisps, that sort of thing.'

Suddenly it's Jay's party. Means they'll get some interesting people coming. People come when Georgina calls too, but when Jay calls they flock to the house. No wonder some of the aspiring politicos of SW1 are jealous enough of him to make up a few stories. Owen tends to do his socialising in the pub. He hasn't learned the knack of saying 'you must come over' and meaning it yet.

Owen finishes his can, wondering if it's learned or innate. Bit of both, like being a musician, or an artist. Jay is a born politician. Twenty-eight and he's better at it than half the Cabinet. Turns on the smile, offers his hand and you like him. You don't know why, you just do. He's got 'Future Leader' written all over him.

'Fine,' Georgina says. 'Thanks.'

She answers the phone with a warm 'Hi' and pushes herself off the sofa to follow Sad Charcoal Guy.

Chapter 5

It's a warm evening. Lights start to come on in the houses around them. Phil has opened the doors to the dining room and turned up Duffy on the midi hifi. Owen rolls the barbecue out of the garden shed, and the men fight half-heartedly about the best way to get it lit. Gradually the kitchen and garden fill up with party staffers, organisers and researchers and a handful of junior special advisors.

Owen sits on the low wall between the stone-flagged patio and the patchy lawn with Archie from the Labour communications team. Usual topic. David Cameron and how to beat him.

They've been fighting over 'just call me Dave' for months, and every time they do Owen feels the knot of anger and worry tighten in his head. Makes it ache. The Labour government is tired, and Georgina and Phil and Jay arriving all bright-eyed and bushy-tailed just as Tony Blair had the baton yanked from his grip can't change that.

Owen has been in the trenches longer than them. He was

working as an office boy at Labour Party headquarters back in the glory days while they were still doing their A-levels. The political bug was in his DNA, but those early years rattling around Westminster had given himself something else – ambition, and a sense of possibility. He got bold, talked his way into a degree course and student politics in Manchester, then back out when he got a sabbatical in London. He'd been here for the golden years of Cool Britannia, through 9/11 and the fucking war.

He notices Cameron's pictures in the papers now and shudders. He is a beast of the apocalypse come to punish the party he loves for its hubris, its naïve optimism. Labour is going to lose the next election. 'Manage the damage' is Owen's secret mantra now. Manage the damage.

Archie grinds out his smoke and drops the butt into an empty can.

'I'm just saying, people will see Gordon as a steady pair of hands in a crisis. And Alistair's calm demeanour is great on TV.'

Owen closes his eyes briefly. 'Archie, you're seriously telling me you think this fucking disaster is going to improve Gordon's chances? And everyone knows him and Alistair are at each other's throats half the time.'

'But why risk the uncertainty of a new government in dangerous times?' Archie looks hopeful. 'Voters want to stick with what they know. Why should that change?'

Owen's stomach actually hurts. 'Because they are the *Tories*! Just because Murdoch let Blair have a go at running the country as long as he behaved himself doesn't mean anything's really changed. In a crisis, trust a toff. It's what people in this country have had force-fed to them since William the Conqueror.' Archie looks irritated, frowns at the deepening shadows at his feet as Owen warms to his theme. He's said it before, it wins him no friends, but he can't help himself. 'The Tories will attack on both flanks. Every picture of Gordon or Tony shaking hands with a banker on one side, and then "Look at Labour, so irresponsible with money" on the other.'

He realises a pool of silence has developed around them. Someone's changing the CD and people are looking at him.

He stares back at them. 'It's true. You know it is.'

A woman in tight jeans with long blonde hair purses her lips. 'We just have to get the message right and stick to it.'

The man next to her nods. 'Yes, "Trust Gordon."'

Owen looks him up and down. The chinos and open-necked shirt, the glass of wine in his hand. He twists back towards Archie without bothering to reply.

Archie shakes his head like he's trying to get water out of his ears. 'They can't do that.' Owen finishes the last of his beer. The CD is changed. Pulp. The opening chords of 'Mis-Shapes' make him feel nostalgic and for a beat or two less alone. But he needs to shift before the twat in chinos starts singing along and ruins it.

'Of course they can. And they will.' He speaks more quietly, as much to himself as to Archie. 'It's what I would do. I'm going for another beer. Want one?'

Archie pulls a fresh Marlboro Light from the pack in his top pocket, flicks a flame from his Bic.

'No, thanks. After half an hour talking to you, I think I'll just go slit my wrists under your hydrangea instead.'

Owen laughs at that. Archie is all right. Owen has to stop getting so pissed off with them all. It doesn't help, letting the frustration build and then blasting out.

He pushes himself up from the wall and heads for the kitchen. It's fair enough. He isn't Mr Sunshine at the moment. No point now telling everyone they should have gone for the snap election as soon as Brown took over. No point telling them they can't lean on the heartlands, not after ignoring them and sucking up to *Mail* and *Times* readers. No point telling them Cameron's bullshit heir-to-Blair stuff is working. Have a drink. Unwind. Sufficient unto the day is the evil thereof.

The kitchen is a crush. Owen shoulders his way towards the beers, but a hand grabs his arm. Georgina. She's flushed, pissed but not too pissed, talking to Jay.

'Owen! Get me one, will you?'

He nods.

'Yeah, for me too,' Jay says.

He makes the final stretch to the beer bucket on the kitchen table, ice water and floating labels, and fishes out three bottles of whatever, listening to the others talk.

'Look, Georgina, it's basic economics.'

He's looking over her head, raises his hand to greet some new arrival.

She pokes him in the chest. 'Don't give me that crap, Jay. You want people to believe this isn't just about saving the bankers and letting ordinary people go to the wall, your team is going to have to come up with something better than "trust us".'

Owen passes them the beers but stays where he is to hear how the fight goes. Georgina and Jay were at Oxford together. Comes up a lot in conversation. PPE – philosophy, politics and economics – and the Labour Club. When they fight, they fight dirty. Neither of them afraid to go for the eyes, or the knee to the balls. It is, Owen thinks, to real discussion what a bar brawl is to ballroom dancing.

Where Owen grew up you didn't take someone down with a memorable insult. You used your fists. The golden rule was the same, though. It was all about who moved fastest and with maximum commitment.

'If you can't explain what's happening to an economics graduate like me,' Georgina is saying, 'how are you going to explain to the average worker? Are you just going to hand the bankers a blank cheque and say, "Steps have been taken" while my members are being chucked out on the street?'

'Oh, *your* members, are they?' Jay says. 'Georgina Maxwell, woman of the people.'

The crowd has pushed them close together; Georgina's eyes flash.

'You couldn't hack it working for a union, Jay. You treat anyone who hasn't got a degree like a clever pet – and that's on one of your good days. It's why half my office calls you "his Lordship".'

That makes Jay snort-laugh into his beer, but it's fake. Georgina has drawn blood. Still, it's not a great show from either of them. Tired boxers in the tenth round.

Someone reaches between them, semi-shouldering Georgina aside to tap Jay on the shoulder. Owen doesn't recognise him. Older guy.

'Jay! Let me grab you for a minute. I've heard a word out of Coventry East I want to talk to you about.'

He smiles. 'That would be brilliant. Give me two secs, though!' Georgina puts out her hand and the older man shakes it. 'Owen, there's someone I want you to meet. Grab another beer. Come with me.'

He does, because when Jay has that look of delight on his face there isn't much else you can do. 'Jay, stop trying to set me up with people.'

Jay puts his arm around his shoulders as he propels him deeper into the kitchen.

'Owen, you carry the weight of the world. Let me make you happy.'

He widens his eyes and Owen can't help smiling back at him.

Jay lifts his hand. 'Christine! This is the guy I want you to meet.'

There are two women whom he doesn't recognise standing by the sink. One turns as Jay hails her and right then, in that moment of seeing, Owen's life changes. He's flattened by a full-on Hollywood lightning strike. The woman is tall, mixed race, with her hair tied back and loose strands of it framing her face with corkscrew curls. She is still laughing at something her friend has just said, and it's the way she shakes her head, the slight twist in her lips. You can see the next question, the next thought or idea ready in her eyes, just behind her lips. She puts a hand on her friend's arm.

Cameron and the banking clusterfuck disappear from Owen's mind like the smoke of a snuffed candle. He breathes deeply to the soles of his feet and tries to remember what it is like to be a nice person, the sort of person he hopes this woman might like. The lights in the kitchen bounce off the darkness outside, giving her a halo.

'Hi, Jay!' Her voice is low, warm.

'Christine, this is Owen,' Jay says. 'Lynch pin of the Labour Party and despite his youth and good looks he's been around long enough to know where all the bodies are buried.'

49

The perfect name. Owen had never realised that before, but it obviously was. The best and perfect name. Jay turns to the friend. 'I'm Jay. Have we met? Do you know many people here?' She blushes and shakes her head and he gives her his full-beam smile. 'Let me introduce you to some of the nice ones and tell you which ones to steer clear of.' She looks delighted at the idea and lets Jay shepherd her away, leaving Owen alone with Christine.

'Hi, Christine.'

He offers her the other unopened bottle and she takes it.

'Thanks, Owen.' She twists round to locate an opener among the wreckage behind her and Owen finds he is staring at the line of her neck like Count Dracula.

She finds it with a little yelp of victory, opens her bottle, hands the opener to Owen, and both clink the necks of the bottles together.

'Cheers.'

She's got one of those non-regional accents. Not public-school posh, but neutral.

'So Jay said you work at party HQ,' she says.

'Yes. You in politics?' He can't decide if he wants her to be a politico or not.

'MP's researcher.'

Owen is sure – like down to his bones absolutely fucking sure – he would have noticed this woman around Westminster if she'd been in the village more than a week. He takes the chance.

'When did you start?'

'Today.'

'Welcome,' Owen says and manages not to add 'to the madhouse', which helps. 'Who are you working for?'

'Jasper Bartlett.'

Owen flicks through his mental rolodex of MPs. A good backbencher, solid on legislation committees and votes with the party. Was against the war, supported Gordon. 'Member for Alnwick South?'

She nods. 'That's him. My local MP.'

'You're from Northumberland?' Owen says. 'I went there once. School took us to the castle. I thought I lived in the north till I went on that coach trip.'

She laughs. 'Yup, you're a southerner.'

Owen tries to think of something witty or charming to say about Alnwick. He fails.

'Born there?'

'Born and raised. Dad was a dentist, Mum a nurse, from Ghana. My sister and I were the only black girls for twenty miles either direction. People were very disappointed every time they asked me something about Africa, and I had to tell them I'd never been south of Manchester.'

Owen reaches for a panic question. 'How do you know Jay?'

Christine smiles at him. A warm smile, but it's at the memory of meeting Jay, not for him. 'He spotted me in the Sports Bar when I was visiting last week, to get my bearings. Gave me his number and told me to get ready to be stuck in the front of team photo ops. He managed to do it in a way that seemed cool, though.'

Owen winced. 'As long as you don't get stuck in the back row for everything else.'

She gives him a serious look. 'I won't be. So are you going to ask me out?'

Fireworks of delight explode in Owen's chest. He owes Jay a pint or seven.

'I was going to go with the "drink to chat about your new career".'

She gives a sharp shake of her head. 'No, if it's a date, it's a date.'

'Then it's a date.'

'Owen! Babe! Can you come save us?'

Georgina is waving at him over the crowd. She comes towards them, registers Christine's presence with a micronod. 'Archie and Phil are trying to do the barbecue and they are going to kill us all – fire or food poisoning.' She puts her hands together in prayer. 'They'll ruin that chicken you made. Please feed us!'

Georgina has a way about her, no doubt of that.

'OK, OK.' He turns to Christine. 'Keep me company?'

'Sure!' Christine pushes herself away from the sink. She has tiny diamond earrings. Owen can't think straight. He doesn't care.

Chapter 6

Tuesday 16 September 2008

A twitchy and intense day at the office. The tension hums in the air, a dropped cup in the coffee area and everyone jumps like a gun has gone off. Owen wades through his call sheets preparing for the conference, but his voice feels unnaturally loud; his chatty and friendly tone a bit forced. Everyone has an eye on the BBC News channel. He hangs on to the memory of Christine. She'd said he was brave when he told her about ditching his A-levels and coming down south, his months living in a squat and how he got the office job at Labour Party headquarters. She went to Exeter. Read French and English.

Owen gets home late and hungry, hoping to salvage supper from the remnants of last night's barbecue, to find Phil at the kitchen table with his head in his hands, bent over the newspaper, a half-filled bin bag of empties and paper plates at his feet.

Jay is rummaging in the fridge.

'I need vegetables,' he says over his shoulder as Owen comes in. 'Can I eat this broccoli?'

'Help yourself,' Phil says and turns over a page. 'Owen, you hungry? Jay is making a stir fry.'

That'll be an adventure. Owen isn't much of a cook, he knows that, but between living off cheap noodles in London as a teenager and feeding himself at university he can cope in the kitchen. Jay, after public school and Oxford, still thinks opening a can of beans is a strange and esoteric art.

'Yeah, sure.' He picks up the bin bag and starts gathering more plastic cups, emptying dregs into the sink and sweeping crumbs off the working surfaces. 'Georgina in yet?'

'Out wining and dining with Kieron and his crew,' Phil says. 'Deciding on conference strategy.'

Owen should ask Georgina about that, see if there's anything he should be worrying about. Kieron has enough power and presence to make life difficult for the government if he wants to. One of the few Union leaders who still does. Sure, he is technically only second in command, but everyone knows he calls the shots at the Public Sector and General Workers Union.

'Jay, I owe you a pint or seven,' he says, peeling a plate off the work surface. It's glued on with dried mustard. 'Christine and I are going out for a drink tomorrow, thanks to you.'

'Thought you'd like her. Smart and takes no bloody nonsense. Deep calling to deep. Aww, shit!' Owen looks up. Jay drops the knife and holds up his finger, a neat slice across the top. He stares at it, seemingly fascinated by the sight of his own blood. It drips onto the cutting board.

'Mate, what you doing?' Owen says, abandoning the bin bag. 'Stop staring at it and run it under the tap.'

Jay switches on the cold with his elbow while Owen fetches kitchen towel and scrabbles for plasters in the 'chuck it in there' drawer.

'It really stings!'

'Let's have a look.' It's not deep. Owen takes Jay's hand, dries it and squeezes it with the towel, unwrapping the plaster with his teeth. 'Think you'll live.'

The blood blossoms through the damp paper. He takes it off, replaces it with the plaster. Jay hisses as he tightens it.

'That's all I need. What if I can't type?'

'Don't act like you lost a hand, Jay,' Owen says, glancing up. Jay frowns, then suddenly smiles at him, looking him in the eye over his damaged fingertip.

'Thanks, Mum.'

'Yeah, yeah. No more sharp objects for you. Clear up. I'll make food.'

'Thanks.'

Jay's phone goes. He fishes it gingerly out of his pocket.

Owen wipes the board clean and attacks the broccoli, then goes through the cupboard looking for odds and ends. He can't be bothered to wait for rice, it's after nine already and he only got three hours' sleep last night. Sod the stir-fry. Pasta will do.

Jay's end of the phone conversation begins to intrude.

'I've already told you. No . . . no, she didn't leave me a message last night. I'm telling you, I have a system! You think I could cope with everything going on if I didn't have a system?' Jay has his back to them, one hand holding his phone to his ear the other stabbing into the air. 'Yes, we did have a few people round, but what has that got to do with anything? She didn't mention it today!'

Phil lifts his head from the paper, catches Owen's eye. They exchange a shrug. Jay is still going.

'We're all busy. No. No ... I'll do it, but there was no message. I'm telling you. Don't give me shit for something that's not my fault! It'll be done by morning. What difference does that make now? Fine.'

He hangs up.

'I don't bloody believe it!'

Phil and Owen both turn to stare at him. 'What?' Phil asks.

Jay is staring at the wall; he spins round. 'Melissa claims she left me two messages to get the stats together for the graphics team last night. Now Simon is yelling for them. She didn't! And Simon's saying I must have missed it because of the party.'

Owen fills the kettle and flicks it on, finds a pan which looks clean.

'So you missed a message, happens to everyone. Particularly after a few beers.'

'I didn't miss it. I was fine. I went for a run this morning! But those stories about me being a party animal ...'

'So it's a fuck-up. How does yelling at your boss help?'

'I didn't yell. I just don't like being spoken to that way. Like I'm the help or something.'

'We're all the help, Jay,' Phil says, still bent over the paper.

'Speak for yourself. And I don't like being accused of lying.'

Owen finds the pasta and a jar of pesto without any fuzz growing in it. 'So don't accuse Melissa of lying, then,' he says.

'I don't know why you are on their side! I don't fuck up. Never.'

'Nice for you,' Owen says. Jay ignores him.

'God, I have to get them together now, it'll take me all night.'

'Food will be ten minutes,' Owen says.

Jay sighs, runs his hands through his hair and flinches as his injured finger complains. 'I don't have time to eat now. Couldn't stomach it.'

He leaves the room and they hear him thump into the dining room. Owen stares at the half-made dinner and half-cleared kitchen. Thanks a lot, Jay.

Phil gets up from the table and picks up the bag; takes over the clearing up.

'What's got into him? Bit dramatic over a missed call,' Owen says and carries on with the food. 'More mysterious whispers?'

'Probably rattled after last night,' Phil says, shaking his head.

'Why?' Owen gets on with the cooking. 'What happened?'

'When I went to bed, Thomas Berkeley was hinting to Jay about a seat. Next election. Coventry East, I think. Nothing certain, but you know that "nod nod, wink wink, play your cards right". It would put me on edge having that dangled in front of me.'

Owen pushes the pasta into the pan way too hard and splashes his wrist with boiling water.

'Fuck!'

Owen came to work for the party ten years ago, has been at the rock face since he was a kid, and no one comes to have a quiet chat about possible seats with him. You'd think that loyalty would earn him something, all that hard graft of organising the conference floor votes. But no, handsome Jay in the fancy suit with his first from Oxford gets the nod. Of course he does. Owen runs his wrist under the cold tap. Returns to the cooker without saying anything.

'Owen—' Phil ties up the bin bag and pulls another off the

roll. 'They need you at headquarters this cycle. You know that. No one knows the constituency parties like you do.'

Phil is a mind reader sometimes. And Owen knows he is right. Maybe, but it's easy to say, isn't it? And hard not to feel passed over. He checks the pasta, finishes cutting up the broccoli and chucks it in to blanch it.

'How are we supposed to claim to be the party of the workers, though, when we keep parachuting in Oxford graduates to every seat that comes up?'

'We are the party of the brightest and best.' They turn round. Georgina has come in unnoticed. 'You can leave the mess, you know, Phil. It's why we pay a cleaner. Is there food? I'll take some to Jay. He's growling over his laptop in the dining room.'

She looks flushed.

'The cleaner has plenty to do. We can make the effort. Had a good evening, Georgie?' Phil asks.

'Oh, spiffing! Using my Oxford-educated brain to work out how to help people keep their jobs or even, you know, actually get a new one while the world tumbles around our ears.'

Owen finishes making the pasta. She takes a plate from the cupboard, holds it out.

'I'll just serve Jay's dinner then,' Owen says and tugs his forelock.

'Give me a break, Owen,' she snaps. 'I've had an evening of Coogan's funny jokes and everyone calling the waitress "darling" and *I'm* the one taking Jay his fucking dinner, Oxford degree or not.'

Owen bites his tongue. Just let it go, he tells himself. He fills the plate, and Georgina grabs a fork out of the drying rack and exits in a plume of indignation.

Chapter 7

Monday 7 March 2022

'Mr McKenna?'

Chloe Lefiami is looking at him patiently.

'Sorry. I lost my thread.'

'We were talking about the day Lehman Brothers collapsed. You had a party at the house. You met Christine Armstrong. You and she were engaged for a while. I believe?'

'That's right. Jay introduced us. We got engaged late in 2009, but it didn't last long. She married an old schoolfriend of hers three years after that.'

'But were things tense in the house at that point?'

Owen thinks it through. 'Everyone was tense. World was falling apart. We were all working too hard, and it was all ... high pressured. For all of us in different ways.'

She nods and Owen wonders what she was doing in 2008 – if she remembers that night.

'And Jay? What about him?'

That was his last night as the golden boy, Owen realises. He's always thought of that evening as part of his own story – his and Christine's. Not Jay's. But now his view shifts and he realises that was the last time he saw Jay and Georgina spar like that, the last time Jay seemed to radiate light out into the room. His last night as the 'real' Jay.

Owen gathers his thoughts. Tries to turn them into things which can be written onto Ms Lefiami's yellow pad.

'He missed a couple of phone messages that evening. His boss, the head of comms on the Treasury team, wanted him to put together some stats for a party press pack. Left a message on his phone. When Jay got in on the Tuesday night, knackered, and hadn't got a clue about it, he got his arse handed to him.'

Chloe looks up from her pad.

'That was all? Just a missed call?'

Owen nods. 'Thing was, if he had just apologised and got on with it, he'd have been forgiven. Everyone screws up sometimes. But he kept insisting no one had left him a message, which sounded like he was calling his boss a liar, so it blew up. He could be stubborn. But then he'd been complaining about stories circulating about him for a while. He was already wound pretty tight.'

Jay was still talking about it when Owen had got in the next evening, high on his first date with Christine. It had killed Owen's happy mood.

'Then his boss said the hangover had probably been to blame and Jay got on his high horse over that,' he tells Lefiami. Those appeals to him and Phil and Georgina. *I wasn't hungover. I went for a run! Even though I didn't get to bed till four! It was you who had the hangover, Owen. Remember?* Owen just wanting him to shut up. Georgina being soothing.

'But yeah. That was where it started. God, I accidentally delete messages all the time. You get a bit fat-fingered . . . everybody does it. We had more important things to worry about.'

Lefiami nods. 'Like the party conference that year?'

'I was in charge of delegate liaison,' Owen says. 'I was pretty tense about it.'

'Important job?'

He grunts. 'I certainly thought so. Yes. We needed to get a clear message out to the voters that we were going to protect their mortgages, their savings, their bank accounts. I had to keep nonsense resolutions off the floor and make sure Gordon and the Cabinet knew which way the votes were going.' He remembers the rushed, intense conversations backstage, open only to those with an access-all-areas pass. The long trestle tables set out for the journalists slithering with cables, the huge silver flight cases of audio and video gear, the sound guys – they were all men back then, dressed in black and wearing headsets.

'And you got Phil Bickford a room for his pamphlet launch too?'

He nods. It was a broom cupboard really, but at least it was in the secure zone.

'Did you see much of Jay then? During the conference.'

Owen pauses. 'As I said, Ms Lefiami, I was very busy.'

She finally closes her pad and leaves him to his remaining emails just after nine. By the time Owen gets back to the flat he rents on the edge of Vauxhall, he is wrung out. Chloe Lefiami had stayed scrupulously polite throughout their meeting, but some of her questions made him uneasy. And it wasn't over yet. She'd be back, she promised with a slow blink, at some point in the future, to discuss the run-up to Glastonbury. He can't think about that, his conscience feels like it is clotting and souring.

Owen lets himself into the lobby of his building and checks his mail. Junk mostly. All the important stuff goes to the constituency office or his pigeonhole in the House.

He looks at his watch. Too late to eat anything, too early to go to bed. He takes the stairs to his flat on the second floor. Small, but well laid out and he has a desk by the window where he can work and look out at the magnolia tree bravely fighting the traffic fumes on the road outside.

He's there an hour later, still typing out replies to his constituency agent, when the door buzzer goes. He checks there's nothing in his diary, then goes to the door and picks up the answer phone. A middle-aged face, freckled and with thinning sandy hair, blinks into the camera.

'Hello?'

'Owen, Hi! It's Greg! I saw your light was on and wondered if you fancied a night cap.' He holds up a bottle of whisky alongside his face so Owen can read the label. Talisker. A single malt and not easy to get these days.

'Come on up.'

He presses the door release, then goes to open the windows, get some air circulating. Seconds later he hears the hum of the lift. Greg Griffen. Not a man to take the stairs. Greg was one of the MPs who thought he had a job for life, then got hoofed out of parliament in late 2019. Owen hasn't heard anything of him since. Does he want back in? Owen is beginning to get calls from former MPs looking for a chance to stand at the next election.

He tells them all he can't help them, that it isn't his job anymore. He is just a backbench MP trying to look after his constituency, keep up with committee work, but they press and he offers advice, his gut instincts, a few names of possible campaign donors, then returns to his own work. If Griffen is prepared to part with a bottle of Talisker for that sort of advice, Owen isn't going to drive him away.

He opens the door as Greg emerges blinking from the lift and stands aside to let him in.

'Nice place. Handy location,' he says. He sees the windows are open and takes off his mask.

Owen nods, hangs up Greg's coat and fetches glasses.

'Just passing by, did you say?'

Greg hands over the bottle and Owen wipes it, then cracks the seal and levers out the cork with his thumbs.

'Passing by on purpose, to be honest,' Greg replies and watches without saying any more as Owen pours the drinks.

There are armchairs either side of the fireplace. Straight-backed ones he and Christine found in a Bermondsey flea market during their brief engagement. She pointed them out and he paid for them. They are still the nicest things he owns.

And now they are settled. It's like being in a corner of the Commons library. The drinks, the chairs.

'What can I do for you, Greg?'

Greg sips his drink. 'Why did you resign as a parliamentary private secretary, Owen?'

Owen savours the drink. 'It's one of those times, Greg, when the official story is actually true. I disagreed with the leadership about Article 50.'

And God knows it had cost him. Fighting 'enemy of the

people' stories on the constituency Facebook groups, making his point again and again that following the will of the electorate on Brexit didn't mean he thought it was right to chain negotiators to an arbitrary timeline. Maybe it had helped, staying in the argument. He'd kept his seat after all when people like Greg had lost theirs.

'A man of principle?' He wears a sceptical smirk.

Owen doesn't reply. He believes the last two years have proved him right. But then everyone else says they've been proved right too and who can pick apart the damage after the virus anyway?

He drags his memory. Someone has said something to him about Greg in the last few weeks and it wasn't about him looking for a seat again. Owen feels his brain wake up. The deadening mental effect of the inbox slowly cleared by the peaty flavour of his drink. He looks more closely. Greg is wearing a suit. All his clothes, shoes too, the coat he was handed on the way in look like Savile Row. Not to mention the whisky.

'So what are you doing these days, Greg?'

Greg widens his eyes. 'Ah, I've crossed to the dark side! Maundrill Consulting took me on in early 2021, all those years toiling on committees paid off in the end. I'm in public affairs.'

'A lobbyist. Doing well, then?'

He nods. 'Became a director six months ago. We work across a lot of different sectors, putting our clients and their projects together with law makers.'

Boom time for lobbyists. The legislation passed as the economy ground to a shuddering halt in 2020 had been rushed, a thousand unintended consequences, and the business of the current parliament is to try and sort it out. The inquiries into the actions and reactions of the government have begun, but everyone is still scrabbling to keep up. The virus, Brexit, the ructions and reactions as the voters discover that things can still get worse. The government squeezes where it can, while fighting a rearguard action on targeted taxes.

Owen puts down his glass. He's tired. He needs to sleep.

'So?'

Greg nods. 'It's simple, really. I heard you tabled a question about the commercial use of NHS data. The upcoming consultation. Some of my clients are the pharmaceutical firms who used that data to save thousands of lives. They wanted me to see, quietly, if you had any particular concerns and to put your mind at rest. I understand their friendly overtures have been rebuffed. And a little bird told me you'd raised the matter with the Select Committee too.'

'Those committee discussions are supposed to be private, Greg. I'm sure you remember.'

Greg is completely unruffled.

'Christine Armstrong put you up to this, didn't she? I hope you've bothered to ask her why. The woman has a bee in her bonnet. You know how it can happen to people who have lost their seats. Some,' he points to himself, 'manage to find fulfilling work and thrive. Others, like Christine, spend their time packing delivery boxes in the back of their husband's little delicatessen and fume about perceived injustices. Past glories. Find a crank to hang their frustrations on, an old boyfriend to manipulate.'

The injustices were real, and Christine did the marketing for her husband's successful shops. Like every story, it's all about how you tell it.

'I have no idea what you're talking about.'

He swills his drink. 'Isn't it time you got back in the swing of things, Owen? A few speeches to the right groups, a word in the ear of the leadership from some of the party's biggest donors. You're wasted off the front bench.'

Yes, he still has ambitions. Then he catches the satisfied look in the eyes of this man whose constituents chucked him out on his ear. He pushes his drink away. 'I'm not interested in any favours from you, or your clients.'

'That's a shame, Owen.' Greg brushes some imaginary speck of lint off his lapel. 'But do think on it. Withdraw the question. Don't push it on the committee. The consultation will happen in due course, when we have our ducks in a row. No need to make a fuss just now.'

Owen stands up. 'Great to see you, Greg. Now sod off.'

'You are still unnecessarily combative, aren't you? Sit down, Owen.'

Owen doesn't.

'We just want to consult, quietly, with interested parties in order to present the case for the commercial use of the NHS data, so in this age of fuck-ups and missed opportunities we do something *right* for this country. You pushing for this consultation now draws attention and confuses matters.'

'Were you always this patronising? How the hell did you get elected in the first place?'

He arches his eyebrows. 'You helped me immensely in 2010. Got me another nine years. Which is why I am bringing you a bottle of very fine whisky and an olive branch.'

'What are you hiding, Greg? The sooner we have this consultation the better. I chased for an answer yesterday, and unless I get an answer I will raise it as a point of order with the Speaker.'

'You've always been a bit resistant to our sector, haven't you?'

'Lobbyists and special interests? Of course I have.' He recognises the name of Greg's company now. He has turned down a few invitations from them over the last month or two. Private openings, a couple of invitations to speak at regional conferences. Pam had told him they looked more like influence sessions than legitimate policy forums and the fees offered had made him uncomfortable, so he had told her to say no.

'Luxury of having a safe seat, I suppose.'

'I like to know where the money is coming from, Greg.'

'Fine.' Greg opens his briefcase and pulls out a thickly filled cardboard folder. Places it on the side table next to his glass. 'Withdraw your question or the story about poor Jay and the campaign you ran against him in 2009 will break. And trust me, Owen, however bad you think it might be, it will be much, much worse.'

Owen thinks he must be getting stupid. Whispers in the corridors about an exposé of what happened to Jay, the leadership investigation, now Greg's visit. The pieces fit together snugly. 'This so-called freelance journalist, Barns, works for you.'

'Let's just say we collaborate on a regular basis. I wanted to get a little something cooking when you began to show how unfriendly you could be. And then I remembered poor Jay. Wasn't much reported on at the time, was it? I suppose you were all nonentities then. But not now. Not to mention how much bad behaviour we tolerated in those days. So yes, I asked him to get the ball rolling, fed him a few truffles and left him to dig up a few more in the tangled roots of Westminster. He's already got enough to get the editors at the *Chronicle* salivating, but I told him to hold fire until you and I had a chance to catch up. And now I have this for him too.' Owen looks at the file and Greg sees it. 'I can stop the story, Owen. If I instruct him to, Barns will tell the *Chronicle* there was nothing there after all. Just unsubstantiated rumours. Click of my fingers and it's gone, then the inquiry will wither away too. Just withdraw the question.'

Owen feels sick. 'What's in the folder, Greg?'

'I won't ruin the surprise, Owen. But if I let Edward Barns publish what is in it, your career, such as it is, will be over.'

He fetches his coat, and lays it carefully over one arm, picks up his briefcase and opens the door into the corridor. He replaces his mask, then looks back.

'Just read the file, Owen. And enjoy the whisky.'

The door closes behind him. The lift hums in the hall.

For a moment Owen stays exactly where he is. Then he grabs the bottle of whisky off the sideboard and carries it to the open window.

'Oi! Greg!'

Greg is just letting himself through the metal gate and onto the pavement. Owen hurls the bottle so it smashes on the pavement in front of his feet. Greg skips backwards but his expensive shoes get splashed anyway.

Owen slams down the window and yanks the curtain shut. That was stupid. Felt good, though.

What had Christine got him into? He's been in politics all his adult life and no one's really tried to blackmail him before.

He's bone tired, but there's no point putting it off. He picks up the cardboard file and switches on the reading light. It takes him a moment to realise what he is looking at. After fifteen minutes of reading he wishes to God he had the Talisker back.

He is holding the complete medical records of Jay Dewan, from childhood to the summer of 2009. Owen has seen files in GPs' offices before – fat envelopes of forms and reports on different-coloured cards all shoved in together with copies of letters, notes and referrals. The file left for him doesn't look like that. It is perhaps seventy pages, crisply printed, stacked together in a solid block – but it contains the same material as those bulging folders behind the receptionist's desk. All the unwieldy and differently shaped forms and cards have been scanned – long file names on the bottom of each page – so even the sections that are handwritten have a machine-like smoothness. You can smell the expensive ink on each crisp sheet.

Lists of Jay's childhood immunisations and ailments, a broken arm when he was ten, his appendix out at eighteen. The regular struggles with his asthma. Not much for Greg to hold over Owen's head there. Then – towards the end – he comes across a stack of pages in looping but legible handwriting, scanned from an original and printed out. Owen is tempted to skip over them at first, still wondering why Greg thought news of Jay's broken arm would matter to Chloe Lefiami, or to him. Then he sees his own name. And Phil's. These are, he realises, looking back through the stack, his mouth going dry, detailed notes from Jay's sessions with a counsellor, starting over Christmas 2008 and into the spring of 2009. These wouldn't be in those standard folders. They would have had to have come from the counsellor's own records, but here they are, between prescriptions for antidepressants and inhaler refills. He hears

Jay's voice lift off the pages and he can't believe what the voice is saying.

If Greg hands this over to his pet journalist, Owen's career will be over.

Chapter 8

Owen is shoving his way through the exhibitors' hall looking for the chair of the Constituency Labour Party of Rickmansworth. He's made dozens of arrangements like this to meet face to face with the people he's been emailing and talking to on the phone all year. It gives him the chance to hear what they don't want to write down, or say over the phone in an open-plan office, and tell the grittier stories from the doorsteps they save until halfway down their third pint.

And this year he's not just picking up doorstep intelligence, he's chivvying and placating and listening on behalf of the whole party. He's access-all-areas and delivering votes on the conference floor. Strength and unity. That's the message of this conference and Owen is making bloody sure it stays that way. He hasn't slept in twenty-four hours, and his eyeballs feel like they are shrivelling in the recycled air, the fuzz of temporary carpeting catches in the back of his throat, but the adrenaline, and the litres of bitter coffee he's getting through are delivering a hell of a buzz.

A couple of the PSGWU boys stop him by the pop-up book stall to tell him Kieron Hyde is pushing for a public inquiry over banking job layoffs and Georgina is working the phones to get 'her' MPs on-side. He thanks them for the heads-up.

'She knows how to stay on the right side of the boss, that girl,' Pat Coogan adds with a leer. 'God, I'd love to have Kieron's job. All those lovely ladies needing a favour.'

Whatever. 'But I can count on your delegation vote tomorrow?'

'Yeah, fine. Kieron says he's OK with it so far. So long as you keep us in the loop. No nasty surprises. And no union-bashing briefings in the papers.'

'Understood. Cheers.'

'Owen!'

Coogan heads off and Owen turns towards the man shouting his name. Ed Kazan. His boss. He's thumbing through a copy of Robert Shrum's memoir of working with Teddy Kennedy. 'You read this?'

'Yes. It's good.'

''Course you have. Don't know why I bother asking. So are we going to win the floor votes tomorrow?' Ed asks.

'No guarantees.'

Owen is ninety-five per cent sure they will win all the important votes, but he's not saying so. If you're wrong, you look like an idiot, and if you're right it looks like it was a foregone conclusion and you get no credit.

There's the Rickmansworth guy. Owen lifts up his hand to

give him the 'stay there, with you in two minutes' sign. Ed is still looking at him. Eyebrows raised. He wants more.

Owen gives it to him. 'If the polls are as crap as we think they are going to be this weekend, the constituency delegates will buy into party unity rather than a big public row. That's what they're telling my team.'

Ed slams the book shut and puts it back on the shelf. 'Good. Get back in there. Listen to what they say. If we still have a banking system next week we'll work out the message then.'

Owen just nods and is about to move off when Ed stops him.

'You know Jay Dewan, don't you?'

'Yeah – we share a house.'

'Thought you did. Is he sound? I've been told good things, possible candidate. Maybe he parties too much, but now I hear something about him being unstable too. Shouting at his boss and now interrupting the Chancellor's calls?'

'Sounds like bollocks to me,' Owen says. 'Jay's solid.' Ed grunts and then waves at someone else in the crowd. Owen is released.

Weird. Three people have told him versions of this 'Jay interrupting the Chancellor' story now. A snippet to have a quick laugh over between sessions, negotiations. Roughly, they say Jay broke in to a call between the Chancellor and the Icelandic Minister of Finance with some bit of nonsense he insisted was important. Doesn't seem likely, but when three people tell you something, even if the details shift a bit each time, you start to wonder.

Owen's given the 'sounds like bollocks' line every time he's heard it, though Jay has been wound tight recently. Anyway, the whole party will be out drinking tonight. Should be plenty of gossip to replace a minor Jay fuck-up by breakfast.

Rickmansworth is a man Owen's own age with a face badly scarred by acne and wearing a shapeless green coat. '*New Statesmen* party?' he says as Owen reaches him.

'Yeah, I got you down as my plus one,' Owen tells him. 'Fill your boots and don't forget to lift some sandwiches for tomorrow's lunch.'

Rickmansworth doesn't answer. Owen looks up and sees Christine is coming towards them. He still cannot believe his luck. He's managed to take her out twice since they met, once drinks, once dinner. The conference has got in the way of things, but Owen is hopeful. Heart expanding, slightly doolally hopeful. It's adding to the buzz, that's for sure, and the frustration of not being able to spend more time with her makes moments like this sharper, clearer. He feels them under his skin.

And he notices people notice her. Like Rickmansworth, struck dumb. Owen says they look at her because she's beautiful. Said it to her last night when they got here and said goodnight at the door to the room she's sharing with a mate. She laughed, then said they look because she's black, then lists the number of times she's been asked if she's Diane Abbott's daughter.

'And anyway, I'm here to work. I don't like being "admired" like I'm a museum exhibit. Let them keep their eyes to themselves.'

It was a brief kiss goodnight. Then he left her to sleep while he made sure the first round of votes were secure.

Fat chance of men keeping their eyes to themselves if Rickmansworth is anything to go by. Owen introduces her to him and she is nice because he looks nervous and geeky and she's a kind person. By the time they are back in the Midland at the reception, Rickmansworth's got over his nerves and is debating policy with her, talking about the latest council by-election results and what the leadership has to do for Labour to win in the Shires.

'Owen! Have you got a minute?'

It's Jay. Owen hadn't even seen him come in. He must have just arrived and headed straight for them. His tie is off and his eyes have an unfocused glimmer. Owen tries to be jovial.

'What can I do for you, Jay?'

'Owen, have you heard this story about me breaking in to a phone call?'

The crowd is shoulder to shoulder and getting louder. Waitresses and waiters, all skinny and pale among the drink-flushed, mostly middle-aged crowd, shoulder through with their trays of mini meatballs and dabs of salmon mousse in pastry cases. Owen can feel the sweat prickling the back of his neck. The smell of warm bodies and breath and fish paste is getting a bit much.

'What? Oh, yes. I've heard it.'

Jay squeezes his eyes shut. 'It's bullshit – utter bullshit and *everyone* is talking about it.'

'Jay, JK Rowling has just given us a million quid. Everyone's making magic wand jokes. No one gives a crap about you.'

Not entirely true. When the big stuff is messy, serious and complex everyone likes sharing a tidbit about a potential star such as Jay making a twat of himself. It's the classic mix of jealousy and *Schadenfreude* which keeps the political world spinning. But still. They are running a country. Not everyone is talking about Jay. Not all the time.

'Georgina said you'd heard it.' Georgina? Owen tries to remember. Yes, she'd asked him, off-handedly, on the way into the Q&A. 'She thinks there is a campaign against me. Owen, take this seriously. This is my career.'

Owen feels his phone buzz in his pocket. A problem with one of the composite motions? He can hardly reach into his pocket to check, the crowd crush is getting so bad. He doesn't have time for Jay.

'Oh well, if it's your career, what the fuck are we doing hanging around? Summon the authorities! Launch an investigation.'

Jay looks stung and Owen feels like a heel. Too much coffee. Too many people.

He can remember the sniggering which followed him around headquarters in the early days when he mispronounced words he'd only ever seen written down, wore the wrong suit or shoes or admitted he didn't like *The West Wing* much while everyone around him was trying to talk like they'd been scripted by Aaron Sorkin.

'Look, Jay. It's shit when it happens, but it happens to everyone.' He puts a hand on Jay's arm. 'Don't go mental about it. Ignore it. Do your job. Laugh it off. If it's rubbish, your team will know that.'

'If!' Jay says it loud enough to make heads turn and shakes off his hand. 'If! I just *told* you it was bullshit. God, Owen. You're supposed to be my friend. You should be out there defending me. At the very least tell me who told you and I can sort it out with them.'

Owen has to get out of here soon. 'Jay, what's up with you? I'm not narking someone out so you can make an idiot of yourself shouting at them too.'

'Owen, it's got worse. Melissa had a go at me in the office yesterday because she'd been told I was calling her a liar. Now there's this story going round and all I did was pass the Chancellor a note. We all do it! It's our job! Someone is out to get me.'

Owen tries to ignore the crowd, concentrate on Jay and make him listen.

'Jay, you're knackered. Everyone is. You've got to calm down. Ignore it, go and charm the pants off a few people and leave this stupid story alone. Think about something else, for God's sake.'

'Wow. Just wow. Thank you for your help, eternally grateful, my old mate,' Jay says and turns his back, pushing past the waiters and heading for the exit. Had that been an attempt to take the mick out of Owen's accent? The arsehole. Let him stew, then.

An MP and a reporter chatting nearby watch Jay go, then look at Owen, eyebrows raised. Owen shrugs – 'nothing to do with me, guv' – and feels a touch on his arm. Christine, thank God. Her touch fizzes up his bloodstream.

'Your CLP man says thanks for the chat and he'll see you round,' she says. 'What's up with Jay?'

'He's being an idiot.'

She accepts this without comment. 'I'm going to drop in on Phil's event then see if I can find Jasper.' Her MP. Jasper gets to spend hours a day with her, the lucky sod. How can he get any work done? 'Though I saw him talking to Georgina earlier, so I'll probably just get twenty minutes on what a remarkable young woman she is.'

Owen grins. 'Jealous?'

'Oh, I know Jasper's a solid guy, but he's a bit of a dinosaur about women. Or "the ladies" as he calls us. And Georgina does sort of flirt with him.' She sips the last of her white wine, considering. She looks composed even in this crowd. 'You know she's ditched the automatic payment system from the Union Political Fund? Used to be the local party would just get a cheque in the post, now they get a personal note, signed by her. And she pops by personally to tell the MPs they've got their reselection votes for the trigger ballots. All "I rang round the branches and made sure they are happy to support you" stuff. And she does it all with the smiles and hair-tossing and they all act like she's their niece who's just turned up with homemade cakes.'

Owen is scanning his messages. Couple of orange flags.

'She's smart. Look, I've got to go.'

'What, and I'm not? Just because I think hard work and actually giving a damn about what I do is more important than biting my bottom lip and acting like every lecherous old fart here is my special "Daddy"? It's not just irritating, it's bad for everyone. It makes them think they can get away with their sexist bollocks.'

Whoa. She is jealous. He half-laughs, risks leaning forward and kissing her forehead. It's cool. He thinks of sea breezes and open skies. 'Georgina is just a great operator, that's all.'

A narrow crease across her forehead, then she shakes it off. 'OK. See you whenever.'

Not their warmest goodbye. Owen wonders if he's done something wrong. Maybe Christine is jealous of Georgina's contacts – all the Oxbridge crowd, or the fact she's done so well in the Union while Christine is just another bright researcher. He watches her leave and is about to follow, check she's not really angry, when a pollster ducks under a plate of mini hamburgers to block his path. Christine disappears.

'Word in your ear, Owen?' He starts talking about just how bloody marginal some of the marginal seats are. 'Long story short, how the money is doled out and spent at the next election is going to make or break us. Strategy is everything. I've told Gordon, I've told Ed. Now I'm telling you. It's going to mean making some brutal decisions about who gets money.'

The orange flags will have to wait until later. It's going to be a long night.

Chapter 9

Tuesday 8 March 2022

Phil's team has spent the last twenty-four hours turning down media requests left, right and centre, which seems to be driving the reporters into a frenzy. Once the senior party MPs saw which way the wind was blowing on the story, they began to troop out onto the green in front of Westminster to echo his words in front of the camera for evening news then breakfast telly.

They say a lot about how Phil represents the spirit and passion of their party in a post-virus age, and depending on their place on the thought spectrum, either praise his no-nonsense style and independence of spirit (the libertarians), or hold him up as an example of the common-sense embrace of difficult negotiations (the patricians).

Phil says nothing – and they clothe him according to their own desires and agendas.

Ian has been elated, deflated, proud, over-eager and

depressed in half-hour bursts since the clip was uploaded. He has also taken to stumbling into the office whenever his mood shifts to share his latest thought with his boss.

Phil looks up from his reading as Ian enters the room for the third time today. He cut himself shaving this morning.

'Phil, I've just had Wilbur Harrison on the phone!' One of the Secretary of State for Health's special advisors. A champion of health care privatisation, free market absolutist. Not a natural ally of Phil's. Not a pragmatic market reformer, oh no. Off the other bloody side of the dart board, really.

'What did he want?'

'He'd love to have a sit-down with you to talk through some of the patient care provisions under possible shifts of the trusts to profit-creating centres.'

Phil initials the document he is reading. Picks up the next.

'But what did he *really* want?'

Ian sits on one of the overstuffed armchairs, pulls out his phone and scans it while he speaks. 'He wants to establish a relationship in case the Secretary of State gets the boot and you get his job, of course.'

Phil makes a note on the margin of the page he is reading. A question about the sample size of a survey quoted in the text. It's the sort of thing he's famous for among his civil servants, this nerdish obsession with where figures come from. They wish he'd just pick his favourite numbers and throw them around like verbal confetti the way most of the Cabinet do, but also there is a weekly pool to see who can get the most ticks in the margin. A question with an exclamation mark is the booby prize and means you have to buy happy-hour drinks for the whole team.

Ian jumps back to his feet again. 'I mean, it could happen, couldn't it? They wait until they see how bad the results of the investigation are. Blame him and then bump you into the top job. New broom, sweeps away past errors.'

New broom? I was there when the Personal Protection Equipment was running out, Phil thinks. When nurses and doctors were dying and terrified they were bringing the bloody virus home on their shoes to their parents and grandparents. I have to take my share of blame for the errors. But to become Secretary of State . . . ? He could really *do* something from that chair.

A possible move, but still unusual. Being a junior minister for health didn't mean you were expected to develop a speciality in the sector then become increasingly senior in it. The way Cabinet reshuffles work you could be in charge of the army one day, health care the next. It was as if the City decided to swap their CEOs every eighteen months or so. Good at running Twitter? Great, from tomorrow you are in charge of this bank. Top job steering your chemical manufacturing conglomerate through the worst economic downturn of the century! Why not try running Aldi? Promotions within a department did sometimes happen, though – especially when the government had some arse-covering to do.

'Calm down, Ian. Nothing is going to happen for now.'

He barked. A short gasp. 'Yes, it is. One way or another, it's sink or swim time, Phil. You've painted a bloody great target on your back. Someone has said the magic words "future leader", the rest of the Cabinet are going to be on you like foxes in a henhouse.'

He sighs. 'Normally one fox, lots of hens in that analogy. Try hounds on a stag.'

Ian shoves his hands in his pockets. 'I bloody won't. How come you grew up in Essex but say things that make you sound like landed gentry with a shotgun crooked over your arm?'

Phil really has to read this next document. 'I adapted to my environment. Tell Wilbur I'd be happy to see him; suggest a coffee in the tea room. Don't want it to look like I'm arranging a coup.'

'Yeah – be interesting to see if he's happy with that.' He pauses and Phil looks up. 'What else?'

'Chloe Lefiami, the investigator looking into the Jay Dewan case for the Labour self-flagellators. She wants to talk to you.' Phil puts the document down. 'You shouldn't see her,' Ian goes on quickly. 'It's suicide. The reds might pin what happened on you, and her investigation has no authority over us. It's a Labour Party matter. Let them get on with shooting themselves in the face.'

Phil rewound to the moment of seeing Sabal in the gallery, the woman with the braids sitting next to him. He turns his eyes back to the page. 'Tell her I'll see her tonight. Here. Nine. You can be here, and tell her we want the meeting recorded.' Ian opens his mouth to protest. 'I can't dodge this, Ian. I did nothing wrong, but avoiding her is going to make me look like a coward.'

'If *they* don't use it, your enemies on *our* side will!' he says.

Phil throws down his pen. 'Of course they will use it! The fact Lefiami investigating in the first place is all they need, me talking to her won't make any difference. They'll be briefing Peston and Kuenssberg over their "doubts" about me the second they think they can get away with it. The only way to do it is fight it publicly.'

Ian sees he's pushed him too far. He puts up his hands. 'OK. Maybe you're right. Such a ball-ache it's happening right now. I'll call her. And I'll be here tonight.'

He retreats, all but backs out of the door, and Phil inhales then exhales very slowly. Future leader. They'd said that about Jay once and look what happened to him. If Sabal and Lefiami hadn't been in the gallery, he wouldn't have made that mistake at the despatch box; if he hadn't made that mistake he wouldn't have left the Chamber angry and humiliated. Wouldn't have spoken to that student as he had, wouldn't be enjoying his hours in the sunshine of pundit approval now. Cause and effect, action and reaction. Luck. Chance.

Chance did for Jay. He should have had a career, a shining future given that brain, his charm, his ambition. He could be on the front bench right now. But chance happened. Phil thinks about his wife embroidering at home, her favourite thing to do after a long day at work, one stitch leading to another: cut out one stitch and the whole thing might unravel. Is that how it was with Jay?

He sighs and returns to the document. He will tell Lefiami the truth. He can stand by his actions. And the ones he can't defend? There's no way she knows anything about those.

Chapter 10

Saturday 20 September 2008
Manchester Central Convention Complex

Philip thanks his interviewee and takes off his lapel microphone to a smattering of not-really-even-trying-to-be-polite applause.

He hands it back to the sound guy who has wandered onto the stage to reclaim it, and the projected image of his latest pamphlet disappears, replaced by a bright blue screen with AWAITING INPUT written on it. Phil's co-author seems unbothered by the tiny audience and the bored, if not contemptuous, reception. But then, he's a political science lecturer at Liverpool Uni, so probably used to small unengaged audiences.

Phil gets up and steps off the low stage of meeting room seven. The lights come up and he notices Christine Armstrong sitting by herself in the second row. She stands as he comes forward, smiles.

'That was interesting,' she says, thrusting her hands into the pockets of her wide-legged trousers. They are bright red. She's going to have to fake sincerity better than that if she's to have a career in politics, Phil thinks.

'Thanks for coming.'

'I'm sorry you didn't get a bigger audience.'

Owen had told him the start time of five-thirty was the only slot available in the secure zone, and he'd grabbed it. Stupid. He should have risked his luck in one of the fringe venues.

'Or a more friendly one,' Phil says, nodding towards a tight knot of staffers from the Public Sector and General Workers Union scarfing the free sandwiches at the back of the room. One, Coogan, looks over his shoulder at Phil and laughs.

'Do you want to get a drink?' he asks.

Christine looks at her watch. 'I'd better find Jasper. Later maybe? Are you leaving the zone?'

Hope not Hate are holding their curry night near the Town Hall, but Phil doesn't think he can face the fuss of leaving and coming back through security again, the queue of pissed-up delegates waiting for their takeaway kebabs to be X-rayed and their bags rustled through.

He shakes his head and she offers him an encouraging smile, a touch on the arm. 'Later then.'

A few of the brutes watch her go. One says something, and Coogan guffaws so hard he almost chokes on his sandwich.

Phil heads towards the table at the back of the room where the food and the neatly fanned copies of the pamphlets are laid out. The remaining sandwiches are beginning to curl and his pamphlets are already covered in crumbs.

The arseholes are getting ready to go. Coogan saunters up to him, puts a meaty paw on his shoulder, breathes a day's worth of free alcohol into his face.

'Keir Hardie would spin in his grave listening to you. Like a top, he would. This is our party. We're not doing Blairite-Tory-lite anymore, and if you think otherwise, you've got another thing coming.'

He drains the dregs from his glass.

'And your free wine tastes like piss.'

He squeezes Phil's shoulder too hard and lumbers off with his mates before Phil can think of anything to say. Idiots. Though he is right about the wine, and Coogan's boss, Kieron Hyde, is famous for knowing his way around a wine list. Keir Hardie? Great – nineteenth-century solutions to twenty-first-century problems. He should have said that.

'I have a question,' a voice says. Phil turns round. It's a journalist he vaguely recognises. Youngish woman. Well dressed with a no-nonsense air about her. She puts out her hand and Phil shakes it automatically. 'Charlotte Cook, *The Times*. I'm doing the "colour" conference columns.'

'Go on,' Phil says.

'I wanted to ask, who do you think would like your pamphlet more: Tony Blair or David Cameron?' she asks.

He brushes crumbs off the pamphlets that can be saved and abandons the grease-spotted ones. Starts loading them back into their box. She takes one off the top.

'They are both welcome to read it. I wrote it to appeal to all market reformers.'

She's opening it, scanning the pages in front of her. 'HEAD OF LABOUR THINK TANK APPEALS DIRECTLY TO CAMERON,' she says. 'Nice headline.'

'Is that what I'm going to read in your column?' Phil asks bitterly.

She glances up. 'Sorry, my love. You're no use to me – not colourful enough. Yet. But I'm going to give your pamphlet to one of Cameron's team. You'll get more of an audience from them than you will from the meatheads here.'

She smiles, it seems genuine, and then she walks off. It's getting noisy out there. Delegates are deciding which fringe meetings to go to, which invitation-only parties they can gate-crash on the first floor of the Midland.

Phil feels a bubble of excitement in his blood and wonders why. He realises, horrified, it's excitement at a pathetic little scenario playing out in his head. One of Cameron's people handing him the pamphlet. 'Some interesting stuff in here, Dave.' Dave reads, looking interested. Christ, the idea of Cameron reading his stuff actually makes Phil happy. His ideas falling on fertile ground. The new future of the centre ground of British politics. He swallows and tries to fold the lid of his box so it won't spring open. If Owen ever suspected a thought like that had crossed Phil's mind, he'd kill him. Then skin him.

Phil dumps the pamphlets in his room, changes into his jeans and heads down to the bar. He spots Jay immediately. Georgina is sitting next to him, her hand on his shoulder, and at first Phil thinks it might be best to leave them to it; it looks pretty intense. But then Jay looks up, sees him and beckons him over.

So Phil gets a round in, a bottle of white wine actually, and a random assortment of nuts in little ceramic pots as it looks like that's the only dinner he'll be getting this evening. He scoots into the booth.

'Have you heard the latest stupid rumour about me?' It's the first thing out of Jay's mouth. Phil catches Georgina's eye over his shoulder. A sympathetic if slightly pained twitch of her mouth. She tucks her blonde hair behind her ear with a free hand, then reaches for the fresh glass of wine like a woman who really needs a drink. Phil's been told the story. It was the pre-event chatter while he was laying out his poor hopeful pamphlets.

'Why aren't you working on Alistair's speech?' Phil asks. 'I heard it wasn't finished yet.'

Jay takes hold of his glass with two hands. 'You *have* heard, then. Who told you? Was it Owen?'

'I can't remember,' Phil lies. 'And Owen is your friend. He wouldn't spread stories about you.'

'He resents me.'

Phil snorts. 'No, he doesn't. He can be a bit rough around the edges, but he's where he wants to be. Right in the thick of the fight. He's having way too much fun at the moment to spend any time resenting you.' That might not be entirely true. He adds in an exaggerated drawl, 'Though it does take a while for him to forgive one for going to Oxford.'

'So he *does* resent me.'

Phil drops the posh voice. 'Swear to God, Jay, I don't believe he's thinking much about you at all this week. He's too bloody busy.'

'I know it wasn't anyone in the team who started the story. At least, I don't think it was Simon or even Melissa.'

'Why aren't you working on the speech?' Phil tries again. Three weeks ago the Chancellor's conference speech was all that Jay could talk about. He thought he'd get a couple of lines in it and was ready to get them embossed and framed if he did.

'I'm going for a piss,' he says instead of answering, and gets up unsteadily. Georgina saves the wine bottle and Phil manages to stop the little bowl of cashews spilling onto the floor. They watch him wander off.

Georgina sighs and takes another long pull at her wine. 'He says they sent him out to "cool down" a bit. Honestly, I don't know what's up with him. It's just a stupid story.'

'Is it true?' Phil asks quietly, like he thinks Jay might storm back and berate him for even asking. Georgina gives him a twisted half-smile.

'I think he shoved a note about something totally unimportant onto Alistair's desk when he was demanding the Icelandic banks stop pulling their assets out of the UK and got his nose spanked. That's what I heard, anyway. I mean, I can imagine him breaking in like that when he gets excited. He says it didn't happen and now he thinks there is a campaign against him.'

Phil leans back against the banquette. 'He's his own worst enemy.' He chews a handful of nuts. Salt and fat and booze. All major food groups covered.

'Tell me about it.' Then she holds up her hand. 'No, actually. Don't. I'm sick of the subject. Tell me about your pamphlet. How did it go?'

He tells her, and her immediate sympathy feels like a blessing.

'Those guys! They can hardly tie their own shoelaces. Coogan only has his job because his dad is a big hitter in our North West branches. His father is a sort of an old-world chivalrous gangster type.'

'Really?' Phil says, eating more cashews.

She wide-eyes him. 'Oh, yeah. He saw me getting hassle from a drunk shop steward in the pub after a meeting and offered to have his crew leave a dead dog on the bloke's doorstep.'

'Wow.' Phil likes to think he knows the world. Not like he grew up in the Ritz, but some of Georgina's stories still shock him.

'Oh, shit!' Georgina exclaims.

He twists round to follow her gaze and spots Jay by the bar. He is waving his hands at two men who have their elbows on the polished wood. They look a mix of baffled and disgusted.

'What now?' Phil says.

'The guy on the right is a new policy guy at Number 10,' Georgina mutters and downs the rest of the wine in her glass. 'I have to get Jay away before he says something . . .'

People are turning to look and Jay raises his voice so they can all hear, even with the slight slur in his voice.

'This is my career, and you dare just laugh at me . . .'

Georgina has half stood up. It's not just the Union hard cases who can be chivalrous.

'No, you smooth things over with them.' Phil necks the rest of his glass and casts a regretful glance at the crisps. 'You've done your stint. *I'll* deal with Jay.'

He's rewarded with a grateful smile. He walks across the bar and puts his hand on Jay's arm.

'Come on, Jay.'

Jay shakes him off. 'I need to know who's spreading the crap, man. I'm sick of it!'

'Your friend's being very rude. Please take him away,' Policy Guy says with a sneer. 'And he's *drunk.*'

He lifts his hand to attract the barman's attention. If he hadn't done that, it would have been OK. It wasn't.

'Don't you turn your back on me!'

Jay shoots out a hand, grabbing Policy Guy by the shoulder.

He swings his arm back, elbow raised, catching Jay on his chin just as Phil is yanking hard on Jay's wrist.

Jay recoils from the elbow blow and staggers backwards against the chairs of drinkers grouped round a table just behind him. His foot catches in the straps of a pile of tote bags someone's snaffled from the exhibition space. Phil lets go instinctively and Jay goes over backwards, arms flailing. Glasses fly off the table as it overturns. Chairs tip over as delegates try and get out of the way and Jay is on his back on the floor, pulling himself onto his elbows. Policy Guy is staring at the wreckage. Smash and clatter, curses and gasps ... then a moment of silence.

Fuck. Fuck. Fuck. Phil takes Jay's hand, hauls him to his feet then shoves him towards the door. He hears scattered laughter and cat calls.

'We're leaving, Jay. Now!'

Jay half-resists, then throws his hands in the air and strides off.

'I barely touched the stupid boy!'

Phil glances back. Policy Guy is proclaiming his innocence at the bar. Delegates are setting the table right, examining their clothes for red-wine stains. Staff appear with cloths and dust-pans and expressions of concern.

Georgina is in the thick of it, hand on the shoulder of a woman dabbing at her ruined blouse. As Phil watches, she turns from her to the Policy Guy offering apologies, contrition, absolution. Damn it! Kieron Hyde and Coogan are off on one side. Not helping, of course, just smirking and watching Georgina deal with the mess.

Thank God for her. Phil hurries off after Jay before he loses him in the crowd.

Chapter 11

Tuesday 8 March 2022

Owen feels like he drank the whole bottle of Talisker when he wakes up in his flat. He hauls himself out of bed and moves through his usual routine. The *Today* programme on, scanning the news sites and marking up stories with his Apple Pencil; shower, shave, coffee.

All the time he's aware of Jay's file squatting where he left it on the side table late last night. It keeps snagging on his vision as he moves around the flat. Does he just leave it there? Glowing radioactively between the armchairs? It feels wrong with it out in the open like this.

He picks it up and carries it to the bedroom, puts it in the bottom of his chest of drawers. He still has the poster from his first campaign at university up on the wall, alongside one from his first parliamentary campaign. They stare down at him. He feels a fool hiding the file, but leaving it out doesn't seem possible either.

He is so close. Twelve years out of government while the world goes to hell, but he's rising in the party again – and the party is ahead in the polls. He could be in power. He could actually do something more than hold the government's feet to the fire on the committee and send letters on House of Commons stationery. And now, just when it might be possible, his entire career, everything he's worked for, waited for, is going to be snatched away. It's zero tolerance on bullying in the Labour Party now, and he cheered when he heard that. Celebrated. Never thought they'd hang this on him. Never thought they could.

He slams the drawer closed, making it stick so he has to shake the damn thing into place. What on earth has Christine got him into now? He reaches the hall and realises he's forgotten his wallet. Goes back for it and sees he almost left his laptop bag too. He's rattled.

He leaves, jogs down the stairs and then heads towards parliament through the back streets to the river and along to Westminster Bridge. The file pulses in his mind, as if he can feel the heat of it, radiating out from the shirt drawer.

The morning is warm already, one of those accidental spring days that feels like a blessing and promise after the dragging dark days of February. He hadn't known Jay was going to therapy. Had Phil known? Had Georgina? Why hadn't Jay told them?

But he's read enough to know the answer to that one. The notes make it clear Jay was convinced Owen was out to get him. That he was racist, classist, homophobic. That he was trying to destroy Jay out of pure envy. That he was orchestrating some sort of campaign. A plot. Owen can't stop hearing the words from the file, repeating in Jay's voice: *I thought he was my friend, but he's destroying me, just for being who I am.*

He catches the fermented-seaweed-and-salt scent of the Thames at low tide on the air. Not many people on the bridge yet this morning. A tour group in matching face masks. Their guide in bright blue gloves is talking into his microphone; some of the group fiddle with their earpieces. Owen swerves round them, manages to nod his good mornings to the security staff at Portcullis House. He grabs a coffee from the modern, breezy barista area and pounds up to his office.

The file is wrong. Owen has never bullied anyone, not even in school. And he hopes he's not racist, classist or homophobic either. Well, maybe on the class side he hasn't worked that hard at understanding the hurt felt by rich self-entitled arseholes. And sure, he hasn't always been the most patient of men. He isn't someone who invites his staff or colleagues to share their problems with him over hot chocolate and baking. Wait, why is he thinking of hot chocolate?

Of course. The house in Lambeth. Coming in one evening and seeing Georgina feeding Jay with fat slices of cake and nursery drinks. Just like Nanny used to make.

Stop it, Owen, they were neither of them that posh, he thinks, just a lot posher than me. The homely smell. The way they both went silent as he came in. A daggers look from Jay, a sympathetic grimace from Georgina. He'd grabbed something from the fridge and retreated to his room feeling oddly spurned.

He hadn't bullied Jay! The idea was nonsense. Jay had recovered a bit after making an arse of himself at conference. One of the special advisors had read him the riot act. Why wasn't *that* in the bloody therapist's report?

'Owen?'

'What?' He re-emerges in 2022. Swimming up through years of loss, austerity, Brexit, the vicious feuding, the world tremor of the virus, and finds his researcher hovering in the door, hands crossed over the pad across her chest. She looks concerned.

'Sorry, Pam. What can I do for you?'

'We have a meeting? To go through the grid for the Budget?'

Owen closes his eyes briefly. This bloody investigation; Christine stirring up trouble when she isn't even in parliament anymore – and all while they are closing in on the most important days in the political year. He's hardly given it a thought yet.

He pulls himself together. 'Of course. Come in and let's get cracking.'

Pam's already found and talked to a range of businesses in Owen's constituency about what they hope for from the Budget, and what they fear. Pencilled in a rough schedule of visits he can make to talk to the owners and workers in person over the weekend after the Budget and the debates, a photographer in tow; 'but no press, so it's a proper listening session.'

Her list is good, a mix of manufacturing and tech, a bakery that managed to survive the virus by doing deliveries locally and a couple of citizen support groups and their clients.

'This is great.'

She flushes. 'Thanks. Liam helped a ton. And Marcie.'

Liam. Owen's stomach twists again. Is Liam going to get dragged into this? He looks at his watch. 'What else have I got today? Other than emails?'

She takes him through it. A committee meeting later. A tour.

'And what should I know?'

'Phil Bickford got a lot of good press.'

'I saw.'

Couldn't miss it really.

'Knock, knock!'

Pam turns round in her chair as Georgina Hyde pushes open the door. She's wearing a powder-blue trouser suit in some sort of silky material and her hair is loose and curled. She looks halfway on a line between Margaret Thatcher and Melania Trump. Pam and Owen both get to their feet.

'Sorry to barge in, Owen, but the guys outside thought it would be OK, and I'm trying to hide from my policy team.' She spots Pam and puts her hand across her chest and bows to her.

'You must be Pam! I'm Georgina. I hear Owen is very lucky to have you working for him.'

Pam blushes to her roots. 'Hi, yes! That's me. Lovely to meet you!'

'Sorry, Pam, it's your meeting I'm interrupting! I'll go hide somewhere else.'

Pam shakes her head. 'No, no that's fine, Ms Hyde. We were just finishing up. I'll get out of your way. Can I get you anything? Tea?'

'Thank you, but no. I had to have about fifteen cups to get me through a really boring breakfast meeting. And do call me Georgina. Ms Hyde makes me sound like an evil Victorian nanny.'

Pam giggles and practically backs out of the room, murmuring her farewells. As soon as the door closes, Georgina flops dramatically into one of the armchairs, and blows her long blonde fringe out of her eyes. Owen laughs.

'How are you, Georgie? I heard you on the *Today* programme yesterday. Good job.'

She swings straight again and he comes and joins her at the coffee table. The emails can wait for a bit.

'Thanks! It did go pretty well, didn't it? I sometimes get really stiff in those interviews.'

'Pretend you are arguing with me, or a friend, then just say what you would say – without swearing.' He considers. 'No, don't do that exactly, just make it *sound* like that's what you are doing. Are you really hiding from your policy advisors?'

She wrinkles her nose. 'A bit. Mostly I'm just having one of those days when if I see a member of the Cabinet I'm just going to scream at them to get out of the way so we can get back into power and start *doing* something. Seen the latest polls?'

He nods. 'Looking OK at the moment, but you can't tell anything until an election is called and that might be the best part of two more years.'

'Ever the optimist. I swear, this is the longest parliament there has been in the existence of the universe. But then I guess a pandemic and a recession will do that.'

She shakes her head and looks at him. She has that gift of turning the full beam of her attention on you. Jay had it too. 'So how are you doing, sunshine?'

'You mean this investigation?'

'Yes, and the story. Any idea why they are coming after you? Come out of the blue a bit, hasn't it?' She is watching him closely.

'It has.' He resists the power of her attention and doesn't say any more. 'I saw you with Jay's dad yesterday.'

She smiles. 'I'm very fond of him. We've kept in touch.'

Then she's back on her feet. Owen is sure she has more energy than she had a decade ago. 'How are Kieron and the kids?'

'Oh, fine. Come and have supper sometime.' She glances at her watch. 'I guess that's my "me" time over. Self-care on speed. Look, Owen, I'm asking around quietly about why you are suddenly villain of the month, but if there's anything you can do to make it go away ... Well, I'd be very grateful. Last thing I want is the tabloids to find pictures of me at Glastonbury with flowers in my hair. Not the image we want as we convince voters we are the party of sound fiscal policy.'

Owen stands up, smooths his tie. 'I've been wondering, why did you come, Georgie? To Glastonbury? You weren't into the music. We could have found someone else to take the ticket.'

She looks surprised. 'You know, Owen? For the life of me, I can't remember. A last fling before I became the model of propriety all female politicians have to be, I suppose. Ridiculous, isn't it? You can have a prime minister who won't confirm how many children he has, but God, can you imagine a single mother as PM!? Besides, I wanted to keep an eye on your boys' club.'

That surprises him. 'If we were a club, Georgie, you were part of it.'

'Sure. Look, if I hear anything, I'll let you know, but if you can squash the story, please do. Going over that time ... It can only hurt us all.' She puts her hands together as if in prayer.

'Of course.'

She rewards him with one of her TV-ready smiles and heads back out into the fray, her head held high.

Chapter 12

Sunday 21 September 2008
The Midland, Manchester

Owen loads a plate at the breakfast buffet as soon as it opens and has the morning newspapers half-read before seven. The polls are worse than they thought. Bad. Party in danger means the delegates will behave. Good. A lot riding on Gordon's speech. Inevitable. Speech is in good shape. Hopeful.

He's so engrossed in one of the *Guardian* reports that he doesn't notice Georgina until she puts down her plate on the table next to him. He twitches a copy of the *Daily Express* out of her way as she unwraps her cutlery from its paper napkin straitjacket.

'You OK with me being here, Owen?' she says, pouring herself coffee. 'I mean, we have breakfast together most days, so I can sod off if you prefer.'

'You're all right. Didn't see you last night. You OK?'

Now the polls are out he feels relieved. Battle lines are drawn and he's ready for the fight. His buzz buzzes at a slightly higher frequency.

'Few drinks at the Midland trying to smooth things over after the Jay incident. Then the News International Party. You?'

'*New Statesman*, then about five hours spreading a message of unity and strength in the Midland. God, Jay's an idiot.'

'They've sent him home. Some excuse about sorting the Chancellor's schedule for next week.'

'Good idea.'

'Thanks,' she says. 'Simon thought so.'

Georgina starts on her breakfast. Smoked salmon, scrambled egg, wholemeal toast.

Owen watches her as she flicks open the *Daily Mail* and starts scanning the coverage. In the months they've lived together, he hasn't got to know her that well, but putting a plan together with one of the senior members of the Treasury team to get Jay out of the way until the story dies down – that shows smarts and access. Better for Jay, too.

'Actually,' she says, turning the page and not looking up, 'I wanted to ask your advice about something. Just between you and me.'

'Sure. Fire away.' He closes the paper.

'Did you know Adam Riddell is definitely retiring at the general, whenever it is?'

Riddell, Coventry East's MP for the previous twenty-five years. Veteran. Owen hadn't heard it was certain yet. 'You sure?'

She nods and sips from her coffee cup. 'Janie, his wife, told me he was definitely standing down last night.'

Owen looks up in the air and gathers his thoughts. 'It's a safe seat. Still hanging on to some of its industrial base. Chair of the CLP is a good bloke.'

'Any women?' Georgina sets down her cup carefully.

He thinks. 'Treasurer of the CLP and membership secretary both under forty and women.'

She smiles at him. 'You're amazing, Owen. Like a walking database.'

Owen almost blushes. 'Yeah, well, I talk to most of these people every week. So, what's your interest? Looking into it for Jay?'

A flinch and then she scrunches up her nose. 'Look, this is delicate, but I've been approached myself. That's why Mrs Riddell wanted to speak to me last night. Would I be interested in standing.'

Owen's buzz is momentarily shut off. First Jay and now Georgina? Thank you, universe. He controls his expression. Tries to. He could just about handle Jay being head-hunted, but Georgina too?

'That's great, Georgina. You want it?'

She looks pained. 'Yes, yes, I really do. I mean, you can do so much more in parliament, can't you? Make a real difference in the world. Ever since I was a child I've wanted to be an MP.'

News to Owen.

'So what do you want to know? I mean, it'll be tough. You're coming out of nowhere.'

'Not quite nowhere. I know some of the locals through the political fund.' He remembers what Christine said last night. Of course. Smarts and access. Georgina hurries on. 'But it's not that, it's Jay. He was born there, you know. So he's a local even if the family did move to London when he was two. I was born and raised in Brighton.'

Owen wipes up the last of his egg yolk and brown sauce with the hotel's thin white toast and eats it.

'And I think he's just expecting it,' she goes on. 'But he's not helping himself. The missed calls, now this Alistair story and a drunken brawl with a senior advisor in the Midland to cap it off!'

'What are you asking me, Georgina?'

She looks him straight in the eye, a sort of dizzying frankness. 'Oh, sorry! I want to know what's best for the party. Me or Jay.'

What's best for the party. The words tattooed across Owen's heart.

'If Jay can get himself together and repair the damage – Jay. If not, then you or someone else.' She looks hurt. 'It's the local thing, Georgina. You are both posh and a bit too New Labour for that constituency, but him being a local boy wipes that out. Some of the locals won't like the fact he's gay, but it's 2008. They won't want to show it. But there is going to be lots of competition for that seat if Jay isn't up to running. You don't have any local connections at all?' She shakes her head. 'Then you're not just posh, you're posh and southern.'

'Kieron Hyde was brought up there, though. He knows everyone. If he supports me, that's got to make a difference.'

'Of course it would. He's a hero in that constituency – anyone who has Kieron's support will probably walk it. But he's unlikely to back one candidate wholeheartedly, even you, this early. Surely he'll spread his favours around until he sees which way the wind is blowing.'

She breathes in sharply, then looks down at her food.

'Rebuilding Britain's manufacturing base. That's what I'll campaign on.'

He picks the paper off the table and starts to read it again.

'Hold your horses, Georgie. Jay's just had a bad couple of weeks. He can recover and like you just said, he was born there.'

She sighs, then puts her knife and fork together.

'Yes. That's true. And the selection process won't even start until after Christmas. You're a good friend, Owen.' Georgina pats her mouth with her napkin. 'I really appreciate it. Don't say anything to Jay, will you? I mean, I haven't decided what I'm going to do next.'

''Course I won't. I'm trying to stay out of his way until he chills out a bit, anyway.'

She gathers up her plate and gets up. Owen picks up his newspaper, but finds he watches her all the way out of the dining room.

Chapter 13

Tuesday 8 March 2022

The call saying that Christine is waiting for Owen at security comes exactly as the reminder on his phone beeps. She was always punctual.

'How much time have you got?' she says as soon as the 'hellos' are out of the way. He leads her through security.

'I've a ton to do, but no meetings till later,' Owen replies. She's looking good. Slim, wearing tight jeans and long boots – an outfit she wouldn't have risked when she was an MP. All the women have to wear some narrow variation on the trouser suit. Her hair is tied up in a rough bun, her face framed by the stray tendrils, just as it was when they first met.

'Let's just get something at the Despatch Box,' she says. The central atrium of Portcullis House, with its fig trees and mix of benches and tables, is a sort of upmarket food court. The escalator leading off the floor doesn't lead to a shopping mall, though, but direct to the Palace for MPs scurrying off to vote.

The tunnel under the road saves them from having to jostle through the 5G protesters, anti-vaxxers, temperature checks and security gates. The integrity of the bubble is preserved.

'I thought you wanted to go to Strangers' Dining Room?'

She smiles broadly, sudden as the sun coming out from behind a cloud. 'You know what? I changed my mind. The thought of all that linen, painted wallpaper and roast meat makes me cringe.'

'They do a plant-based steak for us and the Lib Dems these days, you know,' he tries, and is rewarded with a half-laugh.

'Come on. This will do.'

They queue at the coffee bar with their plastic trays, making small talk. Her husband Rob is well, he's down south, too, at the moment, talking to suppliers. Chris is having some meetings, going to galleries. The children are fine, having a ball staying with Christine's mum and enjoying bracing walks on the beach at Alnmouth.

They are served the salad box of the day by a girl with artfully drawn-on eyebrows. A tattoo of a rose on the back of her hand shows through her thin blue gloves. Her eyes, peering at them over her mask, look tired.

They sit, and the way Christine unwraps her cutlery reminds him of Georgina preparing to enjoy her smoked salmon that morning she first mentioned the Coventry East seat at conference in 2008. But then, everything drags him back to 2008 at the moment. Has Chris heard about the investigation? He wants to ask, but she speaks first.

'So. The question about the data consultation?' Christine says and starts spearing the cubes of goats' cheese in her salad, the baby spinach leaves slick with dressing.

'Chased it.'

'I was worried you'd be distracted by this bullshit investigation, Owen.' So she has heard. 'You had nothing to do with what happened to Jay.'

'I've been going over and over it.'

'And?' Christine asks.

'I'm beginning to think I was a bit of an arse back then.'

She laughs darkly. 'You were a white, twenty-eight-year-old bloke, Owen. Accent on the *bloke*. You were all right, just a bit oblivious. Especially to the small things. But they add up, you know. Lefiami's asked to speak to me too, by the way.'

Small things. He suspects she's being generous.

'What will you tell her? Lefiami, I mean.'

'The truth,' she replies, as if it's that easy. 'Jay was getting more and more paranoid and turning the house toxic. We started avoiding him a bit, then the leak made things so much worse.' She puts a hand, lightly, briefly, on his arm. 'You didn't do anything wrong.'

Yes, he did, and he's got a horrible feeling he's going to be forced to pay for it.

He finishes his salad and pushes his sagging cardboard salad box away. Time to ask the question. 'Why do you want me to push on the medical data so much, Christine?'

Should he add that it could cost him his career? That the newspaper wolves are tracking him through the forest and he's bleeding? There are causes he's willing to fight all out for, causes that would take him onto the streets and up onto the barricades. He's just not sure data security is one of them.

She flicks the ring pull on the can, lifting and releasing it with her index finger, making it twang. 'You're going to be pissed off with me. So can I ask you to remember I've been working on my own: no researchers, no constituency agent.'

'OK.'

She breathes out quickly like someone steeling themselves for a final set of reps. 'This isn't just an "on general principle" inquiry. It's about a young woman with family in my old constituency. She came to me and I've been trying to help her. I believe her family is the victim of a great injustice.'

Bee in her bonnet. Crank to hang her frustrations on. Greg's words from last night clang in his mind. 'Have you vetted her? When did she come to you?'

'Three months ago. And no, I mean, I can't beyond Google, but I trust my gut.'

She was right. He is pissed off. 'Great. You're hanging me out to dry on the basis of one woman and your gut?'

A slight frown. 'What do you mean "hanging you out to dry"? What's happened?'

He could tell her. Tell her about the late-night visit and the file and the ugly allegations in Jay's own words. But he can't. Not now and not here. It would make it too real.

She's still thinking. 'You don't think that this investigation is because of the *question*? They are coming after you because of that? I heard it was to get out in front of something in the *Chronicle* . . . ' She looks – damn her – she looks excited. 'Oh, if they are behind the *Chronicle* story we must really have hit a nerve! We've got them rattled. This is excellent news.'

'Who is "they", Christine? And what do you mean, "our story"? You've stirred up a bucket of shit that means I have to relive the worst year of my life.'

She flinches. 'Owen, it was the year we were together.'

'Yeah and look how that turned out! It was also the year of Jay, the expenses scandal and Phil fucking off to the Tories. Austerity, Brexit. It started there and then in the middle of the banking crisis. Even a few months of being with you doesn't make up for that.'

He gets up and grabs his tray, ready to dump it back onto one of the racks to be removed and cleaned so hard another layer of the varnish will come off. She puts her hand on it so he either has to wait or tip it, the dirty cutlery and shreds of salad into her lap. He can't do that.

'Owen, please. I'm sorry. Come with me now. Meet my girl. Listen to her story.'

No. He doesn't want to. He wants to get back to his office, withdraw the question and get on with his life.

Chapter 14

Thursday 18 December 2008

The party is in full swing. The central lobby of the Public Sector and General Workers Union building off Queen Street has been strung with fairy lights and tinsel, and around the edges of the space cabaret tables are set up with doll-sized Christmas trees and piles of cheap crackers. The Union choir is singing carols at the entrance and the caterers are handing out mini Christmas puddings and turkey and cranberry bites.

Crackers are pulled. Jokes read out. Hats worn. They are generous with the booze, but it's eggnog and punch, not champagne. As the world slides deeper into recession no one needs the UNION BOSSES IN CHAMPAGNE BLOW-OUT headlines. Owen and Christine have found themselves a corner by the plate-glass windows which look over a stark, modernist courtyard, grey with the London winter. Christine is sipping her eggnog and listening to the choir with a slightly daffy smile on her lips.

She's been smiling since they stayed up all night to watch Obama win the US election. She came over and the whole house made a night of it. Jay and Georgina danced together to BB Collins. Phil and Owen fought to out-nerd each other on their deconstructions of American industry and Christine's heady delight lit them all up. And Jay was himself again. Funny, sharp. They were part of something better. Still. Again. At last.

After Obama's speech, Phil, Jay and Georgina went to crash out for a couple of hours before work. Christine and Owen sat on the front step together, just to make this one good day last as long as they could, listening to the city shift towards dawn. Hope. Change. For a few hours Owen felt like he was living the movie version of his life and these were the glorious closing frames. Struggles behind and sunny uplands ahead.

Christine's heading up to Alnwick on Tuesday. Owen isn't leaving London till Christmas Eve, heading up on the train with a sack of gifts from the House of Commons gift shop. His mum loves anything with a portcullis on it. The tins of biscuits are shared with the neighbours, then the tin becomes a store for her sewing bits. Owen's sister likes the mugs.

He's still trying to hang on to the feeling, the Obama buzz, but it's getting harder. Jay isn't here. Relationships between the Union and the Treasury team are a bit strained as rumours of public-sector pay freezes gather momentum. It's party season, though, so no doubt he has some other event, more champagne soaked than this one, to go to.

Phil has come. Even though he seems to dislike all the unions and what they stand for more and more. And the dislike is mutual. Good for him.

Owen spots him as he comes in and waves, then watches as

Phil grabs a paper cup of punch from the waiter at the door and shrugs off his backpack to avoid clobbering the mini puddings out of the revellers' hands as he fights across the hall.

'Nice turn-out!' He tucks the backpack next to the window. 'Hey, Chris.'

'Hey,' she replies. 'Owen, who's that?'

She nods sideways. Under the mezzanine level Coogan is talking to a woman of about their age. He towers over her and has a hand on her upper arm. She has her head down and is shaking her head, her face flushed.

'Don't know her,' Owen says. Coogan glances around, like he can feel them looking, then he puts his face closer to the woman's, talking fast. His grip is making the fabric of her suit jacket wrinkle. She moves her arm. Is she trying to pull away? It's hard to tell through the crowd.

'Looks nasty,' Phil says, rising up on the balls of his feet to try and see better. 'Should we do something?'

Christine pushes herself off her high stool.

'Too bloody right we should. Owen, stay here. Phil, your arm, please. We are now slightly pissed.'

Phil offers his arm and Christine takes it. Owen watches as they make their way, not unsteadily, across towards where Coogan and the woman are standing. As they pass he watches Christine miming recognition of the girl. Coogan says something and Christine, all smiles, replies.

The woman moves and even through the crowd Owen can see the reluctance with which he lets her go. Then everything has reconfigured: Christine and the woman are arm in arm and heading further under the mezzanine. Coogan looks at Phil, then turns and stalks off. Owen watches Phil amble back in his direction, then looks round the room again. Happy colleagues raising a glass of Christmas cheer. A few singing along with the carollers. Then he notices Kieron Hyde, standing in the dead centre of the room, staring at the space where Christine and the unknown female disappeared.

'How did you manage to pull a woman like Christine?' Phil asks him. 'Explain it to me. Is it the brooding thing you have going on? It must be the brooding, strong-man thing.'

'It's my cheerful personality and rugged good looks.'

Phil half-laughs into his reclaimed punch. 'Seems unlikely.'

'So what happened?'

'Christine did the fake "didn't-we-meet-at-the-conference?" thing, swiftly followed by the "can-you-show-me-where-the-ladies'-is" thing.' Phil stares into space, a crease of worry on his forehead. 'Poor girl was eager enough to pretend to recognise Chris, then show her the way. God, I hate Coogan.'

Owen finishes his eggnog. Weird. Like drinking custard. 'He's OK most of the time. Works like a bloody pit pony on Union business. If I had one of him to put in every marginal, we might end up denying the Tories a majority at least.'

Phil's face twists in a complicated rictus.

'Not looking good?'

'No. Every time we update the list of defensive marginals with the private polling, it gets longer.'

Christine is coming back towards them carrying three cups of punch at once, elbows out and biting the side of her lip as she concentrates. Owen takes one carefully from her and feels a frisson as he touches her fingers, her dry smooth skin and the touch of her painted nails.

'So?' Phil asks. 'How was the damsel in distress?'

Chris shrugs and drinks her punch while Owen examines his. It's neon red and has bits of what might be orange pith in it. He hopes it won't make the eggnog in his stomach curdle.

'Didn't get much out of her,' she says. 'Didn't try either, mind you. She seemed pretty shaken up. Owen, do you know what an NDA is?'

'Non-disclosure agreement,' he says automatically. 'They get stuck onto lawsuits sometimes, people settling disputes with their employer sign them in return for compensation. Why?'

'She said she'd signed one. Didn't mention her name, but she told me that. Anyway, she's gone home.'

'She didn't tell you what Coogan was going on at her about?' Phil asks.

'No. Asked me to walk her out. Still, it gave me an excuse to get to the bar.' She glances at her watch. 'We have to go in a bit.'

'What?'

She sighs. Mock exasperation. 'You are buying me and Phil dinner at Tas, remember? You stood us up last week.'

Oh yes. Though he didn't think Phil had minded that much.

'Got to watch your manners, Owen!' She puts her hand on his arm, squeezes it and says more gently, 'Even if we are both terribly grateful for your dedication to saving the country from the Tory scourge.'

Phil laughs. Bit too hard. Perhaps Christine makes him nervous. Owen is not sure how he'd manage without her, even though they've only been together three months. They would make a great team, him and Christine. Him an MP and her running the constituency office. He catches himself. No doubt he's besotted. He hopes she feels the same way, or something close to it. He doesn't want to scare her off back into the forest of Westminster where so many more powerful, smarter, richer men are lurking.

'We should say hi to Georgina, make sure she knows we turned up.' Phil is scanning the room for her.

Christine points across the room. 'She's over there.'

Owen looks. Georgina is standing next to Kieron Hyde and the chair of the Coventry East Labour Party. She has a tinsel halo perched on top of her head and is wearing a tight red business suit. The look is a confusing mix of business professional and naughty Mrs Santa.

An upright piano has been dragged into position under the Christmas tree and a man with a thick shock of black hair is playing the opening chords to 'My Flag is Red'. The choir begins to regroup. As she turns towards it, Georgina sees them and waves. Owen waves back. When the singing starts, Kieron wraps his arm around her waist.

Christine fake-coughs into her punch. 'Daddy issues.'

Owen gives her the side-eye and she tries to look innocent. It's true Georgina does flirt with powerful, older men. Owen's still not sure why Christine looks down on her for it.

'Shall we head?' Phil asks.

'Ah, come on, you misery,' Owen finishes his drink and sets it down. 'One chorus.'

'I don't think I remember the words,' Phil replies.

Chapter 15

Tuesday 8 March 2022

Owen and Christine take a cab and she gives the driver an address in Vauxhall. Owen remembers the feeling of lockdown in London, of being a hamster on a wheel restricted to a world whose limits were a twenty-minute walk from his flat. He finds himself longing to get back to his home in the constituency for the weekend.

It didn't feel like home at first: the terraced house in his target seat was just a place to sleep as he launched his campaign, won that, then lost his argument with his voters on Brexit. He hardly slept during the 2019 campaign, and still his majority was cut by two-thirds.

Then came the virus. The world shrank, came into focus. When he wasn't in London he walked the streets around his house, mask in one pocket, sanitiser in the other, talked to his neighbours over the low garden walls and learned to love the place.

The cab pulls up outside a neat block of flats just off the main road and he follows Christine out and onto the pavement. She's moving fast; she's already rung the buzzer and is holding the front door open for him before he slams the cab door behind him. He resents the ease with which she touches things, then remembers the fear when she and Rob were ill and her mother had to take the kids. Squashes the feeling.

The hall needs a new carpet and the paintwork is scratched, but only the homes of the ultra-wealthy look polished these days. Everyone else, and their landlords, are making do. The air is musty, still.

The flat they are after is on the ground floor. Christine knocks and the door is opened at once. The woman welcoming them into the room is very pale, and very slim and young. Mid-twenties at most, with long black hair.

'Hey, Christine!' She glances at Owen, a mix of suspicion and defiance. 'You must be Owen McKenna.'

He admits it.

'Elsie Collins.'

She's in jeans and a vest top with a lumberjack shirt thrown over it. Geometric tattoos twist out from under them to her wrists and her eyes are heavily made up. She looks like a character in a graphic novel.

Owen looks around while she offers to make tea and Christine tells her they are pushed for time. A light space painted rental beige. An obvious workstation at one side of the living area with two huge computer screens. The pictures on the walls are posters and prints. He spots reproductions of a couple of early communist propaganda posters, admires them. There are a couple of others advertising sci-fi films and twin Chagalls over the TV.

The living space is divided from the kitchen by a dining table. Another computer, a laptop this time, and a stack of cardboard folders half-fill a space meant for six. Another flashback of the table in the old house. Elsie indicates the chairs around it and Owen sits down.

'Christine told me I should start from the beginning, Mr McKenna,' she says as she opens the windows, lets in the purifying breeze. Northumbrian accent, modified by some years down south. It has a rough, unused edge to it. Owen notices the blanket on the sofa, a tea mug next to it. Wonders if Elsie is a long-hauler, one of those whose illness has left a cluster of strange fatigues and random days of pain in its wake.

'Please do.' No reason he should give this woman a hard time just because he's angry with Christine. 'And please, call me Owen.'

A short nod. She looks away, starts to wrap her hair around her fingers, twisting and unravelling it as she talks. 'This isn't about me. It's about my brother. Victor. Dr Victor Collins. He was a computer scientist who founded and ran a small crypto start-up in Newcastle.' She notices him pick up on the tense. 'He killed himself just over a year ago.'

Owen absorbs this. Gives it a beat. 'I'm sorry to hear that.' He catches sight of a photograph hanging to the right of the workstation of a young man, with a slim narrow face like Elsie's. 'Is that him? You look alike.'

She doesn't look round. 'Yeah. That's him. We were twins. Are twins. I never know which to say.'

'Do you work in computers too?' Owen asks.

She half-shrugs. 'I work in visual effects. For the movies. But my brother was the clever one. He got into crypto early, found a couple of engineers he liked and ran his company out of a shed in our parents' backyard for three years.' Owen waits and resists the temptation to look at his watch. She stares at the table for a minute, then looks up and meets his eye. 'Do you know anything about crypto?'

Owen shakes his head. 'I know Bitcoin exists, and I read an article in the *London Review of Books* so I thought I understood it for a while. That illusion didn't last long.'

She twists and untwists her hair again. Owen wants to reach out, still the movement. 'It doesn't matter. You don't really need to. Not in this conversation anyway. I'll give you the layman's version.'

'Do I need to take notes?'

Christine cuts in. 'No. You can read the detail later. Elsie's made you copies of the documents.' Oh joy, thinks Owen. She turns back to Elsie. 'Just tell him the story, Elsie.'

Elsie blinks rapidly a few times as if she wants to clear her vision before she starts talking, then she speaks quickly, like rattling off a list. 'So – middle of 2019 Victor read an article about the government selling off NHS data to anyone who fancied buying it, and the concerns that the system they were using to make the data anonymous was full of holes.' She glances up to check he's paying attention. 'Like, Swiss-cheese full of holes. All you needed to do was write a decent bit of code to match them up with publicly available data – anything from the electoral roll to Facebook – and you could match records to individuals like that.' She snaps her fingers. It echoes. 'Victor thought there might be a crypto solution, and started playing with it. After the virus arrived he worked on it exclusively. Then the government loosened some of the restrictions on how the medical data could be used.'

'To help the research into COVID-19,' Owen interrupts.

'Yeah, whatever. Anyway, then he thought it was crucial. He laid down the basic programming and went to the local MP to see if he could help him get the idea in front of the right people in government.' That would be the man who replaced Christine in the 2019 election, a Brexit fanatic who pumped out thousands of leaflets with the headline ENGLISH AND PROUD OF IT, then acted like an offended toddler when it was pointed out he was a racist twat. He won. By six hundred and eighty-two votes.

'The MP wasn't much help. But Victor talked to one of his old professors from Cambridge. He thought it was brilliant and took it to the health department.'

Owen shakes his head. 'I'm going to need to know more about what this "it" is.'

She plucks at the cuffs of her lumberjack shirt. 'It takes the data the NHS has, separates it from any geo tags, and stores it in remote lines of code that can only be assembled and recombined with the right set of digital "keys". If a company comes to you wanting to know about the effect of a certain drug in patients who are like, over forty-five and diabetic, then the NHS programmer can give you a set of "keys" which will let you access that information, with the matching socio-economic status, activity levels, whatever you need, but won't tie that to the geo information or any of the other hooks and inferences which mean you could match real records to real people and places.'

She lifts her hands, trying to grab the right analogy out of the air.

'It's like building a bank with an infinite number of security deposit boxes. The person buying the intel, for legit reasons, gets his specific keys and that opens his particular box. He gets the data he needs and off he trots. Next person wants different data, he gets different keys, and they take him to a different box where his data is assembled, gift-wrapped and completely anonymised.'

'And what happens now?'

'In layman's terms? Basically it's one key. One door. One data vault. Access all goodies inside. Companies go in and take whatever they want, which tends to be everything, just to be on the safe side. What they do with it afterwards is up to them.'

Owen crosses his arms. 'That can't be true.'

'Just fucking google it.' Owen raises his eyebrows at her and she hunches her shoulders. 'I'm sick of people telling me something can't be true when the evidence is sitting right in front of them.'

'Elsie, let me fill Owen in on those details,' Christine says soothingly. 'You tell the story. Tell Owen what your brother wanted from the government.'

Owen sees the muscles in her jaw work as she gathers herself. 'He needed start-up money to recruit specialist pro-grammers and rent the remote capacity, and asked for a one per cent share of the fees the NHS charges to corporate clients to store and protect the data. He reckoned the system could be up and running in a year and his old professor backed him on that.'

'And what did he hear?' Christine prompts her.

Elsie reaches over the table and opens one of the brown files and rifles through it. Owen catches Christine's eye and points at his watch. *Just wait*, she mouths at him. *Five minutes*.

Elsie gets the letter out of the file.

'Here.'

Owen reads.

Dear Dr Collins,

    Many thanks for your submission of the twenty-ninth of last month and the supporting documentation. This is an excellent initiative and we are delighted to have the opportunity to work with you. We will be discussing your proposals in detail over the coming weeks in the department and following up with the project sponsors. Should you have any questions about this process, please contact my advisor on the following number.

Owen is surprised. The letter is signed by the Secretary of State himself, and that means that they weren't just interested, they were very, very eager. They would have run the idea through their own digital teams and got a thumbs-up too before sending this. Dr Victor Collins was no crank in a shed.

Elsie waits for him to finish reading, look up. Her expression is of intense focus, rage just held back.

'For a week he was on the phone to NHS and government people all day, every day. Then everything stopped. No more calls. No one at the department would speak to him. A fortnight after he started getting the silent treatment, some guy turns up at my parents' house offering to buy the company and all the work Victor had done so far for three-quarters of a million quid. He turned them down. Then the threats started.'

'What sort of threats?' Owen asks.

A bus passes outside, making the windows rattle slightly. It startles her and her eyes flick round the room. She doesn't want to tell him this bit. Owen's been in politics long enough to see when people are picking their words very carefully.

'Victor was a genius. I mean a real genius. Technically I'm one too, but he always left me in the dust. But he had problems. Didn't fit in at university, drank. Some drugs.' She adds something Owen can't hear.

'What was that, Elsie?' he asks.

'I said, he was committed!' she snaps. Then the story comes in a flood, like she's ripping off the plaster. 'He tried to kill himself – had a breakdown. While he was doing his PhD. But he'd got better. Got his doctorate working from home back north. Mum and Dad looked after him, his company was doing really well and he was healthy! But this sleazeball said he either had to sell the company and all the intellectual property to him, or the whole story of Victor's breakdown would be shared with any future investors. He wouldn't get funding for anything in the future. Start-up stopped dead.'

'Did he sell, then?' Owen speaks gently and feels himself being scanned for signs of scepticism.

'Yes. He had to.' She is calmer now she's got that out. She strokes the edge of the table, following the patterns of the fake grain with her close-cut nails. 'Two months later he got in contact with his Cambridge professor and was told the whole idea had been rated "unviable" by the new owners and shut down. He couldn't take that. He walked out of the house and we didn't hear from him again. The police found his car near Marsden Grotto.'

'It's on the coast,' Christine says, giving Elsie a moment. 'The police found his body on the beach.'

Elsie's fingers are starting to scratch at the patterns in the wood. 'I'm just glad *they* found him. Not any of the kids and families who play there. Like Victor and me used to. Can't believe the idiot didn't think of that. But then, I can't believe he gave up either.'

She pulls over another file and yanks out a business card. 'This is the guy who made the offer and the threats.'

'Can I take this?' Owen asks.

She nods. Waves her hand across the table. 'All this is for you.'

He glances at the card – he doesn't recognise the name or the company – and tucks it into the pocket of his jacket.

'Spell it out for me then, Elsie. What are we saying?'

She starts organising the folders into piles. 'These are copies of what I've found. Some of it is from the internet. Lots of stuff about what happens to the NHS data, or what *can* happen when it's repackaged or sold. Look, it's pretty simple. The companies who are buying the data now, some of them anyway, don't want the digital keys that take them to *one* little stack of goodies. They want the whole store. Full and free access to the vault. Victor came along with his idea and someone told these bastards they were about to get their supplies cut off. They couldn't have that. They used his medical records to blackmail him about his past then buried his work. So they could keep selling and reselling the data. They as good as murdered him.'

She thrusts the stack of folders towards him and Owen gets to his feet. 'That clear enough for you?'

Her expression is hostile. She walks past him and opens the door to the hall; he notices her hands are shaking. Nerves perhaps, or exhaustion. She won't look at him.

'Yes, that's clear,' he replies and gets up. 'Thank you for speaking to me.'

Christine picks up the folders, afraid he won't, and he notices her mouthing at Elsie now. *Well done*, and *I'll call you.*

He hails a cab on his phone and this time Christine is hurrying to keep up with him. Two minutes, the app says.

'Owen?'

'I'm going back to work.'

'But what do you think?'

'What do I think?' He turns on her. 'I think if there was a shred of proof of *any* of this Elsie would be talking to a lawyer, not you. I'll bet my last fiver those threats were made to Victor only and that the company have denied them. I bet somewhere in there is a detailed analysis of why his idea would never have worked. I bet his last breakdown involved him telling people that men from the government were after him. I will bet my fucking *life* on the fact there is a lawyer's letter in there telling Elsie to keep her mouth shut or be sued for slander, and a dozen from the Department of Health regretting the fact the scheme proved impractical and top computer experts pointing out "issues" with his methodology. Am I close?'

Christine's expression tells him everything he needs to know.

'That woman is ill! And you've sucked me into this conspiracy bollocks! Christine, it's a good story but there's nothing to back it up.' A thought occurs to him. 'That's why you haven't gone to the leadership with it. You're using me as a stalking horse. Bloody hell, Chris.'

He waves at the approaching car. Checks the number plates match.

'Owen!'

'What?'

'If there's nothing there, then why are they scared? Why are they scared enough to set the *Chronicle* on you? Why are they so nervous about answering a simple bloody question about a data security consultation? If they are golden and this is just bollocks, *why are they scared*? If it was a bad idea, *why did they buy the company?*'

He gets into the car and closes the door, but he doesn't have an answer for her.

That evening his neighbour knocks on his door. A cardboard box on the welcome mat with JUST READ THEM, OWEN written on it in black sharpie.

'Your girlfriend dropped them round,' his neighbour says. Young man in tracksuit bottoms and T-shirt but a professional haircut. 'It's my week working from home.'

'She's my ex-fiancée actually.'

The man's face twists with a series of uncomfortably British expressions of sympathy and confusion.

'Ah. Not a bomb in there, is it?'

Define bomb. Christine is blowing up Owen's career with it. He bends down and picks up the box. It's heavy. 'Thanks.'

'No worries.'

Owen closes the door with his foot and sets the box on the worktop, then glances at the business card on the work surface next to it. The company it names was sold to a company with a different name just before Christmas, a month after Victor Collins's suicide. The name on the card leads to a Linked-In profile showing a white guy in a suit and tie with a cherubic face, but the page is full of dead ends – a list of companies with one-page websites filled with boilerplate copy about investment in innovation. Another ghost. Owen wonders if this man even exists. The photo is probably culled from the biography of some failed real-estate broker. There is something sub-prime about the image. Damn, Christine is beginning to infect him with her conspiracy thinking.

Owen opens the carton. The files are neatly arranged: phone records, bank records as well as thick folders of correspondence and research. The Cambridge University letter of support, a draft contract of appointment. He pulls out the bank records and checks. There it is in black and white: one payment of £350,000, then another three weeks later of £400,000. So whatever else Victor imagined or invented, the money was real.

Chapter 16

Chloe Lefiami arrives in the Central Lobby at three minutes to nine. Ian goes to fetch her.

While Phil waits for her to be shown up, he glances at the side Cabinet where he keeps a bottle of a decent blended whisky for long evenings at the House. He tries to wake up hopeful, but more often than not when it reaches this creeping quiet at the end of the day, all one can really say is that you got through another twenty-four hours.

The MP from the constituency neighbouring Phil's popped in during the afternoon, twirling his iPhone between his stubby pink fingers, to tell him the Secretary of State's people were briefing against Phil 'in a sowing-the-seeds' sort of way. Those loyal to Number 10 were still hanging back, waiting to see who emerged victorious. Phil thought this Secretary of State was a paranoid apparatchik when he arrived in the job eighteen months ago. Seems he was right.

'They are nervous about the second-wave PPE failures that

are bound to come out in the inquiry. The current Secretary of State can't lay that one at his hallowed predecessor's door, and they are afraid the "mistakes were made" line has worn pretty thin,' his informant tells him.

Phil thinks of Toby Dale's threat to make him the sin-eater for the whole department. That would be perfect for the Secretary of State. They might not want to do it today after the toxic glow of his fuck-up at the despatch box was replaced by the golden halo of five thousand Twitter likes on his speech to that student. But it might work tomorrow or the next day. He is on thin ice. And this investigation is like hearing another crack and groan as the waters shift below him. It's reminding them all about his past. Damn it, it should remind them what he did for them too!

Phil returns to another of his briefing documents fat with boasts of the PPE *now* available to the NHS. All well and good, but Phil is still haunted by the portraits of the doctors and nurses who died in those first weeks. Applauding them wasn't enough. A monument isn't enough. Someone has to stand up and say sorry. We were panicked, in denial, scrambling. We tried, but in a Cabinet taught by the last election that just claiming success was as good as achieving something, we thought optimism and an upbeat attitude would carry us through. We're doing better now. Forgive us. How can we move on from giving stuttering, evasive answers without owning up to our faults?

Phil rubs the bridge of his nose, then realises it is the same gesture Owen always made when he was thinking.

A knock at the door, and Ian shows Chloe Lefiami in without waiting for an answer. She looks around with frank curiosity: the high windows, panelling, gruesomely patterned green and cream carpet. They bow, with the light smile the British still wear when they catch themselves avoiding shaking hands. Phil decides against the whisky. This is a formal meeting and should be treated as such.

Ian fetches water bottles and puts them on the coffee table and they settle. Chloe and Phil are opposite each other in the firmly stuffed armchairs with Ian on the sofa against the side wall between them like an umpire. His iPhone on the coffee table and recording. Lefiami notices it, but makes no comment, then wipes down her bottle and opens it. Avoids the glass.

'Thank you for seeing me,' she says.

'I'm happy to help you in any way I can, Ms Lefiami,' he replies.

Her lips twitch into a tiny smile: a 'we both know that's not true' smile.

They talk for a while about the shared house, the 2008 conference. Lefiami seems well informed. She's obviously spoken to Owen, Christine and Georgina. Her questions are calm, concentrating on the factual. No gotchas yet.

'Jay believed Owen McKenna resented his success, Minister, his advantages – is that right?'

The question surprises him. Phil frowns. Takes a moment, peers into the undergrowth of his memory. 'Yes, I heard him say that. I thought he was talking rubbish and said so.'

'Did you resent him?'

'No.' Phil is firm. 'We met at Oxford, after all. And I enjoyed my job at the time, in spite of my growing frustrations with the party. I had no reason to resent Jay.'

'Wasn't easy for you to get to Oxford, though, was it?' she says without looking up.

Phil bristles. 'Straight up the M40 or the train from Paddington. Not that hard.'

Now she looks at him. 'I think you know that's not what I meant, Minister.'

He passes his hand over his eyes. He can't remember the last time he didn't feel tired.

'Ms Lefiami, I was very lucky and my life could easily have been very different, but I'm not ashamed of my background. I didn't resent Jay, or the support he had from his family, his school. I thought he was weaker for it. As a candidate for political office and as a man. He had, of course, to deal with plenty of casual racism.' He holds out his hand as if Lefiami is about to jump in, though she shows no sign of doing so. 'And that's terrible. But I think that it meant he never bothered to think about the societal advantages he *did* have. That irritated me occasionally, but we were young men living in a house together at a very high-pressure moment in our lives. We were bound to irritate each other. I didn't resent him, or even give it much thought. And this was before we all got used to becoming intersectional thinkers. Jay arrived in London looking and sounding like a future star, but when things went wrong he fell apart.'

She doesn't nod, continuing to take her notes, and one of her braids falls over her shoulder. She flicks it back into place. Phil clears his throat.

'Is it worth saying, Ms Lefiami, out loud, that I never plotted to do damage to Jay's career? Never slandered him? When the opportunity arose I tried to give him the best advice I could. We were friends. But I was beginning to break with my party at that period and that consumed most of my thoughts. For better or worse, I was distracted.'

She writes for a few seconds on her legal pad.

'Always worth saying that aloud, Minister. Thank you. I would like to move on and ask you about the leak of the draft minutes of the meeting between the Treasury team and the PSGWU team in early 2009. Am I right in saying things had been improving for Jay? Over Christmas? He was being spoken of as a candidate again, wasn't he? Then came the leak story.'

'And the wrath of Kieron Hyde,' Phil says. 'Have you spoken to him?'

'I have his version of events on record.' Ms Lefiami would make an excellent politician.

'Kieron Hyde was a bully. He represented all that I thought was worst on the Labour left.'

'Did you know him well?' Lefiami asks, her tone pleasant, as if they are making small talk before some charity dinner in the City. When such things happened.

Phil shakes his head. 'No, I occasionally saw the ripples coming out of his office. I didn't like his people, other than Georgina. And of course Georgina talked about him. Obviously, she didn't feel the way about him I did. She always spoke about him warmly, but I can't say I was convinced. And it was him, without a doubt, who really destroyed Jay's immediate prospects in the party. Hyde's reasons may have been sound, or perhaps Jay was just his victim of the week. But it was him who delivered the killing blow that spring.'

Her pen moves smoothly across the page. She is his personal recording angel.

'Now, the minutes that were leaked to Charlotte Cook. You know her quite well, I think?'

'Yes.' Phil straightens in his seat. 'I do. Everyone in politics

132

does, on both sides of the House. She was an established polit-ical reporter even then.'

'But you knew her better than the others by the beginning of 2009, didn't you, Minister?'

Phil feels his stomach churn with the misery and betrayal of that time.

'I don't know what you are insinuating, Ms Lefiami . . . '

'I'm not insinuating anything, I'm asking a question.'

Maybe Ian was right. This might have been a mistake. 'I didn't leak those minutes. Jay did. Jay did it and it destroyed him.'

Chapter 17

Phil lets himself in to the house and the first thing he hears is Jay. Jay shouting. He shoves the door closed behind him and follows the voice to the kitchen.

Georgina is backed up against the door and for a foul, frightening moment Phil thinks Jay is shouting at her. But no, he is on the phone.

'Maybe Owen leaked it just to make himself look like a saviour then!' Jay spins round as he hears Phil come in. His face is flushed and he has his phone-free hand in a fist pressing against his temples. 'I didn't give Charlotte Cook shit. Fine, I think Kieron and all his team are a bunch of wankers—' Georgina leans against the door and covers her face with her hands, 'but I didn't leak. Ask her! Ask her if it was me!'

He takes the phone from his ear. 'Georgina, did you see Owen with my computer yesterday? Phil? Did you?'

Phil is rocked back. What the fuck is Jay talking about?

134

Jay hangs up and taps at his screen. 'Charlotte! It's Jay... I'm terrible today, that's how I am! Tell them, tell the team it wasn't me! No ... Don't give me that ethics crap. You're not protecting your sources, you're ruining my life. Don't hang up! Damn!'

'Jay, calm down and tell me what is happening,' Phil says. Jay looks at him and there is something glassy and blank about his eyes which chills his blood. His laptop is open on the kitchen table, a half-full cafetière and one of their huge coffee mugs sitting next to it.

Jay turns and sweeps at it with his arm. Computer, mug, cafetière and grounds crack and clatter onto the uneven tiles.

Georgina squeals and presses herself against the door.

'Jesus, Jay!'

As Phil stares in shock at it, the glowing apple fades into blankness. He lifts his hands and takes a step forward. If Jay starts trashing anything else, he's going to have to try and stop him.

'He read an email and completely lost it! Like a bloody child!' Georgina says. 'That's what happened!' Her voice is tight with shock and fright. 'Christ, Jay!'

Jay looks at her over his shoulder.

'Fuck the lot of you.'

He pushes past Phil in the doorway and seconds later they hear the front door slam hard enough to make the chain rattle and bounce against the wood.

'Are you OK?' Phil asks. Georgina really does look shaken.

'I'm fine,' she says, and sounds steadier this time.

'Chuck me the kitchen roll.'

She does, and Phil steps over the mess to turn off the

computer power cable at the wall, then mops up the worst of the coffee grounds.

'Shit, the coffee's got right in it.' He extracts the machine from under the coffee and pottery shards. 'Do we have any rice?'

She pulls herself together. 'Yeah. I think, maybe.'

She fetches a kilo of basmati and a baking tray; puts them on the table while Phil shrugs off his coat, hangs it on the back of a chair and grabs another fistful of kitchen towel to wipe the pooled liquid off the half-open keyboard.

Georgina sighs and kicks off her high heels, gets the dustpan and brush and starts sweeping up the broken pieces of the cup as Phil covers the laptop in rice to draw out the moisture. He has no idea if it will work, but these computers cost a grand a piece.

The bin lid clatters as Georgina dumps the pieces. 'Tea?'

'Yeah, thanks, if you're making it.' He wipes off his hands. 'Well, what was that about?'

She puts her palms on the work surface. Stares at the kettle as it boils. It clicks and she drops bags into mugs, fills them.

'He's really fucked up this time, Phil. There's going to be a report in *The Times* tomorrow based on the draft minutes of Kieron's last meeting with the Treasury team.'

'Was it a bad meeting?' Phil asks as she adds milk, squeezes the bags and drops them in the bin on top of the broken mug. 'You were there?'

'Yeah. I was there. Not great. I mean, Kieron was good, strongly advocating for the members. The Treasury team were saying flat out there need to be public-sector cuts and we should start getting ready for it. We talked about trading a pay freeze for job guarantees. Came to an accommodation. So, a bit tough, but, you know,' she sketches air quotes, '"constructive". Then Pat Coogan said something silly about how that works nicely for us as we'll still get the membership dues if there are no job cuts, just a pay freeze. It was in the draft minutes, but not the final version.'

Typical of Coogan, Phil thinks. He remembers his leers and jibes about the free wine he was necking at conference, the weird way he was with that woman at the Christmas party. Yes, keeping jobs and therefore subs and membership numbers was important for the Union, but it wasn't something you *said*. You conceded it, quietly. Certainly not something to cheer about when the bankers were still giving each other bonuses and nurses and teachers were being asked to take the hit.

'And how did it get to *The Times*?'

They sit together at the kitchen table. She blows across the top of her tea. 'Jay's being accused of leaking the draft minutes.'

'Oh,' he pauses. 'By whom?'

'Coogan, of course. Kieron's screaming blue murder. And the rest of the Treasury team have their suspicions, I think. The email that made Jay lose it was telling him to come in first thing tomorrow to "discuss the leak".' She pauses. 'I told him not to ring the team, but he did of course and you heard the rest. Did you know he's been seeing a therapist?' Phil shakes his head. 'I think it's making him worse. More paranoid.'

'Should we go and try to find him?'

She sips her tea. 'Let him walk it off.'

She looks so miserable, Phil reaches out and squeezes her shoulder. 'You've been really patient with him, Georgie.'

Jay had heard Georgina had been approached about the

Coventry East seat; he was bound to in the end. He essentially told her she wasn't even allowed to go there, which was ridiculous, then accused her of flirting with her boss to get the Union's support. It had been an ugly scene which ended with Owen basically ordering Jay out of the room.

'Thanks, Phil.' She looks at him and he feels the full force of her gaze. 'I appreciate that.'

He takes his hand away. '*Did* he leak it?'

'He still hates the Union for supporting me as a candidate, so he's a prime suspect.' Then she shakes her head. 'Apparently, Owen went full Campbell on *The Times*, insisted that Kieron's reply slapping Coogan down was included. He was applauded when he hung up the phone. So my sources say.'

So that's why Jay said that on his call, Phil thinks.

'Who was the journalist?'

'Charlotte Cook. You know her?'

Phil sniffs. 'Seen her around a few times.' At the conference. For drinks. A quiet kitchen supper with her and her husband at their house where Phil also met a couple of Cameron's people. This must be what it's like having an affair, the rush of sneaking about for clandestine meetings, then the guilt and shame waiting at home.

'Don't let that get out, or Jay will accuse you of stealing the draft minutes off his computer and leaking them yourself.'

Phil actually laughs. 'Why would I do that?'

'To "get at him", of course. And there's another reason he's prime suspect. He wrote the minutes. Shared the original with his boss. Closed loop – no one else should have had them.'

Case closed for Phil. Charlotte is a good journalist and can be charming when she wants to. Phil knows he's not the only young political activist being cultivated. Charlotte wants to make friends with anyone who looks like they have a future. Makes sense she would chat up Jay too, if she could. And Jay is a bit of a sucker for friendly attention at the moment.

'I did see Jay and Charlotte in the Red Lion together,' Georgina muses, head on one side. 'I mean, it looked pretty casual, but you know . . .'

She breaks off as the front door rattles open again.

'We're in the kitchen,' Phil calls out.

Owen comes in from the hall, ruffling up his hair where his woolly hat has flattened it. 'It's bitter out there.' He clocks the rice and laptop. 'What's up?'

They tell him.

He whistles between his teeth. '*Was* it Jay? I wondered, but I didn't think he'd do anything that daft. Why did he leak it?'

'You know he hates Kieron,' Georgina says.

Phil and Owen exchange a glance and a shrug. Phil had been thinking Jay was doing better; other than claiming that some people were being weird with him, he'd kept his head down and been working. But then, Georgina knew him best.

'I'm glad Jay isn't here, actually,' Owen says, sprawling into a seat at the table and pushing some of the post aside. 'The chair of the CLP in Coventry East just called in a flat panic. The local PSGWU told him this afternoon if they put Jay on the shortlist, they won't campaign, won't offer any help on the doorstep and no money for leafleting. Georgina, you didn't have anything to do with that?'

She holds up her hands. 'God, no! Of course not! Kieron is really angry and Coogan is humiliated. But I had no idea they'd do this. Must have happened after I left.'

He looks at her for a second then nods. 'Fair enough.'

Phil decides tea is no longer enough. He fetches beers from the fridge. Georgina takes one too. 'What? Before they've even interviewed him about the leaked minutes?'

Owen is frowning. He looks like a sad owl in a snowstorm. 'Which is why they aren't saying anything "officially", but they've let it be known. Yeah, it's pretty stark.'

'What are you going to do?' Phil asks, sitting back down again.

'I suggested an all-woman shortlist in Coventry East. Keeps Jay out with plausible deniability they haven't been influenced by the allegations round the leak.'

'Good idea,' Phil says and drinks deep.

Owen lifts his can towards Georgina. 'All woman shortlist and Union backing. Looks like the seat could be yours to lose, Georgie. Congratulations.'

'Cheers,' she says. 'Lucky me.'

'Jay's denying it then?' Owen asks. They nod. 'He should have just 'fessed up to it: said he thought he was providing background and hadn't clocked the Coogan quote.'

Phil wouldn't have thought of that. Owen's getting better at the ducking and diving, the half-truths of politics every day. He stares at the table-top for a long moment. 'Any chance you could try and soothe Kieron a bit, Georgina?'

She pushes herself up from the table. 'I'll call him. See what I can do.'

She takes her can and her phone upstairs.

'Think she'll have any luck?' Phil asks as she disappears.

'I'm told she can wrap Kieron round her little finger, but who knows.'

'You think Kieron would really follow through with a threat like that?' Phil says. 'Kill off the funding to a constituency party? I mean, I know he has power in the Union, but this is a lot.' He stares at the political cartoons torn from newspapers and slogan magnets stuck to the fridge. Last year, they kept their delegate badges from the conference up there for weeks. Not this year.

'Everyone expects him to be general secretary in a couple of years. They are scared of him.'

'Still, bit of an overreaction, isn't it?'

Owen laughs darkly. 'That's just it. Overreacting is Kieron's favourite tactic. Just go nuclear now and again and you can afford to be a pussy cat the rest of the time ... Keep everyone else in line by once a year picking a victim and breaking them.'

'That's a shitty thing to do,' Phil says.

'I know. Effective, though.' He finishes the can. 'This year it's Jay. Last year it was Julie Coats.'

'Never heard of her.'

'She was rising in the ranks of the Union. Had some star quality so we were looking at her for a speech at the conference. Then Kieron and she had a falling out and he put it about she was unstable.'

'Was she?'

Owen tries to remember the details. 'Single mum, two kids with different men, and she had a restraining order out against the dad of one. We had plenty of good candidates for the slots without the *Daily Mail*-ready baggage.'

'Where's Christine tonight?'

'Spending the weekend with her folks. Look, don't say anything to her about the Jay stuff, will you? I'd rather keep her out of it. She'll want to defend Jay and sometimes these things are best handled quietly. Jay's a good candidate. He'll get a seat eventually. A few months and Kieron will find someone else to pick on.'

'Kieron does a hell of a lot for his members and without his fundraising you wouldn't have the stamps to send out your fancy campaign leaflets, Owen.' Georgina says, coming back in with her phone in her hand. 'And he's got every right to be pissed at Jay.'

Owen lifts his hands in surrender.

'Fair enough! Look, I like it when Kieron's pointing his guns at the Tories, I just wish Jay wasn't in his sights. Any luck calming him down?'

She shakes her head. 'Nope. In fact, I think Jay's in more trouble than we thought.'

Chapter 18

'Thank you, Minister,' Lefiami says. 'So it was after the leak allegation that Kieron Hyde stepped in?'

Phil nods. 'He was bloody angry, and when that man lost his temper he was pretty terrifying. He could scare Owen – and that takes some doing.'

Her eyes flick up whenever he mentions Owen. She must have heard the story about the engagement party, some humiliating version of it anyway.

'Clearing the way for Georgina in Coventry East with an all-woman shortlist wasn't enough. No, he made it clear any constituency party who even *interviewed* Jay as a candidate would not get a penny from the Union Political Fund. Owen managed, with Georgina's help, to persuade the Union to let the message go out quietly rather than making some sort of public declaration. I mean, there weren't many seats available then, let

143

alone winnable ones, so it was just a matter of a few phone calls. Keep Jay undercover until Kieron moved on.'

Lefiami tapped the pen on her pad. 'And did anyone tell Jay that was happening?'

Phil frowns.

'No, I don't think so . . .'

Lefiami raises her eyebrows and Phil feels a cold knot in his stomach. A long pause. Outside they hear a vacuum cleaner being pushed along the corridor. It's getting late.

'Look, I liked Jay, he was clever and he could charm the birds from the trees when he felt like it, but he had a temper on him and he'd never learned to control it. We didn't want him storming into the Union offices and challenging Kieron, or getting in his face at some meeting.' Phil examines the gothic swirls in the carpet at his feet, their geometric interlocking shapes. If only life were that orderly. 'Maybe we should have told him, but his mood was all over the place in those weeks. And you've got to remember how hellish things were. The economy was falling apart, and then in May we had to deal with the expenses scandal. We were all . . . There was so much anger about, and shame. Owen's private list of defensive marginals was getting longer.'

It sounds pathetic and pleading, even to him.

Anger and shame. Humiliation and fear of humiliation. They run through the pipework of the House while idealism and noble purpose white the sepulchre.

'Defensive marginals?'

How did they get onto this? 'Yes, seats which were Labour but the private polling told Owen were in danger of going blue.'

'Why private?'

Phil shifts in his seat. Shame and humiliation. 'Every party has a list, and keeps it secret so their opponents can't use it to shape their own strategy. It makes a big difference to where money is spent, and no one had money to spare in 2010.'

'Thank you.' She makes a note. The recording angel writes on. 'So how do you think it looked to Jay?' she asks and Phil says nothing. 'Basically barred from Coventry East then being blocked from every chance to stand for a seat and no one telling him why?'

Phil feels the cold from his stomach spread through his limbs.

'Let me be clear; you said, Minister . . .' she turns back a page in her notes, 'that you never plotted to do damage to Jay's career. But it sounds to me as if you did exactly that. Hardly surprising that his mental health deteriorated, is it? Now, if we could move on to Glastonbury . . .'

Ian stirs into life. 'Ms Lefiami, I'm sorry but it's after ten and the Minister still has work to do. Can we continue at another time?'

She nods and puts the lid on her pen. 'That would be fine, Mr Livingstone.'

'It will have to be next week,' Ian says, a bit too quickly. 'The Minister's diary is packed.'

'Whenever is convenient to you.'

'I really was . . . we honestly were trying to help,' Phil says as they stand and exchange their shallow bows.

She doesn't comment on that, only wishes him a pleasant evening before Ian shows her out. Phil sits down heavily. He thinks of Jay lying in his tent, the blueish tinge on his lips, the inhaler in his loose grip, the distant thudding sound of music, the shiny pill case. Unintended consequences . . .

Chapter 19

Owen's calendar tells him he has tickets to watch the parliamentary choir at St John's in Smith Square, and that Anna Brooks had agreed to come with him.

Seeing her name on the alert delivers a familiar pang of regret. Owen is finding it hard to be 'just friends'. Their relationship was fractured by lockdown, warped by their schedules and then the local lockdowns which set off small bombs along the way, tangling their plans, but it had been going somewhere. He misses her ambition and her throaty laugh; her unapologetically strange sense of humour, her enthusiasms. They had started talking about next steps: her beginning to attend political events as his official partner, living together, marriage. The practicalities would have been a challenge. Owen thought they could have worked it out, though.

No, she'd stopped laughing as much, then began to disentangle herself from his life when a friend of hers persuaded her to look at what happened to MPs' wives in the press. She told him she just didn't think she'd be able to take living like that. Curtains closed, the fingerprints of the journalists on the living-room window; knowing they were there clambering over the bins to stare through the cracks in the curtains, cameras at the ready. She never wanted to be one of the startled faces on the doorstep or clustered around the TV watching their lives being torn apart in real time.

He texts her, and her reply, swift and affirmative, saying she is already on the way shoots a burst of pleasure through his brain.

He tries to surf the wave out of Portcullis House and across Parliament Square, and joins the snaking queue on the corner of Dean Stanley Street and Millbank. Anna joins him minutes later and that burst of pleasure hits him again. She's cut her hair into a bob, making it look even blacker and thicker. She flashes him a wide smile, puts her hand on his shoulder and lifts herself onto her toes to kiss his cheek, then puts her arm through his and squeezes it.

'God, what a day! If you don't get in soon and sort out the bloody family courts I'm going to stage a sodding revolution myself. I basically had to throw a tantrum today to stop a model citizen being chucked onto a plane and sent to a country he hasn't lived in since he was three. All because he pointed out that his employers weren't even pretending to offer any protection.'

'Did it work?'

'This time. Judge only gave in because he had a queue like this one going out the door.'

'Hello to you too.'

She looks up at him again, amused. 'Yeah, yeah. "Hello."'

So are they doing anything new or is it "hum-along-with-the-classics" night?'

They could power a city off her.

Owen checks his phone. 'Haydn then something from the composer in residence.'

'Is it some mournful tribute to something?'

'No, variations on a piece by Samuel Coleridge-Taylor. Then that's your lot.'

'Cool. God, I miss intervals. And interval drinks. The crush round the bar and downing wine out of plastic cups. Taking culture in these bite-sized chunks fills up the diary, not the soul. So tell me then, how are you?'

The queue is moving now. Down at the front of the line an usher is handing out programmes and face masks, another checks tickets with an electronic scanner, another takes temperatures.

'Fair to middling. Budget tomorrow. Big day.'

'Pfft! Penny on this, penny off that and off to the sunlit uplands tomorrow. Maybe.'

'Thanks, I don't need to go now. Might take the day off.'

She looks up at him sideways to check he's not really offended. 'You should! I'm going wild swimming tomorrow. Embracing my life as a middle-class Englishwoman. It was either that or crafting, and I can't go to court with decoupage glue all over my shoes.'

Anna arrived with her mother and sister in London at eight years old, fleeing Sarajevo. Owen thinks of a day the family sat in a café in Budapest, deciding which way to run, and is still grateful to whoever left a copy of *Country Life* on the table. Anna's older sister thought the trees looked nice, so they came here.

Owen spots Charlotte Cook in the crowd ahead of them and raises a hand in greeting.

'Who is that?'

'Journalist.'

Anna shudders theatrically. 'So are you going to tell me how you are *really*?'

Owen thinks about it. 'Not great. But if you want to rack up another good deed today, can you just tell me about you? I'd really like to get away from it for a bit and it's so good to see you.'

He sees a flutter of sympathy and regret cross her face. 'Swamp sucking at your shoes? Sure. Let's argue about music and I'll catch you up on my "crazy people of the week" stories.'

'Thanks. Do you know a QC called Chloe Lefiami, by the way?'

Anna nods. 'Yeah, she's great. Not a showboater in court, "forensic", though saying that about a barrister is such a cliché these days. And she can turn on the rhetoric when she wants to. Why?'

'She's been asked to look into what happened to Jay Dewan.'

Anna knows the story. Most of it. He told her about it one night as they walked by the Thames. She is the only person he's ever really talked about it with. She hisses between her teeth. 'They are going into that, are they? I'm sorry, Owen, but Lefiami will be fair.'

'She might be, but depending on what gets into the press, I don't know if I'll even keep the whip. Zero tolerance. Leadership may not have a choice.'

Saying it hurts him, physically hurts him.

'They'd chuck you out of the party? God, Owen. Was there something you didn't tell me?'

He shakes his head. 'No, not really. But I never knew how much Jay blamed me.'

'You tried to save him.'

'But I failed, Anna.'

'I know.' She leans against him, resting her head on his shoulder. They are still in a bubble of some sort, then. 'But everyone fails sometimes. It's what we do afterwards that counts.'

He's not sure that's a comfort.

The concert is good. The parliamentary choir provides the chorus, and the music and Anna's face as she concentrates reminds Owen that fresh beauty still exists in the world: the Haydn and eighteenth-century architecture, classical columns and the high vaulted roof; that beauty can survive whatever history throws at it. An hour and it is over, but Owen feels fed. The audience leaves in blocks, hands stinging from their applause.

'Fancy getting dinner?' he says as they begin to file out. Maybe he can tell her about the blackmail, the demons Christine has summoned to his door. He studies his phone for surviving restaurants with capacity as they pass through the main door and start walking down the wide stone steps, tries not to think about how easy it used to be.

'Ms Brooks! Ms Brooks!' A camera flash. Anna recoils slightly against him. Owen looks up and sees a photographer he recognises and a young man he doesn't. The man is thrusting a microphone in their direction. 'Ms Brooks, is it wise for you to be going out with a man who has a history of bullying and intimidation? How would your at-risk clients feel about that, Ms Brooks?'

The demons have arrived in person.

'Keep walking,' Owen says. 'And keep your head up.'

The flash keeps going. Photographer and journalist tap-dance sideways down the steps to keep up with them. 'Are you betraying your clients, Ms Brooks? Is it true you left Owen because of his violent behaviour just like his former fiancée did?'

Bastard. At the front of the queue for cabs the Shadow Minister for Work and Pensions sees what is happening, and shouts.

'Owen! This cab is yours!'

Good man. 'Anna, let's just get in the car.' She pulls away and turns to face the microphone and the camera. 'I broke off my relationship with Owen McKenna because I feared exactly this sort of harassment from certain sections of the press. That was the only reason.'

The taxi comes to them and Owen opens the door. Anna gets in and the journalist steps back. He looks pleased with himself. The quote won't help him, but the photos will be good. Owen follows her in and the driver is Westminster savvy enough to pull away before asking for an address. Anna yanks one of the alcohol wipes out of the dispenser and cleans her hands before fastening her seatbelt. Then wipes them again. Throws the crumpled sharp-smelling rag in the bin provided.

Owen does the same. 'Shall I take you home?'

'Yes, please.'

He asks the driver to head to the Barbican. He has no idea what to say to her. He is texting his thanks to the Shadow Minister when his phone buzzes. Charlotte Cook. She must have been in the scrum.

You've probably guessed, but that's Barns, ex-Daily Mail but now runs his own press agency.

Is he going to run something? Owen types back.

🦇 Word is he's telling the editor he's still gathering background. They're getting antsy with him.

He thanks her then risks looking at Anna. Her profile, the strong line of her jaw, is shaded and lit by the street lights as they pass. She feels him looking, puts out her hand and pats his, but doesn't look round.

'Would this be a bad time to propose again?' Owen asks, and she laughs.

'Too soon, Owen.' Then she turns and looks at him. 'You know the problem. You're ambitious, and I want you to be ambitious. You want power, and God knows I'd rather you had it than the current shower, but I don't know if I could bend myself into a shape which would fit with the life you want.'

The drive is too fast. They are approaching the Barbican estate. She tells the driver which entrance she wants. Then she takes Owen's hand properly.

'I had a good time this evening, Owen. He didn't shock me, he just reminded me that if we got married ... well, there'd always be a bit of me hoping you weren't too successful, because, if you were, that sort of shit would be happening all the time. And that's not a good basis for a marriage.' She releases his hand. Shifts up her tone. 'I'll drink with you, though! And eat. Dinner in a week or two?'

'Dinner then,' Owen replies and she leans in to kiss him on the cheek before bouncing out of the car and walking off without a backward glance.

Owen can still feel her hand on his, the warmth of her

breath. She is the first and only woman since Christine who does this to him.

'Harsh,' the driver says. 'Where next?'

'Yeah,' Owen replies. 'She's not wrong, though.' And he gives the address of the Vauxhall flat.

When he steps out of the lift he sees something waiting for him outside his door. A fresh bottle of Talisker with a bow around it. And a note.

Owen - you have until Friday night.

He takes it inside and puts the stereo on.

Chapter 20

Wednesday 9 March 2022

Owen arrives at the Chamber early enough to be sure of a seat on Budget day. He fills in his card to reserve his place and turns to the wall as the daily prayers are read. The Chamber will be eager for this fight. There will be an election within eighteen months and this is the first serious firing of the guns. Who has the vision to pump some iron into the economic bloodstream?

Owen has read the talking points email. All solid. He'll find his own hooks for them, though, and put them into his own words. Nothing worse than when a bunch of MPs all roll out the exact same phrases like automata, it looks lazy and craven.

There's the usual theatre and usual warnings from the Deputy Speaker. 'Before I call the Chancellor of the Exchequer I must remind the honourable members ...' Whoops and cheers from the government benches.

The Chancellor gets to his feet. He has the ability to project confidence without the blustering arrogance of some of his colleagues. Initiatives to recruit farm labour for this year's harvest include a provision to pause Universal Credit, then reactivate your account when the picking is done rather than be forced into the usual nightmare of re-applying. Not a bad idea.

Owen thinks he can hear the empty rattle behind the talk of bold initiatives and restructuring of supply chains. Food is more expensive, even if money itself is still cheap. Job numbers are increasing, but not fast enough for some people – many people – and the shutters that came down during the various lockdowns on so many shopfronts are now rusted shut.

Most people will just be watching for the headline issues. More money for the NHS, aggressive action against tax avoidance: sounds good, but HMRC still knows it's cheaper and easier to pick an extra twenty quid out of the pockets of every gig worker and sole trader than spend millions going after massive international corporations with their headquarters in tax havens and a wall of lawyers between the tax man and their money.

The Chancellor sits and the Prime Minister and his gruesome colleagues slap him on the back and squeeze his shoulders like he just scored the winning try. Phil Bickford is on the second bench behind the Secretary of State for Health. Too far away to join in the backslapping, so he is nodding with exaggerated emphasis and giving throaty 'hear, hears'. He looks up and notices Owen watching him. His face goes blank, then he looks away.

Habit and muscle memory have got Owen this far through the day. He's managed to keep thinking about the politics, but that moment of locking eyes with Phil and he feels himself collapse internally. Why is he bothering even thinking about all this? If Greg puts that report into the hands of this 'skeezy freelancer' Barns, and tells him to write it up, Owen will be out on his ear. Owen watches the back of the party leader's head as he stands to make his reply.

Owen can make it all go away. Just withdraw the question. If Christine really believes in the Collins story, let her go public with it. Owen can keep his seat, his career.

The Chancellor looks thoughtful, serious. They'll never catch *him* laughing about public-sector paycuts. The Prime Minister huffs and chortles and Owen looks away, a shiver of contempt shaking his bones.

The Chamber begins to thin out. By the time the chairman of the Ways and Means Committee is on his feet the Chamber is as empty as during the first sessions during lockdown. All done.

Pam knocks on his door as soon as he gets back to his office and sparks up the email. He reads her look.

'Don't tell me, you've had journalists calling.'

She sits down opposite him. 'I have. Just one journalist though. Edward Barns. Started asking about bullying and sexual harassment in Westminster "for background" then a couple of "when did you stop beating your wife"-style ones and asking if I've ever felt afraid working for you.' She looks disgusted. 'Guy's an idiot, Owen. If he'd rung me a week ago and told me he was writing an article on what women go through in this building he might have got all sorts of twistable quotes about Owen McKenna's researcher living in fear, but what with the investigation he'll get nothing out of me but "no comment".'

'So is it hacks you're angry with, or just incompetent ones?'

'It adds insult to injury, but I wanted to tell you to watch your back.'

'I shall,' Owen replies. Not much point saying the assassin, Greg, has already outed himself – he's shown Owen the length of the blade he carries and named his price.

'Anyway, that's it. I'm adding all the briefing notes to your cloud server as I get them. You should be able to get through it all on the train.'

She gets up to go. 'Pam?'

'Yes, boss?'

'*Have* you ever been hassled at work? I've never asked you. I mean, I get emails occasionally from the Women in Westminster group. You know, you can always talk to me if there's anything . . .'

She laughs. A note of bitterness, perhaps? 'No thanks. I'd hate to talk to *you* about anything like that.' She sees his confused look and puts out her hand. 'No, not . . . It's just I think if I told you some creep had made a comment or shoved himself up against me at the bar, you'd come over all Dad and go and lamp him one in the Central Lobby.'

He imagines it. Yeah, he probably would. 'And that would be wrong, would it?'

She laughs. 'Yes, Owen. It would.'

'And bullying? I mean, not the sexual stuff . . .'

She leans against the door frame. 'Look, everyone gets shouted at in this building sometimes. It's high pressure. You make it pretty clear when I've messed up, but you don't lose it and you're good at saying so when I've done OK too.' She sighs. 'But some people . . . I mean, it's like a compulsion. They like to humiliate, control. It's pathetic, but when you are employed by the person doing it, it's impossible to fight back. I've sat in the Sports and Social Club with half a dozen researchers in the last year who were in a shit state. You have to work so hard to get here, need so much luck, and we turn up hoping we are going to make a difference and then it turns out your boss is a sociopath who makes Donald Trump look like a teddy bear.'

'Who? Which boss?'

She shakes her head. 'Not my stories to tell, Owen. And you can't say anything about it while this investigation is going on. It'll make you look like you're trying to find cover. Look, just get more women in parliament when you are in power and promote them, not just because it looks good, but because it *is* good. Oh, and if you hear any politician say we need more women in government for the sake of health and family issues, rather than say, the economy, well, them you can hit.'

Chapter 21

Thursday 10 March 2022

The rumours about the Shadow Chancellor start to flourish on WhatsApp just after nine the next morning. Food poisoning? No way. Owen sees the first of the messages as he crosses the floor of Portcullis House and lets out a stream of curses in the shade of an abashed ficus. No. They might as well just hand the next election to those crapulous toads right now. If the Shadow Chancellor gets up looking like he's going to hurl with the leader giving him an alarmed side-eye, all the good work of the last year will be wasted.

He takes the stairs and marches into his office.

'Pam, is this true?'

She barely looks up from her phone, scrolling back and forth and swapping between the groups.

'Yup. Looks like it. He started feeling dicky last night during the strategy meeting and hasn't made it out of his flat this morning. They are putting up Georgina instead.'

Jesus. Poor Georgie. She's being handed a live grenade. Safe pair of hands on the 7.10 a.m. slot on the *Today* programme is one thing. Suddenly, with two hours' prep, being caught in one of the biggest set of headlights in politics is another. He wouldn't be in her shoes.

His phone beeps with a message from the woman herself.

Any advice? 😬

His honest advice would be 'fake your own death'. He types.

Watch the alliteration, don't try to be funny or sarcastic. Project, don't shout. Speak for the party, not yourself.

He pauses. What else?

Their hecklers will be brainstorming ways to rattle you. Ignore them. Microphones won't pick them up. Rise above. Key workers, small business, safe schools. International co-operation. Real leadership not photo-opportunities.

He fights the impulse to keep typing but hits send instead. Seconds later she sends him the thumbs up.

'Do you think Georgina will be OK?'

He looks up to find Pam staring at him hopefully. 'You like her?'

Pam nods. 'She's great. So smart, and without being grand. Her press officer, Emily, just worships her.'

I bet Emily is having a nightmare of a morning, Owen thinks. 'If anyone can manage, Georgie can.'

And she does. Trending on Twitter within twenty minutes of standing up. Gets the Chancellor on the back foot on Universal Credit. The way she raises an eyebrow when he's claiming transparency on the recruitment of new contact tracers and customs officials becomes a meme. Mid-afternoon, the *Daily Mail* publishes a story online about her for tomorrow's edition with flattering quotes from friends and pictures from a shoot she did with *Hello!* last month. Owen is glad the pundits have turned away from Phil. Tries to be happy for Georgina. She is still in the Chamber when Owen leaves Westminster to meet Charlotte Cook.

The pub is huge. Wooden floorboards and a mix of booths, tables and beat-up leather armchairs. Twenty different beers advertised on a chalkboard and menus for pies, or pies with mash and mushy peas, are scattered round the flat surfaces.

The two bar staff break off their conversation as Owen approaches the bar. His basic parliamentary uniform, charcoal suit and tie, makes him feel conspicuous and over-dressed. The back half of the pub is busy with men crouched over board-games. All in T-shirts, most with beards. *Dungeons and Dragons* maybe? The quiet is punctuated by the regular rattle of dice.

'Are you Charlotte's friend?' the woman behind the bar says. She has diamonds in her ears and studding in her nose.

'Yep,' Owen admits.

'She'll be back in a tick. Just nipped out to take a call. She said you should try the Kernel Pale Ale.'

'Great. Pint, then.'

One of the bearded boardgame players wanders up and her colleague takes his order for various pies.

'This place been here long? I used to live near here. Don't remember it.'

She sets down his pint. 'Yeah, well, since 2012. It's our tenth anniversary this year. Bloody hell, did we pick the wrong decade to go into business.'

'You've made it, though? What's Charlotte drinking?'

'By the skin of our teeth. One more lockdown and we are done. For now, we get to struggle on a bit longer. She's drinking mineral water.'

'Let's get one ready for her, then.'

She is setting it down on the bar when Charlotte returns. Her hair is tied back and she's wearing jeans and a loose scarlet sweater. Owen prefers it to her usual Westminster wear. She catches him looking.

'At home writing up my column today,' she says. 'How are you, Owen?'

'You tell me, Charlotte.'

They carry their drinks to a table in the evening sun away from the bar and the boardgames. Owen wipes the table and his hands.

'So this isn't just a social call?' she says as she sits down. 'I admit, I didn't think it was, after seeing you and your friend being chased out of church. But what do I get for confiding in you about whispers I may or may not have heard?'

'My sincere gratitude.'

'Oh, aren't I a lucky girl?' She pokes at the ice in her drink with a straw. The breeze through the window pulls at her hair.

'If it was a reporter I liked, or a colleague, I wouldn't tell you anything. But I think this Barns man is a malicious hack. He's been calling everyone. I would say you are in a fair amount of trouble.'

He sips his pint. 'You know, you could stop all this by just telling Chloe Lefiami who leaked the minutes of that meeting to you, Charlotte.'

'Such ancient history. Anyway, I heard you say at the time Jay leaked it, Owen.'

Owen is startled to hear her say it, then he remembers a night in the Red Lion after Glastonbury. She had sought him out to ask what had happened, and he had told her. Perhaps he had wanted to make her feel it was her fault, that she should have rejected the leak. Unreasonable of him, but then he had been in an unreasonable mood.

'I was sure it was Jay. The draft version of the minutes only existed on his computer. But I've been thinking about him, the house, and now I'm not so sure.'

She keeps poking at the ice. 'About what, Owen?'

'Before the leak, Jay was pretty casual with his laptop. He'd leave it all the time in the dining room if he was working there, or on the kitchen table. We'd all just grab it if we wanted to google something. No lock or code on it. Treated it like communal property. Then, after the leak, when he got his new one, that changed. Never let it out of his sight and he had to type in a passcode every time he opened it.'

'And?'

'Maybe that means it wasn't him who leaked the report? Changing his security habits like that ... why bother if he leaked it himself? But it sounds like what a man might do if he'd been burned. Did he send those minutes to you?'

She looks up, weary and amused. 'Owen, I've been reporting on this snake pit since you were in short trousers. If you seriously think you're going to bat your eyelids and get a source out of me, you have another thing coming. Perhaps some clever pumpkin sent them to me anonymously. It was possible to set up a gmail account even in those dim and distant days.'

'Is that how they sent the minutes to you?'

She crosses her legs and leans against the wall, facing the game players on the other side of the room.

'You know, I can still remember that ear-bashing you gave me over that report. I think if I hadn't included Kieron's line you'd have come straight over to the office, shaking your little fists.'

'You didn't feel bullied, then?'

She laughs, a sharp bark. 'Bless you, dear boy. You were just doing your job. Remember, I had reported through the Alastair Campbell years. You had nothing on him.' Then she looks at him sideways. 'If I tell you something, Owen, will you promise not to repeat it round Westminster? I do not want my reputation damaged.'

'You have my word.'

'I do feel sorry for you. Actual human sympathy! From what I hear, the story is designed to do maximum damage to you personally, and I honestly don't think you deserve it. Believe it or not, I felt sorry for Jay too.'

'Not the revelation I was hoping for, Charlotte, but thank you.'

'So do you want to hear how our friend Edward Barns is spinning his story to the *Chronicle*?'

Owen's been trying not to think about it, doesn't want to

hear it all said into the quiet, slightly sour-smelling pub to the distant tumble of dice, the easy whoosh of the beer pulled into a glass. He has to know.

'Please.'

'They can't decide between the class hatred, racist or homophobic angle. But the story is that you systematically bullied Jay into a breakdown, destroyed his reputation and career, then threw him to the wolves at Glastonbury.'

Owen closes his eyes. And this is before they've seen Jay's file.

'There aren't any wolves at Glastonbury.'

'That's not what the average *Chronicle* reader thinks,' she says. 'And then the editors love the idea of the houseshare. You and Phil Bickford and Georgina in the house with Jay. A sort of "where are they now?" Or a political *Big Brother* house. Wild parties. Georgina's the survivor, Phil's the guy who saw the light, Jay is the victim and you are the villain.'

A good story. And just enough truth in it. He wishes he could go back, grab his former self by the collar and tell him to talk to his boss, to talk to Jay, to stop thinking he was so bloody clever he could just sort things out on the quiet. Perhaps his success managing the floor votes at the conference had made him cocky.

'Christ! It's such bullshit, Charlotte! We were so fucking square in that house. I didn't bully Jay. He was my friend.'

He can feel guilt beginning to corrode his thoughts, though.

'Like I said, Owen. I'm sorry. Also happy to put your side of the story, should you wish to confide in me.'

He shakes his head. If he just withdraws the question, this

165

will all go away. But Charlotte is a proper journalist. If he says anything to her it will be reported.

The hanging basket outside the window swings as a pigeon lands on it then flies away. The Number 1 bus glimmers by on the main road, just visible through the urban landscape, the Victorian townhouses, the yellow-brick council flats, the multi-coloured postmodern blocks with their tiny balconies.

Owen is silent. He is thinking through those pages of notes again.

'You should talk to Phil.'

'What?' Owen has an edge of disgust in his voice.

'I said,' Charlotte repeats with exaggerated patience, 'you should talk to Phil. Compare notes. Isn't it time to get over your issues? You were good friends and it's been twelve years.'

'Thirteen and he betrayed us.'

'Come along, Owen. I've seen you chewing the fat with Tory MPs.'

She is looking at him with her eyebrows raised. The 'it's all just a game, isn't it?' expression which drives him mad. Politics is not just a game. People protect themselves pretending it is, but what happens in Westminster makes and destroys lives.

'They don't know any better. But Phil stabbed us in the back, Charlotte. We knew that Cameron was just another Tory bastard who thought the poor were suffering on purpose to annoy him. But Phil went trotting over there anyway because the cool kids in the Labour Party didn't want to read his bloody pamphlets. And he—'

'And that's why you beat him up?'

Owen slams down his pint. What's left of it. A couple of the dice players turn round.

'I didn't beat him up, Charlotte. I landed one punch and he fell over. He bloody deserved it, too.'

'I was told Georgina had to pull you off him.'

'Not true.'

She finishes her drink. 'I'm rather inclined to believe you. Shame we are on background – that line about Cameron is quite amusing. But honestly, Owen, Phil is a better fit in the Conservatives than he ever was going to be in the Labour Party after Blair.'

Owen rubs his thumb down the side of his pint glass. A yell goes up from the other side of the room. Some dark enemy defeated. She waits for him to speak, but he feels as if he has run out of words.

She stands up. 'Thank you for the drink and if you do ever want to speak on the record, you know where I am. And I am sorry, Owen. Good luck.'

She leaves him staring into the dregs of his beer.

Chapter 22

Friday 22 May 2009

Owen is still up, reading at the kitchen table so as not to disturb Christine when Jay comes in and announces he's been fired.

'Or let go, as they call it! They said they were restructuring the team, but I think it's all been done to get rid of me. I can't fight it anymore, Owen. I can't . . . '

He sits at the table and drops his head between his hands. Owen puts down his book and moves his chair round the table and drops his arm around Jay's shaking shoulders.

'Jay, I'm so sorry. That's fucking awful.'

'This year has just been a nightmare. I've never been fired before, never failed.'

For once Owen isn't irritated by a statement like that. He feels for him.

'I got fired from a call centre once.' He searches for something better, funnier, to say. 'And did I ever tell you how I got fired from my first job? I tried to get a better staff discount at the newsagent's when I was delivering papers.'

Jay snorts. 'That's very you.'

'It's the same shop my mum works in now. She has a bet with herself about how often in a week she can mention my job title to the guy who fired me. If I've had a meeting in Downing Street, she awards herself double points every time she gets that in too.'

He lifts his head. 'Your mum rocks.'

'Yeah, she does.'

Jay tries to wipe away his tears, then he gives up and starts crying again. Owen finally realises he is messy drunk. He fetches him a pint of water and kitchen towel to wipe his face, stands over him until he's got all the water down him.

'It'll all turn out right in the end, Jay. I swear it will.'

'Kieron's got it in for me . . . Someone said at the bar it's down to him I'm getting blocked for seats. The utter bastard.'

'You've been working too hard, Jay. Look, it's Glastonbury in a month. Can you afford to just take the time off? Or take a couple of weeks before you start looking for a new job, at least. You've got to rest, get away from Westminster. Forget Kieron.'

Jay lifts his head again. His eyes are darkly shadowed. 'You don't understand, Owen. Westminster is the only place I've ever wanted to be, and this didn't just happen – someone has done this to me. It's a *campaign*, a campaign against me. How can I fight it if I don't know where it's coming from? And you and Phil never listen. You just roll your eyes like I'm insane or something. Only Georgie listens. I can't . . . I just can't anymore. God, I want to get out of my own head!'

Owen rubs Jay's back. 'Didn't I just tell you? Glastonbury in a month!'

He half-laughs. 'Yeah, I'll get out of my head there. Fuck it, now I'm sacked I might as well get out of my head all the time.'

'All right, mate, come on. Let's get you to bed.'

Owen leads him upstairs and gets him into his room then fetches another glass of water to put by his bed. Jay is asleep by the time he gets back.

Fired. God, that's cold. Surely Kieron will back off now. He turns off the light and closes the door as quietly as he can.

Chapter 23

Thursday 10 March 2022

Owen finds he is walking round the back of Elephant and Castle and tries to slow his pace. Relax his shoulders, lift his head. It takes effort. He turns left and twenty minutes later, the fumes of beer and anger dissipating a little, discovers that muscle memory has led him to the end of the street where he had lived with Jay and Phil and Georgina.

The corner shop has become a Costcutter, though the posters in the window advertising deals on washing-up liquid and canned tomatoes don't look much different. The street itself has smartened up. The town houses which had been converted into flats are, by and large, single-family homes again. The windows and doors are freshly painted and in the narrow front gardens the bins are surrounded by purplish shale or gravel, box hedges and spiky palms. The paths have been repaired.

He finds himself outside the house itself and stops. It isn't just Phil who knows what it was really like in this house. Georgina knows too. And this is Georgina's house now. Georgina and Kieron's. They bought it after Phil left and the market was low. Let Owen carry on living there through his break-up with Christine and through the 2010 election.

He glances up and down the street. No photographers – though Owen saw photographs on the news sites of Georgina leaving home this morning, before her triumph holding the government's feet to the fire. Her children, a boy and a girl both under ten, had come down the steps to say goodbye and the picture showed her crouching to hug them. FIGHTING FOR OUR CHILDREN'S FUTURE, the headline above it had said on the *Mirror* website, and in the background at the door was the out-of-focus frame of Kieron Hyde.

Owen is ringing the doorbell before he's even made the decision to drop by. He's been to parties at the house since Georgina and Kieron remodelled, but didn't pay much attention to what they had changed. He remembers pale walls and a tasteful mix of modern and classic art on the walls. Their boy had taken him upstairs to show him his old room. The wall where Owen had his junk-shop dresser with framed pictures of Jarvis Cocker and Clement Attlee and a cluster of iPod wires and orphaned chargers was now painted with a blue whale mid-dive through a cartoonish ocean. Owen and the boy agreed, solemnly, it was an excellent room with many advantages over the larger one his sister had, then Owen had returned to the party.

When was that? Three, four years ago? Just before the 2019 election. A good evening. The conversation rich with gallows humour and despair about the leadership and the grip the mop-haired Prime Minister had, against all logic, acquired over the British people. That was back in the days when Brexit was their tragedy. Happy times, even though they hadn't known it. Perhaps a dozen of those guests, Christine included, lost their seats as Johnson romped home and the leadership insisted they had won the argument. Like a guy left bloody in the car park after a bar fight who insists he's made his point.

'Owen?' Kieron Hyde opens the door. 'What on earth are you doing here?'

Good question. 'Sorry, Kieron, was just passing by and couldn't resist the temptation. I guess this investigation is making me nostalgic.'

'Come in and have a drink. Georgina's still at the House, but the kids are fed and staring at computer screens in their rooms and I wouldn't mind the company.'

Owen accepts and follows him through the hallway. Same but different. All lighter colours, spotless. None of the usual detritus in the hall you'd expect in a house with young children. The kitchen has changed a lot. The back wall is now a solid sheet of glass, with a huge rustic kitchen table sitting between it and the kitchen proper. Oak cabinets, an oversized range, copper pans hanging from hooks on a sort of rack, and over the table a chandelier, but made in metal and shaped like a mass of oak leaves. Beyond, the glass uplighter highlights different plants and bits of statuary in the gathering dark.

'Nice,' Owen says.

'Red or white?'

Owen opts for red and watches Kieron as he lifts down the correct glasses and gets to work on a bottle of something French with a waiter's corkscrew. Owen hasn't seen Kieron for years. Not to talk to at least. He must be pushing sixty now and looks thin rather than trim. His hair is still thick, but almost completely white, and his jeans hang loosely on his hips.

Owen remembers how bloody scary he seemed in 2008, when it looked like he was certain to be the next general secretary of the PSGWU, surrounded by his hometown minions, a pint in his hand, loud in his approval and disapproval. The sort of man who could send you flying across the room with a pat on the back. An eye for the ladies . . . who had said that about him? Not Georgina.

Owen had first heard rumours they were 'seeing' each other shortly after Christmas from a pissed-up MP who had noticed Georgina coming out of the office looking flustered and found Kieron red-faced and smug.

Shortly after the all-women shortlist for Coventry East was announced, they were unofficially a couple. Got quietly engaged soon after the tragedy at Glastonbury, and married before the 2010 election. Kieron was at Owen and Christine's engagement party as Georgina's date.

He takes the glass.

'Fancy a turn in the garden?' Kieron says hopefully.

Owen nods and as soon as they are outside Kieron produces a cigarillo from his top pocket and lights it.

'Not permitted in the house,' he says. 'But you're not married, are you? Free spirit!'

'I never smoked,' Owen replies. 'What are you making? Smells good.'

'Fish pie,' Kieron says. 'One of the specialities de la maison.'

Kieron smiles a lot more than he used to.

'So has Chloe Lefiami been to see you?' Owen asks.

Kieron bobs his head, taps ash off his cigarillo and carefully rubs it into the lawn with the toe of his shoe.

'Getting our stories straight, are we? Well. Yes. She talked to Georgina at length, apparently. I did a written statement, but I mean, I barely knew the lad. Just some half-Tory smart arse. Too many of those buzzing around then to tell the difference between them.'

He suddenly snaps to attention, takes a long pull at his cigarillo and takes the stub to an ornamental ashtray hidden under the bird bath. Nothing wrong with his hearing. He's pushed it back into its hiding place with his foot before Georgina appears in the centre of the glass doors and thrusts them open. As soon as she notices Owen, her face is transformed by a broad smile.

'Owen! What are you doing here?'

He walks down the slope of the lawn and crosses the narrow patio area. She blows him a kiss, and he holds his hand across his chest and bows.

'I was just passing by and thought I'd stop by on the off-chance to congratulate you.'

'You doll. And thanks for the advice.' Her eyes flick over his shoulder. 'What's for dinner? I haven't had a chance to eat all day.'

'Fish pie,' Kieron says.

'Not again. Fine. Owen, stay and eat with us. Why did you open the red if we are having fish? Honestly. I think you are getting dotty in your old age.' She kicks off her shoes and bends to pick them up. 'I'm going to get changed.'

Kieron follows them into the kitchen again. 'I'll put the beans on. Ready in two ticks. Kids would love to say goodnight.'

She glances at her watch. Thin strap, antique by the look of it.

'Oh, they are probably asleep, and I just can't take story time this evening.'

Owen wonders if he should refuse the invitation to dinner, but he's hungry and something about being in the old house is stirring and shifting his memories.

It's like the only school reunion he went to just after he was elected. He'd thought his recollections of school were complete, clear, but it turned out all he had were the memories he shared with friends, the stories they retold to each other in the years afterwards. Seeing all those other faces, being back in the school hall itself, had brought back a dozen other incidents, dramas, teenage tragedies and victories he hadn't thought of for years. It was unsettling, rediscovering your past like that.

And it's happening now. He can see Jay more clearly than he has for a long time; the quick bark of his laughter, the nerdish enthusiasm they shared for The Clash, late-night arguments – with Phil acting as referee – on the exact degree of veneration or respect that should be accorded to different American Blues musicians. Owen feels a shock in his nervous system. It was Jay who introduced him to the music of Robert Johnson, the man who sold his soul to the devil at the crossroads in return for his supernatural talent. Owen still listens to those recordings all the time but his mind had cut the connection to Jay. It reknits, somewhere deep in his brain, as he watches Kieron top and tail fine green beans on a thick oak chopping board.

Georgina comes back into the room in yoga pants and a loose snow-white hoodie. Kieron abandons the beans to fetch her a glass and fill it from a bottle in the fridge. She sips, shrugs, then spreads her fingers wide on the table top and looks at Owen.

'Tell me everything.'

Ten minutes later they are in the thick of it, talking about the front bench, the quirks of individual ministers, who is up and who is down. She's witty about her colleagues, sharp without being cruel and frank about those she likes, more circumspect about those she doesn't. Owen feels his burdens eased as they settle into the back and forth. He makes her laugh.

Eventually, Owen realises he's eating and breaks off to compliment the chef. Kieron thanks him.

'Well, he's got the time to be a chef now, hasn't he?' Georgina says. 'Though it would be nice to have something other than fish pie occasionally.'

Kieron continues to eat in silence. Owen tries to remember what Kieron is doing now. He got shunted out of the frontline after losing the election for the general secretary.

'How is life in the Union?' Owen asks.

'Fine, thanks, Owen,' Kieron replies, but doesn't say any more and concentrates on his food.

'Not that running the legal department allows you to shape Britain's industrial future,' Georgina says. Kieron doesn't react and Georgina watches him for a few seconds before turning to Owen again.

'So is being here bringing it all back? I have to see Lefiami again next week. She has more questions, apparently. All I need at the moment. Don't suppose you've managed to squash the *Chronicle* story?'

'No, but you shouldn't have to worry too much. According to my sources, Phil is the one who saw the light, I'm the bad guy and you are the survivor.'

Her head flicks up and she looks at Kieron. He keeps eating and something about her expression makes Owen look away. He drinks his wine, suddenly uncomfortably sober.

'I was remembering what a fan of music Jay was,' he says at last. 'I'd forgotten that.'

'Oh yes, president of the Blues Club at Oxford,' Georgina replies, her expression easy and open again. 'Nearest he'd ever get to a Blue of course.'

'Well, there was his asthma,' Owen replies mildly. 'Not much chance of being an elite sportsman, given his condition.'

'God, yes, always searching for his bloody inhaler! Used that to get out of a dozen fights he was losing in seminars at Oxford. "Sorry, just a moment." Breathe out. Breathe in. Inhaler. Hold your breath. It gave him thinking time.' She catches herself and stops. 'Is it going to be bad for you?'

He swallows. 'Yes. Jay thought I resented him. And keeping him off the candidate lists all that spring doesn't look good.'

'Yes, perhaps you shouldn't have done that,' Georgina says, twisting her glass and looking at the patterns of light scattered through it and across the table. 'He was frightened of you, you know.'

'What?'

She shrugs. 'You can be intimidating, Owen. Lots of people say so. I mean, I know you are just expressing your opinion, but it can come across a bit rough.'

Owen puts his knife and fork together. 'That's bullshit. Jay wasn't frightened of me. We were friends.'

'Oh, I think he was. I remember you ordering him out of the room when he was having a go at me once. And we all know you can . . . shall we say snap?'

The wine starts to turn sour in Owen's mouth. Edward Barns doesn't need to try and get quotes out of his researcher, Edward could just call his old friend Georgina.

Georgina waves her hand, like she's shooing away a fly. 'But let's forget about all that! I want to tell you about the three worst ideas my policy team have come up with since the Budget. Honestly, I know they are *technically* brilliant, but they have all the political sense of a spoon. Earth enrichment audits, for crying out loud. I told them, worms don't vote, but they'd been plotting with Clifford's lot in the shadow environment team again, getting themselves worked up.'

Owen wants very much to forget about Jay. Just for a minute.

'Call it investing in Britain's farms. Regenerating the soil – supporting farming communities. Spin it as patriotic. And remember, if you do Clifford a solid now and get it into the Manifesto Budget . . .'

She purses her lips. 'Yes, he'll be a useful ally when we are in government. Well connected, not too ambitious.'

'Are you so sure you'll win?' Kieron says. He eats like a bird, pushing up a mix of pie and beans onto the back of his fork.

'Of course we're going to fucking win,' Georgina says, and Owen believes her.

Chapter 24

Owen refuses dessert, makes his farewells and walks home. The notes in Jay's file repeating in his head. He can hear them in Jay's voice.

He tries to think it through: what's the worst that could happen? He could be scapegoated by the party and press – have any other skeletons they find in the back of the closet in Charlotte Street lashed to his back and then be driven out into the wilderness. Scapegoat or sacrificial lamb? What would life be outside politics? He can't conceive of it.

His phone buzzes.

He doesn't recognise the number but when he answers it, Greg's voice at the other end seems inevitable.

'Owen!'

'Greg. How did you get this number?'

He presses the button on the pedestrian crossing with his knuckle, the traffic eases to a halt and he crosses to walk back towards his flat along the river, his back to the Houses of

Parliament. 'I still have friends around the place,' Greg replies. 'Quite a few, as it happens, and making new ones all the time.'

'How nice. What do you want?'

'You owe me a new pair of shoes, by the way. That lovely single malt didn't agree with the leather. But there we go. I called to ask what you thought of Elsie Collins? I do not understand why young women disfigure themselves with tattoos. Not the sort of thing which goes down well in middle England, that look. And she is rather highly strung.'

Owen wonders if he is being followed.

'I have nothing to say to you, Greg.'

He sighs. Owen hears it as a hiss on the microphone and steps sideways to avoid a pair of young women taking selfies with the Thames in the background, its surface rippled with lights.

'Withdraw the question, Owen. It's perfectly clear how this is going to play out. Suppose you support the Collins family. What then? First, before you can finish typing a press release Edward will publish the story, complete with tragic Jay's own words. What a story!'

Owen stops, leans on the stone wall between him and the river. He finds he is staring at Millbank Tower and has a flash of himself there when he was just a teenager, overwhelmed by the fact he had found a place at the centre of things. Greg is still talking, and Owen can't stop listening.

'Perhaps your friends agreed it was for the greater good, but it was *you* who made the calls, wasn't it? You who let it be known that Jay was not a candidate favoured by the party that year. Not them. Your boss didn't know anything about it, did he? And even if you did drag dear Georgie and Phil into it,

Georgina is the star of the week, and attacking Phil – saying he agreed with you keeping Jay off the lists – I mean, that will look a bit pathetic it, won't it? You made the calls.'

He is right. Owen's spent the last thirteen years trying to forget about it, but bloody Greg is right.

'Dangerous talk, Owen. People remember that. Of course they do. At the time, given how Jay was and what happened, perhaps they all shrugged and thought you were right and got on with their lives. There was an election to lose, after all. But now? Seems a bit different. Imagine if Edward finds out exactly who to call. I hope you noticed Jay rattled off a useful list of the seats he'd applied to. Drove him to distraction, didn't it? Those constant rebuffs?'

Owen stays as still as he can. Truth. A line from a poem floats through his mind . . . *cold and true . . . like a gun quite close to my head* . . . Yes, he did make the calls. Georgina's words in the kitchen, spoken over her glass of wine, come back to him. 'Maybe you shouldn't have done that . . .' not 'maybe *we* shouldn't have done that . . .' Maybe *you*.

He is on his own. He tries to rally himself.

'Whatever you do, Greg, it doesn't change the fact the sale of access to NHS data needs to be the subject of a public consultation. And the allegations of the Collins family should be heard. People aren't stupid. They can understand I was a shit, and know that the questions I'm raising are still valid.'

Feels good saying that. He almost convinces himself for a second.

'Really? Are you quite sure? A marked man, trying to claw back a little glory – or flailing about as I'm sure various columnists will put it – by supporting this damaged girl and her sad story about her crazy brother. A fantasist and a non-issue. My story is better. You have read the files that Christine left for you?'

So, someone *is* watching them.

'Not much there, really? Do it tonight, Owen.'

Then he hangs up.

Owen puts his phone back in his pocket and turns off Albert Embankment and down Tinworth Street. A train rattles over the bridge as he passes below. Nothing Greg has just said is wrong. The case is weak, he's told Christine that himself. And he is on his own. He gets back to the flat and sits in his preferred high-backed chair, takes his iPad out of his satchel and opens it up. Stares at the black mirror of the screen.

No point in dragging it out.

Owen wakes the screen and logs in to the system. It's not a particularly well-designed site, the parliamentary hub. Like parliament itself, it's been patched up and repurposed a dozen times, and because MPs are, nowadays, a bit gun-shy about spending money on themselves as a rule, it's been patched up cheaply. It works though, and Owen has used it often enough to be able to navigate to the right page.

A drop-down menu next to his question. A simple tap with his index finger. The confirmation box comes up.

YOU ARE ABOUT TO WITHDRAW QUESTION 08348. DO YOU WISH TO PROCEED?

He knows when he's beat. He clicks 'yes'. The screen updates.

The box of files from Elsie Collins is still on the worktop. It looks like a rebuke. He doesn't feel any sense of relief, no sense that from now on the past can stay in the past. He puts Robert Johnson on the stereo and listens. His voice is rough and sweet at the same time and Owen sees Jay, back in the good times, a beer in one hand, dancing in the kitchen of the old house, and his grief returns in a wave.

Chapter 25

Friday 11 March 2022

Phil gets up at six to work out in the hotel gym, then has breakfast and reads the papers in a discreet corner of the dining room. One of the advantages of a constituency in Marlow is that he can usually get home even during the week. When he can't – and between the Budget and the sudden interest everyone is showing in him, that's been a few nights recently – he uses the special MPs rate at the Park Plaza. He misses home. He misses the kids. He scans the newspapers, then the emails from the press office Ian has marked as must reads.

Phil doesn't feel his government is worn out, exhausted of ideas in the way the Labour government was in 2010. But then, it's not like one Conservative Party has been in power for the last twelve years, more like three different groupings who all happened to wear blue rosettes. Cameron, Mr Austerity and Responsibility who threw the country into the sacrificial fire of Brexit, then May the non-government of paralysis, then this lot.

The government of charismatic individualists on epic adventures. This lot. His lot, he reminds himself. His colleagues, his party.

He sighs. Talking to Lefiami has shoved him back a decade. He has to be careful; he thinks of his wife saying it, a warning look on her narrow, intelligent face. Your socialist roots are showing, Phil. He scans the front page of the *Financial Times*. Qualified support, but confusion and scepticism over various of the initiatives announced in the Budget. The tax avoidance campaigns are being compared to searching down the back of the sofa for coppers when the rent is due.

That's not the only thing the government is doing, for crying out loud. It's all about balance. Asking for a little ground here and there. Taking advantage of the commercial opportunities available. Phil believes in moderation, evolution not revolution. He believes in the Chancellor too, which makes a pleasant change. Once the population has got over its impatience with Brexit, its fear of the virus – a reliable long-term vaccine *has* to come this year, surely? One that people will trust? – they'll see this is the best way to build their way back out of this murderous slump. Cameron's way, really. Social responsibility, not state control. That was the line in Cameron's speech which got Phil in 2008. It resounded deep within him, like the voice of a loved one.

Phil remembers mouthing along with the words of 'The Red Flag', hating it, hating the self-satisfied faces around them, becoming convinced between his second punch and a Greek meze that the people around him, who still held such sway over the Labour Party, were out for themselves, ready to loot the country at its lowest point to prop up their own power, feather their own nests. That was before the expenses scandal, of course. He remembers them crowing over that. Christ, and he thought the banking collapse was the lowest point. He'd had no bloody idea how bad things could get, and still somehow stagger on.

He's staring at his iPad Pro, seeing but not seeing, when he notices another email. It's an automatic forward from an old, very old, private account. Owen McKenna. Owen McKenna wants to speak to him.

His mind flickers, Owen singing along at the party with his arm round Christine's waist. Then Glastonbury, the horror, mirroring Phil's own, as the music rocked across the camping site, the grief and confusion under the silent flashing blue and reds of the police and ambulance. Owen in the lobby last week with that grin plastered over his face. Phil didn't need to wipe that smirk off his face after all. Looks like Chloe Lefiami has done it for him.

Phil reads the message and his finger hovers over the little bin icon for a good thirty seconds before he replies instead with a time and a place.

Being a minister, even a junior minister, makes it hard to go anywhere unnoticed. Phil thought, maybe even hoped, that this meeting would get cancelled, but no. After a terse reply agreeing to the meeting, the private email account receives no more messages. So Phil calls the host of the drinks reception he is supposed to be attending and says he will be late, then says goodnight to the staff in the office, arranges for his red box to be put in the car and walks briskly across Parliament Square to Westminster Abbey, past the main doors and under the arched entrance into the Dean's Yard.

The Sub-Dean is waiting for him, leaning against the railings and scrolling through her phone. She looks up as he approaches then takes him through the entrance into the cloisters.

'I appreciate this,' Phil says as they walk past the ancient memorials towards the Chapter House. The lawn smells freshly cut.

'Happy to help,' she replies. 'Terribly cloak and dagger. I feel like I'm in a Le Carré novel.'

Phil blushes, afraid he's being mocked. 'I know it seems foolish but it's surprisingly hard to have a private conversation in SW1.'

She shakes her head a little. 'I do know, Phil. Don't think the church isn't riven by factions too, and *we* are supposed to all be on the same side. He's waiting for you. Though I must say he looked a little nervous when I brought him in. As if I were going to forcibly convert him as the price of entry. I assured him the Chapter House is actually English Heritage.'

'Owen's a committed atheist. He was probably afraid he'd be hit by a thunderbolt.'

She allows herself a low laugh. 'Ah! Atheists! Very superstitious bunch, I find.'

They walk through the low vaulted entry hall then up the stairs to the Chapter House itself.

'You won't be disturbed.' A quick nod of farewell and she is gone.

The Chapter House is an octagon, the ceiling supported by one slender column which seems to grow out of the medieval tiled floor, blossoming from its terracotta patterning. The stained-glass windows wash them with colours and shadows, reds, blues. Phil blinks into the changing light.

'How did you swing this?' Owen is sitting on the stone bench which edges the room. He has his legs out in front of him and crossed at the ankles, hands in his pockets.

'Do you know this is where parliament first met?' Phil says. 'Well, the King's Council. Thirteenth century.'

Owen glances around him.

'They could have picked a more cheerful decorating scheme.'

Phil takes in the faded images of the Horsemen of the Apocalypse and Christ's return.

'A reminder we shall all be judged, I suppose. The Sub-Dean and I were at school together. I wasn't the only one in my year to make it out of Chelmsford.' His footsteps echo as he walks across and stands in front of Owen. He's getting some grey in his hair. 'I thought you'd cancel.'

'Why would I do that?'

'I thought it was just an impulse, emailing me, and you'd probably change your mind five minutes later.'

Owen grunts. 'I did. A few times actually. Just kept changing it again. Anyway, how could I miss out on a catch-up with an old friend?'

This was a mistake, Phil thinks. What's the point? The bitterness runs too deep. Then Owen draws his breath in sharply and his voice changes.

'It's an old habit, being pissed off with you. Can't seem to shake it.'

Phil sits down next to him. 'When I saw you in the Members' Lobby the other day I was seriously considering trying to beat you about the head with a notepad. So don't feel too bad.'

A half-laugh in the shadows.

'So why are we meeting?'

Owen sighs and shifts on the stone seat. 'Charlotte told me I should speak to you. I didn't warm to the suggestion, but I don't know ... My conversations with Chloe Lefiami have woken up some old ghosts. This thing is forcing me to remember a lot of stuff I had managed to forget.'

'Such as?'

'Such as I'd forgotten how much fun Jay was when I moved in. Before he started complaining about the whispers. Do you remember when we wanted to dig a pond in the back garden?'

'God, yes!' Phil hasn't thought of that for years. 'You were telling stories about your mum and Jay was laughing so hard he couldn't hold his shovel straight. Lucky Georgie stopped us before we did too much damage.'

'He had a great laugh. That was a good day,' Owen says and falls silent.

'Yeah,' Phil sighs. 'I hate remembering him as he was back then. A proper enthusiast for stuff, almost as bad as you, then how he was at Glastonbury. I wanted to shake him.' He pauses. 'Now what are you grinning at?'

'You don't sound half as fancy as you do when you're speaking in the Chamber.'

'Sod off.' But it's got no heat in it.

'Were we too hard on him? Should we have fought Kieron over his ban?' Owen asks.

Phil feels a cold grip on his chest. 'He was flailing about. I honestly believe we did our best. Does that help?'

'Yeah. I needed to hear it wasn't all my idea and I wasn't just a violent thug out to get Jay because I envied his Oxford education.'

'I guess you know if I thought that was true, I'd say so,' Phil says. 'It's not true. I always got the idea you just didn't like people who thought an Oxbridge education made them super-heroes. Like they got some sort of "leaders of the free world" certificate along with the degree. And I'm with you on that.'

'That's about right.'

The silence stretches out between them. In the Abbey the organ begins to play and they hear the choir begin their ritual pleas for forgiveness from the Lord.

'Are you in trouble, Owen? With the investigation?'

He rubs the bridge of his nose. 'More the story they are trying to get out in front of. And Jay thought it was me who leaked the minutes to Charlotte, that I was secretly homophobic or racist. Charlotte's not saying who actually gave it to her.'

'Bollocks,' Phil says. 'You're not racist and it was 2008. No one cared who Jay slept with. Not in our house anyway.'

'That's not what he told his counsellor. Apparently, people of my background can't help being homophobic and racist.'

'Double bollocks. But how do you know what he told his counsellor?'

Owen shakes his head.

Phil feels a familiar exasperation. 'What? You don't trust me?'

Now Owen looks at him like he's an idiot. 'Of course I don't trust you.'

And they are back there.

'Look, Owen, I followed my convictions,' Phil says.

Owen blinks rapidly. 'You followed your ... I could almost, almost forgive you for that but give me a sodding break. I know *exactly* what you did.' His voice begins to rise. 'The first by-election in a safe seat under Cameron and it goes to *you*? Three months in parliament and you became a PPS? Do you think I'm a fucking idiot, Phil?'

Phil's throat tightens. 'Owen, I ...'

'Maybe *you* leaked the report. You hated Coogan and the Union. Why wouldn't you leak it? He left his laptop lying about, didn't he? Used the dining room as his extra office all the time. Suppose you saw it. You wouldn't be able to resist it. It was Charlotte who got you in with Cameron's lot, wasn't it? Were those minutes your ticket to the inner circle? Then they sent you back in as a spy for another year?'

Phil is suddenly so angry he can hardly think straight. 'That's it? That's why we are here? So you can accuse me of that leak? *Jay* leaked the bloody minutes.'

Owen shakes his head. 'Why not tell his counsellor that? Why did he get so paranoid about his computer afterwards?'

'People lie to their therapists, Owen! Jay was the definition of denial! Yes, we should have talked to someone else about him, but we thought that would make things worse, not better. And we were kids ourselves. How come you saw his counsellor's notes?'

Owen runs his hands through his hair. 'It's all bullshit anyway. The whole thing. If Christine hadn't annoyed your paymasters at Maundrill Consulting with that bloody question this would have just stayed in the past where it belongs.'

Typical Owen. Shifting the goal posts mid-conversation. No wonder it was impossible to have a sensible discussion with him for more than five minutes flat. 'What has Christine got to do with this? Are you cracking up now, Owen? What paymasters? Maundrill Consulting? I answer to the voters of my constituency. That's all. My paymasters are the taxpayers.'

It sounds a bit pious as soon as he says it. Damn. Owen gets to his feet. 'That is the single biggest crock of shit I've ever heard in my life. You are the most sanctimonious priggish arsehole in Westminster, you know that, Phil? Who pays for your party? Half the time it's the Russians and the rest is big business, lobbyists, the vultures who can't wait to tear the juicy body of the NHS apart!'

Enough. Phil is on his feet too.

'What? And your lot are the keepers of the true flame, are you? So fucking deep in the pockets of the unions they can choose your candidates, get Jay fired, write whatever impossible unicorn requests they want into your manifestos and make you say "thank you" afterwards?'

'This from the party that brought us magic Brexit? You betrayed us.'

'I walked away because I didn't recognise the party I joined: you were throwing everything Tony had done into reverse and you could never *listen* to any bloody opinion other than your own. It was all about the party for you, and any thinking criticism was disloyalty. And look what's happened to you since!'

'Brexit is your fault.' He jabs towards Phil's chest with a finger.

This is ridiculous. Phil opens his arms wide. 'Really? You were happy to court the votes of the anti-Europeans and anti-immigration brigade when it suited you! Not to mention using the EU to cover up for the fact you let the manufacturing industry in the country die on its arse on your watch. Even Georgina admits that now!'

'*Now* he cares about industry! Your lot would leave entire cities to die if one of your big data donors told you to.' Owen steps back. He looks disgusted. 'This was a mistake. I'm an idiot. Just because I wanted to be told what happened to Jay wasn't my fault. You betrayed me! Me! I worked that campaign. I *saw* the damage you did. We were friends and I *know*, I know like I know my own name that when you left the house, you took the list of defensive marginals with you. What was it? A couple of clicks with the iPhone as you packed your stuff? God, they must have wet themselves when you handed that over!'

Phil just stares at him.

'After what we had been through, Phil! And we could have hung on. If you hadn't handed over that list, Gordon could have hung on.'

Phil feels something shift within him. 'You blame me. You blame me personally for losing that election.'

'Yes. And for every austerity death which came after it. Every Universal Credit or bedroom tax suicide. You have blood on your hands.'

'And yourself. You blame yourself.'

'Of course I do! If I hadn't trusted you, if I'd had the sense to see you were about to flee and hide under Cameron's skirts I would never have left it where you could see it. I even talked to you about it! Dozens of times. So fuck you, you Tory butcher.'

He walks away across the colour-splashed tiles.

'This *was* a mistake,' Phil shouts at his retreating back. 'And fuck you too, you paranoid Labour scum.'

Owen doesn't stop walking.

Phil stays where he is, staring at the point Owen disappeared. The choir's sweet distant prayers for grace creep into the Chapter House around him.

Chapter 26

Saturday 3 October 2009

Owen announces his engagement over breakfast. Christine is sitting next to him and wearing one of his old T-shirts with battered leggings. A Saturday morning in early October. They haven't looked for a new roommate. Christine has moved in and she keeps the stuff that won't fit into Owen's room in Jay's, in boxes, and pays a fair share of the rent. Jay's family are still paying his rent. His clothes hang in the wardrobe, his posters on the walls.

Georgina is in flannel pyjamas slightly too big for her and eating toast. She drops the slice immediately, bouncing crumbs over the table top, and claps her hands.

'That's amazing! Oh, can we have a party? Let's have a party tonight.'

Christine shakes her head. 'No party, Georgina. I mean, I haven't even got a ring.'

'You didn't get her a ring?' Georgina appears outraged.

'It was a spur-of-the-moment thing,' Owen says.

'Was it romantic?'

Phil watches her and wonders: it's clear Christine and Owen don't want to jump up and down squealing, but Georgina is going full rom-com on them. Phil can't tell if she is genuinely excited or taking the piss.

'We were walking along the river after dinner and I asked,' Owen says.

'And I said yes,' Christine replies. 'Told my mum this morning, she's pleased. Already trying to get us to set a date.'

'June,' Georgina says. 'June is the month for a wedding.'

Owen is squirming in his chair. 'Depends on the election.'

Phil stands up, opens his arms and Owen gets up and accepts the hug. Phil puts his hands on his shoulders. 'Congratulations, Owen. You do not deserve her.'

Owen looks happy, the first time Phil's seen that since Glastonbury. Phil moves on to Christine.

'I have no idea what you're doing, Chris. Did he hypnotise you or something?'

'Must have done.'

Georgina drums the end of her knife on the table. 'Par-ty, Par-ty, Par-ty.'

'Seriously, Georgina. I meant it. No party.' She recognises the tone in Owen's voice, shrugs and starts buttering her toast instead.

'Fine. What about a few people for drinks, then? Just a quiet one. We could roll out the barbecue again. I know Kieron would love to come and offer his congratulations.'

Christine looks sideways at Owen. 'I guess a few drinks would be fine. I could text a couple of the other researchers.'

196

Owen takes hold of her hand. 'As long as you don't mind not having a ring to show off.'

'Honestly, I don't think I even want one. I'd be scared of losing it. I'll wear a wedding ring, if you will. But that's enough.'

Owen reaches for more toast.

'Are you going to have to be a three-house family?' Phil asks. 'A house in each constituency and a place in London.'

'We'll work it out,' Christine says and asks for the butter. Owen passes it to her. Phil sees the look on his face, though. He hadn't thought of that.

When breakfast is done and Christine and Owen have retreated to shower and dress, Georgina looks up from her phone.

'You have to tell him, Phil.'

'I know, but not today. I can't today.'

'Just rip off the band-aid, babes.'

A few people become a few more, and by eight the house is full. Owen takes all the congratulations he can, then comes to help Phil with the barbecue. An autumnal drizzle is keeping the party indoors, and they've rigged a sort of shelter for the barbecue with an umbrella and the hat stand from the hall. Phil turns sausages and looks at him. Owen has a daffy smile on his face and Phil follows his gaze in through the French windows to where Christine is standing with her friends inside.

'Maybe June would work,' Owen says. 'I mean, I'd lay good money the election will be in May. What do you think?'

Phil turns the sausages again and wonders if he should flap

at the coals. 'Sounds like it. You could always go for autumn though, to be on the safe side.' Owen swigs his beer. 'Aren't you getting wet?'

'It's only mizzling. I wish Jay was here.' Phil feels a pang under his ribs.

'I know.'

'He should be standing in this election. I mean, if he had got himself sorted, Kieron would have backed off by now and, God, Phil, the number of MPs who I hear are standing down now after the expenses stuff. He might have got a decent seat. Or a seat with a decent chance after all.'

'Yeah. I know. It sucks. Go and get us a plate, will you?'

Owen ducks into the kitchen and returns with a platter, looking thoughtful. 'Phil, he didn't think it was me who had it in for him, did he?'

Phil puts the platter carefully under the barbecue to keep warm and snaps open another packet of sausages. 'Jay? What makes you ask that?'

'That ginger cake Christine made this afternoon, it reminded me. Just one time I came in and he was in the kitchen with Georgina, a few weeks before he lost his job. The look he gave me . . .'

'I think maybe he did for a while, but that night he got really wasted, you know really wasted and you looked after him? He emailed me the next day, said sorry he'd been a dick about you and he was pissed at himself for thinking you had anything to do with the rumours.' Owen turns away, rubs the back of his neck. 'Owen, I thought you had no idea he was blaming you at all, so I didn't say anything. I'm sorry.'

Someone's turned on the music inside. Pulp again. Owen

shivers like he has déjà vu. 'These people do know other music exists, right?'

'You can convert them later. My credit card is still burning from the last time you took me CD shopping.'

Owen grins, his wide face-splitting grin. 'Did I steer you wrong on any of those bands?'

'You did not.' Phil turns and bows to him, flourishing his sausage tongs. 'I thank you for saving me from the shame of having exactly the same five CDs everyone else I know has.'

'Maybe you should run for parliament this time,' Owen says. 'Lots of opportunity.'

'I don't know.'

'Mind you, better for me if you don't. More time for you to help plan the wedding. You know I'm expecting you to be my best man, don't you?'

Now he has to tell him. He can't say 'yes', and tell Owen afterwards. He puts down the tongs. 'Look, Owen. I resigned from the institute yesterday. I was going to tell you this morning, but your news sort of trumped mine.'

Owen shrugs and lifts his beer to him. 'You were wasted there. Sounds like great news. Are you going to run? I mean, I can get you on the inside track on a couple of seats in Essex. Local boy made good . . .'

Phil shakes his head. 'I resigned because I've got a new job. Policy unit.'

Owen looks baffled, but still pleased. 'Will you be based out of Charlotte Street? That would make this campaign a lot easier to take.'

Owen's hair is damp with the rain, his shirt clinging to his arms in places and he looks so excited for him. *Just say it.*

'Owen, no. I'm leaving Labour. I've had an offer from George Osborne's people. I'll be working for, campaigning for . . . the Conservative Party.'

The punch comes out of nowhere, or it seems to. Phil sees Owen's face turn to thunder and then he sees stars, an explosion of pain, and he staggers backwards and falls over the edge of the umbrella stand. More pain in his back and his hand stings.

'Owen!' Georgina is standing by the door with Kieron beside her. He looks bemused. Phil holds up the hand that doesn't hurt.

'I'm OK, I'm OK.'

Owen shoulders past Georgina in the doorway. They hear Christine call his name and the slam of the front door. Phil clambers awkwardly to his feet. He can feel blood running from his nose and his right palm is scraped and stinging.

'You told him, then?' Georgina says and Kieron laughs. Phil pushes past them both. 'Cook your own fucking sausages, Georgie,' he says. Then he goes upstairs to pack.

He can hear the sounds of the party breaking up downstairs while he fills a bag with clothes and orders a cab. The rest he can come back for later. Fuck, Owen, fuck the party. They had left him, not the other way around. Cameron was the future, not Gordon with his betrayal of the project and the past decade of government weighing him down.

His nose isn't broken, at least he doesn't think it is, but it hurts like hell and his hand stings every time he touches anything. He rams his laptop into the case and swears at the twisting power cable. Owen still has his copy of *The Big Sort*. He's had it for weeks. Phil crosses the corridor and pushes open the door to Owen's room. It is expensive, that book, and Owen will probably throw it on the barbecue now rather than return it.

The book is on top of the bed with Owen's papers and laptop. Phil grabs it, victorious. Then he sees it. Just lying on the bed and covered in Owen's neat blocky handwriting. The list of defensive marginals.

Outside through the shiver and hum of the traffic passing on the wet street he hears his taxi blowing its horn.

Chapter 27

Friday 11 March 2022

Owen distracts himself on the train back to the constituency with Pam's briefing notes, though his blood is still fizzing and thumping from the fight with Philip. He forces himself to concentrate.

He has a surgery on Saturday afternoon, then on Sunday he'll be on this listening session with local businesses. The list is all small businesses, entrepreneurs – the people who are actually going to pull the world out of recession. Not like insurance companies and big data specialists and lobbyists who are making fortunes picking over the bones then hiding their profits where the tax man can't get them.

Like Victor Collins and his start-up? *If it was a bad idea, why did they buy the company?* Christine's question itches at the back of his mind. They only paid three quarters of a million, though. That must be chickenfeed to them. Perhaps it was done with a shrug, and a 'Maybe it'll inspire our tech lads.' Then

Collins – disturbed, over-worked, borderline psychotic Collins – his hopes dashed, cooked up this conspiracy theory.

Jay's medical records ... if they were a result of one of Maundrill Consulting's clients roaming around the NHS data vault, then Victor's claim his own records were being used against him gains a lot of credence. But Maundrill Consulting could have just as easily bribed a receptionist, a doctor. Tabloid hacks used to do it all the time.

Was Victor's idea any good? Owen has no way of knowing. He knows some things: the files Elsie made and Christine dumped on his neighbour included Victor's mobile phone bills. He *did* get a lot of calls from government numbers for a while, four or five times a day, and then they stopped cold. No gradual tapering off as the department lost hope or interest. A sudden screeching halt. Enough. He has made his choice, he withdrew the question and the story will disappear. Lefiami's investigation will conclude that what happened to Jay was tragic, and make a few recommendations on dealing with the mental health of young staffers and then Owen can get back to politics. *Of course we'll fucking win.* And he's going to be there when they do.

The train starts to slow and he gathers his bags and papers. The brakes hiss and eventually the door release button flashes. He pushes it with a knuckle and it sighs open.

The platform is quiet. Most people travelling back from London got home an hour or two ago. The gates at the side of the station building are open and the only movement is the orange on black signs, writing and rewriting themselves with promises of the next train and the current social distancing advice.

'Here!'

Owen turns towards the voice and sees Liam Holdsworth leaning up against his dark red Vauxhall Astra. The last man in England to buy British. British-ish. Last time Owen was in the underground parliament car park, he saw Georgina climbing into a BMW. Even he has ended up with a Volvo.

Liam's in his pub gear. Chinos and a polo shirt which shows off the thickly braided muscles of his arms. Shaved head. Tattoos down both biceps. Owen has no idea how he manages to keep in shape with two kids and a full-time job in an office full of women who adore him and like to show their love through baking. He's worked at Citizens Advice for five years now. He is Owen's eyes and ears in the constituency, among his voters, and his friend.

He pops open the boot and takes Owen's bag from him.

'Nice week at the office, dear?'

'Lovely. What's for dinner?'

Liam presses the boot shut and Owen gets into the passenger seat.

'Beer, of course. The Cock and Magpie?'

Real Ale. Tables out front on the tow path. Quiet.

'Yeah, perfect. So what do I need to know?'

Liam chats to him about the local news as they go up the Coventry Road and round the back of the hospital. Owen automatically checks the verges, hedgerows, roadworks. OK. The council seem to be keeping on top of things, just.

'New campaign on the local Facebook groups about extending the car-free area, and some fuss about drugs in Priory Park. You'll hear about that tomorrow at the surgery, I guess.'

Liam comes to the surgery sessions at the weekend, walking the people who come to see Owen through benefit forms and advising them on how to fight evictions, deal with debt. Owen's constituency agent calls him her extra set of hands.

The headlights catch a FOR SALE sign outside one of the industrial units. It's been there a month now. Not good. 'Sensible taxation for the nation. More money needed for the police, more money for social services,' he says automatically.

'Some bloody jobs would be a nice step forward too,' Liam grunts as he winds past the modern blocks of flats and older single-family houses and turns into the pub car park. He pulls in behind a wall of beer barrels, turns off the engine. 'Anything you can do about that?'

Owen gets out of the car. Slowly. Watches as Liam gets out and shuts his door. 'Do you blame us?'

'What?' Liam says, hitting the button on the key fob. The car park smells of cooking fat, sour beer and behind it the vague green weed tang of the river.

'Us. Politicians, I mean. For the lack of jobs.'

He shoves his keys in his pockets. 'Me personally? I don't know, mate. Sometimes. Not much you could do about the pandemic, but the rest of it? I like you. You've done OK by me, but even when I put a cross against your name, it's because I think your lot aren't as bad as the Tories, not because of any shiny future I see coming over the horizon.'

'Hence Brexit.'

'Hence Brexit.' They walk round the canal side. 'Why are you asking?'

Owen feels embarrassed. 'I've got some stuff going on.'

'OK. I'll get the first round in. You stare at the ducks for a bit.'

Owen does as he's told and takes a seat so he can lean up against the wall of the pub and look at the water, lit in yellow patches by the lights of the pub. A painted canal boat with a family on board chugs past. The little girl sitting at the back waves shyly at him and he waves back.

Liam returns from the bar, shouting something over his shoulder back inside. Owen hears distant laughter.

'Have you heard about the investigation into Jay Dewan?' Owen asks as Liam sits down.

Liam takes a long pull at his pint. 'No.'

Owen lifts his own pint. 'Now I'm dwelling on my past mistakes.'

'Sounds like a laugh.'

You blame yourself. Get the messaging right. Mistakes were made.

Owen feels a twitch of irritation. 'If politicians, if people, can't own up to the things they've done wrong in the past, why should you trust them to try and do the right thing in the future?'

Liam looks sceptical. 'You're off your game, fella. I mean, twenty years in and all of a sudden you've discovered you're a politician?'

Owen is looking at Liam's arm. The tattoos mostly cover the scarring, but it's still there if you look for it. Shrapnel from an IED in Helmand Province 2008. Liam sees him looking and shifts sideways. Shoos his eyes off with a wave of his hand.

'*Sorry.* Doesn't make a soldier feel any better, saying, "Sorry we sent you to war, turns out it was a shit idea." I was out there for the bloke next to me. Not for Tony Blair. So if that's what you're thinking about, don't.' He drinks. 'And all this apologising gets my goat. Why go over it? Let it lie. Never seen this shit do any good for anyone.'

Owen might have said the same thing a week ago when he first heard about the investigation. 'It's not about making people feel better. It's about rebuilding trust.' Exaggerated eye-roll across the table. 'Fuck's sake, Liam. I mean it. And I'm not just talking about the party. If it doesn't start with individual politicians, people like me, then what's the point? I don't want my whole career to be an exercise in arse-covering.'

Liam snorts into his pint. An alarmed duck leaps back into the water at the sound and Liam laughs at it.

'Did you see that! I gave the poor bloody thing a heart attack.' He glances sideways at Owen, grows serious again. 'Mate, I can't think of a job that *isn't* an exercise in arse-covering. Mind you, that makes it refreshing when somebody stands up, I'll give you that.' He goes quiet and waits until Owen is looking at him again. 'I know what happened that night. You know, I know. That's fine. You showed up and helped. That kept my family together. You didn't have to and that means something. Never felt the need to chat about it. I like my privacy.'

'Shall I get the next one in?'

'Yeah, and stop looking at me like you want to kiss me. It's freaking me out.' Owen stands up. 'Tell you what does matter, though.'

'What?'

'Being heard. We've worked hard on that list for you on Sunday. Promise me you'll listen to them, not just stare over their heads and wait for a chance to trot out one of your talking points.'

'Do I do that?'

'It has been known, Owen.'

'I promise.'

Liam folds his arms and leans back in his chair. 'Excellent. You may now buy me more beer.'

Chapter 28

Phil finds himself picking over the fight with Owen in the Chapter House as he nods and bows his way around the drinks reception. It's a 'health care around the world' conference closing party. The room is huge for the numbers, the windows flung open and piles of face masks and hand sanitiser scattered among the table decorations where you used to get bowls of nuts.

One delegate after another tries to whisper in his ear and he palms them off with vague promises of future meetings, working groups. Greg Griffen, an accomplished heckler when he was in the House, gets a nod and a photograph and makes vague congratulatory statements about Phil's great work then disappears back into the crowd. His card says he's working for Maundrill Consulting. Suddenly, Phil can't get out of there fast enough.

He's starts rerunning the fight with Owen on the way home, working through his papers on the back seat while his driver listens to Classic FM, and kicking himself for the chances he had to cut Owen down to size. By the time his driver drops him in front of his house in Marlow, he's fuming again.

Sara, Phil's wife, calls a hello from the kitchen and an offer of gin. His house. Her house. He couldn't afford to live like this on an MP's salary, even with the ministerial bump. He met Sara when he was working in the City after the 2010 election, getting some 'real world' experience Tory HQ had called it, and she had stayed there miraculously accruing wealth even as the rest of the country turned to ashes around them.

'Honey! Welcome home!' The kitchen floor is scattered with Lego. The twins have been on an orgy of construction and destruction. Sara has a gin and tonic on the go already.

'I've ordered Thai. Hope you don't mind. Not feeling very wifey tonight.'

He kisses her, grateful for the smell of her face lotion, the familiar reassurance of her hand on his waist.

She makes him the drink while he goes upstairs to change out of his suit and kiss his two children. They are splayed out on their beds in their shared room, sheets twisted around their legs. Alex is curled up, hands under his cheek and his curly hair falling across his cheeks. He looks like a model for a Victorian postcard. James is lying on his back, arms and legs akimbo. Behold, the man.

He arranges the sheets over them. Kisses their foreheads and goes back downstairs unsure how he got so lucky, the anger with Owen beginning to leak out of his blood but leaving him tired and unsettled.

'What's up?' Sara says as she hands him his gin.

He tells her. Sara has never met Owen, seen him across a

crowded room or on TV from time to time, but never met him. He is a figure in their marriage nevertheless, a ghost in the back rooms of their relationship, their understanding of each other, just as her dead father is. A formative influence, absent and unchallengeable, but still invisibly buffeting your partner's actions and reactions as they move through life.

'Not the conversation you've been hoping to have with him,' she says when he is done.

'No. I don't know what I was expecting. Why I was expecting anything else. When I told him I was joining the Conservatives, I knew he'd be raging at first but I thought we'd be able to talk about it eventually.' He stares at the ice settling in his glass. 'All these years later he's still going for my throat.' He drinks, feels the kick of the alcohol and his own disappointment. 'Everything is so tribal with him. I don't understand why he doesn't get it's that sort of thinking which has brought the world to its knees.'

'That and a global pandemic, my love,' she says.

'Don't patronise me, Sara,' he snaps. She holds up her hands, eyebrows raised. 'Sorry, sorry. I blame Owen. The man drives me mad.'

'Did you do it?' She asks the question very carefully, quietly. 'Did you give the list of defensive marginals to Conservative Party HQ?'

He could give a non-answer. He could bluster. But he loves his wife.

'Yes.'

She gasps, a tiny intake of breath. 'And I thought we got this seat because of my charm and all our hard work.'

They *had* worked hard. The local party weren't wild about

the idea of an ex-left winger from the other side of London and the wrong side of the tracks being parachuted into the constituency. Sara had thrown herself into the work while pregnant with the twins and supporting him financially. She'd bought this house between coffee mornings and school fetes and posed for photographs, hanging on his arm, even while the morning sickness was at its worst.

'You made all the difference.' He means it and he thinks, hopes, that she believes him. 'It was never an explicit quid pro quo, you know. And I was trying to convince myself they wanted me in parliament for myself, not as a result of my past . . . ' he can't find the right word, 'endeavours.'

She swallows, still absorbing the change in perspective. Folding the new information into their story. 'Why did Owen never confront you about it before?'

Phil is raw. 'It would have taken him a while to work it out, and we never spoke again after his and Christine's engagement party.'

'When he punched you.'

'When he punched me. He might have started wondering when he saw how well focused our spending was. Me being selected for this seat probably felt like a confirmation.'

She swills the last of the ice water in her glass. 'Why didn't he tell anyone else?'

'Because it would have made him culpable too. He shouldn't have left the list unattended in the house, even in our house.'

'Poor Owen.'

His anger flares again. 'He would have done *exactly* the same thing if he'd had the chance! He'd have leaped on something like that and spent years crowing about it, no matter who he screwed over to do it. He's never done anything that wasn't about the party and what he thought was best for it. Sod the greater good. The guy is the ultimate machine.'

'Apart from meeting you today,' she says gently. 'Whatever that was about, it wasn't about what is good for the Labour Party.'

'I don't know. Maybe it was, and I just missed it.'

The doorbell chimes softly and she goes to fetch the food while he lays out the plates and cutlery. They set out the cardboard boxes, licking the drips off their fingers. She hasn't put any music on, and Phil unfolds slowly into the peace of it. The garden is dark. A curious fox blinks at them from the patch of light spilling onto the grass from the floor-to-ceiling glass doors, then disappears.

'The stuff about Christine causing problems is interesting. Did you check it out at all?'

There's a reason she's got this rich. She doesn't miss much. Phil looked it up in the car: the question about medical data lying unanswered on the order paper, then withdrawn just before Owen sent him the email.

'That's the only thing I can see out of the ordinary.'

'Go and talk to him again. This weekend, while you are both out of London. Talk about what happened to Jay, about why you left. Confess.'

He stabs at his dinner. 'It would be good to actually see something of my family.'

She snorts. 'Breakfast with the twins at the weekend and you'll change your mind pretty fast. Go up after your surgery. Honestly, there's a football match and a birthday party during the afternoon. It's a taxi duty Saturday. I mean, as long as your civil servants don't discover you have a few free hours a month we'll be fine. Then you can have all the fun of dragging James and Alex to church while I have a lie-in on Sunday.' He nods. Not agreeing to the plan exactly but agreeing to think about it. 'What about this medical data thing? What do you think?'

He shrugs. Still hurting and subverbal.

She pushes away the takeaway box and fishes out her iPad. Looks up Maundrill Consulting and starts reading while he finishes his meal and refills their wine glasses.

'God, they are very, very quiet about who their clients are, aren't they?' she says at last. 'All very vague, industry leader stuff. And they aren't trying to sell themselves here. I get the impression you need to be invited to even ask for their services.'

'The whole thing sounds crazy. Owen blaming his troubles on this?'

She shakes her head. 'No. Not completely crazy if they see the question as a threat to their interests. He's on the Digital, Media, Culture and Sport Select Committee too, I see. Would they oversee data security?'

'It might fall within their remit. Their discussions are confidential though until they've decided what they are going to report on.'

'So if he asked about NHS data security there it would probably leak.'

Sara has learned a lot about Westminster since Phil was elected.

'Perhaps, but it still seems a stretch.'

'That health data has any number of commercial

applications. And geo-tagged info can tell you an enormous amount about a place.'

'Such as?'

'Imagine if you are choosing a place to build a factory, or another bloody distribution centre. This sort of information will tell you a lot more about your potential employees and the social infrastructure than the glossy promos of smiling market traders you'll get from the council.' She sips her wine, still reading. 'Seriously, corporations will pay millions for that sort of analysis. And that's before you even start thinking about how valuable this stuff is to the insurance industry. Who's had the virus? What's the likely vaccine uptake? You can tell that by seeing who gets vaccinations for childhood diseases already. What are the rates of diabetes? And now the government are encouraging employers to offer private health insurance to their staff, this data is going to get more and more valuable. Certain locations will mean higher premiums.'

She pushes the iPad aside. 'Darling, I don't want to end up with my head in my hands again, but shouldn't you know about this sort of thing?'

He sighs. 'It was decided the secondary and commercial use of data would not be overseen by my department.'

'Hmm.' She invests the noise with considerable cynicism.

'So, it's plausible? That just asking the question would send certain concerns after Owen? To shut him down?'

She waves her hand, taking in their home, the imported French wine, the shining appliances and well-stocked fridge. 'Information is king, darling.' She looks at her wine glass. 'You know that as well as anyone.'

He reaches across the table, takes her hand.

'I am so, so sorry I didn't tell you.'

She traces a line on the back of his hand and is silent for what feels like a long time before she answers. 'You were ashamed, Philip. And sometimes shame can make us do terrible things.'

Chapter 29

Saturday 12 March 2022

Phil drives north. It takes him three hours. According to his Facebook page, Owen is due to finish his afternoon surgery in the remains of the local shopping centre in half an hour. Phil parks and finds a bench with a view of the front entrance. He doesn't want to read on his iPad here. Too many people crossing back and forth across the flagged square look pinched and hungry. Tracksuits, pound-shop blouses, and shopping trolleys that double as a sort of walking frame. He buys a thriller from one of the charity shops and tries to read it while keeping an eye on the entrance.

This is stupid. What if one of Owen's people spots him and wants to know why he's here? What if they leak this unannounced visit to the press? What if he ends up having to defend the latest Budget, actually standing in a half-shuttered high street with a camera in his face?

He feels like an idiot. He tries to shrug off the sensation

and concentrate on his book. It half works, then a movement catches his eye.

The security guard checking IDs before he lets Owen's constituents into the surgery is having problems. A woman, late middle age with a floral shopping bag at her side, wants in and her name is not on the list. Phil lifts his head.

'But I'm hungry!' she says, her voice rising. 'The kids are back from their dad's tomorrow and there's nothing in the house.'

The guard says something to her and she backs away, shaking her head.

'I'm not filling in another fucking form! Not another!'

The guard tries again.

'What am I supposed to do? Can you tell me that? I've had my parcels! I've been everywhere. I just walked two miles here in these cheap-arse shoes because I can't afford the bus, and you won't even let me in?'

People are looking. The security guard touches the phone strapped to his arm.

She steps away from him into the bare desert of concrete flags. Someone has drawn a series of messy rainbows in chalk over them. Phil can't remember when they last had an outbreak round here.

She's crying. Ugly crying. 'Fine! Fucking arrest me then, you cunts! What have I got to lose?'

And she drops to her knees on the paving stones and rainbows. 'You think we're animals! So feed the animals! Feed me!'

She's screaming it. Phil notices her hair is brushed, her clothes clean. Like his mum on her way to Iceland when he was a kid. She might only have a fiver in her pocket, but her blouse would be ironed. The woman holds up her arms, her head thrown back. People around the edge of the square are turning to stare.

'I missed one appointment! I called ahead and they sanctioned me anyway!'

The words stop, or they stop being understandable. A tearing yell bubbles up from deep in her throat. Then she draws breath and screams.

Inside the old furniture store, Owen hears the scream, but not the words.

'I'm sorry, Mr Parker,' he says to the elderly man sitting opposite him. 'I better go and see what's going on. You stay where you are.' Mr Parker looks confused, deflated. 'I'll be back. I promise.'

Marcie, his constituency agent, shakes her head. 'Owen! Don't! The police will be coming. Derek can handle it.'

'I'll just be a minute,' he says. Yes, his security guard probably can handle it, but Owen is twitchy anyway. The store still smells of cheap carpet fluff. He needs air. And for God's sake, he's the MP. He can't just hide. Too many politicians do that. He puts a hand on Mr Parker's shoulder as he passes and squeezes, hoping it reassures him that he will be back. He feels the slight shock in Mr Parker's body, and wonders when he was last touched.

'Owen!'

He turns back. 'At least take your panic button!' Marcie lobs it across the hall to him and he catches it. Sticks it in his pocket. He hates the bloody thing, can't look at it without thinking of 2016.

He walks across the old showroom, nods to the people

waiting at the back of the hall. Liam is there, at one of the for-mica tables with a fan of Citizens Advice leaflets in front of him, talking to a woman with a baby on her lap through a handful of Universal Credit forms. He raises his eyebrows. *Need me?* Owen gives a micro-shake of his head.

He steps outside, blinded by the spring sunshine bouncing off the flagstones for a second, then sees the woman on her knees and hears the ugly throat-tearing cry again.

She looks like a painting. Something medieval, a wood-carved pietà, her empty shopping bag across her knees.

Derek semi-blocks him. Politely done, but it's still a block.

'Didn't have an appointment. Says she's talked to the Citizens Advice people already. Stay here, Mr McKenna. Police are coming.'

'Who is she?'

'Don't know. She said she's hungry, got sanctioned. I told her this isn't a food bank. Tried to give her the office number but she just went off on one. Please, Owen. Just let the police handle it. They know it's your surgery. They'll be quick.'

Yeah. Everybody wants to make sure Owen is safe. A young woman holding the hand of a toddler is standing opposite and watching them, horrified. She takes a step towards the woman.

'Not quick enough,' Owen says. 'I'll be fine. Just watch my back, will you?'

He walks cautiously towards the woman. Her eyes are open but he's not sure she's seeing anything. He can't see any sign of a weapon, but then how could he tell?

He crouches down a couple of feet from her. 'Ma'am?'

She reaches out for him, the movement sudden and wild, with a sort of groan.

'I can't . . . I can't do any more,' she says with suddenly clarity. He tries to control the flinch, feels the warmth of her breath on his face, its sour stench.

Derek is jogging towards them. Owen holds up his hand. 'I'm fine, Derek. Stay where you are.' The footsteps stop.

'Ma'am, what's your name? I'm Owen.'

She can't focus. Her mouth works sideways for a second or two, then she seems, finally, briefly, to see him.

'Fuck you,' she says, crisp and clear. She collapses sideways. Strings cut.

Owen makes a grab for her, gets his arm around her shoulder before her head hits the concrete.

'Derek! Ambulance!' Owen shouts, and wonders what in God's name he should do next.

'Owen, mate.'

Liam – and he's got a seat cushion from the furniture store in one hand. He crouches beside Owen and slides it under her head so they can lower her onto it. Liam takes her weight. Not that there's much to her, just that Owen's in this clumsy half-lunge, holding her, and is in danger of going over himself. The weight of responsibility. Owen twitches her skirt so it covers her legs. Her skin is cold.

He takes off his jacket and lays it across her.

'Do you know her?' he asks. 'Derek said she's been to Citizens Advice.'

'Never seen her before in my life,' Liam replies and leans in to take her pulse. 'Thank fuck she's still breathing.' Owen feels the light on his face, he hadn't even heard the sirens. Ambulance, paramedics running towards them. A pair of police officers. Not again. *No long coats*, he thinks, his brain feeding him scraps of

Larkin poetry. *What are days for?* Two of them. Young. A girl with her hair scraped back off her face, a bloke, older, Asian.

'We'll take care of her, boss. If you'd just step back.'

Familiar and strange. Not déjà vu, but a mirror of another moment. *We have suffered a sea-change.* Owen looks up and thinks he's seen another ghost. A glitch in the matrix. His mind is playing crappy tricks on him.

He gets awkwardly to his feet, steps back out of the way.

'Is she OK?'

The male paramedic glances back over his shoulder. 'She'll be all right. Bess, fetch the gurney, will you? This yours, sir?'

He passes Owen his suit jacket and whips out a fleece blanket from his bag, which he arranges over the woman.

'There we go, love.'

Owen hangs the jacket over his arm, looks round the sparse crowd again. He can't decide if he's looking for a familiar profile or camera phones. It's going to be a story. How will it play? Dammit, can't he just *be* here for a second without thinking of the politics. Always the bloody politics.

'Fella?' Liam. 'Me and Derek have got this covered. You get on with the surgery. Folks are waiting.'

Owen looks at the policeman, who nods. 'Go ahead. I don't need you at the moment, sir.'

'She wasn't ... she didn't try to attack me or anything like that,' Owen says. It sounds weak.

'Thank you, sir.'

But he can't leave until he sees the paramedics lift the woman onto the stretcher, strap her in. They've given her an oxygen mask and her eyes are fluttering open.

He thinks of the votes he has taken since he became an MP,

the policies he campaigned for when he was at Labour HQ. The compromises, the failures. Phil.

Did I do this? Do I blame myself? Do I have to blame myself?

They are putting her into the back of the ambulance.

Did I make this happen? Was Jay my fault?

He stays where he is a second longer, then pulls himself together and heads back towards the office and Mr Parker, his worries about his wife's care home, trying to leave the questions outside.

Phil walks back to his car. Fast. He has no idea if Owen saw him or not. He thinks maybe he saw some flash of recognition as the paramedics arrived, but what with the woman and the screaming ... He was about to help Owen himself, on the point of dropping his book and running over, then the shaven-headed guy came running out of the store front, a cushion in his hands, and Phil recognised him: Owen and paramedics and police and there is Liam sodding Holdsworth in the middle of it. How in God's name? He tries to think through what he saw. Liam at the surgery. Liam and Owen working together?

He gets into his car and breathes, leaning forward with his head on the steering wheel, and the memories and the guilt break over him in waves. Georgina with flowers in her hair. A dancer with Minnie Mouse ears. The torches of Shangri-La. He takes out his phone and googles Liam's name and Warwick. There's a bit about him on the website. 'As an ex-offender ... ' Christ.

Phil pulls himself together and heads back to the M40, back towards his wife and his constituency and his home and away from the damn memories. But they come with him, of course.

Chapter 30

Owen gets back to London in time to vote on Monday afternoon. His tour of local businesses went well and he has a draft memo for the Shadow Secretary of State for Business and Industrial Strategy laying out what he heard and making suggestions. Pam is pleased with the photographs and will pepper them across his social media feeds and newsletters for the rest of the month. Being back in Westminster brings him back down to earth, confronting him with the limits of Labour's power while the Conservatives still hold the majority.

The government wins vote after vote, pushing through their various tax cuts and stimulus packages, but the Labour Party want to show they mean business too, so the whips make sure they are all there, temperatures checked, crowding into the 'no' lobby to register their objections, at least.

Owen spots Georgina through the crowd. She is surrounded. A steady stream of congratulations for her performance standing in for the Shadow Chancellor. Everyone wants a moment. She breaks free and comes over to him.

'I've just heard the *Chronicle* story isn't happening! I am so relieved for you.'

'Thanks,' he says. He should be pleased, but the word sticks in his throat.

Georgina heads off to talk to someone else, but her aura of success lingers round him briefly like perfume. A few people turn round to see who has been so favoured. Faces register his presence, some surprise, some cool assessing glances. A couple of backbenchers drift over to ask him his opinion on something. They don't care what he thinks about anything, but they want to stand close to him, to see if they can smell ambition on his skin.

His phone buzzes. An update from Liam. Finally. The woman who collapsed is called Clara Jane Michelson. Clara Jane worked at a bookies shop in the high street until the virus hit. Furloughed, then laid off. Never been on benefits before. Liam adds that he knows the type: new to the system, they fill in the forms wrong, don't know the tricks, knock on the wrong doors. She came into the Citizens Advice office once and spoke to one of Liam's colleagues about credit card debt. Didn't come back, didn't respond to the follow-up calls. He's pretty sure he can get her an emergency loan and will sort out the paperwork so the credit card company won't snaffle half of it straight out of her account. Hospital said she probably hadn't eaten for two or three days.

Update from Pam. The local press have published a grainy picture of him online, caught bending over Clara Jane among the chalked rainbows, Derek in the background. LOCAL MP IN MERCY DASH, the headline says. Mercy grab, more like.

Pam wanted to make a thing of it when the paper called for comment, but Owen resisted. She reluctantly issued a statement, which they've printed.

Owen McKenna MP spoke briefly to a constituent in distress outside his constituency surgery on Saturday afternoon. We are grateful for the prompt actions of local police and ambulance workers and wish the lady in question a full and speedy recovery.

Pam insisted on adding a couple of lines about his post-Budget visits to local businesses, but they've cut that.

He looks up from his phone and wonders how he will cope, sitting in the Commons and looking across the government benches tomorrow. How many of them have caught a starving woman in their arms recently?

But that's not why he is still feeling like crap. Just because the story has gone away doesn't mean he won't have to talk to Lefiami about what happened at Glastonbury; her investigation is ongoing. And Jay's father, Sabal, shouldn't read what Owen has to say in a report. There's something Owen can do about that, at least.

He digs out Lefiami's business card from his wallet and dials her number.

Chapter 31

Tuesday 15 March 2022

Sabal Dewan lives in a solid Victorian terrace on the edge of Hampstead Heath.

He opens the door and says something Owen doesn't catch. Then he leads Owen through the hall and into the sitting room. The bay window is thick with branches in their spring green bright in the early morning light. High ceilings lined with bookshelves, studded with art and above the fireplace a porcelain Ganesh, the elephant God, with a saucer for offerings in front of him. Above him is a double portrait of Jay and his older sister taken in their mid-twenties. It's a cheesy, 'portrait studio session for Mum's birthday' sort of thing. It breaks Owen's heart to look at it.

Chloe Lefiami is waiting for them and she stands as Owen comes in.

'Thank you for arranging this,' Owen says, 'And for letting me come to see you, Sabal.'

'I am glad you asked to come, Owen,' Sabal replies as Owen chooses a seat that puts him opposite Jay's photograph and the steady regard of Ganesh. Sabal has the trace of an accent still, a slight cadence to the words. 'You look exactly the same, I think, as when my late wife and I visited with you and Jay, and Philip and Georgina in happy times.'

'I was sorry to learn your wife is no longer with us,' Owen replies. 'I know Jay loved her very much.'

Sabal accepts this with a nod.

'I've told Mr Dewan what I know, Mr McKenna,' Chloe says. 'Jay made mistakes and attracted the hostility of some important people, including Kieron Hyde. In a misguided attempt to shield him from that hostility, you helped blacklist him as a candidate for the upcoming election. Is that fair?'

'Yes,' Owen replies. So there we are. One of his biggest regrets summarised in what, twenty words? He turns towards Sabal.

'I'm here to apologise, Sabal. I let Jay down. If I had been wiser, more observant, just a better friend, I would have seen the state he was in and I might have been able to help. I should have tried a lot harder than I did, and I've been avoiding admitting that for a long time.'

Sabal bends forward and covers his face with his hands. Owen waits.

'Thank you,' he says at last. His voice sounds suddenly raw and rusty. 'You were not the only person to fail Jay. We did too. I had no idea he had ever taken drugs. He did not even tell us he had been dismissed from his employment.'

Owen chooses his words carefully. 'He was only an occasional user of drugs, Sabal, though I wish he had never taken any at all. And I do believe, though he was going through a bad time, he would have come out the other side of it in the end.'

Sabal nods.

'I'm also here to tell you about Glastonbury,' Owen goes on, 'what I saw, and how I remember it. If that is what you want.'

Sabal lifts his head, looks at him.

'Yes. I want to know, Owen.'

Chapter 32

Friday 26 June to Saturday 27 June 2009

Georgina will have her own tent. The boys — Phil, Jay and Owen – will share. It will be tight, but none of them are expecting to spend much time sleeping.

Phil seems to be the most excited of them all. For the first time since Owen has known him, he doesn't want to talk about politics.

Dragging their gear behind him on a bouncing trolley from the car park to the site, Owen realises Phil hasn't wanted to talk much in depth about policy stuff for a few weeks now. It's weird.

Owen looks over his shoulder. Jay is walking next to Georgina, and it looks like they are arguing about something. She says something to him then puts her phone to her ear. As always. Now she's certain of the Coventry East seat and has handed in her notice at the Union, it is permanently clamped to her ear.

Jay has gone from hostile and defensive to morose as his phone calls go unanswered, his applications for available seats ignored. And now, since he was 'let go' by the Treasury team due to 'internal restructuring', he's drinking too much, staying out late in the Westminster hangouts claiming he was fired because of the whisper campaign against him. Phil keeps trying to jolly him up at the house, suggesting other jobs. Jay is not receptive. Owen finds it hard to look at him; every time he does he feels sick with guilt and confusion. He tells himself things will change. Jay will get a new job and be in a better position for a seat next time for having been out in the world a bit. If only he would stop making everything worse.

Phil is trying to read the festival guide as he walks and keeps shouting band names over his shoulder at Jay, seeing if he can get a spark of interest out of him. Nothing. Owen is betting on time. Jay just needs time.

Phil finds them a site – they are among the later arrivals and it's way at the edge of the field, then getting the tents up takes a while. It would have taken even longer if not for help from a bloke in the neighbouring tent, an ex-squaddie who watched them for five minutes then put them out of their misery and took command over the squabbling.

Owen gives him a beer from their stash, and the guy's stories from Helmand manage to draw Jay out of his shell for twenty minutes. Turns out Jay has a second cousin who was out serving at the same time. Owen hates war stories. Not that they aren't interesting or important, but he can't deal with being reminded about the war in Afghanistan. Not when he can see the battles he's going to have to fight himself coming up.

The squaddie shakes their hands, making an elaborate show

of kissing Georgina's fingertips, then heads off. Owen's hungry and Jay volunteers that he fancies a death burger. Georgina and Phil want to find the cider bus.

And for a while it looks like it's going to be OK. During a rain shower on Friday night they hear Michael Jackson has died and Jay sounds like his old self for a bit, rating each album, each track. Owen thinks he might have taken something, but if it makes him happy for a while Owen isn't going to argue. Then on Saturday morning Jay and Georgina have a massive fight about her relationship with Kieron Hyde that ends up with her storming off in tears saying she wishes to God he'd go home. Owen and Phil stay with Jay.

'Jay! Leave her alone. It's not up to you who she falls for.'

Around them the constant cabaret of Glastonbury rolls on: a guy on an old upright piano he has strapped on a rolling platform so he can play and pedal at the same time; stilt walkers and Morris men mix with witches and Disney princesses.

'She hasn't fallen for him!' Jay spits out. 'I think it's just politics. And that's disgusting.'

'Steady on,' Phil says. 'This is Georgie you're talking about!'

Jay lifts his hands. 'I know! And no, no I won't stop talking about it. Not till you listen to me! The way that Kieron Hyde treats women. I've heard some stories, I tell you. Since people realised he has it in for me, they've talked to me. I don't know why the papers aren't on it.'

'Jay, you've got to stop saying stuff like this, it doesn't help,' Phil tries.

'I have names, guys! Chapter and verse. Debra Brooks is just the latest in a long line, that's what I'm hearing.'

It's too much for Owen. 'For fuck's sake, Jay! Leave it, for

God's sake. If you make an arse of yourself going to the newspapers with vague rumours about the next general secretary of the biggest union in the country, you'll *never* get into parliament.'

'People should know what a shit he is.'

Owen feels the frustration and guilt rising in his gorge.

'Jay, stop it!'

'You never listen, Owen! You never bloody listen!'

And he walks off into the crowd. Owen lets him go.

Georgina is all sunshine a couple of hours later. They all try Jay's phone through the afternoon without success. Georgina doesn't seem worried, but Owen feels gradually worse. Bloody Jay. His ticket cost him over a hundred quid and the weekend feels sullied.

Phil comes back from a cider run and reports spotting Jay heading towards Shangri-La after Dizzee Rascal's set.

'I saw him from the queue. He was with some people,' Phil adds. 'Looked like he was having a good time.'

'We've got to go and talk to him,' Owen says. They are sitting on the grass as the darkness thickens around them and the site is lit by washes of colour from the sound stages and the neon signs of the stalls and side gigs.

'Oh, let him dance it out of his system,' Georgina replies. 'Shangri-La is too trippy for me anyway.'

'Na, Georgie,' Phil says. 'Owen's right. Let's go and make friends again.'

'Maybe he's just gone home,' she says hopefully. 'We'll probably just find a note in the tent.'

'He didn't look like he was thinking of leaving when I saw him,' Phil replies and Georgina shrugs.

'I guess we'll find out,' Owen says. They finish their drinks, Georgina takes forever over her cider. Then he gets up, puts out her hand and hauls her to her feet.

'That guy!' Phil says, pointing to a boy in shorts and neon rainbow braces. 'Jay was with him.'

They are deep in Shangri-La. A blade-runner, disco-dystopia vibe. Above them on the main stage, pyrotechnic torches bubble with flame in time to the beat. Dancers, their faces slashed with fluorescent bands of colour, strike pose after pose, like animated hieroglyphs. Owen leads the way, peering over the top of the crowd.

'Watch it, petal!' The man checking him is wearing a horse-head mask.

'Sorry, mate.'

The Horse makes the peace sign. Owen bears right, and, catching a glimpse of the neon braces again, reaches through the crowd stumbling on the uneven ground, makes the connection.

Neon Braces turns and offers them a wide and unfocused smile. Some of his teeth are painted silver.

'Do you know where Jay went?' Owen says, shouting against the music. Neon Braces leans closer and points at his ear.

'Jay! Asian guy? He was wearing a Ramones T-shirt. He's our friend, we've lost him.'

Neon Braces lifts up his arms. 'Yeah! Jay! He was here, like a second ago.'

'Where is he now?'

A girl with Minnie Mouse ears and fluorescent lipstick slips her arms around Neon Braces' waist, slow dancing with

233

him while he shifts his hips to the trance beat. It seems to work for them.

'He said he was going back to his tent,' she shouts. 'Looked like he'd had a bad pill or something,' she adds.

'Oh yeah! That dude. No, his pills were good. It was his inhaler!' Neon Braces pauses to whoop as the beat changes. The dancers spell out the secrets of the universe. Some of the crowds, arms raised and swaying, look like they are getting the message. 'Yeah, he said his inhaler was out – going back to get his spare, he said.'

'Who had the bad pill then?' Lipstick asks.

'You did, baby. Yesterday.' She brightens, then looks at Owen again.

'Tell him to come back to Shangri-La. He's hot.'

'Slut,' Neon Braces says affectionately and kisses her.

Owen promises to pass it on and works his way sideways through the press of dancers. The horse heads are everywhere. The UV lights pick out dark tattoos, and his vision trembles with glow sticks and strobe lights.

'Here!'

Phil is waiting for him where the crowd thins. The noise dies quickly in the open air but Owen's ears are ringing. He tells Phil what Minnie Mouse and Neon Braces told him.

'His reliever inhaler was out?' Phil says. 'If he uses it more than three times a week, he's supposed to go to the doctor. Shit. Have you heard him moving around at night, back home?'

'Couple of times,' Owen says. 'But I've been at Christine's most evenings.'

'That's bad. And he's on pills? Idiot.'

Georgina rocks up out of the dark. Someone has put a garland of flowers in her hair.

'I almost got picked up by a unicorn!' she says and doubles over with laughter. 'I told him I wasn't a virgin, but he said that was cool. I was so wrong – this place is amazing. Come on! Let's dance!'

'I'm going to check on Jay,' Owen says. 'Georgina, those two said his inhaler was out. He went back to the tent.'

Georgina slumps forward. 'But that's miles away!'

'Why didn't he just go to one of the first-aid stations?' Phil asks.

'Maybe he did.' Georgina is playing it up. 'He'll be back in a minute probably. Do we have to go, Daddy? I'm having fun.'

Owen shakes his head. 'You can stay and flirt with the unicorns if you like, but I'm going to go and check. Does he even have a torch?'

'He's probably got a glow stick and he has an excellent sense of direction,' Georgina pouts.

'Come on, Georgie,' Phil says and put his arm round her shoulders. 'They said he's on pills too. He could be in trouble.'

She steps back. 'If he's got pills, I'm not going anywhere near him!'

Phil shakes his head. 'I want to check on Jay. Stay if you want.'

'Fine!' she says. The outsized dungarees help with the whole 'thwarted little girl' act. Owen is suddenly glad Christine isn't here. Glastonbury is Not Her Thing. Still, he can feel her rolling her eyes at Georgina from three-hundred-odd miles away.

As they pick their way back to the path and head out towards the campsite, Phil is worrying – Owen feels it coming off him in waves – and Georgina is still sulking and muttering about pills.

They reach the edge of the field. Even in the darkness they have a decent idea of where they are going by now. Solar torches show the path, and some of the tents are lit from within, making them look like Chinese lanterns scattered through the dark.

'Do we shout for him?' Phil says as they head towards the fringes where they pitched their tent.

Owen shakes his head. 'No need to piss everyone off. Let's just check. If he's not there, we can start looking again.'

He hits redial on the phone. No answer.

'He's probably back at Shangri-La by now,' Georgina says. 'Probably run off with my unicorn.'

'There.' Their tent is still a hundred yards away in a more isolated part of the field, but they can see a faint glow within. Owen leads the way. He finds himself breaking into a jog.

'Jay? Are you all right?'

He pulls back the unzipped flap. The tent looks like a bomb has hit it. Jay's rucksack is on its side, spilling T-shirts and socks. One of the camping torches gives off a feeble light and casts shadowy monsters. Toiletries are scattered over the three sleeping bags. And Jay, dressed and curled knees to chest, is lying there, facing the watery blue nylon wall. He is not moving.

Chapter 33

'Jay?'

No reaction.

'Is he asleep?' Phil asks, leaning in. 'Fuck, why's he been throwing his shit around?' Owen crouches down and shakes Jay's shoulder.

'Come on, Jay.'

Jay tips onto his back. His lips are ashy. His inhaler drops from his loose fingers.

'Jay? Jesus!'

Owen puts his fingers to Jay's neck. Is that how you take a pulse?

Phil groans and stumbles into a half-crouch next to him.

Jesus. Jesus. Owen can't feel anything under his fingers. Jay's chest doesn't seem to be moving. 'Phil, call an ambulance!'

Phil falls backwards and Owen tries to think through his panic-blocked brain.

'Nine-nine-nine, Phil! Now! He's not breathing.'

Georgina crowds into the tent, sees Jay and screams; it's an ugly, terrified sound but somehow it gets Owen's brain working again.

Owen did a first-aid course last year. A boring day in a windowless office when he had a million other things to be getting on with. DR something. ABC. Danger, Response. Airways, Breathing, Circulation. Shit. Shit. Shit.

He listens at Jay's chest, checks his mouth, settles and bends over him, pinches his nose and breathes into his lungs, watching to see his chest rise. It does. Does it? It's dark and Georgina is crying. He can hear Phil on the phone, giving directions. He puts one hand on top of the other, pushes down on Jay's chest to the rhythm of 'Stayin' Alive', eight times. Then another breath. He hates that song.

There is movement around him. Georgina crowding him, saying Jay's name again and again.

Is he pushing too hard, or not hard enough? Is he in the right place? Phil asks him something, he replies and hears Phil repeating what he says to the voice on the phone.

'Is this his spare inhaler? Or this one?' Phil says. 'Should I give it to him? Fuck, they are both empty. OK. OK.' He turns to Owen. 'She says just keep going. Medics are two minutes away.'

But that's an eternity. 'Fine. Georgina, what are you doing? Get out of the way!'

He breathes into Jay's mouth again, trying to believe this is working. Georgina and Phil are moving around behind him, making the tent shake. Phil is still talking to the 999 operator, telling her where to send the medics.

'Just get out! Both of you! Look for them coming!'

Did he feel a rib crack? Why can't he see? He realises he's

crying too; he tries to wipe his eyes and nose without losing the rhythm, knocks his glasses sideways. It's so hot, he's sweating, yet Jay's skin feels cold under his mouth.

He can hear Phil outside now, catches in the corner of his vision the light of his phone being waved back and forth.

'Here! Over here!'

For God's sake, please come. Wake up, Jay. Wake up.

Owen can still hear the music in the distance. Breathe. Then push again. He feels an arm on his shoulder. He tries to shake it off before he realises it's a paramedic, a pale youngish bloke with too much product in his hair. The nylon of his jacket makes a swishing noise as he moves.

'Let me take over, my friend,' he says gently. 'You've done good.'

Owen falls away from him, then feels Phil take his arm and yank him out of the tent. The other paramedic goes in. Owen's sweating and the sudden chill of the night air makes him shiver. He can hear the paramedics talking to each other, saying things into their radios.

One of the medics reappears, tells them to stay where they are and heads off at a jog for the ambulance. It's twenty yards away where the tents are more thickly pitched. The lights flicker over the nylon and canvas, highlighting the sleep-soaked faces peering out and the unsteady couples and groups meandering up the pathways, staring at it with dazed curiosity.

Owen looks at his hands; they glimmer red and blue. The crowd are still cheering in Shangri-La. The night smells of damp grass. He shivers again and Phil gives him his coat.

'Where's Georgina?'

'Here!' She steps out of the shadows. Her voice is strangled and she has lost her flower crown somewhere. 'Is he dead? Is Jay dead, Owen? Oh, God!'

Another set of flashing lights. The paramedic is coming back with a stretcher and in her wake is a pair of policemen.

'Georgina?' Phil says quietly.

'It's fine,' she snaps.

Owen is not sure what is happening. The stretcher is at the entrance to the tent, then Jay is on it. There is an oxygen mask over his face. That has to be good, doesn't it? Now Owen is watching them push it over the uneven ground and, stupidly, he thinks it looks uncomfortable, being rattled around like that.

'Is he OK?' Phil shouts. 'Can we come with you?'

'He's in a bad way,' the one with the hair gel shouts back. 'No room for you in the ambulance.'

'But that means he's alive, doesn't he?' Georgina is pulling on Owen's arm. 'I mean, "a bad way" means he's alive?'

He wants to tell her he did a day course in first aid, not a medical degree. He wants to tell her Jay's skin felt wrong, strange, that he couldn't see if his breath was getting into Jay's lungs. He just shakes his head.

'I don't know.'

The ambulance is on the move now, the siren burping occasionally to force the returning campers off the track. Owen watches it turn onto the tarmac road and pick up speed. Its sirens wail continuously over the horizon.

'We should call his family,' he says. His voice feels strange and he wipes his mouth, convulsively, angrily.

They both look at Georgie. She shakes her head. 'I can't! I can't. There's no point waking them. We should wait until we know something.'

Phil takes out his phone. 'I've got their number.'

'Evening.' One of the policemen is with them now. His fluorescents are too bright. Owen finds himself studying the details of his uniform, the handcuffs on his belt. He takes their names and Jay's. Owen is aware of Phil telling him what happened.

Owen interrupts to remind Phil of what Minnie said about his inhaler being empty. He hears the policeman ask about drugs.

'He might have taken an E,' Owen says. 'I don't know for sure.' Georgina is clinging to him, half-burying her head in his jacket. Phil's jacket.

'I have to call his dad,' Phil says.

'If you give me their details, sir,' the policeman replies, 'we can take care of that.'

'But don't you think I should . . . ' Phil protests.

The policeman shakes his head. 'We can give them the news from the hospital, son. Now, were you all sharing the one tent?'

Owen lifts his head. 'Jay, Phil and I were in the big one. Georgina's got the small one next door.'

'OK if we just take a look, sir? Just to get the lie of the land.'

Owen doesn't care.

The policeman sticks his head in, then re-emerges.

'Bit of a mess in there. Was it like that before?'

'No,' Phil says. 'It wasn't.'

'Looking for his inhaler?' the policeman says.

'He always keeps a spare in his washbag,' Owen says. 'Carries another. And he had it. It was in his hand, Phil said it was empty . . .'

And he can't speak anymore. The policeman nods to his colleague. He's asking about their jobs now and when Phil tells them, he raises his eyebrows.

'Advisor at the Treasury? Young lad like that?'

'Junior advisor,' Georgina mutters. 'And he got fired a month ago.'

'Owen,' Phil says. 'We've got to tell London. You've got to. This will be a story.'

'Oh, shit,' Georgina squeals.

'Officer,' Owen says. 'Phil's right. It's important I let the government know what's happening, and we want to keep this out of the press until we know how Jay is and his parents have been informed.'

'Naturally, sir.' Has the quality of that 'sir' changed? Owen can't tell if it's more careful, or has a sneer on it. He wonders if this is the sort of man who is going to get in his car and sell the story to the *Sun* for a grand. Take the kiddies somewhere nice.

'I think we should take you all down to the station to take your statements, though, do this properly. A sudden collapse like this, at an event like this. Especially if the young man might have taken a pill. I'm sure the government would agree.'

'Yes, of course. Sure. Whatever you need.'

He nods and speaks into his radio, ordering up another car. 'Sarge?'

Owen twists round. The other policeman is holding something up and Owen catches sight of it in the twist of the blue lights. A small pencil case, silvered leather but with LVs written all over it. He recognises it, it's Jay's: he's seen it on the dining-room table a dozen times.

The policeman unzips it and fishes inside, extracts a clear baggy and holds it up delicately with his blue-gloved fingertips. Owen glimpses half a dozen pills in the blue wash of light.

'Just on the inside. Plain view.'

'That's not my tent,' Georgina says in a sort of yelp. 'My tent's on the other side.'

The two policemen are looking at each other.

'Oi!' The squaddie who helped them put up their tents. He's powering towards them.

'What the fuck are you doing?'

The policeman is putting the pencil case and baggy into an evidence envelope. The one who has been questioning them steps between the squaddie and his colleague. 'We found what appear to be drugs in your tent, sir?' He points at the pencil case. 'Is this yours?'

'No, it isn't!' he rages. 'Now piss off out of my stuff!'

'If you would just calm down, sir.'

Of course it's not his, Owen thinks. And now this bloke is going to get himself in trouble. He takes the magic half-step forward. 'Officer . . .'

Georgina's grip suddenly tightens on his arm. 'Owen, don't!'

He looks down at her. 'But that case is Jay's. I've seen it at home.'

He tries to pull his arm free of Georgina, but she holds on.

'Millions of people have cases like that. It must be that guy's. God, you've already said Jay might have had a pill. Now you're going to get him done for intent to supply or something!'

'This is an illegal search,' the squaddie is shouting. 'I serve my country and I come home to this. You bastards! Get away from me!'

'If you would just calm down, sir.'

One of the younger coppers comes up behind the squaddie and puts a hand on his shoulder. Bad mistake. The reaction is instantaneous.

The squaddie swings at the guy who touches him and his fist catches him on the side of his head and sends him stumbling. For a second the squaddie looks confused, like he doesn't understand where he is, or how he got here. The policeman who had been searching the tent tries to get the squaddie round the chest, pinning his arms to his side. Again, as soon as he is touched, the squaddie reacts. He elbows the man behind him hard in the gut.

All hell has broken loose. A crowd has gathered to see the show.

'Christ,' Phil says.

'It's not his fault,' Owen says. 'They need to back off.'

A girl in flip-flops is running towards them from the main trail. 'Babe, stop!'

Another wail of a siren and another two more fluorescent jackets are crossing the field at a sprint after her. The squaddie pauses, turns towards the woman's voice and the first officer grabs something from his belt and sprays him. He grunts, swears, falls to his knees.

The lads in the crowd jeer. Shout, 'Bad luck, mate!' Someone grabs hold of the squaddie's arm; he's trying to get the pepper spray out of his eyes and lashes out.

'Baby! Stop!'

One of the police has pulled a taser from his belt.

'Jesus!' Owen shakes Georgina off his arm. 'Give him some space!'

The girl in flip-flops rushes past the man with the taser and drops onto her hands and knees in front of the squaddie.

'Baby, stop fighting!'

And he does. Owen can see his shoulders go limp.

He is dragged to his feet again.

'That case. Do you recognise it, Phil?' Owen says.

'I told you, Owen, there are millions of cases like that,' Georgina interrupts. 'Have you seen Jay with it here? No, of course you haven't. Because his is still in London.'

'Phil?'

Phil hesitates. 'Leave it. He just assaulted a police officer. He's got bigger problems now.'

They have led the squaddie off to one of the squad cars: he's shaking his head, trying to get the crap out of his eyes. They guide him into the back seat. Slam the door.

The older policeman is coming back towards them. Georgina grabs hold of Owen's arm again.

'I swear, Owen, it's not Jay's! Don't complicate things! The press will have a field day with this without you dragging in some random guy's drugs into it. What will they say about Jay? What about me? What about my seat? What are you doing?'

'Are you OK?' Phil asks the policeman as he gets closer. 'Is there any news on our friend?'

The policeman avoids his eye. 'I'm to take you to the station. Let's go.'

'Our stuff!' Georgina says. 'I can't remember where my wallet is. Did Jay have his wallet on him? What if someone steals it?'

'We'll leave someone here to keep an eye on everything, don't worry, miss.'

'But our friend ...' Owen tries again. 'Any word on our friend?'

The policeman wets his lips. 'Let's just get you to the station.'

Phil covers his face with his hands, and Georgina releases

a sort of moan. Owen's mind suddenly feels empty, as if the bowl of his skull has been hollowed out. He takes out his phone and dials.

'Owen McKenna here, I need to speak to the Duty Press Officer immediately. Yes, it's urgent. Who is on call?'

Chapter 34

Owen finishes. Stares at his hands.

'And when you got to the police station, did you try and do anything to help the soldier?' Chloe asks.

Owen shakes his head. 'I was on the phone to the press office in the waiting area most of the time. It seemed to take hours for them to take our statements and then we heard the news about Jay. We gave our witness statements for the assault, that's all. I didn't tell them what I suspected about the pill case. It was easier to tell myself I might have been mistaken. I asked if they thought he might be suffering from PTSD. It was something about the way he reacted. They said they'd consider it.'

'Poor man,' Sabal says. Owen feels it, the grace it must take to think that, say that, think of anything else, having heard the details of what happened to Jay.

'He was going through a difficult time,' Owen says. 'He'd seen two of his friends killed by an IED, was injured himself at the same time and left the army. He was finding it hard to adjust. Anger issues. He served six months and got treatment for his PTSD after his release. Re-trained. He's a great deal better now. Married his girlfriend and they have two kids.'

'You know a lot about him, Mr McKenna,' Lefiami says.

'Yes. I tracked him down after the 2010 election. He works for Citizens Advice, in my constituency. We're friends. His name is Liam Holdsworth.'

'And he has forgiven you?' Sabal asks.

Owen shrugs. 'I told him I was sorry once, for not stepping up. He told me it wasn't my fault he lost it and hit the policeman.'

'A generous man,' Sabal replies and Owen agrees. 'Owen, it is up to God to forgive, not me. Perhaps if you had been a better friend, my son would be alive. But he was not without fault. And we cannot ask forgiveness for our own sins and expect perfection from everyone else. Again, I thank you for coming to speak to me.'

It feels like a conclusion, so Owen gets to his feet. 'I'm sorry it took me so long to do so. I think I assumed Georgina would have told you everything. But that's just an excuse. I failed Jay, and I didn't want to face you.'

Sabal stands too and bows. 'Georgina and I concentrate on happier times. Would you like to come and see him, Owen? Would you like to come and visit Jay? We can go now. The home is not far away. I wanted him close.'

'Yes. Thank you. I'll come.'

Chapter 35

Sunday 28 June 2009

They give Owen tea in an actual mug, and the policewoman assigned to take his statement has a Somerset burr to her voice. As soon as he sits down, Owen realises how exhausted he is. Beyond exhausted. Shattered. The fabric of him feels cracked, like a broken mirror still held together by its frame, in spite of the terminal damage. The grind of the last months, the fear of the last few hours. His hand is shaking and the tea tastes of cardboard.

'Thanks for coming in, Owen,' the policewoman says, tucking a stray lock of blonde hair behind her ear. 'Normally we wouldn't be so formal in the circumstances, but the young man is quite important, and of course there are always some who want to paint the festival as some sort of crime and drugs farrago, so we have to watch ourselves a little. Isn't it a shame about Michael Jackson? I just love his music.'

Owen likes the way she says 'farrago'. He even finds comfort in the tea. Maybe they'll let him stay here. He doesn't want to go outside, look at the others.

'Do you have any news on Jay?' he asks.

She puts down her pen and folds her hands over each other on the table.

'He's very poorly, I'm afraid. The doctors are working away, but we don't know how long he was like that before you found him.'

Owen tells himself to breathe. They should have gone looking for him earlier. They should have taken better care of him. They should have been taking better care of him weeks ago. He has an impulse to weep. No. If he starts, he won't be able to stop.

The policewoman asks him questions and he answers them. They go through the assault first 'while it is fresh'. He tells her about how the squaddie reacted and his conclusions. She nods understandingly. Then they go through the rest of the weekend. When he arrived at the campsite, what sets they saw, the times when they were with Jay and when they weren't.

'Now, I know in your line of work this is a bit delicate, Owen, but were any drugs taken? Beyond a few ciders, I mean.'

'Not by me,' he says. 'It's not just being in politics; I don't trust them.'

'You should watch the cider too,' she says dryly. 'Especially the organic stuff, in my opinion. Now, what about Jay? Did he ever dabble?'

'It was an asthma attack, wasn't it?' Owen puts down the tea. The colder it gets, the more the cardboard flavour comes through. 'If it was an asthma attack why are you asking about drugs?'

'Sort of thing the coroner likes to know,' she says, then sees his expression, 'and of course we are all praying like ballyhoo it doesn't come to that, dear. But we still have to ask. In case it does.' She pauses. 'So did he? Dabble?'

Owen stares at the mug. 'I don't know. A bit, perhaps. He's been drinking more. Lost his job recently.'

She looks at her notes. 'But you've never actually seen him take anything? He never offered you a pill?'

He shakes his head. 'He knows what I think about all that.'

'You're a sensible lad,' she replies.

Suddenly he wishes she was more aggressive, more challenging. This gentleness is going to kill him.

'How come you weren't together this afternoon and evening? Sounds like you'd been sticking pretty close before then.'

'We had a fight. Not a bad one, not really. But he was talking about work. Very intense, sort of hectoring.' The words start tumbling out of him. 'He's been like that all year. He marched off and we let him go.'

She purses her mouth. Her lipstick is the coral pink Owen's mum used to wear in the nineties.

'So your friend – who's been depressed for a while, not looking after himself and has had quite bad asthma since he was a child – and you had a bit of a set-to, then he marched off into the festival, upset, and stopped answering his phone. And you and your friends only thought to go looking for him,' she glances at her pad, 'ten hours later?'

'He's been really hard to live with.'

Owen feels as if he's folding in on himself, he's going to disappear into the dark.

She keeps writing. 'My sister has depression, Owen. And you

know sometimes I could just slap her. Makes people awfully self-centred, doesn't it? You trying to live your life and there's them refusing to put one foot in front of the other. That's when they need us most, of course, when they need us to listen however much we'd like them to quiet down. Not much virtue in being kind to people if they make it easy for you, is it?'

Owen covers his eyes. He is not going to cry. This is not fair.

'It's not my job to look after Jay.'

'Not sure whose job it was, then. We all have to try and look after each other, don't we?'

She sighs and writes something else down. 'Well, I'll get this typed up on the computer and you can sign it at the desk. You wait out front with your friends.'

Owen stays in the chair, can't face moving. She goes past him and opens the door to the corridor, then puts a hand on his shoulder.

'Try and do better next time. And I hope your friend recovers.'

Chapter 36

Tuesday 15 March 2022

They take Lefiami's car. The permanent care home is near Trent Park not far from Sabal's house, but on the other side of the North Circular. Its gardens give it an almost country feel. Oak trees and ash fringe the lawns. London plane trees lining the drive. Tarmac paths, easy for wheelchairs, cross the lawns and edge the flower borders. A section to the right of the house seems to have been converted into a wild flower meadow. Owen watches a care worker in a burgundy uniform pause so the patient in the wheelchair she's pushing can admire them.

Lefiami pulls up and Sabal lets himself out. They haven't spoken since they got into the car, and Owen, once he had sent a message to Pam to say he'd been called away, has been staring out of the window. Whenever he glanced towards the front seat, he saw Sabal, watching him in the rear-view mirror.

Owen has been to permanent care facilities in his constituency, the publicly funded ones. They don't look like this. It's another stab in the gut. Creeping privatisation of the NHS, all done under the banner of efficiency, but a child could see through that. Scare those who can afford it into the blossoming private insurance market, and sell off the NHS slice by slice. He thinks about the data. He's ignored three calls from Christine since he withdrew the question. One thing at a time.

Owen clambers out of the back seat, brushing crumbs off the edge of his coat. Lefiami sees him.

'Sorry about the mess,' she says.

She looks less like a nemesis today, more like a busy professional mother.

'Don't be daft. How many kids do you have?' The back seat is scattered with toys and battered books, thin volumes with neon covers.

'Two. Michael Junior is twelve, Lizzie is six.'

They follow Sabal up the steps.

'Nice place,' Lefiami says. Owen walks alongside Lefiami into the marble-tiled lobby.

Jay hadn't recovered. They'd got his heart beating in the ambulance, but it had stopped and it took thirty minutes to get it started again in A&E. By the time Georgina, Phil and Owen arrived at the hospital, he had been put in a medically induced coma. He was like that for a fortnight and when he was weaned off the machines it became clear the brain damage he had suffered was severe.

Sabal signs in at the desk, and Owen and Lefiami do the same. At least, they give their names, the nurse with a pleasant smile does the actual writing, then takes their temperatures and offers them masks. They all have their own. Lefiami's has a Jamaican flag on it.

Jay's room is on the ground floor. It's huge, with floor-to-ceiling windows opening out onto the lawns. The bed is one of those complicated ones, designed to lift and tilt the body through a range of positions. The sheets are a rich burgundy. It holds Jay in a semi-seated position facing the open French windows. The air smells of the lavender growing along the edge of the path outside. Sabal and Lefiami go in, but Owen stops in the doorway. He can see a shape under the sheets, a flash of the side of Jay's face, then his view is blocked as Sabal walks up to the bed.

'Jay, I have brought an old friend to see you,' Sabal says, then beckons to Owen. Owen steps forward and the door eases shut behind him. Sabal puts a chair by the bed, then moves aside.

Owen walks forward as if in a dream, and looks down onto the bed.

Jay, but not Jay. His hair is black as ever, but the muscles of his face seem slack. His eyes are open, but vacant. Owen feels them flicker over him.

'Jay, it's Owen.' Now he's read the notes from the counsellor, he almost expects Jay to react, to show some sign of rage or fear. Nothing, just that skittering gaze.

'Sorry it's taken me so long to come and see you, mate.' He sits down and, before he realises what he is doing, he takes Jay's hand. Jay's fingers lie loosely across his own. 'It's good to see you.'

This is better than wondering about him, wondering if anyone would even tell him if Jay had died, wondering where he was or fighting to suppress any thought of him at all. Jay is wearing pale blue pyjamas with a thin white stripe. They are ironed and laundered.

He doesn't know how much Jay can understand. Owen hopes to God he isn't capable of thinking of what might have been, hopes that the brain damage that has stolen his ability to move, to speak, has also taken his capacity to suffer. Then why is Owen here? If the visit is just some sort of performance for Sabal and Lefiami then Owen is contemptible, the sort of hypocrite he tells himself he despises. But he can't know what Jay does or does not hear. So he needs to say it.

'I'm sorry it's been so long. And I'm sorry I was a rubbish friend. I should have done things differently, should have listened.'

He doesn't know what else to say. Jay's fingers twitch, a pressure perhaps, Owen looks at his face and perhaps, just perhaps Jay looks briefly back across all those years and all the space between them.

'I was stupid. But Jay, I never stopped believing, not until well after that night, not until we realised how sick you were . . . I never stopped believing you were going to be party leader someday. I had this idea: I'd be like the Gordon Brown to your Tony Blair.' His mind could be playing tricks on him, of course, but Jay's fingers do move a little. Owen blinks. 'I mean, I hoped we'd get on better than that, of course. But even when things were bad in the house, I still believed that was where we were going to end up.'

He can't do this anymore. It's too much.

'Sorry, mate. I'll see you later.'

He gets up and walks out through the open French windows and across the lawns. No idea where he is going or why. He just needs to move. He makes it to the tree line, plucks off his mask and, his back to the home, leans against the trunk of an oak.

Time passes, seconds or minutes.

'Owen?'

He turns. Lefiami is a few paces away from him on the grass. 'How are you doing?'

'Great. Perfect. I mean, in comparison. Christ! I mean, I knew, but ... Sometimes I wonder if ... '

She holds up her hand.

'If you are going to say you think you did the wrong thing saving his life, then don't.'

He points back towards the home. 'Really? You think he'd want to live like that? I mean, what sort of life is it?'

She shakes her head. 'I'm a Christian, so I have to believe that every life has value and deserves respect. As a politician I think it's important you do too.'

He turns away from her again makes his hand into a fist and presses it into the bark of the tree.

'You don't have to be Christian to value life, Ms Lefiami. But it's important if you are a politician not to accept suffering with a shrug and a line about God's plans either.'

'I don't do that.'

He presses hard enough to feel the pain in his knuckles. 'Was this God's plan? For me to be a crap enough friend not to see he was in danger, but remember enough of my first-aid training so Jay could spend the next thirteen years in this state?'

She takes off her mask and puts it back into her pocket. 'I don't pretend to know His plan. Maybe this is supposed to teach you something.'

'Teach me what? That it's a really good idea to have health insurance if you can afford it these days? That even when people who are depressed or *in extremis*' – he feels the weight of the

woman in his arms again outside the surgery – 'are difficult or irra-
tional, they should be listened to? Even when you don't want to?
Fine. Got it. Why make Jay suffer so long for that? God could have
sent me a greetings card with that stamped on it in swirly writing.'

'I don't know. But I doubt God's telling you to buy health
insurance.'

She has every reason to be angry with him, but her voice is
wry. Owen breathes out, turns to face her.

'Sorry, Ms Lefiami. I've no right to take this out on you.'

'I can take it, Owen. Sabal is staying for a while. He'll get a
cab home and I've signed us out. Want a lift somewhere?'

'Yes. Thank you.'

They start walking across the lawn towards the drive. She
takes out her keys, starts swinging them in her hand.

'I worked on a number of cases involving brain injury. I think
one of the mercies is the injured brain often doesn't know it is
impaired.'

Owen does not want to be comforted. 'Are you telling me he
isn't suffering?'

'I'm telling you it's impossible to know either way. Sabal said
he thought Jay knew you. And was glad to see you.'

He doesn't know what to say, but the words hurt. If Jay can
be glad to see him, it means he's aware and surely awareness
is suffering in his condition. She beeps off the alarm and they
climb into the car.

'Thank you for inviting me to be here when you saw Sabal. I
don't know how much this investigation is worrying you, but I
think it's only fair to mention that though my report will say it
was foolish of you to help keep Jay off the candidate lists at the
time, my conclusion is that it was not malicious.'

258

So now he is doing what Greg tells him to and Lefiami has decided he is not a monster, Owen is in the clear. And he's faced up to the demons of guilt which have been chasing him for years. Great. So why does he still feel like shit?

'You don't think it was me who leaked the minutes of that meeting?'

She puts the car in gear and they drive slowly down under the avenue of plane trees.

'No. From what your colleagues say about you, that doesn't seem to be your style. But then I don't think Jay leaked them either.'

They reach the main road and she indicates, leaning forward over the steering wheel to check the road beyond the high brick walls.

Owen thinks of Phil. Maybe he was right to accuse him in the Chapter House. He remembers the party, what Phil said about Jay's emails.

Lefiami swings out into the road and changes gear, checks her mirror.

'Did you ever have a chance to go through Jay's emails?'

'I went through his work correspondence, electronic or otherwise. Or rather, one of my assistants did. They showed a young man under pressure who, for all his brilliance, had a tendency to blame others,' she replies.

'He had a gmail account too. We all did, and used them for non-work stuff.' He messages her Jay's old address. 'I'm glad you've judged me not guilty, Ms Lefiami.'

'I'll look at the other emails. Thank you. And we're all guilty, Mr McKenna. I've just said you didn't bully Jay. But *someone else* definitely did.'

'Really?'

She nods and slows to let someone creep out of one of the side streets.

'I talked to the people who were with him on the Treasury team. They were constantly hearing stories about Jay, about his drinking, drug taking. His sex life.'

'What? That's bullshit! Yeah, towards the end he drank, and yes, a couple of times I saw him I thought maybe he'd taken pills. But he was a monk, sex wise. Who was spreading the stories?'

'You know what it's like chasing down rumours, rumours over ten years old? It's impossible. Everyone just says it was "something they heard".'

'What about the Union, though?'

'I was asked to look at you, Owen. Not the Union. My remit is limited. I have no authority to compel anyone to talk to me. You and Georgina have to meet me because the Labour Party told you to. Mr Bickford saw me out of courtesy, and he told me about the campaign to keep Jay off the candidates list. And freely confirmed you all agreed it was the best course of action. That was his choice. I had a brief statement from Kieron Hyde, but the Union politely refused to let me talk to any of their people. The investigation is a Labour Party matter. They just pointed me to the rules about workplace relationships, including bullying and what they call "romantic involvements", which they drew up in 2016.'

'I didn't realise they'd published new guidelines.'

'More than guidelines. A list of sackable offences.'

'2016 was the year Kieron Hyde lost the election for general secretary,' Owen says slowly. 'I thought he'd be the boss well before then, but the previous gen sec stayed on after we lost the 2010 election.'

The traffic is getting heavier. Another strange fracture of COVID. People drive when they can to avoid the closed-in atmosphere of the Tube – those who can afford to, anyway. So Kieron's ambitions for leadership were finally crushed, and then the Union brought in new rules. He thinks about Jay talking about the Union on the last day in Glastonbury. *You never listen.* He was listening now.

'What are you doing today, Ms Lefiami?'

'Working, of course. Why?'

He tries to put it together in his head, make the jumbled memory of guilt in his mind form into words, a plan. 'The last time Jay and I spoke he was trying to talk to me and Phil about Kieron Hyde and the Union. We didn't want to hear it ...'

'And?'

'We should have heard him out. But it was a pain, *he* was a pain. Georgina was getting ushered into the seat and we were still dealing with the fallout from the expenses scandal. All of Westminster was in fight or flight mode. We didn't even want to consider there might be something rotten at the PSGWU.' He looks out of the passenger window at the rows of shops, some shuttered. 'Even while Kieron was blacklisting our friend, getting me to help blacklist him. Then Kieron and Georgina got together and after that ...'

'After that, what?'

'Kieron seemed to drop all his bullying tactics. It made it easy to forget what Jay had been telling us.'

He twists round in his seat so he can see her properly. She's frowning, staring at the traffic ahead.

'Look, Chloe. I think there is someone I could call. Someone we could talk to about the Union at that time.'

'Give me a moment, Owen.' Lefiami indicates left, and they turn off the ring-road into a half-empty parking lot. A motel, garage and chain café. She parks.

'OK, Owen. Make your calls. I'll get us a coffee.'

Chapter 37

It takes four calls in the end. One to confirm the name, Debra
Brooks, then three more to find someone who knows a current
number to go with it.

'Look, I'll try. But I don't know if she'll want to speak to you.
Shall I give her the number you are calling from?'

'Yes. Will you do that right away, please?'

The woman hangs up with an exasperated 'Fine'.

Lefiami emerges carrying disposable coffee cups and packages of sandwiches. Owen leaves the car and joins her on one of
the metal picnic tables up against the blank wall of the motel,
puts his phone on the table and they eat in silence staring at it.
When it finally buzzes, they both start. He answers.

'This is Debra Brooks. Why do you want to talk to me,
Mr McKenna?'

Her voice is high and she's speaking fast.

'Ms Brooks, you're on Speaker. I'm with a barrister called
Chloe Lefiami. She's been looking into the bullying of a young

man who worked for the Labour Party in 2008. Jay Dewan?'
Silence. 'The thing is, Jay mentioned your name to me just
before he became ill. He was making accusations about the
Union and he mentioned you. I didn't want to listen at the time,
but I think I should have.'

'Ms Lefiami has been investigating *you*, hasn't she, Mr
McKenna?' The voice on the speaker says. 'That's what I've
heard. Just you. Are you just trying to shift the blame for what
happened to Jay?'

Chloe and Owen look at each other.

'This is Chloe speaking. Ms Brooks, I think Owen did some
foolish things, but I don't think he was a bully. I feel like I've
been looking in the wrong direction.' More silence. 'Did you
know Jay?'

'No. Look, I signed an NDA.'

Chloe leans in. 'Debra, we can discuss that when we meet,
but a lot has changed about non-disclosure agreements and
how they are enforced since 2008. You have my word I'll keep
anything we say confidential. It'll be up to you if anything you
say ever gets written down or discussed beyond the people on
this phone call.'

'I've got the kids today. You'll have to come to me.'

Owen feels a sudden burst of triumph, then he realises Chloe
is looking at him. He nods. Pam will be angry with him for
cancelling the whole day, but he has to do this.

'That's fine. Where are you?'

'Between Brockley and New Cross.'

Chloe looks surprised. 'That's where I live too.'

'I know. My girl goes to the same school as your son. I saw
your picture on the news, in Westminster. I almost spoke to you.'

'How about the park, on Telegraph Hill? Owen will text you when we're close.'

'OK.' Debra cuts the connection.

When they arrive, the sky is overcast, the sort of London afternoon which could easily tip into showers or sunshine. On their way across the city, Chloe talked to Owen a little about what they might expect. He is thinking about it as he sits on the bench. He's on the edge, by the bins. Chloe takes her place next to him, then there is the gap for Debra, if she comes. Owen hasn't had a reply to his text saying they've got here.

A couple walk past with a pushchair, and a curious-eyed infant with her mother's curly hair examines the world like it's his first time out. The man walking with them has a china mug of tea in his hand.

'Chloe?'

Chloe looks up and Owen sees the recognition in her face. 'Hi, Debra. Yes, I recognise you from school. This is Owen.'

Debra looks like she is Owen's age, late thirties, on the pivot of middle age. Same age as Christine, as Georgina, but she has none of their gloss and glamour. She has lines around her eyes and streaks of grey emerging from a rough ponytail. Her long cotton coat is smothered with embroidered roses.

'I know you too!' she says, looking at Owen. 'You were at that party, with the girl who got me out of there.'

Owen stands up and bows slightly. 'That was Christine Armstrong. She was my girlfriend at the time.'

She sits down again, and Owen does the same.

'I thought ... I thought when I heard there was going to be an investigation about bullying, it was going to be about me. I've

265

been waiting all week for someone to call, like an idiot. And then Patsy, she still works for headquarters, she told me it was a Labour Party investigation, nothing to do with the Union and just about Jay Dewan. I couldn't believe it! An investigation into him! Just a posh boy who went partying and forgot his inhaler.'

Owen keeps his mouth shut, trying to learn his lesson from the car rather than leap forward to defend the Labour Party, or Jay. Chloe was talking about this woman, about women like her, as they crawled through the city traffic. A woman who was told to get over something, who tried to get over it and found she couldn't, and now looks back at her bruised and damaged life and is caught between a sense of failure and anger. They make bad clients, bad witnesses; they lash out, Chloe said. Juries and tribunals look at them and see cause for their dismissal, their problems, confusing the effect with the cause.

'We heard someone was writing a story about Jay and the party talked to Sabal Dewan, Jay's father. He felt the matter hadn't been examined properly at the time so the Leader's Office asked me to look into it, but I have no power to make the Union talk to me at all. Until Owen told me, I'd never heard your name.'

The woman gave a short laugh. 'Of course you hadn't heard of me. I signed an NDA. They said they'd destroy me if I didn't, if I spoke up. Then I found I was destroyed anyway.' She looks at Owen. 'Your girlfriend was good to me that night. And I called a couple of people who'd said you're OK, and I have to talk to someone. I have to.'

'I'm glad you called me, Debra,' Owen says. The air smells of damp grass, a slight tang from the over-stuffed and fox-ravaged bins.

Chloe takes a breath. 'Debra, without looking at the actual document I can't say for sure, but you may well be breaking the terms of that NDA if you tell me your story.'

Debra covers her face with her hands and twists sideways like someone trying to avoid the heat of an approaching flame. Chloe keeps talking.

'But, Debra, listen to me now. I swear I will treat this conversation as confidential. I won't take any notes, not at the moment, and then, depending on what you tell me, we can discuss your options. Until then, we are just people sitting on a bench, watching the world go by. Isn't that right, Owen?'

'Yes, of course.'

Debra wipes her face with the back of her hand. Owen isn't sure how much is going in. Now they are close he can see the pink capillaries around her cheekbones. Perhaps she drinks. Cause and effect. Shame.

'I thought . . . I thought after everything that's gone on in the last few years it had to come out. After Weinstein and all that, I thought someone else would speak out. I thought that after he lost the election for general secretary too, mind, I thought *now* they'll tell the truth and get the bastard. No such luck. Then I thought it again when I heard about the investigation, but no. And I just can't take it anymore. He's still there. Getting a nice fat salary while I scrape by as a teaching assistant. My husband works at the Royal Free as a hospital porter. We're hardly managing. He's still not right – he had the virus, of course he got it – the flat's damp and the landlord just says he's got no money to fix it and he . . . he's in bloody *Hello!* with Georgina! It's disgusting after what he did.'

Owen feels his heart sink in his chest. Weinstein. Oh hell!

Had he suspected? Maybe. The signs were there, but he had chosen not to see them. He remembers Coogan at the conference – *all those lovely ladies, looking for a favour.* He thinks of Kieron in the kitchen, eating his fish pie, washing it down with a good white wine, and feels a wave of disgust. But where did Jay fit into this picture? He was victim of a whispering campaign, a power play by Kieron so he could get Georgina into the seat. Nothing like Weinstein.

Debra bites her lip, trying to hold back the words. 'I confided in her! In Georgina! I thought she was my friend. I thought that as it was happening to her too – then I get the lawyer's letters and a year later I find out she's his girlfriend! She married him! She'd never have got that seat or hung onto it without him. She's a whore, a fucking whore. And she made me feel like one. As much as he did.'

'Georgina *knew*?' The question bursts out of him.

'She knew everything. She knew about me, and Julie Coats. She acted like she cared, all sympathy, but she was just covering for him and out for herself.'

No way poor Georgina knew. Or if Debra spoke to her, Georgina couldn't have understood what it meant. She would never have married Kieron if she knew about this.

'Debra, I am so sorry this happened to you.' She glances sideways at him and flushes. 'Do you mind if I just speak privately to Chloe for a moment? Then I think I should leave you to talk. Again, I'm so sorry this happened to you.'

He watches her carefully. A flicker of mistrust, but then she nods and hunches her shoulders. He stands up and Chloe follows him a few steps from the bench. You can see the whole city from here.

'Can you help her, Chloe?'

'Yes, of course. I know some excellent solicitors if she wants to pursue this further but I'll have to talk to the Leader's Office and give them the heads-up.'

'What about the NDA?'

A breeze whips between them and she pulls the collar of her coat closer.

'NDAs are complicated – it depends what they are for. If they are to prevent the theft of copyright, they still have plenty of power, but after Weinstein people hardly even bother defending them if they were used to cover criminal assault, and my sense is that is what they were being used for in this case, would you agree?'

'I would.'

Chloe nods and they walk back together to the bench.

Debra eyes them suspiciously and Owen bows. 'Debra, I'm so sorry I didn't listen to Jay when he tried to tell me about you.'

For the first time since the bloody pandemic started, the bow feels right.

'It's OK,' she says and pulls her shapeless coat around her more tightly. 'Nobody wanted to hear it. Do better next time, yeah?'

Just what the policewoman said. 'I swear I'll try.'

Chloe takes a seat back on the bench again and Owen heads down the hill towards New Cross Station. That's what, the third time he's promised to listen, to do better, in the last few days. He doesn't believe it is God teaching him a lesson, but it feels, at least, like the universe is making a point.

He thinks of Elsie Collins, Christine and the story they've been telling him and of the mysterious man who disappeared like smoke as soon as he bought Victor's company. He pauses at the bottom of Erlanger Road and gets out his phone, looks up a photo of Marsden Grotto where Victor's body was found. It is beautiful, bleak. High cliffs and white sand.

Point taken, universe. He leans against a low stone wall of someone's garden as the buses and vans speed along Queen's Road and spends a few minutes on the parliamentary secure app, then scrolls through his calls received, finds the number he needs and dials. Greg picks up straight away.

'Owen, how wonderful to hear from you! How can I help? The editors at the *Chronicle* were apparently very sad to lose the story, but we've looked after Barns. No need to fret, in case that's why you are calling.'

'Hi, Greg. No, I called to say "fuck you". I just resubmitted the question. Do your worst.'

He hangs up. The trees shiver their new spring growth about his head. It sounds like whispers. It sounds like a gathering storm.

Chapter 38

'Where have you been?' Pam says as soon as Owen walks into the outer office back at Portcullis House.

'I've been visiting Jay Dewan with his father and Chloe Lefiami, Pam.'

Her face falls. 'Oh, I'm sorry. I didn't . . .'

'Don't apologise, I shouldn't have gone AWOL without giving you any notice. I'm sorry. Come into the office for a minute.'

She picks up her pad and follows him. When he sits at the coffee table rather than the desk, she looks confused, but picks the armchair opposite him and waits.

'I need to fill you in on a couple of things,' Owen says. 'Then I need to make some calls.'

'What's the headline?'

'That story is coming out, about me bullying Jay, and it's going to be grim.'

She puts her pad on her knee and takes the lid off her pen. 'I can take it. I'll put on your work-fast playlist on Spotify and prepare for trolls. But Christine Armstrong has been ringing. A lot. She's still in London and wants to meet you. She's at the Café Nero downstairs, by the Tube station.'

Christine has to wait a while longer. Owen's first call is to Elsie Collins, and this time he does not look at his watch. It is almost an hour later when he joins Christine. They get takeout from a hassled barista and Owen glances out of the window; Parliament Square has been surrounded by tractors as farmers protest the latest trade terms with the United States, and the air is thick with blasting horns and chants.

Christine is being strangely quiet.

'We can't talk here,' Owen tells her. 'Let's go over the bridge, sit and watch the river. Are you here to give me a hard time about withdrawing the question?'

She shakes her head, and doesn't say anything until they are halfway over Westminster Bridge. The jam caused by the tractors means the cars are almost stationary. At least the tourists on top of the bus have a decent view.

'Owen, I came to apologise.'

'Really? Not your style, is it, Chris?'

'I don't know.' She smiles briefly. 'I've stayed married seven years. You can't do that unless you learn to say sorry and mean it.' They walk down the steps onto the relative calm of the Embankment.

'If you're really going to apologise, I'd better sit down.'

He points to one of the benches, raised up on a plinth so you can sit on it and admire the mother of all parliaments on the other side of the river, and they get settled.

'Go on then. I'm ready.'

She leans forward and puts her elbows on her knees. High boots and jeans again today. 'Yes. Look, when I started this, and then when we had lunch and I took you to see Elsie . . .' She blows out a lungful of air. 'I thought when you mentioned the story it was just some bullshit fishing expedition. I didn't think for a second there was any basis in it, so it didn't worry me.'

'I did call round, tell people not to interview Jay for possible seats, Christine.' Damn, honesty can become a habit. He can feel her looking at him, doesn't look back.

'You never told me that, Owen.'

'I told myself I didn't want to get you involved, but, I don't know.' He looks at the Thames. Occasional pleasure boats pass by, but they are still rare. He realises the river probably hasn't been this empty of traffic in five hundred years. The waters still flow on at their own pace, though. 'I was probably afraid you'd tell me we were doing the wrong thing, that we should challenge Kieron, and I didn't want to hear it.'

He tells her about Jay's file and Greg's threat. An office worker passes them on an electric scooter. He's in his sixties perhaps, wearing a mask in the same dark navy pinstripe as his suit.

'Yeah, you should have told me, but I'm still going to apologise,' Christine says.

'That journalist, Edward Barns, tracked me and Rob down while we were visiting suppliers on Thursday afternoon. I could tell by the questions just how bad the story could be. He asked Rob if he had rescued me from an abusive relationship with you.'

Owen met Rob a few times while Christine was an MP. A Geordie with a loud laugh and a passion for good food.

'And what did Rob say?'

'He told Barns if he wanted to see what a violent man looked like, he should ask him about his wife again. He slunk off. Anyway, I got it then. I called you to say you should withdraw the question, then to say I was glad you had.' She blinks rapidly. 'I should have thought . . . Trouble is, I knew them, Owen. The Collins family. Victor and Elsie's parents live near the shop, and they came in most weeks. Elsie too, when she was visiting. Rob delivered to them all through lockdown, except when we got sick. I even met Victor once or twice and he seemed sweet. Bit otherworldly, bit intense maybe. But not mad. And his company was doing well before he tried to do us all a favour and he ended up dead. I was too close to it to see what you might be bringing down on your head. I was asking too much.'

Owen thinks of the young man in the photo above Elsie's workstation. 'No, you weren't. You were asking me to do my job. I'm still an MP and on the Select Committee which handles data and the internet. That counts for something. Even if the party withdraw the whip and I get deselected by my local party – it'll take time. Before then, I have the weight of that beautiful monstrosity behind me.'

He points at the gothic pile opposite them.

'What do you mean, if you lose the whip? I don't get it,' Christine says. 'You withdrew the question. The story will be shut down and you'll be fine.'

Owen shrugs. 'I tried that and it felt shit. What does "fine" mean? I wouldn't be "fine" walking around parliament knowing that Greg had that hanging over me. I wouldn't be "fine" watching his friends slice up the NHS and hand over the people of this country to big data. Fuck "fine" if that's what it looks like. Let them publish. Jay's dad knows what happened, knows that I liked Jay and never meant him harm. I trust Lefiami to be fair. I resubmitted the question.'

She pushes the hair back from her face. 'Owen!'

'And I spoke to Elsie again.'

Christine brightens. 'And? What do you think?'

He thinks of her anger, vibrating through the air as they spoke, her sharpness. But then she also has passion and conviction, and her love for her brother, her belief in him, is unquenchable.

'She's not a good witness, and the story is as unprovable as it ever was. But you're right, the whole thing stinks. The key thing is, I'm going to try and counter the claims Victor's tech turned out to be faulty, go and visit Victor's professor from Cambridge.'

'Elsie said he wouldn't speak to her.'

He points emphatically at parliament again, which makes her laugh. She has a good laugh. She puts her hand on his arm. 'But Owen, have you thought this through? Even if the official report is broadly supportive, if the story is really bad ...'

'Too late now, I asked the question, and you know what, Christine? It feels good.'

Chapter 39

The online version comes out just after six in the evening. First Owen's WhatsApp notifications blow up, then the phone starts ringing. Pam comes into the office with her iPad and sits on one of the armchairs while Owen stays at his desk and they read the article at their different screens. She manages not to say anything out loud until he pushes himself away from the desk with a grunt of disgust, but he hears her intakes of breath. Their phones buzz and twitch.

It was what they were expecting. HORROR HOUSE IN LAMBETH, shouts the headline. MP OWEN MCKENNA ACCUSED OF DESTROYING THE CAREER OF RISING STAR, JAY DEWAN, LEADING TO HIS TRAGIC DECLINE. Phrases swim up into sharp focus as he reads. Scan the article quickly enough and it sounds like Owen tried to murder Jay. *Jay Dewan is now cared for in an £8,000 a month permanent care home on the outskirts of London.* Most of the quotes are from anonymous sources. *'His background is very macho, very hard man. I'm not surprised* he had issues with a brilliant Oxford-educated gay man like Jay.' Another source has volunteered that he had to hauled off Phil Bickford during his own engagement party. *'I'm not surprised his fiancée ran for the hills.'*

Innuendo. Cruelty. Someone has snatched a photograph of Jay, glimpsed through the window at the home. Next to it is one of Jay looking handsome but waif-like in a suit and tie on the first day of the conference, below them an ancient shot of Owen at a local football match, his arms raised and his mouth open in a shout. Thug. Victim. No quotes from Sabal, nothing from Christine. Nothing from Georgina, at least nothing attributed to her, but she emerges as a survivor. *'No wonder she can cope in the Commons after living in that house.'*

The article includes a brief statement from the Leader's Office. *'We take all allegations of bullying extremely seriously and the accusations levelled at Owen McKenna are being thoroughly investigated.'*

Then, the killer last line. Jay's own words from his counsellor's notes, the ones that have haunted Owen since he read them. *'I thought he was my friend, but he's destroying me, just for being who I am.'*

It is what Owen was expecting, but he wants to cry. Hit something. The injustice of it all. He clicks onto the notifications, knowing he shouldn't, knowing it's a stupid, stupid idea, but he does it anyway. *'I always knew he was a thug. Look at the state of him. That poor boy! Destroyed by a racist. Typical Labour. Just want to drag everyone down.'* Screeds of obscenity.

'I've started a statement,' Pam says quietly.

It breaks through. He closes the window onto the screaming hellscape and looks up at her. Her face creases with concern and he takes a breath. Pulls himself together. There is no mention of Anna anywhere, at least. He is glad of that.

'Go on.'

'The gross distortions of this article are an insult to me and to the memory of my friend, Jay Dewan. That said, I will always attempt to acknowledge my mistakes and await the Labour Party's own investigation into the tragic events of 2009.'

He rubs the side of his nose. 'Good, but put this in too.' He waits until she has turned the transcription mode of her phone on then speaks. 'In a foolish attempt to shield Jay, I told a number of chairs of Constituency Labour Parties that he should not be invited to interview for possible seats. It was a stupid thing to do and the consequences for Jay and his family have been terrible. He was a young man of great promise and if he had had more mature and sympathetic friends I am sure he would be serving in this house with distinction even now.'

He thinks of Jay dancing in the kitchen, then of how it might feel to be passing him in the corridors on the way to vote, serving alongside him.

She clicks off the microphone. 'Is that too much, Pam?'

A second's hesitation. 'No, it's good, boss. I'll write it up.'

Another alert pings on his screen.

'Hang on, there is something from Sabal on the *Guardian* live blog.'

She comes round the desk and looks at it over his shoulder. A photo of Sabal outside his house in Hampstead and below it, indented and in italics, his statement. '*Owen McKenna visited me yesterday, and in the presence of Chloe Lefiami, QC, who has been leading the investigation into my son's case for the Labour Party, he gave a full and frank account of his friendship with my son. He then*

accompanied me to Broadfields Manor where my son is in perma-
nent care. I am grateful to Owen for offering such a full account of
the events, and though my family and I live with Jay's tragedy every
day, we feel an increased sense of acceptance and peace. Jay's sister
and I will remember Owen in our prayers with gratitude.'

Owen's throat closes up and Pam rests her hand briefly on his shoulder.

'You called him,' she says, 'told him what was coming.'

'I had to warn him. Still incredibly generous of him to come straight out with a statement this evening.'

She's looking at her phone again.

'Yes! Statement in support from Phil Bickford!'

'Really?' He thinks of Phil's face as he left the Chapter House. 'Qualified support?'

Pam shakes her head as she reads. 'Nope. Short and punchy. *"The account in the Chronicle is totally at odds with my recol-lections of the events of 2008 and 2009. Whatever my political differences with Owen McKenna, I never saw him display any signs of homophobia or racism and I believed, and still believe, that he always tried to protect Jay as well as his party during a difficult time."* Then some stuff about his faith in the Labour Party's own investigation. Blimey, his lot won't like that. It'll make it much harder for the Tories to put the boot in. Wow. He could have just stayed quiet! What's he up to?'

Owen stands up, thrusts his hands in his pockets and turns away. That's why you should have a window in your office, gives you somewhere to stare when your brain is churning and you can't look the people you are with in the eye. The icy blast of the air-conditioner tightens his skin.

'It's possible he might just think it's the right thing to do.'

'This is still Westminster, isn't it?' Pam says. 'I didn't skip into a parallel universe when my phone overheated?'

'OK. I don't know what he's up to.' He turns back. 'It helps, though, doesn't it?' He hears the appeal for reassurance in his voice.

'Bloody right it helps! And all of this within an hour of the story breaking. It means tomorrow's papers will have to include these quotes too.'

'Get that statement out sharpish.'

'On it.'

As soon as the statement is out, Owen sends Pam home in a cab, instructing her firmly to keep her phone off until the next morning, and summons another to get him back to his flat. He sees the pack on the pavement outside under the street lights. The broadcasters won't have sent crews to his house. These are the stringers and freelancers hoping for a shot to sell, a quote. A few seconds of video to flog to the news sites for a hundred quid. Or a grand if he loses his temper.

'Good luck, mate,' the cabbie says, pulling up on the road alongside a couple of parked cars.

Owen breathes deeply, steps out. They start screaming his name.

'What's wrong, tough guy? Give us a smile!'

'Do you hate gays, Owen?'

They are all men. There's a cluster of them between him and the door.

'Did you beat up your girlfriend?' Just keep moving, he tells himself, head down slow and steady. He has the key in his hand.

'What's up? Sad because your little gay friend's a cabbage?'

He looks up, his face suffused with loathing, towards the voice and hears the fluttering of the shutters.

The key feels heavy in his hand; he tenses his muscles. This is the closest he's come to throwing a punch in more than a decade. He can't. It'll ruin him and make the man who gets the shot a small fortune.

'Watch out, lads, I think he's going to blow. Was it because I said "cabbage"? You sorry for the cabbage?'

'Owen?'

The door is opened from the inside and the man from the neighbouring flat to his is beckoning him in. Owen staggers through the crowd, the adrenaline running through his veins turning toxic. He should have slept in his fucking office. Christ, if his neighbour hadn't been there he wouldn't have got the key in the lock. His neighbour slams the front door on the pack. They go through the lobby to the bottom of the stairs.

'Thanks . . . Sorry, I don't even know your name.'

'I'm Matt. Shall I call the police?' he asks. 'Get rid of them?'

Owen feels the shaking exhaustion that comes after an adrenaline spike and they start to climb the stairs, slowly.

'No point. That lot – they'll keep coming back until the story dies. Sorry, if they've been bothering you.'

They start up the second flight. 'Fuck, don't worry about me,' Matt says. 'I've never seen the like. They were ringing on all the doorbells. Someone let one of them in an hour ago and he was banging on your door. I told him to clear off.'

Owen pauses as they get to their landing. 'Thanks.'

'It's OK. Swear, I never had any idea what they could be like. I mean, you see it on the news, but up close like this? It's freaky.' He pulls himself together. 'Anyway, you must be shattered. If there's anything I can do ...'

'You already saved my life coming down and opening the door. Well, my career at any rate. I nearly lost it out there.'

Matt still looks shaken. 'Sure there's nothing else I can do?'

'I am.'

'Don't let the bastards grind you down, I guess.' He gives Owen a half-wave and lets himself back into his flat.

Owen opens his own door and shuts the curtains before he turns on the light. The fresh bottle of Talisker that Greg left on the doormat is now sitting by the sink. Owen grabs it and pours himself a large measure. Imagines what that picture they took will look like on the front pages tomorrow. He lifts the whisky to his lips, but he can't bring himself to drink it. He pours the damn thing down the drain. Watching it swirl away is comforting. He empties the rest of the bottle after it. What will the leadership do? Yes, he has Sabal's statement and Phil's, but the story had Jay's actual words accusing him. And the policy is zero tolerance.

He calls his family, texts Sabal to thank him. Talks to Marcie, his constituency agent, and to the chair of his local party, then to Liam, who is supremely confident the news will be chip wrappings tomorrow. 'And if not, my brother is on the lookout for truck drivers. Get your HGV licence and you'll be sorted.'

Anna sends him a text, just sending her love, so he calls her too, and by the time they hang up she's offered to buy him dinner as soon as he has a free evening. He wonders, hopes, if now she's seen the worst that can happen, the press doesn't horrify her as much as it did. Dangerous stuff, hope.

The story is out there in all its foul and slippery glory, but so is Sabal's statement, so is Phil's and so is his. He turns on the stereo. Not much chance of sleep, but he won't torment himself reading the overnight reactions to the story. He wonders if there is a stereo in Jay's room at the care home.

Thinking of Jay steadies him. Whatever he is going through, he is where he always wanted to be – in the middle of things – while Jay is there. A home like that has to have a way to play music for its patients. He starts thinking of the music Jay might have missed and starts working on a series of playlists, one per year. It absorbs him the way only music and politics can, as his mind picks quietly at the past and present.

He tries to tell himself, sitting there, that he doesn't care. Even if he finds he's not an MP anymore, after this, so be it. He needs to able to look in a mirror. But he *does* want to be an MP, be part of a new Labour government. He wants that very much. This is his blood and bones, politics. The sport and struggle of it, the battle to get something done, to leave some significant mark. If people are turning against him, buying into the idea of him as a thug, then the rest of his life will focus on playing and replaying this moment. He won't even have the shock of the fall to wipe it out.

It's out of his hands. He opens his email and taps out an email to Phil's old address.

Thanks, you Tory bastard. This time he doesn't delete the footer that includes his mobile number. The reply comes back almost immediately.

You're welcome, Labour scum. Now get some rest.

Chapter 40

'Are you insane?'

'Good morning, Ian. Hope you slept well,' says Phil.

'I didn't,' Ian replies. 'I've been working on this rant all night, so now I'm asking you how, when you are vulnerable, when the Secretary of State has his knives out for you and all the Brexit fanatics in the Cabinet are looking for reasons to mistrust you, you send out that statement in support of Owen McKenna! He is everything we hate most about the left! We were shaping up for another nice bit of Labour bloodletting and you handed them a bandage. So I think you must be insane. Are you insane?'

Phil glances at his watch. He guesses his breakfast meeting is waiting in the Central Lobby and Ian is keeping his visitor waiting just to yell at him. He'll have to give him an answer just to be allowed to get on with his day.

He thinks of seeing Liam Holdsworth outside Owen's offices. Owen must have tracked him down, got him a job. He is beginning to remember that under his persona of a tough, take-no-prisoners political operator, Owen has a strong sense of right and wrong.

'Politically speaking, probably yes, I am insane. I told the truth. Now if you've got that out of your system, could you show up whoever is waiting to see me?'

'If you're going to start telling the truth on a regular basis, I better start looking for a new job.'

And with that he stalks out of the room. Ian is right, Philip was in a dangerous position before and he's just made it worse.

Chapter 41

Phil can't stop his leg shaking. In the end he stands up and walks in tight circles around the rows of bolted-down plastic chairs in the waiting room.

'Oh, sit down!' Georgina says. 'This is worse than the jiggling.'

He does, next to her. 'Georgina, that case they found in the squaddie's tent? That *was* Jay's, wasn't it? I saw it while Owen was giving him mouth-to-mouth.' She ignores him. 'Georgie? What did you do? That poor guy!'

'Shut up, Phil! He hit a policeman.'

'Why in God's name did you throw it into his tent?'

Finally, she looks at him. All the flower-girl sweetness has disappeared. She seems older, sharper, the skin drawn tight across her cheekbones. 'I'm going to be selected for the Coventry East seat. I will not let Jay screw that up.' Phil hasn't seen this look in her eyes before. He does not like it. Then

286

her expression softens. 'And I did it for Jay! You think he'll get another job, a chance to restart his political career, with a possession charge?'

'What about the soldier?'

'I didn't know that stupid policeman was going to look in the wrong tent.'

'This is wrong, Georgie. Tell the truth or I will.'

'The truth? I've never seen that case before. No idea how it got in that man's tent.'

'But you just said . . . '

'You're going mad. I can't even remember what happened, really, I'm so upset. But I know I've never seen that case.'

She is holding his gaze while she says it, and Phil feels something strange under his skin, a creeping rippling sense of fear.

The double doors into the depths of the station open with a slight rubbery sucking noise. Owen comes into the waiting area, a policewoman following him.

'Miss Maxwell? If we could have a word.'

'Never seen it,' Georgina hisses through her teeth as she bends down to pick up her bag. 'Think about it, Phil. Your career, Owen's, mine, Jay's. All on the shit heap because of something you are just making up in your own head.' She stands up and smiles at the policewoman. 'Hi! Yes, of course, just coming.' Then she turns towards Phil and hisses, 'He hit a policeman. Keep your mouth shut.'

Owen calls Christine while Georgina is giving her statement. She answers, her voice thick with sleep, and snaps into wakefulness and shocked disbelief. They can't talk long and maybe that's a good thing. After the policewoman, Owen thinks

Christine's sympathy might break him entirely. The office is trying to call him. They tell him Jay is in intensive care, that Jay's parents have been notified and are on their way to the hospital. They read him a short statement saying Jay Dewan, until recently an advisor to the Treasury, was taken ill at Glastonbury with what appears to be a severe recurrence of asthma. They all wish him a full and speedy recovery and send their sympathies to the family.

'Sounds fine.'

'No need to mention your names in connection with this now. We'll see what happens.' The Senior Press Officer sounds like a Captain in a World War Two film, Owen thinks. All that assurance. 'Now, anything else I should know?'

Georgina is ushered back into the waiting area and the policewoman asks to speak to Phil. He stands up as Owen replies.

'An ex-soldier in the tent next to ours got into a fight with a policeman while Jay was being taken away,' he says.

Owen looks between Georgina and Phil, trying to read their expressions, the phone still pushed to his ear. They are still. Georgina gives the tiniest shake of her head.

'Were any of you involved in any way?' The Press Officer's voice is sharpened.

Owen feels crushed by it all. He sees the squaddie on his knees, his arms held behind his back.

'No, we talked to him earlier in the day, but we weren't involved.'

'Thank God for that,' the officer says and hangs up.

Chapter 42

Owen is back at Portcullis House by eight the following morning. A couple of shouted questions on the street which he ignores, but he's too early for the main press pack. Pam is there before him.

'How are we doing?' he asks her.

'Well, I wouldn't look at Twitter if I were you. Or the comments section below the articles. The *Daily Mail* loves it. The *Guardian* and BBC News are sounding more cautious, though.' As good as he could expect. 'You doing any interviews? Everybody is asking for you.'

'Nope. Just tell them we're awaiting the conclusions of the Labour Party's own investigation, and don't have any further statement at this time.' He pauses. 'If Charlotte calls, though, tell her I'm grateful for Sabal's statement.' She makes a note. 'Anything for us from the Leader's Office yet?'

'Nothing more since the statement in the article.'

'What about Georgina?'

'I haven't seen any comment from her.'

Pam leaves and Owen stares into space, then picks up his phone. Georgina had wanted him to damp down the story, kill it, and he had let it blow up in their faces. He hadn't even warned her.

Debra must be wrong. Georgina couldn't have known what Kieron had done, but now Debra is talking to a solicitor. The sort of shit Owen has just ploughed through is likely heading for Georgina now. He calls her and she picks up straight away.

'Owen! What do you want? There's nothing I can do about our bullying policy, you know.'

'It's nothing like that. Look, Georgie. I've been thinking about Jay, what he was saying at Glastonbury, about Kieron. Do you remember the name Debra Brooks?'

Her voice becomes less sharp. 'Vaguely. Oh yes, she and Kieron had some disagreement about her contract, I think. Odd woman. Why?'

'I thought you should know, I introduced her to Chloe Lefiami.'

Georgina doesn't say anything at all for a few seconds. 'I see.'

'Chloe doesn't have any authority over the Union, of course. But she's taking Debra to talk to a solicitor about getting round the NDA she signed. Some of things she said, Georgina ... '

'"Chloe" is it now? Look, I have a meeting. Thanks for the heads-up. Take care.'

She hangs up and Owen stares at the handset. Proud feminist, champion of women. She couldn't have known. But if she didn't know what Kieron did, why in God's name hadn't she asked what Debra had said?

*

He tries to sort out the wreckage of his diary and go through his email. His second cup of coffee is cold when his phone twitches to life with a number he doesn't recognise. He shouldn't answer it, not today, but he takes the chance.

'Yup?'

'It's me.'

'Phil?'

'Got it in one. How are you doing?' He sounds like he means it.

'I'm hanging in there.'

'Good. Look, I've got something to say to you, and in an ideal world I'd say it to your face, but I don't think I can swing a private meeting today. That said, I've just left a committee meeting in Portcullis House, I'm grabbing a coffee at the Despatch Box and I can feel your lowering presence in the building.'

'I'll come down. How's the sell-off of the NHS going today?' Owen stands up from behind his desk and walks out of his office. 'And thanks again for the statement.'

'Just peachy, and no problem. Hey, funny story.'

Owen heads down into the atrium of Portcullis House. 'Yeah, what's that?'

He catches sight of Phil sitting by himself with a coffee in front of him, phone to his ear. Owen crosses the hall and sits on one of the long planters filled with actual trees where Phil can see him too.

'Apparently an honourable member drove all the way to Warwick to finish a fight with you, then saw a ghost and turned tail and ran.'

Owen laughs. 'So it *was* you. I thought I was going barmy.'

'Yup.' Phil crosses his legs. 'I've noticed there hasn't been any mention of Liam anywhere. I saw him outside your surgery.'

'Did you now? Yeah, a small mercy. He wouldn't want to get involved.'

'You got him a job?'

'Yes. And we're friends. He's a good person. He tells me when I'm being an arse.'

'Most people have to get married for that.'

Owen smiles in spite of himself.

Charlotte Cook crosses the atrium between them, talking to one of the Shadow Chancellor's aides. Phil and Owen look away from each other. Owen rubs his fingers over the glossy leaves of the ficus nearest to him. 'Is that what you wanted to tell me? About your road trip?'

'No. I wanted to apologise.' He pauses. 'You were right. I did give Cameron's team the list of defensive marginals.'

Owen leaps to his feet then turns to stare at him across the half-empty tables. 'You fucking *bastard*.'

Phil meets his eye across the space between them. One of the cleaners pushes a cart between them, picking up disposable coffee cups with his gloved hands. Spraying detergent on the tables and turning the plastic marker in the centre of each one to 'sterilised'.

Phil waits until the man has gone. Owen can hear him breathing. 'Yeah. And I've regretted it ever since. Owen, I don't think it won us that election, but that doesn't matter. I did it, and it was a shit thing to do.' Owen feels the rage radiate off himself. Phil should be able to see it, like heat waves in the air. 'It was an impulse. And I don't suppose you'll believe me, but I was never spying in the house. I'd even tried to stop talking strategy with you once I decided I was going to leave the party. But I saw it, and the temptation was too much.' Owen finally breaks his gaze and sits down under the trees again. The air-conditioning makes the leaves above him shift a little and the air smells of burned coffee and UHT milk. 'But I didn't leak those draft minutes to the *Chronicle*.'

'OK,' Owen says and looks up. Phil is sitting forward at the table, looking in Owen's direction, but with a carefully blank and unfocused expression.

'Anyway, that's all I wanted to say . . . '

'Hang on, Phil.' Owen rubs the back of his neck. 'Did you take the list before or after I punched you?'

He laughs. 'After. Immediately after. I went to get a book from your room when I was packing for my hasty exit, and it was on your bed.'

Cause and effect. Chains of circumstance. Humiliation. Anger. Rage. Unintended consequences. The dance of events.

'I noticed the story broke just after you asked the question about medical data again,' Phil goes on. 'I assume those things are connected?' Owen watches him look at his watch and stare up at the glass and steel curve of the roof. He's checking he can't be overheard.

'You have been paying attention. Yes, they are.'

'And did you know I married a brilliant woman?'

Owen stands up again, thrusts his hand into his pocket, turns away a bit.

'I heard you married a rich one.'

'The first thing led to the second. Anyway, she thinks there might be something going on with the NHS data.'

'Too bloody right there is. Doesn't she manage a hedge

fund?' Owen asks. 'Surely she's the sort of person making a fortune out of this shit.'

'She works on foreign currency derivatives mostly. Owen, you said you had the notes from Jay's counsellor?'

Oh, what does it matter now? The story is out. 'I was gifted his entire medical file. They threatened to use it in the story, and give it to Lefiami if I didn't withdraw the data question. I did some hard thinking over the weekend, then saw Jay and I just couldn't be doing with it. So I asked the question again, and bang.'

'Fuck.' Phil's voice changes and Owen glances over his shoulder. He is finishing his coffee, getting to his feet. 'Can I send someone to pick it up? The file at your flat? This afternoon sometime. Text me the address. Does your block have a concierge?'

'No, but I've got a neighbour. I'll get my researcher to pop out and leave it with him now.'

'Can you trust her? Your researcher?'

'Yes. Why do you want it?'

'I was in the house. Like you, I was too busy with my own life to help. I want to look it in the eye.'

'OK. Look, Phil, I think something else is coming down the track. Allegations about Kieron, and women at the Union. Worst sort of shit, by the sound of it.'

'Jesus, poor Georgina!'

Owen hesitates. 'I know, and Phil . . .'

'Yeah?' He's paused in his walk towards the entrance to the tunnel back to the Palace proper.

'Thanks for calling.'

'I should have done it ten years ago,' he replies, then cuts the connection and disappears down the escalators.

Owen goes back up to his office and on impulse writes down what he knows about the Collins case and Greg's blackmail threat. While he's writing he gets an email from Victor's professor at Cambridge with a reluctant agreement to meet the next day at his London home, so he includes that. Then he puts the note in an envelope and sends Pam to his flat to add it to the folder and leave it all with Owen's neighbour. The habit of trusting Phil seems to have come back with full force, yet he's keeping all this from Georgina. *I confided in her!* 'What did you do, Georgie?' he says to the empty air. He gets no answer.

Chapter 43

Sara is waiting for Phil in the Central Lobby when the day finally ends. She kisses him and bows to Ian.

'You staying in town tonight?' Phil asks her.

'If I'm welcome.'

'Always.' He hands Ian his red ministerial box, the traditional briefcase ministers carry, stuffed with reports from the civil service.

'Can you give this to my driver and tell him to take it to the hotel?' Phil says. 'My wife and I will walk.'

Ian grunts his agreement and departs.

'He seems particularly vinegary today,' Sara says, fitting her arm through Phil's.

'He's still angry about the statement I sent out in support of Owen,' Phil says. 'Some of my colleagues are accusing me of playing the centrist card.'

'But you are a centrist.'

'Worst thing you can say about anyone in politics, as you

well know. It's good to see you. What did you do with the children?'

'Well, I'm proud of you. They are on at-home days for the rest of the week so your mum volunteered to have them. Till Sunday morning.'

Phil looks unsure.

'Phil, they love it there. Your dad lets them watch gameshows and takes them to proper football matches. I don't want to breed snobs.'

It's true, his kids seem to have a better time at his parents' house than he ever did. 'OK.'

'You have work to do, I take it?'

'I can spare a couple of hours. And I got Jay's medical file from Owen. I think I should read that too.'

A sharp nod. 'Let's just order room service at the hotel, then.'

They pass the member for Newcastle North West in St Saviour's Hall. He puts a hand on Phil's arm to stop him.

'You are a lucky bastard, Bickford.' He's been at the bar; his face is mottled pink and his breath stinks of bad red wine. For a moment Phil thinks he is referring to Sara, but no, he's not staring at her chest the way he normally does.

'I am certainly blessed, Paul.' He looks pointedly at the man's hand on his sleeve. He doesn't move it.

'I heard the *Daily Mail* was going to do a piece about you and your old Labour cronies after that pathetic statement you put out last night, but now Georgina Hyde's going to blow the bloody doors off something and every drop of newsprint is going to be about her.'

'Blow the doors off what?'

He sneers. 'Haven't you been checking Twitter? Some

women's issue in the PSGWU. Sounds like she's leaving dear old Kieron. Didn't you have a thing for her? Might be your chance. You better watch yourself, Mrs Bickford.'

Sara doesn't seem particularly worried. 'I'm trembling in my tiny shoes. Now please stop sweating on my husband's suit. It's only just back from the dry cleaners.'

He takes a step back, and Phil leads his wife away.

'Now, what on earth is this about?' he says once they are out of earshot.

'I suppose we better watch the news with everyone else,' Sara says.

The policeman at the turnstile wishes them a pleasant evening.

Chapter 44

Emily Fremantle has worked for Georgina for three years. It is, she explains to the friends who never see her, whose weddings and baby showers she misses, to her proud but confused family, her dream job. Georgina is her mentor and friend, and she is Georgina's confidante, her sounding board. They are partners.

Georgina's policy team – Gabriel, who tears his hair out when she changes his speeches to make them understandable or, God forbid, newsworthy, and Samuel who huffs over his homemade marmalade when Georgina drops the nuance and uses her interviews on the *Today* programme to go for the government's throat – do not understand just how important Georgina is. She is not just some empty vessel to carry their policy ideas about. She is a leading member of the opposition, a rising star and obvious Secretary of State in the next Labour government – she is also an inspiration.

Emily's friends ask her if she resents working eighty-hour weeks for pay that means she can't afford more than the rental on a studio flat on the fringes of Mile End, and she laughs at them. Of course she does nothing but work. When work is this exciting, this important, why would you do anything else?

And she is needed. Georgina relies on her, tells her so half a dozen times a week. And today Emily is needed more than ever.

Just after lunch, or rather the hour people who have time to eat lunch, eat lunch, Georgina messages Emily and her executive assistant Constance to cancel her appointments and hangs the DO NOT DISTURB sign on the door. It's not a real sign, but Georgina will take no calls, no drop-in visits, and if the building is on fire, they should wait until they smell smoke to get her.

Emily and Constance don't know what is happening. They check their Twitter alerts and leave the auto-refresh feeds of the most gossipy online journalists open on their screens.

It's a distracted, nervy hour, then one of Emily's friends at the *Guardian* calls and asks her about the allegations against Kieron Hyde. Emily promises an exclusive quote in due course in exchange for anything the journalist can tell her right this minute. The journalist says, 'Nothing solid. Looking a bit Harvey Weinstein though,' and hangs up.

She won't get a fucking quote for that. Emily feels her heart rate increase like she just jumped off the high board and plunges back into Twitter with a bunch of new search terms, Kieron Hyde, PSGWU, MeToo and a fistful of misspellings just to be on the safe side.

Constance brings her coffee and breaks out the homemade flapjacks. Her equivalent of taking a hammer to the safety glass.

A swirl of speculation sweeps across Twitter like a breeze through dried leaves. Two names, Julie and Debra, drift across the internet like the perfume of someone you just missed on the street corner. Who are they?

Emily watches, trying to sort out the journalists who are attempting to sound like they are in the know from the people who actually might be. The fat black phone on her desk has been turned to silent and she decides to let everything go to voicemail for the time being. Tells the others in the office to do the same. Gabriel is about to complain, until he catches the look in her eye, and Samuel looks at his own desk phone in mild surprise as if he's slightly shocked to see he has his own extension.

Serious contacts will send Emily WhatsApp messages anyway. At the moment, everyone she knows is just sending question marks and Munch 'Scream' emojis. Another light on the phone blinks red and holds steady. She glances round. They are all still staring at their screens. It has to be Georgina dialling out. The call lasts twenty minutes. It blinks off, then on again. Another, shorter, conversation.

Minutes tick by. The *Guardian* journalist messages. Defo HW. Assault. Poss rape. NDAs. Harassment. Comment?

Emily messages back: Details? Dates? Sources?

The scrolling dots and she just gets Later.

Fine. The comment can come later too.

Finally, Georgina opens the door and asks Emily to come in. Emily leaps as if she's been scalded.

Georgina goes back into her office, but before she follows her, Emily addresses the whole room.

'Right. We have to switch the phones on again or they'll say we're hiding.'

'What's going on?' Samuel asks. She ignores him.

'But the line to the media is we have no comment at this time.'

That's it. Everyone else – take a message. And I mean everyone, including the Leader's Office, though when they call tell them we'll call back as soon as possible, obviously.'

'Emily?' Constance is pointing at her screen. Emily goes to look. It's paparazzo footage of Kieron Hyde outside the house in Lambeth. He is loading an overnight bag into the back of the BMW. Reporters are shouting about assault allegations. Kieron ignores the questions and climbs into the driving seat, then pulls away from the kerb.

'When was this taken?'

Constance points to the flashing 'live' button. Emily wonders where Kieron is going. Not back to the constituency house, she hopes. Nowhere associated with the family, she prays to God.

'OK. Call the school and tell them to watch for photographers. Some might try and get into the grounds, but they will definitely be there and waiting when school closes.' She checks her watch, it's two o'clock now. It can be done. 'Send a couple of people over to help them. Does the nanny have a car?' No one knows. 'Gabriel? Do you have your car today?'

The policy genius nods, suspiciously.

'Good. Go to the house and pick up the nanny. She's called Sonia and she'll probably be shit scared. I'll text you her number. Go and pick up the kids with her and get them home. But *do not* drop them all at the front door. Use the back route through the neighbour's garden on Drake's Road.'

'What people do I send to the school?' Constance asks.

'Google personal security and use the most expensive ones,' Emily snaps, 'use the office credit card.' Then goes into Georgina's office.

*

Georgina is sitting at the desk with her head in her hands. Emily closes the door softly behind her and she looks up. She is dry-eyed.

'Emily, babes. I've called my parents. They are coming up to London from Brighton right now.'

'Do you know where Kieron has gone?'

'Norfolk,' Georgina says, and Emily breathes a tiny, invisible sigh of relief. 'He will rent a cottage in the Broads. Well off the beaten track.'

Emily looks at the time on her phone. 'What do you want to do? A statement? Ask for privacy?'

Georgina snorts then crosses her legs, swinging her chair to one side. 'As if *that's* an option. No. We have to get out ahead of this. I need to read the files, the original complaints, and I need you to dig out my diaries for 2008 and 2009.'

'I have the diaries – we had to send copies to Ms Lefiami.'

'Of course we did. God, this *bloody* investigation.'

'I don't know how we can get the reports out of the Union, though,' Emily says. 'And the terms of the NDAs. I don't have many contacts in the Union.' She covers her mouth. 'Kieron was head of legal!'

'Getting the reports is not a problem,' Georgina says. 'I just better check them for landmines. You should too.' She passes Emily a memory stick. It is emblazoned with the logo of the kids' old nursery. 'They will leak around seven. By eight we'll need a statement. I'll draft that once I'm done with the reports. You read it for the press pack and distribute copies, then an exclusive interview for *Newsnight*, I think. Millbank studio will be fine.' She nods, satisfied, then catches the look on Emily's face. 'All shall be well, Ems.'

'But you have to go home,' Emily blurts out.

'Why?'

The memory stick feels hot in her hand. 'The children. They'll be frightened by the press outside and need to know where their dad has gone.'

Georgina raps her fingers on the top of her desk, then gives a short, sharp nod.

'Good point. In my office at home, then. And make sure the interview is live. Me at home, Kirsty or whoever in the studio.'

'I hope the reports *don't* leak. They'll be able to identify the women, and they will be besieged.'

'They'll leak.' She pauses. 'Perhaps the police should advise them to leave their homes for a day or two. To avoid the journalists. Yes. The Leader's Office should be able to make a call and recommend that. Call them. Suggest that, tell them what we are doing.'

Emily wets her lips. 'What is the statement going to say, Georgina?'

Georgina has turned back to her screen and is reading, a yellow pad like Chloe Lefiami's at her right hand. She makes a note with a sweep of her fountain pen before looking up again.

'What?'

'The Leader's Office will want to know what the statement is going to say. At least some sort of idea.'

'Oh.' She waves her hand. 'Distraught, dismayed, shocked. Kieron Hyde has left the family's London home while Ms Hyde absorbs the magnitude of these horrendous accusations. That sort of thing.' She hesitates. 'Maybe Ms Maxwell-Hyde ... No. Too soon and the constituents hate double-barrelled names. Keep it Mrs Hyde for the time being.'

She checks the time. 'And call the house when Mum and Dad have got there, will you? Warn them when I arrive I want Mum on the top step. No jewellery.'

Emily makes another note. 'What about hair and make-up this evening, Georgina?'

She pauses. 'I'll do it myself. As soon as you've made the statement, follow me over to the house.' She looks up at Emily from under her lashes. 'I'll need you, Emily. My whole family will.'

Emily relaxes her shoulders. 'Of course, I'll be there, Georgina.'

Her attention returns to the screen. 'Excellent. Well, do what you do, Emily.'

Chapter 45

The PSGWU reports and NDAs do leak. It's clear from the initial summaries on the news sites that the journalists are reading the same pages as Emily. Then they publish the complete documents, with some of the names redacted. Emily wonders if Georgina leaked them herself to control the narrative. She puts the thought aside and keeps reading.

It's shocking and sickeningly familiar at the same time. Kieron Hyde had a series of sexual relationships with workers and members at the Union. Some were consensual, but seem to shade into the coercive. On at least three occasions women complained they had been assaulted – promised confidential help with their complaints about their employers or advice on how to progress within the Union and Kieron had . . . a hand on the knee, a bottle of champagne, then an insistence his hearing wasn't great, so he had to sit close to them, somewhere they could be alone. The comforting touch became aggressive. The hand on the thigh turned to fingers creeping under the hem of a skirt. And on being challenged, laughter, compliments. The woman was too hot, too beautiful. He couldn't help himself. They were friends, weren't they? On the same side? When Debra protested, and tried to leave (her statement read), she was pushed up against the wall and Kieron tore the zip on her skirt as he thrust his hand into her knickers. Then he laughed again and accused her of being hysterical.

Emily reads as calmly as she can. She's heard stories like this before, read the Ronan Farrow book, watched the Roger Ailes film, and she's been angry and wondered what she would do in the circumstances. But this is so much closer. It is right here. She's been in Kieron's house a hundred times. He's made her coffee while they were waiting for Georgina in that lovely kitchen, chatted about politics, and he's told her war stories from the campaigns. She's watched him with his kids – bright, happy-looking kids – and seen him gaze at them with such fatherly pride. Emily has, often, admired the way Kieron takes on so many of the parenting duties men of his age usually shirk. But this ... could this ... ? She keeps reading. Of course this is what happens. This is always what happens. While everybody is pointing to the madman in the bushes, the serial killer down the dark alley, this is what is happening.

She starts again, reads again, trying to harden herself to it, and this time looks for the specific mentions of Georgina. They are there. Debra says she confided in her. That's a bomb all right. The language is dry, but it seems after he assaulted her Debra refused to be in the same room with Kieron. Georgina came to find out why; or was she sent? Either way, Debra claims she laid out her accusations and Georgina had been so sympathetic, cried with her, insisted on the need for justice, then in the same conversation backtracked, pointing out how horrendous these investigations were for the victims, how it was impossible to prove anything. Georgina had advised her to handle it all through the Union.

'I believed her,' the quotation read, 'because I thought Kieron had done the same to her. It was common knowledge what went on in their "meetings".'

Christ.

Emily has read statements on camera before. She uses a clipboard and clamps her arms to her side in case she starts shaking. The statement is brief.

'After hearing the allegations and believing them to be credible, I have asked my husband of twelve years to leave the family home while investigations continue. I have also been examining my past and my conscience in light of these allegations and, like my friend and former housemate Owen McKenna, I am seeing this period in a very different light. We have learned so much from the courageous campaigning of women who have suffered at the hands of predatory men in positions of power, and the reporting of brave journalists and investigators who have allowed them to tell their stories. I am very proud of the work my party has done to re-examine past mistakes and I am ready to take part in that process, a vital first step on the road to recovery and healing. I am certain that the PSGWU, which has done so much over the years to support the rights of all workers and which I served with pride, will take that as a model. I ask that the press bear in mind I am the mother of two young, confused children. And I wish to thank my parents for interrupting their own busy lives to come and help care for them at this difficult time. I aim to be as open as I can, and am grateful for the opportunity to speak. I shall, however, continue to hold the government to account at every opportunity, knowing that my first duty, after that as a mother, is to my constituents and the people of this great country. It is a pleasure and honour to serve on the front benches, and I shall continue to do so at the discretion of my leader as long as my service is of value.'

Emily finishes reading. As soon as she lifts her eyes from the page, questions are shouted at her. Constance hands out printed copies of the statement, and in the office Gabriel hits send and the electronic version appears in inboxes, Georgina's Twitter feed and Facebook pages.

She said no questions. She waits thirty seconds, not responding to the barrage, but letting them get the footage of her not scuttling immediately back into her office. Then she retreats, she hopes with dignity, and orders a car to take her to Georgina's.

Chapter 46

She asks the driver to take her into the parallel road, but she can see the press pack outside the house from the end of the street. A policeman has been installed at the gate. He's masked and gloved, keeping them at the end of the path and occasionally reminding them not to cause an obstruction. One or two windows in the street are open, with curious neighbours leaning on the sills and looking at the fuss. No doubt a few will offer comments to the journalists who knock on the door. Some are popping up on Twitter already, though they all seem to be along the lines of 'He seems such a nice man'. One or two are claiming they felt a creepy vibe. Emily doesn't believe them. She never got a vibe from Kieron like that, and she knows creeps. There are still enough men in parliament who love to put a lingering hand on your lower back as they pass.

Emily lets herself into the garden of a three-storey Victorian townhouse with her own key, glances up at the window and waves at the elderly woman who owns the place. She waves back.

Georgina made this arrangement when she first reached the front benches. This side gate allows access to the old woman's garden, and at the back of her lawn is a gate which opens into Georgina's back garden. In exchange for a few spare keys, Georgina and Kieron pay to have the old lady's garden maintained. It's beautiful – rose bushes and lavender she can see from her window, a scrubbed patio area where she can sit out in good weather. And Georgina can sneak past the press pack whenever she feels like it.

When she came home this afternoon, though, Georgina went to the front door. Her mother opened it, took a step out into the sunlight, and now every photographer has a choice of shots of the lovely Georgina being embraced by her grey-haired mum. Her daughter is hovering in the shadows just behind them. Three generations of women in crisis. The headlines write themselves.

Emily walks down the path towards the plate-glass windows at the back of Kieron and Georgina's house. She sees movement inside and recognises Georgina's father as he pushes the sliding doors open for her to come in.

'Hello, Emily. Tea?'

'God yes, I'd love some. Where is everyone?'

'The camera people are setting up in the study and Georgina is getting changed. My wife is with the kids in the dining room.'

Emily hesitates. 'I should go and see Georgina.'

He is pouring from the pot. 'You have five minutes, dear. You did very well on the TV, I thought.'

Emily puts down her bag and slides into one of the chairs around the edge of the table while he puts a Cath Kidston mug of tea in front of her.

'Thank you. It's a strong statement.'

'Yes.' Dr Maxwell runs water into the sink. Emily notices the remains of a nursery tea piled on the sideboard. 'Very well crafted.' He switches off the tap and leans on the edge of the sink, head down. 'I never liked him, never understood the marriage, but I got used to him over the years. Found him quite companionable while he was sneaking his cigarillos under the pretence of looking round the garden. Now I want to kill him.'

'I liked him too,' Emily says and he returns to the dishes. 'How are the kids?'

'Nice to hear someone asking,' he replies. 'I have no idea. They ate. But they are being very quiet. Waiting to see how the land lies, I suppose, as we all are.'

It's a pandemic-style framing. The bookshelves behind Georgina's head show off a mix of modern literature, classics, non-fiction. They established a base during lockdown, and freshen it up every month, books and family photos. The ones featuring Kieron have been removed. Emily did that, and part of her is looking forward to seeing if anyone notices it. An 'a-ha' moment in a blog post or think piece.

Georgina blinks at the camera. She is wearing an earpiece, and occasionally nods at the screen. Agrees something. 'Yes. That's fine . . . I might not be able to go into details . . . No, I'm not answering that.'

Emily sits behind the camera with the producer and he hands her a set of headphones; the feed from the studio control booth in one ear, the broadcast as it goes out in the other. The titles are running, a voice in the studio counts down and the presenter hits her cue. Behind her chair is Georgina, sitting in this room, her hair loose, her make-up light, wearing a white hoodie. She always appears on TV in a suit jacket and blouse – the house has rooms full of them but, Emily realises, Georgina wants to look more 'ordinary' today. She is the mother who got in a couple of hours ago, has seen her traumatised kids through teatime and bath time and is now ready to get back to work in her home office like thousands of other high-flying mothers.

The screen on the producer's laptop cuts to a pre-recorded package. Archive video clips of Kieron speaking at Labour Party and TUC conferences, a lawyer explaining how, after the Weinstein case, enforcing NDAs that cover complaints of harassment and assault has become impossible. There is a short statement from the law firm now representing the two women, and refusing to confirm their identities, even if they've been doxed all across the internet. There's the familiar footage of Kieron packing his car, then, Emily sees with a jolt, they play the tape of her reading Georgina's statement. She hates seeing herself on screen, but it does work from a professional point of view, at least. Emily looks pale – that's just the lights, of course – and in shock. Which she was. The camera can see what you are thinking ... who said that? Someone who knew. Emily looks like someone struggling to take in bad news, someone who is reeling and angry and terribly worried about the person whose words she is speaking. It's impossible to fake and it gives the words far more impact than they had on the page.

The package ends, and the presenter turns towards the video wall full of Georgina looking vulnerable yet resolved in front of her bookshelves. Emily holds her breath. Which way have they decided to jump? She wishes she'd heard the pre-interview. Either Georgina will be seen as a victim, or not. A twist, a kink in the narrative, and they could be fighting a rearguard action against making Georgina into a conspirator, the cold-hearted enabler. What would the women have said? If they had been caught on camera, describing Georgina as an opportunist, the manipulator who kept them from going to the police, allowing the abuse to continue ... Emily suddenly realises it is a very good thing the press frightened them off. The stage belongs to Georgina.

But still. It depends on this moment; are they going on the attack?

'Mrs Hyde,' the presenter says, 'thank you for speaking to us this evening. How are you holding up?'

Emily closes her eyes and enjoys the moment of relief, breathes in and focuses. At least seven more minutes to go. Give it ten minutes after that for the hot takes to come in. Then they'll know what they are dealing with.

Chapter 47

Georgina looks good when she is tired. Owen scans the bookshelves behind her head: a lot more fiction than he reads.

'... I think, I think what I want to say more than anything else is how grateful I am to the campaigners who made me reassess this period in my life. I told myself that it was my fault, that Kieron might have been a little rough with me, but that was only because he was carried away by passion, didn't know his own strength. It was what he told me, after all.' She looks off camera for a long beat. 'I was in love with him, and I wanted to believe what he said. Sometimes we can only see the shapes of our lives, looking back from a distance. I'm inspired by men like Owen McKenna who are willing to examine past mistakes, challenge their own histories. And by women like those who made complaints against my husband, and are speaking out now.'

'They tried to speak out then,' says the interviewer. 'They confided in you, they wanted assurances things would change at the Union. But those changes took a long time, didn't they? And you were part of a very small group of people who knew about these complaints and hushed them up, allowing your husband to run for the role of general secretary. He was very useful to you in your political career, wasn't he, Mrs Hyde?'

Not a flicker. Of fear or anger. You could study this footage frame by HD frame and you wouldn't find it. She nods slowly as if considering the question, then puts a finger just below her eye as if to control a tear.

'I think . . . Yes, he helped me enormously and I was so grateful. I loved his family too, his home. I suppose what I am trying to say is that I have had every advantage in life, I had a stable background, a privileged education and a challenging, exciting career. But I allowed myself to be bullied, coerced. I no longer trusted the evidence of my own eyes and ears. I believed what Kieron told me. And then, after we were married, there were to my knowledge no further complaints. I told myself this was proof the stories about my husband were wrong. Misunderstandings or even, God forgive me, the complaints of jilted women.'

'So you were gaslit into a remarkably successful political career.' Was that a flicker then, thought Owen? 'What has changed, Mrs Hyde?'

'The investigation into the case of Jay Dewan forced me to recall in detail that terrible period personally, then I found myself thinking of those complaints in a different light. I actually pulled them from the Union records two days ago to reassess them in light of what we know now about abusers like . . . Kieron.' The name is said softly, dripping with pain. 'I was on the point of reaching out to the women, through my lawyers, to see if they wished to revisit the complaints, when one of them got in contact with the investigator appointed by the leader of my party.'

'And do you think similar cases are ongoing in your party or the Union movement?'

Georgina tosses her head and there is anger in her eyes now, but not directed at the interviewer.

'I am sure there have been dozens of similar cases where women have found themselves in the power of abusive partners, bosses, colleagues. The trade union movement is not immune to abuses of power. I hope any man who has treated women in this way will be living in terror tonight, and that any person who thinks they can exploit and degrade another in pursuit of their selfish or sadistic pleasure, hears this:

'We can see you now, and we're coming for you.'

'Fuck me. I'm going to need another drink after that. Will they bring a single malt up if I ask nicely?' Sara presses the button on the remote and the TV emits a short declining pattern of electronic notes, a digital sigh, and goes dark.

Sara is lying on the bed, chin in her hands, stockinged feet crossed at the ankle.

'You look like Holly Golightly,' Phil says, free to look at her now he's released from the spell of Georgina's interview. He's still holding the briefing paper he picked up before the section on the Hyde family scandal began. He realises the thick linen page has crinkled slightly with the sweat of his fingers.

Sara rolls onto her back while he puts it down and orders the drinks on the room service app.

'That's nice of you, dear, but do remember Holly was a teenage prostitute and I run a hedge fund.'

'Noted.'

'But that was quite a performance, wasn't it? From conspirator to victim to warrior in five minutes.'

She picks up her iPad and starts scrolling. 'It's playing well on Twitter. Huh.'

'What?'

'Someone's clipped that last bit and made her eyes flash. Quick work.'

A knock at the door. She gets up and opens it, takes the tray from the masked porter and thanks him. Proper glasses.

She gives Phil his and stands behind him. 'Have you read Jay's records yet?'

He shakes his head.

'May I read them? Unless you're worried that I might find out some other deep, dark secret of yours?'

He turns to face her properly. 'You know my worst secrets now. No, but I know those records shook Owen and I don't want you to think any worse of me.'

She smiles. 'After ten years of marriage, I don't think there are *many* surprises left.' He hands her the file and she carries it to one of the armchairs, picks up her drink. 'Even that thing with the list. I didn't *know* you'd done it, but I wasn't *surprised* that you had, or that you were ashamed of it. Even if I don't know the specifics, I do know what sort of man you are.'

She gestures towards the black screen of the TV.

'It's why I find this story of Georgina's a bit ... troubling. They've been married longer than we have, raised children. Either she was so obsessed with her work she really didn't ever think about those accusations again, even while the whole Weinstein thing was unravelling, or she knew perfectly well what and who he was and that whole interview was a crock of shit.'

Phil puts his pen down. 'But you still sound as if you admire her.'

'I think I'm slightly in awe. And a little afraid. But not as afraid as her husband has been for the last ten years, I would think.'

'I can't imagine Kieron being afraid of anything.'

She waves her drink at him. 'Exactly! Look, suppose she knew exactly what he was when they married – and note there have been no complaints since they married. Just imagine the strength of will, of character, it must take to keep a man like Kieron Hyde, a powerful predator what, fifteen years older than her, on a short leash.' She raised her eyebrows. 'God and to have children with him! That's terrifying.'

Phil thinks about Georgina, her brilliance at university. 'She never had many female friends.'

Sara gives a gurgling laugh. 'Not surprised. We women have to develop a much more sensitive radar for super-predators than men do.'

He doesn't have an answer for that. She picks up the file and an envelope slips out. She holds it up. No name on it so she shrugs and opens it.

It's midnight when she speaks again.

'Honey?'

He puts down the page he is working on.

'What?'

'I hope that whisky hasn't dulled your brain.'

'Why?'

'Because this thing Owen has stumbled into is a toxic hell-hole and we are going to need a strategy.' She looks at him and her usual expression of wry amusement is gone. She's deadly serious. 'And you might need to do the right thing again.'

He listens with a blossoming sense of dread as she tells him what Owen has so far. No wonder Greg was ready to go to extremes to try and keep Owen quiet.

'If the Secretary of State for Health has done this, Phil, there must be evidence in the department somewhere.'

Phil feels sick. He doesn't want to know.

'I don't think they get together and write down the details of their conspiracy in a handy email chain, Sara! Hey, Mr Secretary of State, just a quick email to confirm that we'll keep donating vast sums to your party and rolling out fat speakers' fees if you'll just crush this data initiative thing.'

'Wouldn't that be nice?' She finishes her whisky and looks sadly at the glass.

'Do you want another?'

'No, got to think.'

He taps the submission he just read together and returns it to the red box. What is he supposed to do now? If Owen's right he has to do something. Somehow it's a relief to find he believes that. Perhaps he is still more human than politician after all.

'That's it! Paper!'

He closes and locks the box. 'You've gone insane. Shall I fetch someone?'

'Ssh, I'm having a moment. I know they are always trying to modernise the House, but it's still medieval really. There is paper about this Collins deal somewhere. The ministerial box!' She claps her hands together. 'Your civil servants put stuff in it, you read it and make notes on it and give it back, yes? But what happens to those notes?'

'They are filed in the department.'

'Look, honey, go at it from the other end!' She swings her legs round and sits crosslegged among the papers on the bed. 'There must have been a ... what do you call it?'

'The papers from the civil servants? A submission.'

She shrugs. 'Don't know why you don't just call it a report like reasonable human beings, but look, there must have been a *submission* about the Collins project, mustn't there?'

'Probably several, if Owen's information is correct. One when Collins first got in touch and they decided the idea was plausible, then another when they'd drawn up a letter of agreement they wanted signed.'

She holds up Owen's note again. 'And that agreement was ready to go! Owen says Collins had his copy, but then the department went dark and there followed three weeks of silence while Greg's bosses and their minions got ready to blackmail Collins into selling his company.'

'So the Secretary of State must have told the Head of Procurement to put a hold on it.' He catches some of her excitement.

'And isn't there a chance that he would do that in response to a submission? Wouldn't that be the best way just to stop things in the department? He wouldn't want to call a meeting on it where he could be challenged, would he?'

'There's a chance.'

'Then we should take it.'

'It's impossible, Sara. They are looking for an excuse to stick the knife in. If I get caught going through the Secretary's files, I'll be crucified.'

She waits. But if it is there ... If Owen's information is

correct ... Owen had just brought all the furies down on his own head over this, and politics is his entire life. If Phil does get caught, does get thrown out of the party and parliament, what will he be left with? His kids, his home, his wife, who'll still be able to look at him the way she's looking at him now.

'Fine. I'll try.'

Chapter 48

The professor's house is a pleasant two-storey building on the edge of Southwark Park, not far from Canada Water Station. His narrow front yard is full of geraniums.

'No car? No security?' says the man who opens the door to Owen, looking up and down the street.

'Professor Graves?' He nods. Graves is in his late sixties and wears a collar and tie under his thin sweater. Owen thinks he looks like a retired naval officer, the sort whose shoes are still polished to a gleam every morning. 'I'm just a backbench MP, we get a panic button and a travel card.'

That surprises a reluctant smile out of him. He watches as Owen gets his mask out of his pocket and puts it on.

'Come through. We can talk on the patio and then you won't have to wear that thing.'

Owen follows him through the house. A woman, the same age as the professor, is filling the kettle. 'My wife.'

They exchange their bows and then Owen hurries after his host out onto the patio area beyond the kitchen.

Graves gets straight down to business. 'I can only tell you what I told Victor's sister when she contacted me,' he says as soon as they sit down round a wrought-iron garden table, looking over a long narrow garden. 'It was made very clear to me by the people Victor sold the company to that if I talked about the abandonment of his work, I would suffer for it. I signed an NDA when Victor first came to me, with his company. Of course I did. So when Victor sold his company, that NDA went with it.'

The patio is decorated with pots of herbs, and Owen can smell rosemary on the air as the breeze shifts. This man is obviously not the sort given to small talk, and Owen guesses he will not be given long to make his case. And he needs Professor Graves. If the government and the company who bought Victor's intellectual property can just keep repeating the line Victor's work was no good, then Owen will have gone through this for nothing.

'Last weekend when I was at my surgery a woman collapsed in my arms. She hadn't eaten for days. Some kids had chalked NHS rainbows all over the pavement and she just keeled over among them. She's in hospital recovering now.'

'What does that have to do with me?' Graves is caught between defensiveness and curiosity.

'Doesn't that woman deserve her dignity, her privacy? God knows the pandemic and the crappy social security system in this country have taken most of it all already, but doesn't she deserve to be more than a datapoint in some health insurance database?' Graves frowns but says nothing, so Owen ploughs on. 'Elsie has a copy of the letter you wrote in support of Victor's project. I don't pretend to understand the technical details but you also spoke very passionately about the need to protect patient data in the way Victor suggested, and how whole communities could be victimised by its improper use. "Human beings are not commodities. When they are treated as such we are in danger of treating our fellow citizens as mere units of value to be bought and sold."'

'You memorised my letter?'

Owen shakes his head. 'Only parts of it. You still believe that, don't you? And in Victor's work?' Graves crosses his legs, folds his arms. 'Because if you were wrong, Professor, and his work was faulty, I should leave.' He starts to stand up.

'I wasn't wrong! Victor was brilliant and his work was exceptional. Ground-breaking but beautifully engineered and I have absolutely no doubt about its quality or the practicality of his proposals. And the current use and abuse of the data is a scandal, or it damn well should be. Sit down, Mr McKenna.'

Owen lowers himself back into the chair. 'Then now is the time to speak up, Professor.'

'But what about me? And my wife?' Graves' voice rises. 'I do not want to spend my retirement savings on lawyers! What if I read stories about myself in the media to discredit me? It's one thing for you . . . I mean, *you* signed up for this sort of nonsense. What if they set their trolls on *me*? I wish to be left in peace and you want to set me up in front of a firing squad!'

'Honestly, John,' Professor Graves' wife comes out from the kitchen. She is holding an oversized mug in both hands. 'You haven't been living in peace since you heard the news about Victor.'

She pulls up a garden chair next to him and sits down, puts a hand on his knee.

Owen looks out over the neat garden. An orderly life and one he has no right to disrupt. It's not me who is threatening it, he tells himself, it's Greg's clients and the shifting tides of money and influence behind them. Time to push.

'Professor, it's not just my job to do this. It's yours too. It's everyone's job. We only get to live in a free country if we are willing to fight for it. That doesn't just mean being ready to sign up the way our parents and grandparents did. It means standing up and telling the truth, even when doing so has consequences. It's lonely and messy, much less clear than just heading out for the barricades or to the front line in a troop train, but it's still our duty.'

The word 'duty' hits hard. Graves studies the wrought iron of his picnic table then looks at his wife. She takes his hand and squeezes his fingers.

'Poor Victor,' Graves says at last. 'He was so brilliant, but fragile. A butterfly broken on a wheel. Very well, Mr McKenna. I'll be your expert witness. What do you need me to do?'

Owen calls Elsie on the way back to Canada Water Tube Station. When she answers he is standing in the lee of the modernist library on the edge of the old timber pond. He tells her the professor has agreed to vouch for Victor's work; it sounds like she will cry.

'Thank you, Owen,' she says after a moment. 'Thank you so much.'

'We've got a long way to go, Elsie,' he says quietly. A woman goes past him pushing a pushchair with one hand and holding a small child with the other. They pause a few yards away from him and the child starts throwing oats to a pair of swans. He is trying to make sure, Owen realises, that they get equal shares. 'When we go public with this story, the danger is the people who have come after me will come after you too. Even with the professor onside, it's going to be hard to prove his work was knowingly suppressed. If we can't do that, then the more we ask questions the more you and your brother will be smeared. If the stories about me keep coming, I could also lose my seat in parliament, and any power and platform that goes with it.'

She sounds defiant when she replies. Owen pictures her, sitting in her room in front of the picture of her and her brother, lifting her chin. 'Victor was on his own. I've got you and Christine and now the professor. We press on. Have faith, Owen.'

They make their farewells and Owen pauses a little longer to watch the swans being fed. He wonders if Phil has read Jay's file, if he has read the notes Owen sent with it about the Collins case and what in God's name he'll do with them.

Chapter 49

The Secretary of State's offices in the department are on the same floor as the main boardroom, the floor below Phil's. Phil shuts down his computer and puts on his suit jacket, pushes open the door, lifts his coat off the stand. His private secretary looks up.

His red box is open on her desk. Submissions must be made by five p.m., that's their rule. He eyes it suspiciously.

'Not too bad tonight, Minister. I promise.'

'You've said that before, and I've found I have the equivalent of *War and Peace* to get through before breakfast.'

She types something on her computer as she replies. 'I'd say it was more *Crime and Punishment* tonight.'

He glances at his watch. 'Don't let it get out of control. I'm going to show my face at the boardroom. It's Gibbons who is leaving, isn't it?'

'Yes, poor man's got a promotion into International Trade. The party is supposed to be a celebration, but I suspect he'll be choking on his sherry.' She notes his coat. 'Shall I send the box to the car when it is ready?'

'Yes, please. Though it does seem foolish to be driven across the bridge. I'm at the Plaza again tonight.'

She nods towards the battered red case. 'Well, we have to keep an eye on the paperwork.'

'And I thought you were all just worried about me. Goodnight.'

'Goodnight, Minister. Enjoy the sherry.'

He takes the stairs down to the main floor. The main working area looks like any other large office, with suites of offices like his own, the open-plan area and the boardroom where he can see a small gathering sipping sherry and enjoying the view towards parliament.

He takes his coat off and walks into the Secretary of State's outer office.

The Secretary's private secretary smiles tightly at him.

'Minister? Are you looking for him? He's got a meeting for another hour or so, then will be making an appearance at the boardroom.'

Phil lifts the bundle of his long wool coat. 'No, I don't need him. I was hoping to leave my coat here while I pop in and raise a glass to Gibbons.'

She nods. The gunmetal-grey cabinets of the live files are in a wall behind her. Sara has sent him on a search for a needle in a haystack. He has an image of himself tossing folders over his shoulders, scattering memos and submissions and confidential data across the nylon carpet tiles. He puts his coat on the bank of grey nylon chairs which mark the informal waiting area opposite the secretary's desk then heads for the boardroom, his heart thumping. He is not cut out for espionage.

The boardroom party gives him a warm greeting, warmer than he was expecting. The civil servants gathered in the room perk up when he arrives. If he was in the House itself, among the politicians and their staff, he would be beset with questions about Georgina, Owen and Jay. This lot have been trained against indulging in political gossip and he can't help admiring their restraint, even while he notes their interest.

'Sherry, Minister?' Gibbons is playing host.

'Thank you, and congratulations.'

Phil hates sherry. It reminds him of Christmas at his grandmother's house, trapped for hours in her over-heated living room. Even if they serve a much better vintage here than Nan did, the taste still twangs uncomfortable chords in his memory.

He wants to ask his host what people gossip about here. Their colleagues, probably. Instead he asks about the promotion Gibbons has just received. A safe space. His private secretary was right. Gibbons doesn't look too pleased about it.

'Apparently, there is a lot of travel. My wife isn't happy. She doesn't trust the infection figures coming out of Thailand.'

How long does he need to stay here? 'I thought everything was done by Zoom.'

Gibbons shakes his head. He can't be over thirty, but has the jowly face of a much older man. 'The Minister insists on the importance of face-to-face meetings.'

Phil can imagine. The Minister believes if she stares someone down in a meeting room, entire governments will just see sense and do what she wants them to.

He manages twenty minutes. The Secretary of State will still be in his meeting. Phil's secretary will have sent the red box down to the car. It's now or never.

He makes his farewells. There's another waiting area outside. A chair, a pot plant, a coffee table. He sees the photos on the front page. A three-column-wide image of Georgina, and below it one of Kieron packing his bags into his car. He can see yesterday's front page next to it. Owen at a football match, arms raised. Christ, what are they doing? Phil keeps walking and turns into the Secretary of State's outer office again. He makes to pick up his coat, then sits down heavily on the chair.

'Minister?'

He glances up at her. 'Sorry, it's been a tough few days. I'm sorry to ask you this, but do you think there's any chance you can chase my driver for me? He occasionally pops out for a smoke out back. I told him I'd be longer than this at the party and he's not answering my calls.'

She looks at the filing cabinets behind her. 'I shouldn't leave these unlocked, Mr Bickford. Even for a minute.'

Phil gives his best weary smile. 'I promise I'll keep an eye on them until you come back.'

He can see the little war going on behind her eyes. Protocol says she should lock the cabinets, but then Phil is a minister, and he's promised to keep an eye on them. It has to be OK.

She gets up and picks up her keycard. 'By the car park? Under the balcony?'

Phil nods like he hasn't even got the energy to speak and she smiles sympathetically then exits into the main office. He counts to ten. All quiet, apart from the hum of the supercharged air-conditioning and the distant chatter from the boardroom.

Then he gets to his feet and heads for the filing cabinets.

Collins. Papers could be filed under anything, but he's going with his gut and guessing Collins is the best bet. He pulls open the first drawer of C. CA to CO. His fingers are sweating. There are five files at the back marked COLLINS, COLLINS MANUFACTURING, COLLINS ENGINEERING. What was the company called? Forward one. COLLINS COMPUTING. That's it. It's thick. How long has she been gone? He can measure her journey in his mind's eye. Two flights of stairs, passing through the back corridor where the building IT department monitor their intranet for Russians and data activists, fighting back the incursions of anti-vaxxers who are searching for proof of a campaign to insert micro-chips into the population with the latest vaccine.

He lifts the file out and shuts the drawer. Someone laughs. He looks up to see two of the men from the cocktail party pass by the open office door. He should look like he's waiting. He grabs the file and places it by his coat, opens it. Sits with his back to the door. As he takes out his phone he feels a sick lurch of memory back to Owen's room in the house and the list of marginals. Does he photograph every page? If only the fucking Secretary of State had clearer handwriting, he'd be able to see which notes were important at first glance. Sheets of Commons notepaper, thick stock and embossed with the crowned port-cullis, are attached with bulldog clips to the submissions in the file. He hasn't got time to try and read. He starts to take pictures of every note he can find along with the pages they are attached to.

She must be on her way back by now. She just has to open the back door, look right and left. It's not a big area, she'll see immediately that his driver isn't there. A thicker document;

he catches the title in type, GATEWAY REPORT. Another note attached, slightly longer. The damn phone focuses on the floor as his hand shakes. He moves it back till the ink is crisp in the lens. Takes it, then lifts the camera higher to take in the whole page. Is it legible? Should he take more?

The clunk and hum of the lift.

He taps the papers back into shape and puts his phone in his pocket, takes the file back to the cabinet and opens the file drawer again. It sticks. He rattles it, pulls it out. Another laugh and he turns round. No one there. Just sound bouncing along from the increasingly merry sherry drinkers.

Not between ENGINEERING and MANUFACTURING. In front of that. God, he can't even remember his alphabet. There. You'd never know. He slides the drawer shut.

'Minister?'

He turns round. She is in the doorway. 'He wasn't there.'

He lifts up his phone. 'Yes, so sorry. Turns out he was in the café, just didn't catch my call.'

She's still blocking the doorway. 'Were you looking for something, Mr Bickford?'

She did see. And he's on thin ice. All she needs to do is mention this to the Secretary of State. Do they have CCTV in here? They could demand his phone. Should he lie? Should he brazen this out? Try the high-handed, looking-down-his-nose attitude and say 'I have what I need'? No, she wouldn't have this job if she was easy to intimidate. He just stares at her.

She steps inside and round her desk, sitting down without looking at him.

'I meant to say, Minister. I thought it was very brave of you to stand up for your friend Owen McKenna yesterday. Even though he's not your friend anymore. It's nice to see a man of principle.'

'Thank you. Not everyone in the building would agree with you.'

He moves away from the filing cabinet and reaches for his coat.

'I'm sure they wouldn't. But I thought how good it was, seeing someone do the right thing.' She swipes her computer mouse from side to side and looks at the screen, then back at him. 'Have a pleasant evening.'

Phil picks up his coat and puts it on. 'You too.'

The sweat prickles under his collar.

Chapter 50

Friday 18 March 2022

The buzzer on his front door wakes Owen just after midnight. The press pack has deserted him to haunt Georgina, so he ignores it at first, assuming it's a drunk who has forgotten their keys, but it persists. After a while, struggling out of his half-sleep, he realises that someone is amusing themselves tapping out the Fibonacci sequence on the ringer for a minute then starting again. Not a drunk, then.

He stumbles to the door and lifts the receiver. The little camera screen flutters into life and he finds himself looking into the face of a woman he doesn't recognise.

'I'm Sara Bickford,' she says. 'Thought it might be time we met.'

He's too sleep-addled to do anything other than buzz her in, then leaves the front door open as he stumbles back into his bedroom to get dressed.

By the time he gets back the woman is in his flat, peering down his sink. He notices she's opened the windows.

335

'You're pouring away Talisker?' she says. 'Are you insane?'

'Greg Griffen left it for me.'

She recoils. 'Enough said. Got anything else to drink?'

'There's beer in the fridge.'

'Thank fuck for that. Do you want one?'

He shakes his head. 'Too early for me, or too late. What are you doing here?'

She opens the fridge door. 'You mean what are *we* doing here. Say "hello", honey.'

'Hi, Owen.'

Owen starts and stares at the phone on the table next to his chair. It's on speaker. Sara closes the fridge door, opens the can and drinks, examines the label with approval and then sits down in the other armchair.

'Should anyone want to see phone records,' she says as she settles herself, 'they'll see Phil had a long, late-night conversation with his devoted wife. Very touching.'

She points back at the counter. 'I brought your files back, or rather I brought Jay's files back. They were definitely copied from the central NHS data site. The long file names at the bottom of each page were a bit of a giveaway. I checked quietly with a health industry colleague. Just, you know ... FYI.'

'I see,' Owen says and rubs his eyes with the heels of his hands, trying to wake up. 'Thank you, that's helpful.'

'Darling, do you want to tell him the rest?'

'Sara also has a thumb drive,' Phil's voice says out of the phone. Sara produces it from the pocket of her coat with a flourish.

'This is like being on *Charlie's Angels*,' Owen says and Sara laughs into her beer. 'What's on it?'

'A lightly smoking gun,' Sara tells him and puts it next to the phone with a click. 'Tell him, Phil.'

'Sara and I read your notes about Greg and Maundrill Consulting. We thought if the Secretary of State had put a stop to the process of the government investing in Victor's company, the most likely place to find evidence of that would be in the live files, where the civil service stores the red box submissions ministers have commented on.'

'Seemed it would be a more discreet way of stopping things without too many questions being asked,' Sara says.

It made sense. 'And?' Owen asks.

'We were right,' Phil sighs deeply. 'Though I wish it were all nonsense. That thumb drive has photographs of the notes he made on the gateway submission the Head of Procurement prepared for him, and the contracts of appointment they wanted to sign with Victor. It says, and I'm quoting here, "Useful. I have developed serious doubts however about this proposed solution to the data issues and will provide further details when I have the opportunity. For now, do not proceed on any front on this project." It's dated the day before you say the phone calls between the department and Victor stopped.'

'That will lead to some awkward questions. How did you get it?' Owen asks.

Phil tells him, and Owen whistles softly. 'Thank you. The professor is on-side, too. He'll vouch for the tech. You got cover?' Owen asks.

Phil hesitates. 'No, not much. I'm betting that if we do this right, they'll be so busy trying to put out the fire, they won't be looking for the guy who gave you the matches. Ideally, go to someone in the press who will know how to ask the right questions while shielding the specifics which could land me in jail. I'd appreciate that.'

Owen is impressed. 'OK. Are you doing this because of the marginals list, or because I looked after Liam?'

'Bit of both maybe? Not to mention the fact it's just wrong.'

'Shall I punch Owen on the shoulder for you, honey?' Sara says into the phone. 'That's the man version of a tearful embrace of reconciliation, isn't it?'

'Stop enjoying yourself so much, Sara,' Phil says. Owen suppresses a smile.

'Fine. But I did have some fun with the Register of Members' Interests today,' Sara goes on, more serious. 'Or rather one of my researchers did. The current Secretary of State for Health, in the eighteen months since he took the job, has accrued a large second income through making very short public speeches. It's quite clever. He hasn't been paid huge sums by companies who buy and sell NHS data, but other Maundrill Consulting clients *have* paid a lot for his time. The Russians did something similar to smuggle cash out of the country. Works like this: Maundrill Consulting tells their clients who to pay and how much, and you can rest assured that some other person of note you want to influence is getting a similar amount of cash from a different Maundrill Consulting client. Makes the connections between favours and payments much harder to trace.' She kicks off her shoes and curls her legs up on the armchair. 'I don't know why I say influence, I mean *bribe*. The person of note you want to *bribe*. Plausible deniability all round.'

'And you are just giving this to me?' Owen says at last.

'Obviously,' Sara replies. 'My researcher's notes are on the thumb drive.'

'Why? What do you think you owe me, Phil, an election?'

Owen hears Phil suck in his breath suddenly. 'Like I said, Owen, because it's just wrong. We don't agree on much anymore, but we agree on that.'

Owen gets up and goes to the sink, fills the kettle and switches it on. Sara leans over the handset. 'It's OK, honey, he hasn't exploded. Just making tea.'

'So we need someone who knows how to look after their sources. It's got to be Charlotte, hasn't it?' he says as the kettle clicks off. 'Christine is still in town. We'll go and see her together.'

'Do it,' Phil says. 'Tread carefully, Owen.'

'I shall, and thanks, Phil.'

Sara crushes her can and puts her shoes back on.

'Right, I'll hang up on you, Phil, and send for the car.'

'Bye, Phil,' Owen calls, then looks up from his tea. 'You came in the ministerial car?'

'I have my own car service, Owen,' Sara says, an edge to her voice. 'I'm the reason Phil can't be corrupted by all that nasty cash.'

Shit. 'Sorry. I swear to God I am trying to get better.'

She bows. 'Good for you.'

When Owen wakes up in the morning, the flat seems strangely empty. He wonders at first if he dreamed the whole thing, but he sees his mug in the sink, Sara's can in the recycling, the file on the table and the thumb drive.

He turns on the TV news and sets it to mute, then Radio 4. Georgina and reactions to her story echo around the room. He opens the window to let in some fresh air. Other snippets of trade deals and a new outbreak in Middlesbrough. But it's mostly Georgie. He looks out onto the street. People still coming and going, a bus hissing past. People adapting.

When he checks the phone after he's showered himself into near consciousness and is finishing his first coffee, there is a message from Christine and another from Charlotte agreeing to meet. A coffee bar on The Cut near Waterloo in an hour. He packs the box of Elsie's files and Sara's thumb drive and orders an Uber.

At the café he presents Phil's evidence and Sara's research, gives his account of Greg's attempt to blackmail him, then leaves Christine to take Charlotte through the details. 'I'll report the blackmail attempt to the police this morning, then be in the Chamber this afternoon.'

'This is quite the story, Owen,' Charlotte says. 'I'll get a couple of researchers on it and we should be good to go to print Monday. You are sure the professor will back up the technical worth of the project?'

'He will. And you'll be careful how you use those photographs?'

'My eyes only. It's easy enough to suggest they might have come out of NHX or from a disgruntled civil servant. God knows there are enough of them about.'

She taps her notebook. 'So I have bribery, blackmail, suicide. Plenty there, but do people care about their data being sold in this way?'

'They should,' Owen says. 'You have to make them care, Charlotte.'

She lifts her hands. 'Help me out.'

He takes a second. 'It's all in Elsie's notes, when you pay

340

attention. Read the professor's letter too. This government doesn't want to pay for a National Health Service, not really. They've frightened as many people as they can into taking out private insurance, and are hoping that selling our data to insurance firms and pharmaceutical companies will refill the coffers. That's what's happening here. Patients are being treated as commodities, as assets to be bought and sold.'

She nods. 'OK. I can do something with that.'

Chapter 51

The interview with the police is brief and civil. Owen makes his way through the protestors and flag wavers in Parliament Square – no tractors today – then through the halls and into the Chamber itself for the debate about the urgent repairs needed on the parliamentary estate.

He is in time to hear one of the members opposite quote Phil on the importance of parliament, how it has grown and changed as an institution over the centuries, and use it as a clarion call to avoid leaving this place, and allowing essential repairs to happen all around them. Another offers a litany of problems from the creaking sewers to the faulty electrics. Owen wonders if they remember the whole thing burned down in 1834. The building they are sitting in is a newcomer by London standards.

Georgina slides in alongside him, close enough to talk.

She speaks to him, while looking forward. In the moments they are caught on camera she will look like she is paying attention to the debate, while exchanging comments with an old friend.

'I hoped I'd catch the hero of the hour here,' she says. 'From almost losing the whip to candidate for the front bench in seventy-two hours. I'm impressed.'

Candidate for the front bench? Interesting.

'No one was interested in me once the Kieron story broke.'

'So glad the wreckage of my family could help.'

'Georgina, I didn't mean . . .'

'I know – your thoughts are with me at this difficult time. I read your statement. And now I hear we're topping it all off with a government scandal which could bring down a government minister. *The Times* will go to print on Monday and I'm going to lead the charge from the front benches. They really aren't wrong when they say a week is a long time in politics, are they?'

'Charlotte called you?'

'Obviously. We're close.'

That wry tone, with just an edge to it. He looks at her sideways, his beautiful, talented friend. He bends sideways towards her, still watching the honourable member talk about the danger of crumbling stonework. He has to ask her. That's what this room is for, isn't it? To ask questions.

'Georgie, tell me you didn't know. Please. Convince me that you didn't understand what Kieron had done. I want to believe you weren't complicit in what he did. I don't want to think you helped cover up his crimes, and in exchange he supported your political career. Tell me you had a marriage, not a devil's bargain.'

'Of course I had no idea. I loved him and I was taken in completely.' Her voice is flat. It's like she's not even trying.

His heart sinks. 'You're cleverer than that, Georgina,' Owen says. 'You always have been smarter than the rest of us.'

She nods slowly as if agreeing with the point being made on the floor of the House. 'Did you know during the English Civil War they published woodcuts, like political cartoons, and the image they came up with to symbolise the utter horrific chaos of the time was a parliament of women? That was the most abhorrent thing they could imagine. It disgusted them! Is that it? Do women like me and Christine offend you? Have you met Phil's wife, Sara? I have once or twice. She runs a hedge fund. Does that horrify you?'

'Don't talk bollocks, Georgie. We're talking about you and Kieron and if you helped cover up his crimes in exchange for his political muscle. His support was critical for you! What were you willing to do for it?' She doesn't reply. 'But I admit seeing you gain more power is beginning to frighten me. I have always supported women in parliament.'

She smiles, pats his arm as if he's just said something funny. 'As long as it didn't cost you anything. You used to know Coogan; no one ever spent more than ten minutes with him without him saying something foul about women. Did you ever challenge him? Did you ever, just you two men together, tell him not to talk about his colleagues as if they were pieces of meat? Or was that inconvenient? Didn't you and Christine have a massive fight when you finally worked out she wanted to stand for parliament? She came to me in tears, and you know how upset she must have been to do that. Your blank incomprehension. Then your argument that it would be impossible for you both to be MPs and have a successful marriage. And your assumption that it should be you who got priority.'

There's a cold hard truth in that.

Now one of the Labour MPs is speaking in support of the idea of moving parliament out of the building. It will be more efficient and be a greater saving in the end. A lone voice, crying in the wilderness. In this contracted, sickened economy that no one is going to support presenting the taxpayer with the butcher's bill in one bite. Better to spend five billion, quietly over the decade, than four and face the truth all at once.

Another touch on his arm and Georgina gets up to leave, just as the Minister steps forward, thanks the members for their contributions and promises another review. Owen watches her go.

Chapter 52

Monday 21 March 2022

Chloe Lefiami is working from home today. Her office on the first floor is tiny, a box room really. Her desk faces the window, which gives her a view over South London, and the two long walls give her the shelf space she needs for her files and reference works. She mostly uses the online versions now when she needs to look something up, but their physical presence makes her feel grounded by the memories of sweating over them at college, and the posters on the back wall from the Chronic Love Foundation remind her that she didn't just study.

She is finishing her report, so it's only when she goes downstairs to make another coffee and escape her ergonomic chair for a minute that she flicks on the radio.

'Fresh shockwaves hit Westminster today after *The Times* published a story asking if the Secretary of State for Health corruptly colluded with lobbyists in a blackmail scheme which cost the life of one businessman and brought about a massive setback in the attempt to protect data held by the NHS on millions of UK citizens.'

Chloe picks up her phone and opens Twitter. Clips from Sky News and BBC show Christine Armstrong and Charlotte Cook alongside a young woman with long dark hair, lit by the repeated camera flashes. Chloe makes coffee then turns on the TV for the top of the hour. An earnest-looking young man stands on the green outside parliament talking into his micro-phone and fiddling with his earpiece. He doesn't appear to be saying anything he couldn't say in a studio, but Chloe supposes the gothic sweep of the Palace of Westminster behind him makes for a good shot.

He is saying that the sensational stories which emerged in the *Chronicle* only last week were, in fact, the result of an attempt to silence the MP for Warwick South, Owen McKenna. The anchor in the studio asks about 'communications from the Secretary of State putting an end to the project having been paid off by clients of Maundrill Consulting . . .' The young man says very seriously that there are serious questions which need serious answers. They are calling it 'cryptogate'.

The screen fills with speaking fees various MPs have accrued over the last couple of years, all while millions of people are struggling to find work, and food gets more expen-sive every day.

They cut back to the man outside parliament. He has Georgina Hyde with him now.

'This issue is vital to all of us,' she says. 'Data on our health should never be traded in the marketplace as it is now. This scandal is about the right we have to live in a free and fair society and the need to protect and support the work of remarkable, brave members of parliament like Owen McKenna and former MP Christine Armstrong, whom I hope we will see back in the Chamber very soon; it is about fighting corruption and cronyism wherever we find it – and most of all this is a fight for justice.'

Chloe puts down her coffee cup and stares at Georgina. When she interviewed her in her Lambeth house she had thought Georgina sincere. Sincere when she had said, sadly, that yes, Owen did have a temper, that yes, Owen had resented his housemates, Jay in particular. Chloe had been convinced, but she's spent time with Debra Brooks since then and she's read Jay's private emails. Her report includes extracts from a few of them where he speaks fondly of Owen and berates himself for ever suspecting McKenna of being out to get him. She's spoken to Jay's counsellor too. He told her the same story as his emails: that Jay blew off steam about his housemate being out to get him over Christmas, but had decided he'd got that wrong by March or April. He was also very angry that extracts from his notes made it into a newspaper.

She takes her coffee upstairs, reads the report one more time, then presses send.

Owen tells the media pack outside Portcullis House that he had spoken to the police about the attempt to blackmail him and has no further comment at this time. His WhatsApp begins to silt up with congratulations and bomb emojis.

When he gets to his office he emails Marion and the chair of his local party promising an update. He emails Liam too. Then he asks Pam to come in and he tells her the whole story, or most of it. There's no mention of Phil or Sara. He carefully credits

Charlotte with finding the evidence about the involvement of the current Secretary of State for Health.

Pam's a professional. She knows he's never going to tell her everything that's going on, but he can see she is torn between hurt at what he's been hiding and excitement.

'It's a massive blow to the government, though, isn't it?' she says. 'And I know that *The Times* is wielding the sword, but Charlotte seems to be making sure you and Christine get the credit you deserve.'

She's drinking a latte today, her drink of cautious optimism. 'I don't deserve much credit.'

Pam's smooth brow is furrowed. 'So the *Chronicle* story, this Maundrill Consulting toady Greg planted it to discredit you?' He nods. She puts her head on one side. 'Backfired a bit, didn't it?'

He laughs for what feels like the first time in weeks.

'Yes. It did. To be fair, he didn't expect me to grow a conscience. If I hadn't been to see Jay, I might have kept quiet.'

The dance of events. Unintended consequences.

Pam 'tsks' into her coffee. 'Maybe his mistake was being a soulless, blackmailing sell-out bastard.'

'Yeah, that too.'

She smiles over the lid of her mug. 'He's had the press at his door too, you know. Another shamed-bloke-loading-his-stuff-into-a-car-and-buggering-off clip for the archives. And Georgina is really harrying the government on the TV shows. She's so natural on TV.'

She smiles fondly as she says it.

He thinks about Debra, about how Georgina spoke to him in the Chamber.

'Georgina is a remarkable politician, but, speaking as some-one who has known her a very long time ... Don't trust her, Pam.' He thinks it through. 'If she or her staff offer you guid-ance, or mentoring in the future, take your opportunities but never, never let yourself be in a position where she has power over you. Never tell her or her staff anything you wouldn't say under your own name on Twitter. And if she or her staff do or say anything that gives you a moment of unease, talk to me. Wherever I am, even if we aren't working together anymore.'

She looks confused and upset. 'Owen, you make her sound like Satan incarnate! And why wouldn't we be working together anymore?'

'You're going to end up running the country someday. I'll keep you as long as I can, but talk to me about where you want to be in five years and let's see what we can do to get you there. What do you want to do in government?'

'Green New Deal. How to improve the economy with-out destroying the planet. Economic policy and growing innovation.'

'Right. Let's talk about that then.'

Her phone pings. 'Lefiami has submitted her report. Blimey, the Leader's Office have published it already.'

Fresh headlines roll in over lunch. TRAGIC JAY'S STOLEN RECORDS. LABOUR REPORT CONTAINS WARNINGS, BUT LARGELY EXONERATES MP OWEN MCKENNA. JOURNAL-IST AT CENTRE OF BLACKMAIL SCANDAL INSISTS HE WAS INNOCENT DUPE. A dupe maybe, Owen thinks, but hardly innocent. He watches clips of Professor Graves talking about crypto security, Christine talking about how she came to know the Collins family and get involved in the case, and a reporter doing a piece to camera from Marsden Grotto while the screen flashes the number of the Samaritans hotline.

He hasn't heard from Phil, not directly, but Sara sends him an emoji of a shark.

The government takes until late afternoon to circle the wagons. The Prime Minister makes a statement from the Number 10 briefing room promising an immediate investigation, in a performance of outrage, sorrow and concern. He manages to thank Charlotte Cook and her colleagues for bringing the matter to light, staring into the camera with his best shocked and serious expression.

The Secretary of State for Health resigns in time for the six o'clock news. He is photographed leaving Number 10 with his head down and issues a short statement insisting on his innocence of any attempts to thwart any initiative which could safeguard public health.

The call comes late that evening. Phil has stayed in town and is trying to clear his desk without making it look like he really expects anything. His parents still have the kids and Sara has come to the office to wait with him. She sits in one of his armchairs, working at some complicated piece of needlework and occasionally taking calls from New York to discuss the hedge fund's positions.

Ian puts the call through while they are watching the resignation letter being read out by the news anchor. The anchor's voice as he reads sounds sceptical.

Sara pauses in her work and watches her husband as he

answers. 'Yes, yes, Prime Minister. I would be honoured.'

He hangs up. 'Seems I have to make a quick stop at Downing Street before we go back to the hotel.'

'Secretary of State for Health?'

'Yes.'

She snips a thread. 'Don't let him catch you examining the drapes.'

He looks up and is about to deny any aspirations for a higher position than he already enjoys, then decides it's probably wiser not be caught in a lie within three minutes of taking the new job, and says nothing.

He gets up and is putting on his jacket when Ian practically falls into his office.

'He's off to see the PM now,' Sara tells him. 'Make sure he doesn't beam at the cameras. Sober leadership, that's the impression we are after.'

Ian cries with delight and disappears into the outer office. Almost immediately they hear whoops of delight from the rest of the team.

Sara gets up and brushes the front of his lapels.

'Well played, darling.'

'Thank you. You too.'

Chapter 53

Emily makes Gabriel drive Georgina home. She goes with them, just for the time in the car. Gabriel complains about having three advanced degrees and being treated like an Uber driver, but he only does that in front of Emily. Not when Georgina is within earshot.

Georgina has been on the media round all day. She shimmers with a mixture of exhaustion and febrile energy. The outer office silted up with roses, gifts of comfort, condolence, support – the thanks of victims and advocates, their understanding and faith in floral form. Emily has kept the cards, and one bunch for the coffee table in Georgina's office. The rest she sent with Georgina's compliments to the nearest nursing home.

They go through the media schedule for the next day. The Leader will ask the questions in parliament, but Georgina will be sent out in front of the cameras tomorrow, grinding the government's face in the scandal. Georgina is pleased.

'And Charlotte Cook called,' Emily adds. 'She would like a

word. She said you aren't responding to her messages today … understands it's a busy time, but is keen to hear from you.'

'No time. Let her concentrate on the reporting. If she calls again, fob her off.'

Emily glances at the front seat. Gabriel is listening to a podcast and arguing with the presenters as he negotiates the traffic. 'Is that wise?'

Georgina raises an eyebrow. A danger signal. 'Why do you say that? She's just another journalist.'

We all sometimes make decisions about what we choose to know, and choose to ignore, thinks Emily, but she has noticed the times that a drink with Georgina is followed by a scoop from Charlotte. She suspects she is not the only one. And the controversy around what Georgina did and did not know about her husband is bound to bubble up again at times. Emily wonders exactly what Charlotte knows about that. 'Yes, but … '

Danger signal flashing orange. 'But what?'

Emily speaks very calmly. 'I've been wondering, Georgina, that perhaps, thinking longer term, it might be a good idea to address some of the issues that may keep resurfacing about Kieron in long form.'

Georgina turns in her seat, and Emily feels the power of her attention. 'I'm listening.'

'We are in the thick of it now. The Collins case, the whole Kieron situation, the divorce, how you are managing to balance the demands on your time as a senior member of the opposition and as the mother of two distressed children. Just looking ahead, perhaps a book laying out your experiences would be a good idea? And of course, you'll be far too busy to write it yourself, but Charlotte could be an ideal co-writer, don't you think? A respected reporter, but someone who knows you very well.'

Georgina turns away to study the lights of London. 'Yes. We could both do well out of that. You will go far, Emily.'

Emily exhales. She wants to go far, she is just not sure she ever wants to go as far as Georgina.

Owen walks home as usual, ducking through one of the lesser-known exits from parliament to avoid the press outside Portcullis House. He walks across Westminster Bridge and along the river and feels, for once, that he has done something of use.

He turns off the Albert Embankment under the railway arch into the deep dark and then out into the refracted glow of the streetlights beyond.

'Nearly home at last, you fucking arsehole.'

Owen turns round. A man leaning on the brick wall where the pavement widens staggers upright and follows him out of the shadows.

'Greg. I thought you'd be run out of town.'

'Couldn't possibly leave without seeing my dear old friend, Owen.'

He lurches forward and Owen steps back. Greg starts to laugh.

'I'm not going to *attack* you, Owen. No need to be *frightened*!'

'You're drunk, Greg. Go home.'

Greg has his hands in the pockets of his trenchcoat. Owen thinks about the fights he's been in, the victims he's spoken to, and readies himself in case Greg is crazed enough to be carrying a knife in the pocket of his expensive coat, or a razor. No doubt it would be a superior brand. 'I'm not leaving without giving you my farewell message. Guess what it is?'

'You going to swear revenge?'

Greg steps forward again, puts his arm around the base of the streetlight and Owen relaxes a fraction. 'You know, I actually was! Clever boy. Not just poor little me, though. You've made a lot of enemies this week, Owen. Lots and lots and lots of very rich, very powerful enemies. Not good. They have long memories.'

'This is ridiculous,' Owen says. 'Just piss off, Greg. I'll deal with your rich angry friends when I have to.'

Greg jabs a finger in his direction. 'Oh, you'll have to one day. Trust me on that, and they won't try and help you at first like I did, won't try to be friendly.' He stumbles forward. Owen braces himself again – no matter what, he's not going to run from this arsehole – but Greg halts as they are face to face. Owen can smell the rot and drink on his breath. 'They will come right for your fucking throat.'

The threat shimmers in the dark between them and the shadows are full of shifting, whispering monsters. Owen watches, waiting him out, and finally Greg reels away and grabs onto the high metal railings that edge this stretch of pavement. The monsters retreat.

'But you know what the really funny thing is, Owen? And this is *really* fucking funny. You still don't know who was bullying Jay, do you?' He waits a second. 'Not a clue. You have no idea which malicious shit in the painted and primped cesspool of Westminster slandered him till he couldn't think straight and then leaked those minutes, brought down the wrath of Kieron Hyde . . . ' He laughs now, brief and bitter. 'Do you even care, you self-righteous prick? As long as you are in the clear!'

Owen feels that faint horror of truth again.

'But *I* read Lefiami's report this afternoon, you see.' Greg taps the side of his nose. 'You didn't read the medical file properly, did you? I did. I bet Chloe Lefiami would have done, but you didn't give it to her. I could tell. Moron. Bitch.' He's almost talking to himself now. 'Though I think almost killing the poor bastard was going a bit far.' He lifts his hand, miming the press of an asthma inhaler plunger. 'Pfft, pfft!'

'You're fucking insane, Greg,' Owen says and walks away.

Chapter 54

Jay's medical file is back in Owen's shirt drawer. Owen has no intention of looking at it because of the ramblings of a ruined criminal drunk like Greg – until he finds he is standing in the bedroom and holding it in his hands.

For the police. That's why he's taken it out. The police have asked him to drop it by when he has the chance and he's told himself that he hasn't had a moment to do so as yet, but now, after that mad ramble of Greg's, he's wondering if he's hanging onto it for some other reason – if something in there has been snagging on his consciousness.

He takes it through to the main room and sets it on the side table where Greg first left it a fortnight ago. He's read the counsellor's notes a dozen times now and they've been picked over in the press since then. It's not that.

He is still looking at it when his phone rings. Chloe Lefiami. He answers.

'Evening, Owen.'

'Chloe, good to hear from you. I haven't read the report of your investigation yet, but I hear you are very even-handed.'

He hears her shushing a child in the background. 'Of course, and those emails from Jay's gmail were pretty conclusive. But it's all a bit redundant now.'

Owen holds the phone to his ear with his shoulder as he fetches a beer from the fridge and opens it. 'Your investigation mattered a great deal to me. And it did mean Kieron Hyde has to answer for what he has done, even if we got there in a slightly roundabout way. Why redundant?'

He hears something muffled about biscuits and a child's cry of victory, then her voice becomes clear again. 'I don't think the newspapers will cover this, what with everything that's going on, but Kieron Hyde has just sent the Leader's Office a statement through his lawyers stating he was responsible for the whole bullying campaign against Jay – the whispers about his sex life, spreading stories at the conference, leaking the report to Charlotte Cook; the whole thing.'

'Really?' Owen pours his beer into a glass and thinks of Kieron in the garden of his home a little more than a week ago, his biggest concern that his wife might catch him smoking and his casual dismissal of Jay. He could have been lying, of course. 'A whisper campaign doesn't sound like Kieron,' he says. 'And how did he get hold of the minutes? It was just Jay and Jay's boss who had the version which leaked.'

'Secret visits to Georgina, apparently,' she says. Her voice is neutral. Owen carries his beer to the window and looks out into the street. No press pack today, just people coming home from work on half-empty buses. Some office workers carrying shopping bags.

'Do you think Kieron was behind the whisper campaign, Chloe?' It would be convenient to believe so. Kieron was rotten to the core after all, deserved all the opprobrium that could be heaped on him – a perfect sin-eater for the party.

'I don't know. No one is going to tell *me* where those rumours began,' she says and then hesitates. 'But Owen, I know I'd say just about anything to keep access to my children.'

'Yeah,' Owen replies. 'Yes, any parent would, I suppose.'

They make their farewells and he picks up Jay's medical file with a sense of dread and a foul feeling that he now knows exactly what he is looking for.

Five hours later Owen is in a dark corner of the executive lounge of the Park Plaza hotel. Phil joins him after twenty minutes, in jeans and a tatty grey T-shirt. His feet are bare.

'I swear, I thought you'd come down in a velvet dressing gown and striped pyjamas, Minister,' Owen says. 'Congratulations on the promotion.'

The hotel is silent and Owen has chosen a place where they can't be seen from the door. Phil still looks around carefully. The bar is deserted.

'Very funny. Yes, I thought I was going to celebrate with a full five hours' sleep, but no such luck. What the hell are you doing, Owen? If anyone sees us together, they'll put two and two together and I'll be out on my ear.'

'It's important.'

'I mean, I can trust the security team, but still I'm not very fucking pleased about this.'

'Phil, I said it's important.'

Phil stops himself. 'OK. Tell me then.'

'Did you hear Kieron Hyde is claiming responsibility for bullying Jay?'

Phil rubs the sleep out of his eyes and hunches forward in his chair. The lighting in the executive bar is at a two-a.m. minimum, the pools of darkness smudged by the lights outside. 'Well, Kieron was threatening to rain hell down on him, wasn't he? That's why we kept Jay off the candidate lists, so as not to provoke him any further.'

'That's what we were told, wasn't it? By the Constituency Party in Coventry East, from our trusted sources in the Union. But I never heard Kieron say it himself.' He watches Phil's face in the gloom. 'And he's claiming responsibility for the whisper campaign and leaking the minutes too.'

'Bullshit!' Phil says automatically. 'Not Kieron's style.'

'That's what I thought,' Owen answers. 'Look, Phil, what if it was Georgina?'

Phil shakes his head, sits back. 'No, no way. I mean, I wonder sometimes what Georgina is capable of, but not this! She held his hand, Owen! She was right in the middle of it. No one knew better than her how much he was suffering.' Owen waits, watching as Phil puts it together. 'But if one of Jay's colleagues at the Treasury had got to his computer and leaked the report, why would Kieron claim responsibility?'

'And remember, Phil. I spoke to Debra Brooks from the Union. She thought Georgina was her friend too.'

Phil folds his arms around himself as if he's cold, though the ferocious air-conditioning is keeping the air circulating at standard hotel temperature.

'And there's Liam, of course,' he says eventually.

'What?' Owen asks.

Phil tells him, awkwardly, avoiding his gaze, about how Georgina reacted in the police station when he asked her about the pill case and how it got into Liam's tent.

'Shit, I knew it.' Owen's never felt so tired in his life. Tired and wired, a dangerous combination. 'I'm glad it wasn't you, though.'

'Can you find a way to tell Liam I'm sorry for not speaking up?'

'Will do.'

They see a movement by the door and both look. One of the hotel staff. Owen sinks back into his corner and Phil's bodyguard ushers the man away. They wait until everything is silent again.

'But it's part of the same thing, isn't it?' Owen says. 'She was desperate for that seat. Desperate enough to throw Jay's pills into the tent next door. Fine, heat-of-the-moment, maybe. An accident. But I'm beginning to think she was desperate enough to marry Kieron and help him cover up what happened at the Union because she needed his political muscle too. If she would do that, spreading crap about Jay and leaking the report doesn't seem like much of a leap to me.'

'Fuck,' Phil says, massaging his forehead with his fingertips. 'She's been my friend for years. Even after I left the party she never cut me off. She'd call me.'

'Do you remember that fight we had with Jay, after Georgina stormed off, when he was trying to tell us about Kieron?'

Phil nods. 'Of course, I can't forget anything about that day. I've tried.'

Another movement catches Owen's eye and he looks towards the door. Just Phil's bodyguard again, shifting his weight. Phil is going to be watched twenty-four hours a day from now on. If Owen is ever going to tell him what he found in the medical files tonight after Chloe's call, it's going to have to be now.

Chapter 55

Wednesday 6 April 2022

Owen senses a holiday mood in Portcullis House with the arrival of the Easter recess. The government are keen to retreat and lick their wounds while the Labour MPs have developed something of a spring in their step. He takes the tunnel across to the Palace of Westminster for the last appointment on his calendar before heading back home to the constituency – an all-party reception in Westminster Hall to celebrate the new exhibition there. His last work appointment anyway; he's having dinner with Anna again tonight.

The long walls of the ancient hall are lined with artwork, all responses to the COVID-19 pandemic. On the north wall are commissioned works from new and established artists, to the south are pieces created by the public at large, and between them the politicians and power brokers, researchers, assistants and the servants of the house move to and fro, trying to assess what has been gained or lost.

'Owen, I'm glad I caught you.'

Owen turns round and finds the Labour Chief Whip at his elbow.

'Judith! What can I do for you?'

She leads him over to a quieter corner of the hall, swiping a glass of white wine from a passing waiter.

'You can stop asking questions about who was behind those rumours about Jay for one thing, cookie.' She pulls off her mask to drink. 'We've had one investigation already and that's enough. The whole trade union movement is checking its closets for skeletons.'

'Good thing too,' Owen replies. Phil is coming down the shallow steps at the end of the hall. Sara is with him.

'Yes, yes, of course.' She catches the look in his eye. 'I mean it, Owen. Christ! I spent years telling women that being harassed by lecherous old farts was just part of the job – my generation were just so pleased to have a seat at the table! To tell the truth, I'm rather in awe of this younger generation who've refused to accept that. Good for them. But that is beside the point. Stop stirring things about Jay. It's done.'

Georgina is coming down the stairs now, with the leader. She says something and he laughs. Judith follows Owen's gaze. 'I said it's done, McKenna. We are talking about you as Shadow Business and Industry Secretary in the next reshuffle, but I need to know you've heard me.'

'It was Georgina, Judith, I'm certain of it. Kieron's statement is rubbish.'

Judith is watching Georgina too now. She seems to feel them looking and smiles in their direction, offers a little bow. Judith smiles and waves back.

'And I've learned, Owen, not to condemn people on the basis of speculation and rumour.' That stings. 'Enjoy the exhibition.'

She leaves him, and Owen starts touring the artworks, zig-zagging between the professional and amateur. Each wall offers a swirl of grief and hope. Photographs, embroidery, delicate brushwork, angry or joyous slabs of oil paint; faces of confusion and determination, isolation and community swim up through the colours.

Sara wanders across to join him in observing a painting of the community around St Thomas' Hospital. The huge canvas is awash with figures, each with their own story. She speaks without looking at him.

'Phil says hi.'

He keeps his eyes on the painting. 'Tell him "hi" back. And that no one is willing to point the finger at Georgina for the bullying. I've been warned off.'

She nods. 'Can't say I'm surprised. Are you going to say anything to Sabal?'

He focuses on the figure of a child chasing a pigeon across the canvas. 'I can't, Sara. I just can't. Georgina's been visiting Jay for years and Sabal thinks of her as a second daughter. Part of the family. Apparently, she went to him "when she learned what Kieron had done" and he believes her. I can't take another child from him, even if it's Georgina.'

She is quiet for a moment. 'You've been to see Jay again?'

'Yes,' Owen says. 'And I'll keep going. I tell him about the music I'm listening to, play a few tracks. Read to him a bit. I have no idea if he is aware I'm there or not, but sometimes I think he is.'

'OK. Time for me to go. Watch your back.'

'You too.'

She steps back as if taking one final look at the whole image. 'By the way, have you seen that Charlotte Cook is here? She and Georgina are working on a book.'

She leaves before he has time to reply. Owen glances at his watch, looks around. As far as he can tell, no one noticed them talking, then he goes to find Charlotte. She's near the exit watching people come and go from the half-shadows, and as Owen approaches she looks up from her phone.

'Owen! You'll be shocked to hear Maundrill Consulting has just announced it is to cease trading. Seems the tactic of claiming Greg was running the whole operation failed to fly in the end. Oh, and the firm that inherited Victor Collins's company has hived his work off to a new company. They've announced they are hiring your Professor Graves as a consultant. No doubt the new Secretary of State for Health will make sure Victor's work is supported and made use of.'

'I'm sure he shall. Charlotte, it was Georgina who leaked the minutes to you in 2009, wasn't it?'

She looks vaguely amused. 'You know I'll never answer that question, Owen, so stop asking.'

'I don't think I shall stop. I'm certain she was behind everything that happened to Jay, but you are the only person who knows for sure. I'm sure she didn't tell you at the time that the leak was intended to damage Jay, but you've read Lefiami's report. You must realise the truth now.'

'So?'

'So for the love of God, don't do the book. She's too dangerous.'

Charlotte studies her phone again. 'Do you know what

journalists get paid these days, Owen? I'll let you into a secret: it's bugger all, and you should see what we are being offered for the book. My agent says it's a frenzy. And you sound hysterical.'

He has to try. It was Charlotte who warned him about the story and the investigation. 'I believe Georgina was behind *everything* that happened to Jay, Charlotte.'

She looks at him now. 'What on earth are you taking about?'

'Jay refilled his prescription for his inhaler the day before we left for Glastonbury. Then he started trying to tell us about Kieron. We shouted him down and Georgina stormed off. Think about it. Phil and I weren't listening to him then, but we might have done the next day. What better way to make him go home than emptying his inhaler?' Owen takes a drink from a passing waiter. He needs it. The image of Georgina in their tent, emptying Jay's spare inhaler, has been tormenting him since the night he saw Greg and checked through the files. He tried to convince himself it was impossible, but Phil remembered Georgina storming off too, telling Jay she wished he would go home.

Charlotte is shaking her head. 'Maybe he packed the old inhaler! State he was in! Maybe the new one was still back at your house.'

He finishes the glass and sets it down. A waiter sweeps it away.

'I packed his things for him when we finally got it through our thick skulls he wasn't coming back home. No new inhaler.'

Georgina is moving through the crowd towards them now. 'Charlotte, you know I'm right. And you're about the only person who really knows who she is. For God's sake, be careful.'

'Owen! Lottie! What are you two gossiping about?' Owen and Georgina have hardly spoken since that encounter in the

Chamber, though in public they keep up the appearance of cordiality. She puts her head on one side and Owen notices the beginnings of a frown. 'Come on, confess.'

A young woman bustles across to them and touches her elbow.

'What, Emily?'

'The Leader wants you – we're doing those photos.'

She beams at her. 'Of course! Sorry, guys, we'll have to catch up some other time, Owen. Bye, Lottie!'

Her advisor shepherds her away towards the waiting cameras. Charlotte exhales, then looks up at Owen. 'I don't believe a word of it,' she says, then heads off into the body of the Hall.

'Yes, you do,' Owen says to himself as he watches her go.

Chapter 56

Georgina is sitting by the bed, holding Jay's hand, enjoying the scent of lavender in the air.

'How are you, babes? You look good. I'm doing OK. Mum and Dad are moving to London permanently after Easter, which will be so useful with the kids. And they'll supervise during Kieron's visits too. Much better that way, I can't bear to look at him.'

Georgina bends over and kisses Jay's forehead. Squeezes his hand. They've dressed him in his green pyjamas today. They suit him.

She thinks she sees a flicker in his eyes. Perhaps it was the mention of Kieron. They've tried in the past to see if he can use gaze direction to communicate. The results were inconclusive, but they keep trying in between bouts of physical therapy, cleaning and feeding. Georgina is sure he understands her.

'Charlotte and I are writing a book. I thought I might

dedicate it to you. I don't think there will be much need to mention the leaked minutes. Now the story is about poor Victor Collins and blackmailing lobbyists, everyone's lost interest in our little household and our dramas again.' She thinks of Owen, his expression when he watches her, and wonders what he suspects. It will be easier to keep an eye on what he is up to when he is on the front bench. 'But if I hadn't taken a *bit* of the shine off you, I wouldn't have stood a chance. And it's not my fault you left your laptop lying around.'

She sketches shapes over the back of his hand.

'And at Glastonbury – why did you keep going on about the Union? You shouldn't have done that. It was such an important time for me! I needed Kieron! You see that, don't you?' She knocks a tear away from her eyelash. 'I didn't mean to empty it completely. I just couldn't stop, honestly it was like an out-of-body experience. Like it wasn't even me doing it at all. So strange. Then I was sure you would check and notice before you *needed* it. Such a tragic accident, my poor darling.'

She sits with him a while longer, enjoying the quiet, then she kisses his forehead again. Jay's eyes track her out of the room, then flicker up towards the clock.

The nurses at reception take a second to watch Georgina leave the building, heading for her car, pressing the button on her key fob without breaking her stride. They admire her devotion to Jay, the flowers and food she leaves in the staff room as a thank you for all they do for him. She's the first person they call, after Sabal, if there is any change in his condition.

'They should put her in charge,' one says with a sigh.

'Oh, they will one day,' the other replies, ticking her out. 'Prime Minister Georgina Hyde. Sounds good to me.'

Acknowledgements

Many thanks to our agents Broo Doherty and Rory Scarfe for the guidance and support throughout. We are also very grateful to the fantastic team at Sphere for their enthusiasm and patience. Particular shout-outs to Thalia Proctor, Stephanie Melrose, Lucy Malagoni and most of all to Ed Wood for bringing us together in the first place.

As always, our thanks to the writing community on and offline for keeping us sane while grappling with the past and the future – and to Ned: thanks for the cheese. This book could not have been written without the MPs, journalists and civil servants who forever remind us that politics is still a noble profession.

Finally, much love to Malachy, Saoirse, Gabriel, Rafa and Manny.